Joseph Warren Keifer

Speeches - in part - of Hon. J. Warren Keifer, of Ohio

in the House of representatives, Forty-fifth and Forty-sixth Congresses Vol. 2

Joseph Warren Keifer

Speeches - in part - of Hon. J. Warren Keifer, of Ohio
in the House of representatives, Forty-fifth and Forty-sixth Congresses Vol. 2

ISBN/EAN: 9783337267933

Printed in Europe, USA, Canada, Australia, Japan

Cover: Foto ©Andreas Hilbeck / pixelio.de

More available books at **www.hansebooks.com**

Joseph Warren Keifer

Speeches - in part - of Hon. J. Warren Keifer, of Ohio
in the House of representatives, Forty-fifth and Forty-sixth Congresses Vol. 2

ISBN/EAN: 9783337267933

Printed in Europe, USA, Canada, Australia, Japan

Cover: Foto ©Andreas Hilbeck / pixelio.de

More available books at **www.hansebooks.com**

SPEECHES

(IN PART)

OF

HON. J. WARREN KEIFER,

OF OHIO

IN THE

HOUSE OF REPRESENTATIVES,

FORTY-FIFTH AND FORTY-SIXTH CONGRESSES,

AND

CERTAIN PARLIAMENTARY DECISIONS MADE BY HIM AS SPEAKER
OF THE FORTY-SEVENTH CONGRESS

1877—1883.

———•◀▶•———

WASHINGTON:
GOVERNMENT PRINTING OFFICE.
1883.

90 A K

SPEECHES

OF

HON. J. WARREN KEIFER,

OF OHIO.

— —

(Forty-fifth Congress.)

RESUMPTION OF SPECIE PAYMENTS.

November 16, 1877, the House having under consideration the bill (H. R. No. 805) to repeal the third section of the act entitled "An act for the resumption of specie payments"—

Mr. KEIFER said:

Mr. SPEAKER: I think at this late hour in the discussion of this most important of all subjects to the American people I might well content myself with silence. I do not think any member can be converted now. I prefer, however, to go upon the record, so that in after years when the problem of practical resumption is solved, and that myriad of men who now go about the country prophesying evil continually have had their prophetic lips sealed, and that other numberless multitudes of men have come forth and broken their silence by crying through the land "I told you so!" I may not be accused of, at the proper time, hiding my light under a bushel.

I do not, however, propose to attempt a general disquisition on finance or on the wisdom of early resumption as an original question. We must deal with the law as it is, not as we might wish it had been made. I differ only with some of my colleagues from Ohio, who have enlightened the House on this question, as to the proper course to take now, in view of the condition of the country and the present state of the law.

I agree with them that we must resume specie payments, but I believe it possible to resume on January 1, 1879. I believe that when the Government issued the United States Treasury notes to meet a great exigency created by the war and promised to redeem them or make them the equivalent of coin, (gold and silver,) the faith of the whole country was pledged to keep good that promise. I further believe that the act of March 18, 1869, "to strengthen the public credit," reaffirmed the original promise and renewed the faith of the nation to make such notes the equivalent of coin, and also that the resumption act of January 14, 1875, was a like promise that these notes should not be dishonored. Of the wisdom of these laws I need not now speak. We deal with the question as we find it. On the faith of the original sacred promise and these acts of 1869 and 1875, the people of this country have dealt in these notes.

It is conceded by those who have stoutly contended that the bonds of the Government were payable in paper money, that since the "public-credit" act of 1869 it would be bad faith to not pay them in coin.

There is the same pledge given in that act, with the additional one given by the resumption act of 1875, for the payment of the United States notes in coin. Here let me say in passing that the public-credit act does not require the United States Treasury notes or other obligations to be paid in gold coin, but, in terms, they are to be paid in *gold* and *silver* coin.

In defining my position on this resumption question, I wish to say that I should vote for the pending bill, notwithstanding the evils which would flow from its becoming a law, if I believed that we were to have the present United States notes at once withdrawn from circulation.

I agree with the member from Kansas [Mr. PHILLIPS] that greenbacks are the best paper currency we have ever had, provided we appreciate them and bring them up abreast with coin. In answer to the member from North Carolina, [Mr. DAVIS,] I say the paper currency of this Government is honest money, unless we dishonor it. I regret that the advocates of this bill seem disposed to strike down the resumption *act* rather than favor its amendment.

There is a necessity for auxiliary legislation to enable the Government to resume and to make definite and certain that which may be fairly regarded as doubtful in the construction of the third section of that act.

My colleague [Mr. GARDNER] from Ohio has by fair and legitimate reasoning sought

3

to show that when resumption comes cancellation and destruction of the notes redeemed must follow. He thinks the use of the word "*redeem*" in the parts of the act relating to fractional currency and to the excess of United States notes beyond $300,000,000 (when clearly the fractional currency and such excess is, when redeemed, to be destroyed or withdrawn from circulation) furnishes a conclusive argument in favor of the view that when the remaining $300,000,000 of United States notes are redeemed they also must be withdrawn from circulation. This is a legitimate but not a conclusive argument. The context shows, independently of the word "redeem," what disposition is intended to be made of the fractional currency and such excess of United States notes ; but the act is purposely silent (as appears by the history of its passage) as to the disposition to be made of the $300,000,000 when redeemed.

The word "*redeem*" is not used in conjunction with the same phraseology of language throughout the act, and hence it is not safe to look to that word alone in construing the different parts of the act.

Since paper currency was known the word "*redeem*" has had a well-settled meaning, and it has been understood to only mean, when applied to such currency, that its payment by the party issuing it did not prevent its reissue.

However, there should be a law passed giving a construction that would relieve this act from doubt.

The amendment offered by me I now send to the Clerk to be read.

The Clerk read as follows :

That nothing in the act to provide for the resumption of specie payments, approved January 14, A. D. 1875, shall be so construed as to authorize or require the Secretary of the Treasury to retire and cancel any United States legal-tender notes outstanding which may be redeemed on and after January 1, A. D. 1879, under the provisions of said act, or which may then be in the Treasury of the United States uncanceled, or which may thereafter come into said Treasury otherwise than by redemption ; but said act shall be held and construed to authorize and require said Secretary to return said notes to the said Treasury, to be paid out from time to time at their par value in payment of all debts and demands against the United States or in exchange for coin or bullion, and for other purposes, as the exigencies of the public interest may require ; the said notes to continue to have the same legal-tender character now given to them by law.

Mr. KEIFER. It will be observed that this amendment, if enacted into a law, would put an end to contraction of the greenback currency, and continue it, with all its attributes, in free circulation, at the same time appreciated to a coin value. It could still be used by national banks to redeem its currency and as a reserve in such banks. I would amend the national-banking act so as to require the banks (after January 1, 1879) to redeem their currency, on presentation, in gold, silver, or legal-tender notes, at their option. This would bring practical resumption of specie payments by the banks and actual resumption by the Government. This would preserve the volume of the currency substantially where it now is, unless contraction should come through national banks withdrawing their circulation because it was not demanded by the wants of trade or because of unfriendly, unjust, and invidious legislation. It is not my purpose here to speak for national banks.

The burden of the argument so far has been to assume that a repeal of the resumption act would make the poor richer and the rich poorer. There are those on this floor and elsewhere who pretend to believe that depreciated money is easier to get and worth more to the country than good money; that men are more likely to go into business with a paper currency at a discount than with a paper currency at par with coin.

Most of the advocates of irredeemable paper currency assume to speak for the poor and the laboring man, as though these classes of our people were not entitled to be paid their hard earnings in a sound currency. Daniel Webster once wisely said—

Of all the contrivances for cheating the laboring classes of mankind none has been more effectual than that which deludes them with paper money. This is the most effectual of inventions to fertilize the rich man's field *by the sweat of the poor man's brow*. Ordinary tyranny, oppression, excessive taxation, these bear lightly on the happiness of the mass of the community compared with the fraudulent currencies and the robberies committed by depreciated paper. Our own history has recorded for our instruction enough and more than enough of the demoralizing tendency, the injustice, and the intolerable oppression on the virtuous and well-disposed, of a degraded paper currency authorized by law or any way countenanced by government. A disordered currency is one of the greatest political evils. It undermines the virtues necessary for the support of the social system and encourages propensities destructive to its happiness. *It wars against industry, frugality, and economy, and it fosters the evil spirit of extravagance and speculation.*

The effect of the unconditional repeal of the resumption act would be to give the country no more money, but only a poorer paper currency. Such repeal would not start another wheel or spindle in a factory; would not cause another furnace to blaze; it would not open another new coal or iron mine, or give an additional laborer employment. Since the decisions of the cases of Hepburn *vs.* Griswold, (8 Wall., 603) and Knox *vs.* Lee, (12 Wall., 457,) it seems to be conceded that a distinctively new issue of legal-tender notes cannot be authorized by law.

This being the case, we are now engaged in an attempt to depreciate our own currency and destroy its purchasing power, without adding a dollar to the volume of our currency. It is the quality, and not the quantity, of the currency which will be affected by the repeal.

I commend the advocates of repeal to the member from Pennsylvania [Mr. Wright] who, as I understand, is in favor of the Government making and giving to his constituents some millions of dollars. When that policy is entered upon we shall all enter the lists and claim a few millions of the nation's bounty for our constituents.

To the scarcity of money in the country every evil is attributed. I will endeavor to show that this, too, is far from the truth. We now have a currency, *per capita*, more than double the *per capita* of currency at the most prosperous times before the war. I have here a statement relating to the circulation of paper currency at different periods of our country's history before the war. It is as follows:

Statement showing aggregate circulation of paper currency and circulation per capita for the years named.

Year.	Circulation of Bank of United States.	Circulation of State Banks.	Aggregate.	Population.	Circulation per capita.
1811	$5,400,000	$28,100,000	$33,500,000	7,454,000	$4 49
1815		45,500,000	45,500,000	8,369,000	5 43
1816		68,000,000	68,000,000	8,614,000	7 89
1820	3,589,484	14,863,344	18,452,825	*9,658,453	5 02
1830	12,924,145	61,323,898	74,248,043	*12,866,020	5 77
1834	19,208,379	94,839,570	114,047,949	14,373,000	7 93
1835	17,339,797	103,692,495	121,032,292	14,786,000	8 19
1836	23,075,422	140,301,038	163,376,460	15,213,000	10 74
1837	11,447,968	149,185,890	160,633,858	15,655,000	10 26
1838	6,768,067	116,138,910	122,906,977	16,112,000	7 62
1839	5,982,621	135,170,995	141,153,616	16,584,000	8 51
1840	6,695,861	106,968,572	113,664,433	*17,069,453	6 66
1851		155,165,251	155,165,251	23,995,000	6 47
1860		207,102,477	207,102,477	*31,443,321	6 59

* Enumerated ; for all other years the population is estimated.

EDWARD YOUNG, Chief of Bureau.

Bureau of Statistics, *November* 16, 1877.

I also here give a statement showing the amount of, and "*per capita*" circulation of, paper currency during the years 1861 to 1877, inclusive :

Year.	Aggregate circulation, bank-notes, legal-tender and fractional currency.	Population.	Circulation per capita.	Year.	Aggregate circulation, bank-notes, legal-tender and fractional currency.	Population.	Circulation per capita.
1861	*$202,205,000	32,064,000	$6 31	1870	$683,878,000	†38,558,371	$17 83
1862	*332,794,000	32,704,000	10 17	1871	721,582,000	39,555,000	18 24
1863	297,736,000	34,395,000	8 92	1872	731,385,000	40,604,000	18 01
1864	562,072,000	34,046,000	14 74	1873	740,799,000	41,704,000	17 75
1865	628,692,000	34,748,000	18 09	1874	777,538,000	42,856,000	18 14
1866	708,031,000	35,169,000	19 95	1875	769,840,419	44,060,000	17 47
1867	693,090,000	36,211,000	19 14	1876	717,241,912	45,316,000	15 82
1868	678,745,000	36,973,000	18 36	1877	689,618,578	46,624,000	14 79
1869	676,508,000	37,756,000	17 92				

* No fractional currency included.   † Enumerated, all other years estimated.

EDWARD YOUNG, Chief of Bureau,

Bureau of Statistics, *November* 16, 1877.

The last statement does not include demand notes, and the large part of the apparent reduction from 1875 to 1877 is caused by the substitution of subsidiary silver coin for fractional currency.

It will be observed that in 1864, when the paper currency had reached the highest point during the war, there was $17,546,578 less than there is at present.

It will be observed that the *per capita* of currency is now more than it was at any time during the war, and, as already stated, more than double as great as under the administration of Buchanan.

James Buchanan became President in 1857, at a time of great financial distress, and with the volume of currency as already indicated. In his first message to Congress, in

December, 1857, he charges the then hard times exclusively to the existence of an irredeemable and fluctuating paper currency.

I ask the Clerk to read from that message the paragraphs indicated.

The Clerk read as follows:

The earth has yielded her fruits abundantly and has bountifully rewarded the toil of the husbandman. Our great staples have commanded high prices, and, up till within a brief period, our manufacturing, mineral, and mechanical occupations have largely partaken of the general prosperity. We have possessed all the elements of material wealth in rich abundance, and yet, notwithstanding all these advantages, our country, in its monetary interests, is at the present moment in a deplorable condition. In the midst of unsurpassed plenty in all the productions of agriculture and in all the elements of national wealth, we find our manufactures suspended, our public works retarded, our private enterprises of different kinds abandoned, *and thousands of useful laborers thrown out of employment and reduced to want.*

* * * * * *

It is our duty to inquire what has produced such unfortunate results and whether their recurrence can be prevented. In all former revulsions the blame might have been fairly attributed to a variety of co-operating causes; but not so upon the present occasion. It is apparent that our existing misfortunes have proceeded solely from our extravagant and vicious system of paper currency and bank credits, exciting the people to wild speculation and gambling in stock.

* * * * * *

The framers of the Constitution, when they gave to Congress the power "to coin money and to regulate the value thereof," and prohibited the States from coining money, emitting bills of credit, or making anything but gold and silver coin a tender in payment of debts, supposed they had protected the people against the *evils of an excessive and irredeemable paper currency.* They are not responsible for the existing anomaly that a Government endowed with the sovereign attribute of coining money and regulating the value thereof should have no power to prevent others from driving this coin out of the country and filling up the channels of circulation with paper which does not represent gold and silver.

It is one of the highest and most responsible duties of government to insure to the people a sound circulating medium, the amount of which ought to be adapted with the utmost possible wisdom and skill to the wants of internal trade and foreign exchanges. If this be either greatly above or greatly below the proper standard, the marketable value of every man's property is increased or diminished in the same proportion, and injustice to individuals as well as incalculable evils to the community are the consequence.

* * * * * *

It is this paper system of extravagant expansion, raising the nominal price of every article far beyond its real value when compared with the cost of similar articles in countries whose circulation is wisely regulated, which has prevented us from competing in our markets with foreign manufactures, has produced extravagant importations, and has counteracted the effect of the large incidental protection afforded to our domestic manufactures by the present revenue tariff. But for this, the branches of our manufactures composed of raw materials, the production of our own country—such as cotton, iron, and woolen fabrics—would not only have acquired almost exclusive possession of the home market, but would have created for themselves a foreign market throughout the world.

Mr. KEIFER. It will be noted that the sage of Wheatland was a believer in gold and silver coin as the only sound money for this country, and he deprecated all paper inflations. I commend this message to the member from Pennsylvania, [Mr. KELLEY.] Nor did it ever occur to President Buchanan, or any of the wise statesmen of the time of his administration, that the way to turn an evil into a blessing was to enlarge the evil. The financial crisis of 1837, the most terrible in its consequences of any this country has ever witnessed, was laid at the door of an overissue of an irredeemable paper currency and a suspension of specie payments. President Van Buren was constrained to call an extra session of Congress (on the suspension of specie payments in May, 1837) to meet September 4, 1837, to consider the financial affairs of the country. In his special message of date of September 4, 1837, he attributes all the business disasters of the country to an unsound and irredeemable paper currency, and asked Congress to legislate to contract such currency and to secure universal specie payments.

The *per capita* of currency in this country in 1837 was about one-half what it is now and one-third more than in Buchanan's administration. President Van Buren contrasted the financial revulsions in Great Britain and the United States, and traced their causes to the same source, an overissue of paper money.

An extract or two from that message may be instructive. I read:

The history of trade in the United States for the last three or four years affords the most convincing evidence that our present condition is chiefly to be attributed to overaction in all the departments of business; an overaction deriving, perhaps, its first impulses from antecedent causes, but stimulated to its destructive consequences by excessive issues of bank paper and by other facilities for the acquisition and enlargement of credit.

* * * * * *

However unwilling any of our citizens may heretofore have been to assign to these causes the chief instrumentality in producing the present state of things, the developments subsequently made and the actual condition of other commercial countries must, as it seems to me, dispel all remaining doubts upon the subject. It has since appeared that evils similar to those suffered by ourselves have been experienced in Great Britain, on the Continent, and indeed throughout the commercial world; and that in other countries, as well as in our own, they have been uniformly preceded by an undue enlargement of the boundaries of trade, prompted, as with us, by unprecedented expansion of the systems of credit. A reference to the amount of banking capital and the issues of paper credits put in circulation in Great Britain by banks and in other ways during the years 1834, 1835, and 1836 will show an augmentation of the paper currency there as much disproportioned to the real wants of trade as in the United States. With this redundancy of the paper currency there arose in that country also a spirit of adventurous speculation, embracing the whole range of human enterprise.

* * * * * *

In view of these facts it would seem impossible for sincere inquirers after truth to resist the conviction that the causes of the revulsion in both countries have been substantially the same. Two nations, the most commercial in the world, enjoying but recently the highest degree of apparent prosperity and maintaining with each other the closest relations, are suddenly, in a time of profound peace and without any great national disaster, arrested in their career and plunged into a state of embarrassment and distress. In both countries we have witnessed the same redundancy of paper money and other facilities of credit; the same spirit of speculation; the same partial successes; the same difficulties and reverses; and, at length, nearly the same overwhelming catastrophe. The most material difference between the results in the two countries has only been that, with us, there has also occurred an extensive derangement in the fiscal affairs of the Federal and State governments, occasioned by the suspension of specie payments by the banks.

After the suspension of specie payments in May, 1837, the premium on American gold went up to 12 per cent. On the resumption of specie payments, May, 1838, it went down to a half per cent. The Democratic remedy in 1837 and 1857 was to contract or extinguish paper currency and to require specie payments by banks and the Federal Government.

I do not contend for contraction of the currency, but for the maintenance of it at its present volume, brought up and kept alongside with coin in its purchasing power. Let the increase of the quantity of money come through natural causes and by the increase of gold and silver coin, which a remonetization of silver and a healthy foreign commerce will certainly produce. The facts relating to Great Britain, given us by the member from Pennsylvania [Mr. KELLEY] the other day, from Tallis's Illustrated Atlas of 1851, to prove that a large volume of paper currency, regardless of the quality, was the touchstone of prosperity, will bear looking at again, when I trust the honorable gentleman will confess that they prove the reverse of what he claimed for them.

I send the same statement to the Clerk to be again read.

The Clerk read as follows:

Year.	Bank paper.	Effects.
1818	$17,727,000	Prosperity.
1819	41,358,948	Distress.
1820	35,129,105	Distress.
1821	28,669,500	} Great distress; county meetings calling for relief.
1822	26,743,260	}
1823	29,562,422	
1824	33,124,658	} Great prosperity and speculation.
1825	34,220,738	}
1826	30,911,323	

Mr. KEIFER. It will be observed that in 1818 Great Britain, with a paper currency of $17,727,000, enjoyed "prosperity," and in 1824, when that quantity had been reduced about one-third, that kingdom enjoyed "*great prosperity and speculation;*" and also in 1819, when that country floated a paper currency of $41,358,948, it suffered "distress," but when one-fifth of that sum was cut off, it enjoyed "*great prosperity.*"

Here, it seems, is a conundrum for the honorable member [Mr. KELLEY] to work out.

At the period of "*great prosperity*" spoken of, in 1824 and 1825, the population of Great Britain was 21,280,000, and her paper currency *per capita*, as shown by these same figures, was about $1.60, and in 1818, when it was at its maximum, the *per capita* was only $2.30. The United States, with a present *per capita* of currency of $14.79, is said to be in great distress for want of more paper money. This is fallacious; it is for want of more business enterprise, which can only be secured by a sound currency. The resumption act was passed in answer to the promise given to the noteholder, in response to the demands of the country, to defeat the predictions of the Democratic party through its leaders, during the war, that the legal-tender notes would become worthless, and to carry out the wishes of that part expressed since the war. The Republican party discovered in the Constitution the power to issue the United States legal-tender notes; it created and wrote on them a promise to make them good, which should and must be kept. Good faith should be the pole-star of a nation as well as of an individual.

In 1864 Governor Seymour sent a message to the Legislature of the State of New York, deprecating the consequences that would follow from the payment of the bonds of the State of New York in paper money, and exhorted them to set to the State and to the nation a good example in the matter of paying all its obligations in gold and silver. Mr. Seymour was made the candidate of the Democratic party in 1868 upon a specie-payment platform. I can only briefly refer to facts.

We come along up to 1872, when we had this condition of things in the country; we had three great parties in the country, all of whom stood upon a specie-payment platform. The Liberal convention that met at Cincinnati, composed, it was said, of all the virtue, of all the overflowing effervescence of virtue, of all the parties in the country, met and adopted a platform; and the plank in regard to specie payments reads thus:

A speedy resumption of specie payments is demanded alike by the highest considerations of commercial morality and honest government.

Sixty-odd days afterward, the Democratic party, having considered the subject well, and considered it not upon the report of a committee, readopted that platform in the light of a specie-resumption letter of Horace Greeley. They readopted it in words and terms. A speedy resumption of specie payments was demanded by the Democratic party, in 1872, "by the highest considerations of commercial morality and honest government."

In 1875 this Congress gave to the country the resumption law, which did not promise resumption until seven years after speedy resumption had been demanded by all the parties of the country, the Republican, the Democratic, the Liberal and all the other parties; and yet we are now told that we forced this matter hastily upon the country.

Since the passage of the act the Democratic party has continued to demand specie payments. Governor Tilden was made the standard-bearer of that party only one year ago. He had always favored specie resumption. He recommended, immediately after the passage of the resumption act as governor, and the New York Legislature passed and he approved, a bill, now the law of New York State, which requires all taxes to be collected in *gold*—no silver—and all contract obligations payable in the State of New York to be performed by payments in coin after January 1, 1879.

Tilden was placed on a platform which favored resumption of specie payments and which arraigned the Republican party before the bar of the world for not having resumed specie payments on the surrender of the insurgent armies. Lest some may be prone to forget that platform, I read an extract from it, as follows:

We denounce the failure, for all these eleven years of peace, to make good the promise of the legal-tender notes, which are a changing standard of value in the hands of the people, and the non-payment of which is a disregard of the plighted faith of the nation.

That platform only denounces the resumption act and demands the repeal of the resumption clause of the act as a hinderance to resumption.

To further make clear the true interpretation of that platform, I read an extract from Mr. Tilden's letter of acceptance:

"Reform is necessary," declares the Saint Louis convention, "to establish a sound currency, restore the public credit, and maintain the national honor;" and it goes on to "demand a judicious system of preparation by public economies, by official retrenchments, and by wise finance, which shall enable the nation soon to assure the whole world of its perfect ability and its perfect readiness to meet any of its promises at the call of the creditor entitled to payment." *The object demanded by the convention is a resumption of specie payments on the legal-teader notes of the United States. That would not only "restore the public credit" and "maintain the national honor," but it would "establish a sound currency" for the people.*

It will be observed that he, too, thinks resumption necessary to restore credit and maintain the national honor.

On this platform, thus interpreted, the whole Democratic party stood one year ago. The majority of this House was elected on this specie-resumption platform, not excepting the member from Ohio [Mr. EWING] who has charge of this bill.

We should address ourselves to the work of perfecting the law and not to its repeal.

I have said enough on this question. I have sought to show that good money is better for the whole people than depreciated currency; that overissues of paper currency have in the past brought about speculation, extravagance, and extended credit, which when the pay-day came brought disaster and ruin, and that the present in this respect is not different from the past.

I have shown that the law was passed not only to secure the redemption of the nation's sacred promise most solemnly made, but for a wise purpose and in answer to a demand of the great parties of this country, and especially the Democratic party.

It is common to hear the Republican party charged with the passage of this law, and as a consequence with all the financial disasters of the country. The member from Tennessee [Mr. RIDDLE] gives us a summary of financial disasters for four years during the war, when people were just embarking in speculation on account of sudden paper inflation, and for four and a half years since the war, chiefly prior to the resumption act, and he contrasts the two periods. He ignores the real fact that the disasters of the latter period are but legitimate results of the course taken by speculators in the former. The repeal of the resumption act will not pay the debts of a bankrupt, nor start him again in business.

He also states that in 1865 the circulation reached $2,200,000,000; that is, $55 *per capita*, and that the Secretary of the Treasury reduced it $1,200,000,000. This is the old method of perverting figures on the stump to scare the people. The facts do not bear the gentleman out. No such contraction has ever taken place in our currency proper, as I have already shown. Bonds bearing interest, which are included in this statement of the circulation and reduction, were, when due, paid off or interchanged for other bonds by the Government, which never entered into the common currency of the country. We have still in this country a mountain of debt evidenced by bonds which represent in part the cost of a preserved Union. But it is said that bonds have been sold in foreign countries.

Grant it. This was because they, together with the other promises of the Government, were decried and their repudiation threatened until we had to go to the money marts of Europe for purchasers.

Had the bonds been bought and held by our own people as a permanent investment, more money would have been withdrawn from business enterprises and there would have been less employment for the laboring-men. The money arising from the sale of bonds abroad has been made available in business here. The honorable member also assails the Republican party for pernicious and dishonest legislation, invidious to the laboring-man, in favor of the creditor and against the debtor class.

The record of the Republican party has been written and has passed into history. From its birth to the present hour it has battled for the rights of man and the elevation of the enslaved, defenseless, and weak against the oppressions of the aggressive and strong.

I draw no invidious distinctions here; this is neither the time nor occasion; but I may be permitted to say I have never yet seen a Republican who did not believe in giving every man an equal chance in the race of life and the freedom to enjoy the earnings of the sweat of his own face.

Mr. Speaker, to the resumption act all financial disasters are laid. We must remember that the panic of 1873 came two years before its date.

When the army of Northern Virginia surrendered to Grant at Appomattox the price of gold was $1.52 in currency. On July 11, 1864, just after the Democratic party had declared the war on the part of the North an "experiment and a failure," it reached $2.86. When the resumption act was passed gold was only $1.12½. It is to-day only $1.02½. Shall we, by the passage of this bill, again raise the price of gold? Shall we, when we are trying to give the country a bimetallic currency, appreciate gold or depreciate our paper currency?

Had we not better devote ourselves to the work of hitching the three together and abreast? They have been driven tandem long enough.

It is a siren song to sing in the ears of those unfortunate men who are out of employment that financial legislation has brought about hard times; but it is delusive.

Many causes concur in putting an end in this and many of the great manufacturing and commercial countries of Europe to a demand for laboring-men. I can only name one or two of these causes. The labor-saving machinery now in use in manufactories and on farms has driven the laborer from the shops and fields.

It is estimated that England, with a population of thirty-six millions of souls, has, through her machinery, a laboring power equivalent to six hundred millions of able-bodied men; and the United States, with a population now of about forty-six millions, has, through her machinery, a working power equal to two hundred and fifty millions of men. Through the inventive genius of man more men have been left without employment in America and on the continent of Europe than through all other causes combined.

From a state of war, recklessness in business enterprises, extravagant living, and unusual and extraordinary expenditures on public improvements, we have emerged to a period of peace and comparative steadiness in business, economy in living, and a necessary cessation of public improvements. Individuals with wealth have curtailed their expenses in every way, all of which tends to lessen the demands for labor.

The million of men engaged during the war on either side in consuming and destroying returned to fill up the ranks of men seeking civil employment and to become producers. The United States is no longer the principal paymaster to the hundreds of thousands in its employ, to the growers of the products of the soil, or to manufacturers. The South has not yet had time to recover from the devastation of civil war. The purchasing power of our currency is now 33 per cent. greater than when the war closed. Shall we, by enacting this bill into a law, contract the purchasing power of our money to what it was when the war closed?

To all those who believe resumption of specie payments must and should come; to all those who are opposed to repudiation of the nation's sacred debt; to all those who are in favor of a sound and stable currency for the poor as well as the rich; to all those who have the truest and best interests of all classes of persons at heart. I appeal and implore them to stand firm and hold the ground gained, and unite in legislation which will put this country upon a sound financial basis. With many who here support this bill I might agree as to a lack of wisdom in the resumption act as an original question, but if evil has flowed from the operation of the act we have tasted of that evil, and we should now gather the ripe fruit just within our grasp. Gold, silver, and paper money are closing their ranks together; let us do nothing to reopen the breach. If in the future it should seem that the date for resumption is fixed too soon, I will vote to postpone that date to a more opportune time, but let us here do our duty by first perfecting the existing law.

WIGGINTON vs. PACHECO.

On February 6, 1878, in this election case, Mr. Leonard said that in civil cases where there are only two judgments possible, if the testimony is evenly balanced the plaintiff must be nonsuited, and that if there are three judgments possible, a judgment in favor of either one or the other claimant, or a judgment in favor of neither, and there is a conflict of testimony between the claimants, neither is entitled to judgment unless he makes out his case over the other claimant beyond a reasonable doubt—

Mr. KEIFER said :

Let me ask the gentleman from Louisiana where he finds any rule applying to civil cases in this or any other country which justifies him in making that statement.

The distinction is broadly drawn between the testimony in civil and in criminal cases. Such is not the rule, as I understand it, under the civil law in the gentleman's own State. It is not the rule which applies in the Supreme Court of the United States nor in any of the States of the Union, so far as I am aware.

On the same case, February 7th—

Mr. KEIFER said :

I rise for the purpose of disclaiming any purpose to be discourteous to the gentleman from Louisiana, [Mr. LEONARD.] As to the gentleman's rule of evidence I may have been emphatic on yesterday, but I certainly did not intend to be discourteous. I am glad that the gentleman now disclaims that he intended what he said; but I want to say that I entirely differ with him as to the rules of evidence that should apply in this case. There are a contestant and a contestee in this case. First let it be understood that the contestee comes here under a certificate from the officers of his own State, which certificate these officers were compelled under a mandamus of the supreme court of the State of California to issue. Now, that makes his title good, at least for the *prima facie* case if not more; it certainly ought to make more than a *prima facie* case for the contestee. Now, as I understand it, the contestant should overthrow that *prima facie* case by proof—a preponderance of proof. Now, how is it to be done ?

In the estimation of some gentlemen it is done by offering *some* kind of proof in the matter, and then the parties get upon a par and that is sufficient to infer that neither is entitled to the seat. Now, how do we get at this ? I desire as an illustration to quote one single case as a means of overthrowing the claim of Mr. Pacheco. I find in the report of the gentleman from Illinois [Mr. SPRINGER] this sentence in the case of Charles Gilbert. I quote from the report of the committee:

A person cannot be compelled to state for whom he voted ; and the Supreme Court of the United States has expressly decided that when a witness cannot be compelled to answer he need not be called. (6 Peter's Rep., 352, 367.) But Mr. Pacheco might have called the voter, and if he had not claimed his privilege he could have made it clear for whom he did vote. Mr. Pacheco not having done so, we may infer that Gilbert, if produced, would have corroborated the witness whose deposition is in the record.

I would like to know where they find any law in this country that would allow a man to refuse to state before a committee of Congress or upon the witness-stand for whom he voted; but if there is such a law, at least the contestant has never called this witness, and no reason is given why he did not call the witness. On this state of case the majority of the committee reject Mr. Gilbert's vote and deduct one vote from the number counted for Mr. Pacheco.

Well, this testimony would amount to nothing in any court of justice; it would not be received anywhere before any tribunal that has any regard for arriving at truth, for it is absolutely incompetent evidence. Upon this testimony Gilbert's vote was rejected and counted among the votes that had been given for Pacheco, because Pacheco did not call the witness to prove that he did not vote for him. How many thousands of men were there in that district who were not called to swear how they voted? It is conceded by the gentleman who presents this report that the testimony is not competent to prove for whom he voted; but because Pacheco did not call him to prove that he had voted for him he must be counted against him. On the other hand, we might say with equal propriety that Mr. Wigginton ought to have called him and asked him for whom he voted.

But the committee proceeded on the idea that Mr. Pacheco ought to have proved that the man who illegally voted for him, as was alleged, did not vote at all, or otherwise the vote was rejected. That is as far as I desire to go. There are other examples of a like character, but I intend to stop here.

Mr. LEONARD. Suppose there is this case before the House : There is a reasonable well-founded doubt as to who was elected, and a doubt as to whether anybody was elected or not; what ought the House to do?

Mr. KEIFER. I should say that in this case there was a *prima facie* case for the contestee. If the contestant does not make out a case to overcome it, then the contestee being in his seat the House should not act affirmatively to put him out.

Mr. LEONARD. Suppose there is a doubt as to whether he was or was not elected; should he be allowed to retain his seat?

Mr. KEIFER. Yes; he is in the seat, and should not be removed unless a case is made out against him.

APPOINTMENT OF CIVILIANS.

February 13, 1878. The Military Academy appropriation bill was under consideration.

Mr. KEIFER said:

I move to further amend section 2 by inserting after the word "civilians" the words "except such as are regular graduates of the United States Military Academy and who have been honorably discharged from the service"; also to insert after the words "shall only be made" the words "in time of peace."

Mr. DURHAM. So far as the Committee on Appropriations are concerned they are willing to accept that amendment.

Mr. FINLEY. I ask that the section as proposed to be amended be read.

The Clerk read as follows:

That appointments of civilians, except such as are regular graduates of the United States Military Academy and who have been honorably discharged from the service, to be second lieutenants in any of the regiments of the Army, shall only be made in time of peace when more vacancies exist in the Army than will be required in the assignment of the next graduating class of cadets at the United States Military Academy.

Mr. KEIFER. I understand that the gentleman having charge of this bill [Mr. DURHAM] is willing to accept this amendment. I do not desire to take up the time of the Committee of the Whole by speaking in favor of it, except to say that it may often be of very great importance to the Army in time of peace to appoint skilled men and military men, men who have graduated at West Point and who from misfortune or other cause have left the Army after having graduated—it may be important to appoint them to places in the Army when they desire to return, being fully prepared to discharge the duties of officers in the Army.

Let me say that in the proper exercise of their judgments the Secretary of War and the President of the United States may very often make these appointments in anticipation of further vacancies occurring before the time when the graduating class at West Point may graduate, and there would be no objection to making the appointments in that view. In other words, it will not affect the appointment of the next graduating class of West Point to fill places in the Army.

Of course, it is quite obvious that the second branch of my amendment, to insert the words "in time of peace," is a very important one. This section should apply only to times of peace. In time of war, if an exigency should be pressing, such a limitation as this might greatly embarrass the President and the War Department.

Mr. BRAGG. Will the gentleman accept an amendment to insert the word "and" after the phrase "in time of peace," so as to read: "In time of peace and when more vacancies exist in the Army," &c. This will limit the appointments to cases of actual vacancies. With the word "and" left out, there is no such limitation.

Mr. DURHAM. That is right.

Mr. KEIFER. I have no objection to the modification, though I do not see its necessity.

DISTINGUISHED OHIOANS.

March 13, 1878. On the consular and diplomatic appropriation bill.

Mr. KEIFER said.

Mr. CHAIRMAN: This seems to me a good time to say a word in the interest and on behalf of some other distinguished gentlemen from Ohio who have been assailed, in my opinion unnecessarily. I wish, however, in the first place to indorse, from a very good opportunity to know the truth, what has been said to-day and on a former occasion by my colleague [Mr. JONES] in favor of Colonel Alfred E. Lee. It does seem to me that because Colonel Lee happened to accept the position of private secretary to Mr. Hayes, when governor of Ohio, he should not be excluded from taking a position which he is well qualified to fill in a foreign country.

Mr. TOWNSEND, of New York. He belongs to the wrong family of Lees. [Laughter.]

Mr. KEIFER. Mr. Chairman, I was a little astonished to hear the distinguished member from New York [Mr. HEWITT] say that he knew nothing or heard nothing of General Comly, of Ohio, now minister to the Sandwich Islands. Why, sir, General Comly has been a distinguished man, not only as a soldier but as a civilian; and he has stood at the head of his profession as a journalist.

Mr. FINLEY. He was the editor of a paper and the first person to suggest Mr. Hayes for the Presidency.

Mr. KEIFER. I do not wish to be interrupted on this occasion, as I have a very few minutes. General Comly would do honor to this country anywhere. The present occupant of the chair [Mr. COX, of New York] knows him. He is known very well all over this country; and it seems to me that the gentleman from New York did not do himself justice when he said he did not know him. Because he edited a paper at the capital of the State of Ohio, it does not follow that he is incompetent to fill such a position as he now holds. I might dwell further upon General Comly, who is a man of head and heart, but I have not the time.

General Noyes is also assailed as though he were distinguished for but one thing on earth, and that the fact that he stood upon the rostrum in the national Republican convention at Cincinnati in 1876 and nominated Rutherford B. Hayes for President. I wish to remind the gentleman from New York that Governor Noyes was a graduate of Dartmouth College. He was a distinguished lawyer in the Queen City of the West. He entered the Army early in the beginning of the late war. He staid there, going through the campaigns of Missouri down to the capture of Island No. 10. He came over and was in the movement upon the capture of Corinth, Mississippi. He was in the battle of Iuka, under General Rosecrans. He was in the Atlanta campaign; and in celebrating the 4th of July, 1864, at Resaca, he lost a leg, suffering from the injury two amputations. He has since held the position of city solicitor of Cincinnati with great credit. He has presided as judge in that city; and certainly it is not to his dishonor that he was governor of Ohio. He has been distinguished as a scholar, and he has taken great interest in all public affairs in this country. When he was appointed minister to the court of France, he was worthy of the position; for there was not a blot or a stain upon his record anywhere, his revilers to the contrary notwithstanding. He needs no defense; but when I hear him assailed on this floor by the member from Mississippi [Mr. SINGLETON], who has charge of this bill, and by two distinguished members from the State of New York [Mr. HEWITT and Mr. COX], I think it quite proper that I should say a single word in his behalf.

    *   *   *   *   *   *   * .

I am glad that my friend from Kentucky [Mr. BLACKBURN] enters a disclaimer for his side of the House—a gentleman beside me suggests river, but I say House—in relation to these Ohio appointments. But my friend seems to speak somewhat ironically when he comes to talk upon the subject. [Laughter.] He is evidently not in earnest. He would not have the country to believe that he was candid, and therefore I do not credit him with being candid now.

The gentleman starts off by saying that Ohio has a General of the Army. I have heard so much from that side of the House about civil-service reform that I am not a little astonished to hear that remark made. It may not be civil service which made General Sherman the General of the Army, but it was military service. There was competitive examination for that appointment. [Applause.] It was competitive examination with those who were in the Union and fighting for it; it was competitive examination with those who were trying to get out of the Union and fighting against it which made Sherman, the son of Ohio, whom we are proud to honor, General of the Army. I may take another instance. We are told that we have a Lieutenant-General, (Sheridan.) I know he too was born in Ohio in an humble station of life. I believe he used to be connected with the most humble people of our country. But he went into the competitive examination also, and he kept on in his examination, stopping nowhere, standing behind no person, except it be General Grant and General Sherman, until he became by this same kind of competitive examination the Lieutenant-General of the Army, a position which General Sheridan has well earned and fills well. And if there be any person on this floor who thinks he did not fairly earn his place, then I do not think such a person fought for the Union. Now let me say one word further. We have a President from Ohio, and the people of the United States are responsible for that. [Cries of "No!" "No!" and laughter from the Democratic side.] And let me say, Mr. Chairman, with some pleasure the other day, the distinguished gentleman from New York [Mr. HEWITT] say he had a perfect title.

Mr. BLACKBURN. Will the gentleman answer a question for me?

Mr. KEIFER. I will try to do so.

Mr. BLACKBURN. Did the President, the present Executive of the United States, succeed to his office by means of a competitive examination like those other Ohio men?

Mr. KEIFER. Yes, undoubtedly. Mr. Chairman, I would be glad to answer that in the same way, if you gave me time. I know from personal knowledge how he acquired his high-standing, not only as a civilian, but as a soldier. He, too, did his duty in the field, trying to uphold its flag and preserve the integrity of his country. I should be glad to speak further of the President and of the distinguished men of Ohio to whom reference has been made.

BARTHOLOMEW AGRICULTURAL SOCIETY.

March 29th, 1878.   On the bill for the relief of the Bartholomew Agricultural Society—

Mr. KEIFER said:

Mr. SPEAKER: I might answer the inquiry just made by the gentleman in regard to the loyalty of these persons in this way: that in an unreported case recently in the Supreme Court of the United States, that court held that where there was a contract to pay a party, made by the United States, which was valid, it was not important whether the party was loyal or not loyal.   I refer to the case of Clark *vs.* The United States.   I have no doubt about the loyalty of these men, but I need not stop to discuss that matter.   The sole question involved here is whether this contract was binding on the Government.   If it was, then if we refuse to pass this bill to pay this society for, as the report states, the time that the grounds of the society were occupied as a rendezvous for the organization of troops, we simply say that we repudiate a Government contract.

Now, one word further.   It has been intimated that this contract was a forgery in this: that it was interlined so as to attach additional obligations to the General Government after it had been executed.   Now, any person who will examine the contract, the original of which the gentleman from Ohio [Mr. FINLEY] holds in his hand, will be able to see, on the most casual inspection of it, that the signatures, or at least some of them, were written over that part which is claimed to have been interlined.   It is clear beyond doubt that the name of Thomas Wilson was written there after the interlineation was made, for it extends over a part of that interlineation.   Now it happened in this way: the contract, without those words, was sent to Washington by the officers of the Government who were authorized to make this contract: but the society refused to make with the Government any such contract as was proposed.   The Government subsequently, through its officers, put in conditions that the society was willing to have put in and then the contract was executed.   The Government occupied these lands before the change was made in the contract, and they are now bound to pay for that use of the property. It ought to be distinctly understood by the House that the society, by virtue of the language claimed to have been interlined in the contract, gains nothing under this bill.

Mr. JONES, of Ohio.   I desire to ask the gentleman one question, for I want to get at the truth in this matter.   I would ask the gentleman whether it is not a fact that this agricultural society filed its claim for the use and occupancy of its property up to May, 1864, and then, whether they did not file another claim in October, and whether both claims were paid or not?   I ask now further, whether the society did not, at that time, concede that the General Government occupied their grounds from May to October, five months, and whether this bill does not propose to pay them for that time?

Mr. FINLEY.   I desire to ask my colleague [Mr. KEIFER] a question.   Does not this committee undertake to pay this agricultural society for the use of these grounds for one month and twenty-eight days before the contract was ever made?

Mr. KEIFER.   I am informed in relation to the last question asked me, that the contract was sent out and the society surrendered their grounds to the United States, and the Government occupied them for quite a time while there was a little controversy about the execution of the contract, and that explains that trouble.   But the gentleman from Ohio [Mr. JONES] asked me a question which I will endeavor to answer.   I was not a member of the subcommittee which examined the papers, but my information is that no concession was made by this society that the Government had not occupied or controlled their grounds for any part of the time which it is now proposed to pay for. The gentleman is perhaps partly right when he says that some claims were presented and paid.   That is true, and the committee have deducted that amount from the bill.

PENSION AGENTS.

April 11, 1878.   On the pension appropriation bill—

Mr. KEIFER said:

For two days I have listened here to a discussion which seems to me has spread over almost every phase of this question, and at last, when the members of the Committee on Appropriations are brought up to the point, they cannot give us the facts upon which they ask the Congress of the United States to legislate in a matter which is to affect directly over two hundred thousand of the people of this country, and indirectly hundreds of thousands more.   The gentleman from Iowa [Mr. PRICE] yesterday seemed to be startled at the idea that we were paying the pension agents of the country from ten to sixteen thousand dollars a year simply for vouchers, and then the gentleman from Pennsylvania, [Mr. SMITH,] who is a member of the Committee on Appropriations, put a statement in the Record of what had been paid for these purposes, and it is upon that kind of a statement that we are asked to vote for this bill.

Now, let me state that it is an absolute fact that the man who is put down on that list as receiving the largest sum for the payment of vouchers cannot make, after he pays his clerks, his office rent, stationery, postage, and other expenses, $6,000 a year.   I know that he does not make that much.   I had it from his own lips.   The statement put in the Record by the member from Pennsylvania shows that the agent at Columbus receives over $26,000.   There is nothing furnished to show what he pays out.   We are expected to go into important legislation without the facts and for the reason that the Committee on Appropriations get one side of a statement and leave out entirely the other side.

Mr. PRICE.   Will the gentleman allow me to ask him a question?

Mr. KEIFER.   I have so short a time and there are so many gentlemen who wish to interrupt me that I must decline to yield to anybody.   My colleague [Mr. BANNING] rose and spoke a few moments ago about the pension agent in Ohio.   That pension agent in Ohio extends facilities to the thousands of persons who have to be paid in Cincinnati, but my colleague said that because he did not have sufficient information as to the pay of the agents he thought he was in favor of the bill of the committee.   Do we not know that agent goes either in person or by a clerk to Cincinnati on the 4th of each month, when pensions are due, and remains there as long as it is necessary to pay off the pensioners, for the sole purpose of accommodating these thousands of men and saving them from expense and delay and from distress among themselves and their families; and does this out of his own pocket?   And yet we are told that he is receiving twenty odd thousand dollars a year when he is really expending a very large portion of the amount in the interest of the pensioners who need their money and need it promptly.

Now, it is said by the gentleman from Illinois [Mr. FORT] that those pensioners who are in the soldiers' homes are paid direct from Washington.   They amount to but 6,000, and if you want to legislate in their interest then you must not impose upon the Department here the labor of paying all the pensioners throughout the country, because that would prevent them from receiving their pay as promptly as they now do.

Mr. PRICE.   They get their pay from Washington now.

Mr. KEIFER.   The 6,000 in the soldiers' homes do; but if you require the Department to pay the 200,000 the same machinery will not answer with the niggardly legislation of this Congress in the direction of allowing clerks.   Do we not know of the great delay, day by day, week by week, month by month, in giving a few additional clerks to the Surgeon-General's Office that is now being asked for in order to hurry through the decision of the large number of applications for pensions?   Congress stands quietly by and witnesses this delay, and yet it is proposed now to cast additional labor upon that Department.

LEGISLATION IN APPROPRIATION BILLS.

April 30, 1878. Pending the legislative appropriation bill—

Mr. KEIFER said:

I do not propose, Mr. Chairman, to undertake to answer in a general way or a special way many things said here on this subject. I want, however, to say that I should like to see this House and the Congress of the United States go one step further than has been advocated by the distinguished member from the State of Pennsylvania, the Speaker of this House; I should like to see the time, and I trust I will see the time, when no appropriation bill will contain or be permitted to contain any general legislation. I have very recently looked at most of the constitutions of the States of the United States, and I believe that in twenty-four of the States of this Union they have found it wise to say in their organic acts in effect that all legislation in an appropriation bill other than that which pertains directly to the matter of appropriation shall be void. It would be found to be the highest kind of wisdom to have a rule, a constitutional rule, that would inhibit all legislation in an appropriation bill, save such as pertained directly to the appropriation of money.

I want to say further that we should stop legislation of every character in an appropriation bill, and then it would become the duty of an appropriation committee to look to the existing laws of the land and legislate with reference to them in their appropriation bills. I wish to say a word more. I am one of those that are classed here to-day as belonging to a "herd" that are voting against economy. I deny the charge. I deny it because I do not believe that stinted legislation in the way of paying for what we ought to pay for, in the way of making appropriations for the construction of public buildings in this country, is economy at all. I know that now we are paying in the shape of rent in the city of Washington larger sums annually than would pay the interest at 20 per cent. on all the money it would take to build good fire-proof buildings to preserve all the public records here. I know, too, that we could build these buildings here, and if needed elsewhere over the country, at this time when material is cheap, when labor is being tendered all over the country and is going without a demand anywhere, and in so doing would relieve many thousands of people. And if any man says it is economy to say we should pay out large sums in rent instead of building the necessary buildings; if any man says it is economy to let these hundreds of thousands of men go without work when we could furnish the work by erecting the necessary public buildings, I say it is not true economy; it is the meanest kind of economy, if it can be called that at all. That is what I think about it. Parsimony is not economy; in politics it is demagoguery.

The Democratic party, by failing to make the needful appropriations in the Forty-fourth Congress for public buildings, threw out of employment many thousands of laborers. I am in favor of economy, that is, paying only the proper and ordinary wages to men who are employed by the Government. I do not believe I would pay Congressmen any more than they are paid now. Yet the gentleman [Mr. RANDALL] who has spoken of the party I belong to as a "herd" voting against economy, has stood on the floor of this House and advocated the payment of $7,500 a year, including two years' back pay, to himself and others. [Applause from the Republican side.]

TAXING INVENTORS.

An amendment was pending to require patentees to pay, in addition to the fees allowed by law, the actual cost and expense of printing their respective patents.

Mr. KEIFER said:

I am utterly opposed to putting any further tax upon the men of genius of this country who are inventors. Most of them, according to my observation, are poor men, or men who at least have become poor, if not poor originally, in carrying out their experiments, on that which they hope to make valuable to themselves, but which at the last inure to the benefit of mankind. I do not think it wise policy for the Government to undertake to tax that class of men in this country to raise revenue.

I believe the fact is the $100,000 of surplus revenue which has arisen from the tax upon inventors has been used in erecting buildings for the Interior Department. There is now in the Treasury, unexpended from this revenue, nearly $12,000,000. There was about, in round numbers, $16,000,000 standing to the credit of the Patent Office, all of which has been taken from this class of people. I would be glad to see the law so changed that you could command the best talent in America to put into this office—I mean the highest talent. It is a fact that ninety-nine out of a hundred of the patents coming out of that Patent Office for the last twenty years are absolutely void when they have passed through the crucible of the courts. The complaint comes to us from abroad that we are issuing patents in name and not in fact. There is some error in our system; perhaps we have not employed the right men. In England and France they do not issue a patent because some man imagines that he has made a new and useful invention, and hence they do not have their courts flooded with suits of patent cases.

That is not the worst of it. These men obtain patents and go out through the country and make the people believe that they have valuable patents, and they tax the public with them. A person charged with infringing upon one of these patents says : I cannot undertake to go through a lawsuit in a United States court, which is a great distance off, and therefore I will pay the penalty. Many of these patents are utterly void. I know in my own experience that old machinery that has been standing in my country unused for fifty years has been gathered up and a patent obtained upon it and the whole country is required to pay tribute to it.

90 A—K——2

CLAIMS OF LOYAL CITIZENS.

May 10, 1878. On the bill for the relief of Richard Heater—

Mr. KEIFER said:
It was the policy of this Government to provide the method of settling claims of loyal citizens. It was the policy of the Government to allow the Quartermaster and Commissary Departments to settle claims of citizens living in the loyal States. It was the policy of the Government to remit all other claims of loyal citizens to the commissioners of claims to settle all claims for commissary stores and quartermaster stores taken or furnished, to use the language of the statute, from residents of insurrectionary States.

Now, Mr. Chairman, let me state the peculiarity of this case, and I have here before me the original papers.

Mr. BRAGG. If this property was taken by order of the Quartermaster's Department, so as to charge the Government, would not the quartermaster have issued a voucher to the citizens from whom he took the property, so it could be presented to the proper Department and be paid?

Mr KEIFER. The answer to that is, he would if he was prepared to do it, but he was not bound to do it; and the second answer is, that if he had issued the voucher to this man Richard Heater, in the State of Virginia, the Government, by no machinery that has been provided up to the present hour outside of Congress, would have ever paid for it. The voucher would have stood for naught. I understand this man Richard Heater in his life-time presented his claim for these stores and this property to the Quartermaster's Department, and there it was considered. I have the report upon my table. The quartermaster held that while as a matter of fact the property was taken from the citizen in an insurrectionary State, it was still taken from a farm belonging to Richard Heater, in the State of Maryland, a loyal State. While the quartermaster found the property was taken, and that the Government of the United States had the benefit of it, and that it should be paid for, yet under the law, the man himself living in an insurrectionary State and his property in a loyal State, he had no jurisdiction to make an allowance.

Then Mr. Heater went with his claim to the commissioners of southern claims. There he thought they had jurisdiction. There the testimony was retaken. The property was found to have been, taken and used by the United States, and ought to be paid for. The commissioners of claims held that the property was taken in a loyal State and not in a disloyal State, and therefore they had no jurisdiction to grant relief, merely because the property was in the wrong State. In the first instance the man was in the wrong State, while in the last the property was in the wrong State, and there was no relief to be obtained except from Congress. I will now yield to the gentleman for a question.

Mr. BRAGG. How happened it that this claim lay dormant until there was a law passed prohibiting the Quartermaster's Department paying it?

Mr. KEIFER. This claim went into the Quartermaster's Department while the law was in full force as the letter from the Quartermaster lying upon my table shows. It states the reason why he did not order it to be paid. It was because the man lived in an insurrectionary State, and the Quartermaster-General therefore had no jurisdiction to pay him, and it made no difference whether the law was passed taking away the power from the Quartermaster's Department or not, because that Department never had the power under the law and the construction given it by the Quartermaster-General to grant relief.

Mr. BRAGG. Does the gentleman say this claim was presented before 1861?

Mr. KEIFER. Yes, sir.

Mr. BRAGG. How early?

Mr. KEIFER. I do not know that. I cannot give the precise date; but it was presented in due time and considered and rejected, because the Quartermaster's Department held it had no jurisdiction under the law to grant him relief, as he lived in an insurrectionary State. Then Mr. Heater went before the commissioners of southern claims, there presented his claim, there took all the testimony, and had the case fully heard; but the commissioners found, because the property was taken in a loyal State, notwithstanding Mr. Heater lived in an insurrectionary State, they could not grant relief. Their report lies here before me.

Mr. BRAGG. What is the proof showing the amount of each kind of grain that was taken?

Mr. KEIFER. The proofs are all here and are ample to show the amount. And if the gentleman will examine the report he will see that the Committee on War Claims cut down the values and did what is regarded by very many people in the South, perhaps also in the North, as a great injustice—they reduced good cedar rails to cord-wood and put at the ordinary rates for which cord-wood sells here on the Potomac River; and fences made of good cedar timber and buildings which had been used for fuel. All this was put down at the rate for cord-wood and not according to the real value of the material. The prices allowed are the minimum prices adopted by the commissioners of claims, who have been in the habit of allowing for such property the value at the time; and it was very low. Three dollars per cord was only allowed. Wheat is put in at a dollar a bushel and corn at seventy cents. The other things are rated exactly in accordance with the allowance uniformly made by the commissioners of claims and the Court of Claims.

Now, let me say one thing further. This claim was kindred to other claims that have been presented to the Quartermaster and Commissary Departments and that have come before the commissioners of claims, and hundreds of thousands of dollars of claims like this have been paid; and this would have been paid but for the simple fact that neither the Quartermaster's Department nor the commissioners of claims had jurisdiction to allow and pay it.

Mr. EDEN. Did not the commissioners of claims find this claimant loyal?

Mr. KEIFER. Yes, sir.

Mr. EDEN. And did they not find the fact in his favor about the property being furnished?

Mr. KEIFER. The Quartermaster's Department and the commissioners of claims each found everything in his favor, save and except the fact that the claimant lived without their jurisdiction or that his property was without their jurisdiction.

The gentleman from Wisconsin suggests that I am a convert to the payment of this class of claims. Let me say first for John Heater who is now in his grave, the testimony showed most conclusively and the fact is well known that he was a loyal man. He gave his son for the cause of the Union. His son went into the Union Army with his own consent and gallantly served in it during the war.

I do not intend the gentleman shall classify me at all on this subject of paying these claims. I have my own views about it. I believe in paying such claims as this. I believe in a liberal rule, and I do not care what the views of other gentlemen may be from a regard to political considerations. Whatever others may do, I believe I shall advocate on the floor of this House as I have advocated in the committee, and gentlemen of the committee will corroborate me in this statement, a liberal rule as to the payment of claims of loyal men living in the South. I am not to be classed among those opposed to paying. And I desire—although I do not wish unnecessarily to take up the time of the House—to send to the Clerk's desk some paragraphs from a speech made some years ago in the Senate of the United States by a distinguished Senator, a man of both head and heart, Senator Morton, of Indiana, on this subject of the payment of claims of loyal citizens of the South.

The Clerk read as follows:

But, Mr. President, let me take the case of a Union man in the South who has borne the heat and burden of this civil war, who has been persecuted, and who has sustained all those hardships that we know were incident to a Union man in the South during the war. To say that we will treat him as a public enemy, and that we will refuse to pay him for his property deliberately taken by the Government, where under the same circumstances we would pay a man living in the North for his property taken by the Government, is revolting to the plainest principles of justice. I cannot subscribe to any such doctrine. Why, sir, I know that where a camp was organized in the State of Indiana, or Ohio, or Pennsylvania, for the purpose of collecting and preparing troops, the owner of the property was indemnified by the Government for the damage done to it, or where forage and provisions were taken for the purpose of subsisting those troops the parties were indemnified for their property. To say that we will not pay a Union man in the South where his property has been taken under the same circumstances is revolting to the common principles of justice. I would throw to the winds all these technical rules by which the Union man of the South is to be treated as a public enemy and by which we shall refuse to do him that justice which we would do to a man in the North, of doubtful loyalty, who was living in peace, comfort, and safety.

Mr. President, there was one authority referred to, I believe, by the Senator from West Virginia [Mr. Willey] which perhaps might even cover all the cases, and I think that was in Vattel. He can correct me if I state incorrectly. That authority was that even, for example, in a loyal State or in a part of the country where the insurrection did not prevail, if the Government deliberately took property, as a house or a garden, to make a rampart or fortification, or if it took forage or subsistence deliberately, the Government was bound to make payment. According to that authority, as I understand it, when General Lee invaded the State of Pennsylvania and the army of General Meade was falling back, if in the course of a march or a battle they destroyed the property of loyal men, that would be an act of war for which the Government would not be liable, even in a loyal State.

And, sir, applying that principle to the Southern States where General Sherman on his march, or in the course of a battle, passed over and destroyed the property of Union men the Government is not liable; but if General Meade in the course of expelling Lee deliberately destroyed property which became necessary for a fortification, or seized the forage and provisions of loyal men around him there, the parties would be paid, and under the same circumstances they should be paid in the South, always upon the condition that they are true and loyal men.

Then, does not the rule reduce itself down to simply this, that wherever a loyal man in the North would be paid for his property which was deliberately appropriated by the Government, a loyal man in the South should be paid for his property deliberately appropriated by the Government and where in the North a loyal man would not be paid for property destroyed in the course of a march or of a battle, so in the South a loyal man should not be paid for his property destroyed in the same way.

Can we afford to make any other rule on this subject? We might save some money by making another rule; but it would in the end be penny-wise and pound-foolish economy. After having expended some $5,000,000,000 to keep the South in the Union, and after all our labors to build up a loyal party down there, shall we come here making shipwreck in the end by declaring upon the floor of the Senate that the loyal men, whose hardships and sufferings we can never estimate, shall be treated as public enemies, and that we will not pay them under the same circumstances under which we would pay a man for the taking of like property in the North. I can never consent to it.— *Congressional Globe*, volume 71, page 362.

Mr. KEIFER. The gentleman says in the last campaign I undertook to make capital out of the payments of this sort of claims. I never did. Everywhere and always I contended that the Government ought to be just to all those men who stood by it during the war, whether they were from the South or the North. And when the gentleman makes that statement it proceeds from a spirit that lies deep in his own bosom, the spirit of demagogery. He merely imagined we would do it.

Let me say further that I have heard that speech about John Sherman down at Marietta twice since I have been on the floor, and I do not know but it was repeated twice here to-day. The gentleman is utterly ignorant of the law under which that $100,000,000 spoke of by Mr. Sherman was paid. After the pardon was granted by the general proclamation of Andrew Johnson, it was held by the Supreme Court of the United States that that pardon remitted all persons who had property taken from them in the South, under the abandoned-and-captured-property act, however disloyal, to receive from the Treasury of the United States the moneys derived from the sale of captured and abandoned property. And in that way many millions of dollars were paid, and rightfully paid, because I submit the decision of the Supreme Court of the United States was right.

Now, the gentleman has got that summed up here and included in that statement, and undertakes to throw it in the face of the gentleman from Tennessee [Mr. THORNBURGH] when he rises to speak for his loyal constituents and on behalf of them on this measure. I am sorry the gentleman from Ohio [Mr. McMAHON] has left the Hall and gone off to correct the record while I am attempting to reply to him.

Let me say further that I do not intend to submit here to be driven from my line of duty by any such taunts as have been thrown out by my colleague who has just left the Hall, or my colleague who spoke a few minutes ago, [Mr. FINLEY.] He, too, gave as a reason why he did not dare to do his duty here as a member of the House, that the Republican party had voted to pay loyal claims in the past and was now trying to make capital out of war claims by a Democratic House. He contented himself with saying— for that was the logic of his whole speech—that he was opposed for that reason to all these measures and these bills. I hope, sir, this Congress will not be moved by any such low and disgraceful motive, either on the one side or the other.

I did not myself believe that we should undertake to pay damages occasioned by the war, such as are classified under the general head of ravages of war by either army. I challenge the consistency of my colleagues from Ohio, [Mr. McMAHON and Mr. FINLEY.] In vain have I listened to hear from them the announcement of some principle of law for excluding loyal men's claims for supplies furnished to the United States during the war. They each assail the Republican party for having paid in past years claims of loyal men. No political sin of that kind lies at their door. The magnanimity of many Southern men who were against the Union, and some of whom fought valiantly in the Confederate army, contrasts favorably with them. Whatever may be said of the reconciliation of Southern men in giving in their adhesion to the Union in good faith, nothing can be said for some Northern Democrats. [Applause.]

I know that many of these questions were presented here in 1872 before a commission that was appointed partly by the United States and partly by Great Britain—appointed under what was called the Washington treaty, by the twelfth article of which the United States agreed to pay all legal claims of Her Britannic Majesty's subjects growing out of the war. Count Louis Corti, of Italy, presided over that commission ; Judge James S. Frazer, of Indiana, formerly a justice of the supreme court of that State, was one of the members of that commission ; and the Right Hon. Russell Gurney, of Her Britannic Majesty's privy council, I believe, represented Great Britain. That commission unanimously found, when there were claims presented on behalf of subjects of Great Britain before it for losses of property during the late war, that there was no legal claim under the rules of international law against the United States for any losses by the war that came from the ordinary devastation or ravages of war. Before that commission the liability of the United States to pay all legal claims was admitted. No question of loyalty was involved. And therefore we stand upon that rule. I stand on it for other reasons. In effect it has been decided frequently by our own Supreme Court, and the rules of international law are well settled in regard to it. But when it comes to a question of taking a loyal man's property and the United States getting the benefit of it, appropriating it, using it for the purposes of the Government in the prosecution of the war and in putting down the rebellion, I see no reason why the United States should not pay a loyal man without reference to where he lives or where his property was.

I am informed that after the vote was taken in December, 1872, on the passage of the bill in favor of the College of William and Mary, when the bill was voted down by the exact vote I stated a few moments ago—yeas 36, nays 127, not voting 78—a motion was made to reconsider, and that was laid on the table. But subsequently to that time, near the close of that session, a new bill was introduced which did pass. To that extent I was mistaken. But the bill was voted down by the exact vote I stated in December, 1872, and another bill was passed subsequently.

POWER OF APPOINTMENT BY COURTS.

May 20, 1878. A question of the power of judges of the supreme court of the District to appoint certain officers was under discussion.

Mr. KEIFER said:

How does the bill read?

The SPEAKER *pro tempore*. The bill reads "shall be appointed by the judges of the supreme court of the District of Columbia." It is proposed to strike out "judges of the supreme court of the District of Columbia" and insert "shall be appointed by the President, by and with the advice and consent of the Senate."

Mr. KEIFER. Then, Mr. Speaker, the point I was about to make I still insist upon. That is that there is no constitutional power to vest in the judges of a court as distinguished from the court itself the right to make any such appointment as this. The distinction is very plain, and certainly will be very well understood by lawyers, that power cannot be conferred upon a judge or all judges that constitute a court unless it be conferred upon them as constituting the court itself.

Now, it is attempted here, as I maintain, in violation of the second section of article 2 of the Constitution of the United States, to confer a power upon judges, not upon the court. That section has reference to the powers and duties of the President, and the clause I call attention to reads thus:

But the Congress may by law vest the appointment of such inferior officers, as they think proper, in the President alone, in the courts of law, or in the heads of Departments.

Not in the judges of the courts, but in courts acting as courts; and I insist, so far as concerns this vesting of appointment in the judges, this act would be held to be a nullity, being a violation of the Constitution. I am in favor, therefore, of the amendment submitted by the gentleman from Minnesota.

I wish to state another thing. I am unable to say why it is that the committee desire to change the mode of appointment of this particular officer, a higher officer than many others that are required to be appointed by the President of the United States and confirmed by the Senate of the United States. It is sought here to consolidate two offices, to bring them together, and to vest in certain judges of the District an appointing power over which there is no review, of which no confirmation is required. It looks to me as if there was a singling out of this office for some special reason.

Mr. CLAFLIN. There is no objection, I think, to the amendment of the gentleman from Minnesota.

Mr. KEIFER. Let me just add that I always find that where there is special legislation sought there is something wrong about it. It may not crop out on the surface, but sooner or later you find there is an ulterior purpose in it.

22

THE UNITED STATES ARMY.

May 22, 1878.   On the Army appropriation bill—

Mr. KEIFER said:

Mr. CHAIRMAN: I do not defend the Army of the United States and here speak for its preservation because I come from a region of country or State which hitherto has had to appeal to that Army to preserve the peace and good order of the community. We were fortunate enough in Ohio, within the last year, to have a Governor (Hon. Thomas L. Young) patriotic enough, strong enough, brave enough, and with moral courage enough, to declare, when there was danger in our State, (to use his own words,) "I will not call on the United States for troops until every able-bodied man in the State of Ohio has been whipped." And he went through on that declaration. But we saw in the East, in Maryland and West Virginia, Democratic governors appealing to the President of the United States for troops to preserve peace and order and property in their respective States.

In the West we witnessed the same thing, a Democratic governor of Indiana appealing to the President of the United States for troops for the same purpose. In all, ten governors in the last year have made requisition upon the President of the United States for troops to quell disorders. The State of Ohio took care of its own troubles when danger threatened.

But it is not my purpose to pursue this line of argument. It is my duty, as I deem it, as a member of this House to look to the interests of the whole country, and not confine myself to merely local considerations.

The Committee on Appropriations have assumed to report a bill to this House for the reorganization and future government of the Army. The chairman of the Military Committee [Mr. BANNING] said in his speech on yesterday that it became the duty of Congress each year to provide an Army. This is as I understood him. His speech is not in the Record this morning. Is it possible that the Army and Navy of the United States have annually to depend for existence on the action of Congress or a single branch of the National Legislature?

The gentleman from New York [Mr. HEWITT] who has charge of this bill indicates that he borrowed his work from the chairman of the Committee on Military Affairs.

This is a warning to the country of what is to be the future policy of the dominant party in this House. Our Army is to be dependent from year to year on the will or political whim of Congress. It may be valuable to examine the history of the proposed legislation in this Congress. It must not be forgotten that the policy of the last House at its last session was to have an army without pay. Upon failure of appropriation again, the Army is to be disbanded. But let us look to the proposed legislation of this House in chronological order.

The chairman of the Military Committee, [Mr. BANNING,] on October 29, 1877, (see Record, volume 26, page 179,) introduced a bill (H. R. No. 293) to repeal section 1218 of Revised Statutes, prohibiting the appointment of persons who have served in the civil, military, or naval service of the so-called Confederate States. I give the section proposed to be repealed hereafter.

The repeal of this section indicated to the unsophisticated an ardent desire to open the doors to an enlargement of the Army. Such persons could only see in this that the honorable chairman had concluded that it was impracticable to get good officers from graduates of West Point and from late officers of the Union Army (or from civil life) without selecting from those who have served in some capacity in the Confederate military, naval, or civil service.

On January 28, 1878, the member from Ohio, [Mr. BANNING,] in his capacity of chairman of the Military Committee, introduced a bill to reorganize and reduce the Army. It had many remarkable provisions. Section 42 of that bill provided for the repeal of section 1104, which authorizes the enlistment of two cavalry regiments of colored men; of section 1108, which authorizes the enlistment of two infantry regiments of colored men; of section 1218, already referred to; of section 1258, which limited the number of officers on the retired-list to three hundred; and of section 1316, which excluded from appointment as cadets at the Military and Naval Academies persons who had been in the Confederate service. I will give these sections here:

SEC. 1104. The enlisted men of two regiments of cavalry shall be colored men.

SEC. 1108. The enlisted men of two regiments of infantry shall be colored men.

SEC. 1218. No person who has served in any capacity in the military, naval, or civil service of the so-called Confederate States, or of either of the States in insurrection during the late rebellion, shall be appointed to any position in the Army of the United States.

Sec. 1258. The whole number of officers of the Army on the retired-list shall not at any time exceed three hundred, and any less number to be allowed thereon may be fixed by the President in his discretion.

Sec. 1316. No person who has served in any capacity in the military or naval service of the so-called Confederate States, or of either of the States in insurrection during the late rebellion, shall be appointed a cadet.

Here is the section of the bill of the chairman of the Military Committee proposing the repeal of the foregoing sections:

Sec. 42. That sections 1104, 1108, 1218, 1258, and 1316 of the Revised Statutes, and all other acts and parts of acts inconsistent with the provisions of this act, be, and they are hereby, repealed.

[Here the hammer fell.]

Mr. McCOOK was recognized, and yielded his time to Mr. KEIFER.

Mr. KEIFER. My time will not allow me to speculate on the motives for, purposes and designs in, blessings intended by, or evils which are expected to flow from the repeal of these sections now or in the future.

Section 41 of the bill of January 28, 1878, and a section found in a subsequent bill, is the most extraordinary ever proposed, so far as I can learn, in the annals of the American Congress or any other parliamentary body in the civilized world. I give the section here:

Sec. 41. That the troops herein provided for and all others authorized by existing law, including all officers of every grade and in every department of the Army, shall be retained in the service of the United States so long as Congress shall provide for their support, by specific appropriations therefor, and no longer; and if Congress shall refuse or neglect to make the necessary appropriations for that purpose at or before the expiration of the last preceding fiscal year for which such appropriations have been so made, such refusal or neglect shall be deemed equivalent to an express act for the abolition of the military establishment, and the Army shall forthwith be disbanded.

The section if enacted into a law would leave it in the power of Congress or a single branch thereof, by a failure to do its duty in making appropriations, to wipe out the entire Army of the United States. Such is the design of the section, plainly appearing by ts language.

This section proposes to legislate in reference to our own violation of duty as members; to legislate in view of a violation of our oaths and the Constitution of the United States. We are required by our constitutional duty to make appropriations to carry on the military arm of the Government.

Now, I have gone hastily over this legislation for the purpose of saying that it is not economy that moves some of these men to strike at the military strong arm of the Government. Nor is it the desire, as I think, to relieve the people of the country from taxes, as some of them say. It is not that, Mr. Chairman. If you look into this bill and examine it closely, you will find that it provides for something not known before, or rather it omits to provide for something. It omits to provide for the promotion of officers in their regular order to the highest rank in the Army. The thirty-fourth section of the bill reported by the gentleman from New York, [Mr. HEWITT,] the repealing clause of the bill, repeals by implication all the sections I have referred to and leaves the field open in case major-generals die or resign or vacancies happen for the appointment of others in their place without reference to whether they were in the Union Army or out of it.

[Here the hammer fell.]

Mr. CANNON, of Illinois, was recognized, and yielded two minutes to Mr. KEIFER.

Mr. KEIFER. Thanks to the member from Illinois. Under cover of a provision for promotions there is a proviso that second lieutenants shall be appointed from the graduates at the Military Academy or non-commissioned officers in the Army; but very adroitly the committee have left out of the bill any provision for promotions in the line of officers of the Army. It provides that all officers below the rank of colonel, before they shall be promoted to brigadier-general, shall first submit to an examination before a military board. There is no provision in the bill that a colonel or any other officer in the regular line shall be promoted in the order of his rank to the position of a major-general or any other higher office in the Army. We can see underlying this that which more plainly crops out in the proposed legislation of the distinguished gentleman from Ohio, the chairman of the Committee on Military Affairs.

I am very sorry I have not time allowed me to fully elaborate the vicious and dangerous legislation now proposed in this House.

AGE OF PAYMASTERS.

May 21, 1878. On an amendment to the Army appropriation bill fixing the age at which persons shall be appointed paymasters—

Mr. KEIFER said:

There is a great deal of fine distinction in determining the age which unfits a man for service in the Army. We know that during the late war many men, both in the southern army and in the northern army, over sixty years of age went into the field and discharged their duties there under the most trying circumstances and discharged them well, breasting the storms and facing the dangers not only of the battle-field but of the weather at all seasons of the year.. Yet in the year 1878 we find ourselves so dwindled down in manhood and strength that we are afraid to trust a man over forty-five years of age to go to New York or New Orleans or on the Pacific coast and pay troops, although many men of greater age go there merely as a matter of pleasure-seeking. It is true that in a very few cases these paymasters have to go to remote places on the plains, but in those places the climate is healthful and they generally go under escort, and if obliged to remain out of doors they are protected by tents or otherwise.

It seems to me there is something invidious in this limitation to forty-five years. It must be meant to cut off some persons. It is but a short time since that a gentleman born in the last century was urged for the place of standard-bearer of the Democratic party, and in my section of the country he had a pretty good following. He had been governor of Ohio, and, so far as I know, had discharged his duties pretty well. But when we come to provide for a mere paymaster in the Army to, discharge ordinarily only clerical duties, we say that a man over forty-five years of age is utterly unfit to discharge such duties on account of age.

Mr. Chairman, the only plausible argument against the amendment of the gentleman from Minnesota proposing to strike out "forty-five" and insert "fifty-five," is that men who are appointed at so late an age as fifty-five may soon be retired. I wish to call attention to the fact that it is proposed mainly to select paymasters from officers of the Army—officers of the line. Now, gentlemen argue that after passing the age of forty-five these officers will be too old for paymasters; yet they are willing to keep them in service in the line, in command of troops in the field. It is argued that after this age these officers are utterly unfit to become paymasters, in which positions they might occasionally get rest and relief from service in the field; but at the same time it is proposed to require them to stay constantly in command of troops, performing service which is very much harder, more dangerous, and more likely to break them down.

UNPAID TAX ON DISTILLED SPIRITS.

June 1, 1878. Bill to amend the internal-revenue laws—

Mr. KEIFER said:

I think the gentleman who has just taken his seat [Mr. TUCKER] has made a very good argument, if it were applied properly. But I think it will go further than he suggests. All that he refers to would be competent evidence tending to prove knowledge, and not alone a "reasonable ground to believe," as the bill provides. The objectionable words which the member from Tennessee [Mr. RANDOLPH] proposes to have struck out are these: "Or having reasonable grounds to believe." They appear in the clause of the bill which reads as follows:

Or who shall purchase or receive or rectify any distilled spirits which have been removed from a distillery to a place other than the distillery warehouse provided by law, knowing or having reasonable grounds to believe that the tax on said spirits, required by law, has not been paid, shall for every such offense be fined not less than $1,000 nor more than $5,000 and imprisoned not less than six months nor more than two years.

It will be noted that the penalty for "having reasonable grounds to believe" the tax on spirits has not been paid before purchasing, receiving, or rectifying is very severe; and this in the absence of knowledge. The bill makes it a crime for not knowing the fact when the accused had only reasonable grounds for knowing it, or for not believing a thing to be true when he ought to have believed it, or for not having sense enough to believe a fact which he ought to have had sense enough to believe.

I would like to know if we are coming to a time in this country when we will be so barbarous in the administration of the criminal law that a man will be held guilty of a crime in the absence of guilty knowledge. Let me put a case. Suppose that under this section of the bill, if it should become a law, an indictment is found charging a man with having reasonable grounds to believe that the tax had not been paid on certain spirits when he purchased them. Suppose that is the charge. Sir, when we have found him guilty under such an indictment we have struck down the greatest safeguards for the innocent known to the criminal law. We have struck down the rule of the criminal law which has stood the test for hundreds of years in England and in every other civilized country, that a man is entitled to two presumptions: first, that he is presumed to be innocent until proved guilty, and, second, that he must be proved guilty beyond a reasonable doubt before he can be convicted. The Committee of Ways and Means think guilty knowledge, the *scienter*, need not be proved. Under this bill, proof that the accused ought to have known a fact which he did not know is made to take the place of actual knowledge of the fact upon which the crime rests.

The very point under such an indictment on the trial would be to offer proof to raise a presumption of reasonable grounds of knowledge as distinguished from knowledge.

A single word as to the illustration used by the gentleman from Indiana [Mr. HANNA] in regard to counterfeit money. The very fact that a man has been told a bill is counterfeit is in general, when he comes to be put on trial, sufficient proof under the criminal law that he had knowledge the note or bill was counterfeit. Or take the case of a man to whom spirits are offered at 20 cents a gallon, when, if the tax were paid on them, they would be worth, as everybody would know, a dollar or more per gallon. If a man buys spirits under such circumstances, such proof, on his trial, might be sufficient in law to raise a legal presumption that he knew the tax had never been paid. Any such evidence as that would be competent to go to a jury as tending to show the guilty knowledge of the party. The trouble with this bill is that it undertakes to authorize some lower class of evidence which would only tend to show that a man is guilty of a high crime when he had reasonable grounds only to believe a thing and yet did not in fact believe it. If the bill does not mean this, it is simply nonsense. It makes it criminal to purchase, receive, or rectify spirits, knowing the tax thereon had not been paid.

Mr. TUCKER. Will the gentleman allow me to put a question to him?

Mr. KEIFER. Certainly.

Mr. TUCKER. How do you know what I know? [Laughter.]

Mr. KEIFER. Well, for the purpose of the criminal law, if the gentleman states a fact to me and I go on and act without reference to it, not believing it, and I am afterward arraigned for my act, it is competent to prove that the gentleman told me such was the fact, and to argue therefrom that I knew it. In such a case I act on my own responsibility if I do not believe it.

It is not unfair to say that, taking the bill as it reads, a person might be found guilty of purchasing, receiving, or rectifying distilled spirits upon which the tax had been paid, provided a jury could be convinced that the purchaser, receiver, or rectifier had reasonable ground to believe the tax had not been paid.

There certainly is nothing in the history of criminal law that furnishes a precedent for this extraordinary provision in this bill.

Mr. TUCKER. Will the gentleman allow me?

Mr. KEIFER. Certainly.

Mr. TUCKER. I admit that there are direct modes, such as he mentions, of proving knowledge; but are those the only modes in which I can ascertain what the gentleman knew?

Mr. KEIFER. Not by any means.

Mr. TUCKER. If I see his act, which speaks louder than words, and which shows he has in his heart certain knowledge, is he not to be supposed to have reasonable ground for belief?

Mr. KEIFER. That would be reasonable evidence, not only to show the state of my belief, but also to show the state of my knowledge, and might be given in evidence for that purpose. I go one step further than the gentleman from Virginia. But the members of the committee want to take a lower grade of evidence; they deem it sufficient evidence of criminality to raise a legal presumption that the accused ought to know what in fact he did not know, and perhaps, with his comprehension, could not know. Under this bill, unless amended, a jury will be required to find a man guilty if they find he was too big a fool to believe what in their opinion he ought to have believed.

June 3, 1878. The House resumed the consideration of the bill to amend the laws relating to internal revenue.

Mr. TUCKER. I will now propose, looking to the sentiments which have been expressed, to amend the proviso by striking out the word "heretofore," in line 25, and all after the word "made," and inserting "prior to January 1, 1871;" so that it will read:

Provided, That no tax shall be remitted or refunded under the provisions of this section under any assessment made prior to January 1, 1871.

Mr. KEIFER. I wish to ask the gentleman from Virginia a question. Why should we grant relief to men who were required to pay this tax in 1871 and not to those who paid it in 1873? What difference is there between them?

Mr. TUCKER. I am about to answer that question. It is in accordance with the principle of the statute of limitations. If you go further back there is greater room for fraud. If you go back to January, 1871, only, the transaction is more recent and is more capable of explanation.

Mr. KEIFER. I wish to make a suggestion in answer to the gentleman from Virginia, [Mr. TUCKER.] He suggests that his amendment is in the nature of a statute of limitations. How can this be? If these people who have paid a tax unjustly have never had the right to apply for its return, can it be said they are cut off by a statute of limitations? The gentleman's proposition is to give to all persons who have been compelled to pay such a tax since January 1, 1871, the right to recover it back; but persons who paid such a tax before that time and who have never had a right to make a claim for its return, are to have their claims cut off by what the gentleman chooses to call a statute of limitations. Statutes of limitations are made to cut off rights or remedies where they exist. It is a hard rule to say to persons who have just and equitable claims against the Government, but who never had the right to present them under any general law, that their claims are too old for payment, and others who have similar claims but of a more recent date should be paid or have the tax unjustly collected refunded. If it is right to pay any of this class of claims they should all be paid. You might very properly say to the persons who claim they have paid tax on account of whisky or spirits which they never manufactured, that they must present their claims within a particular time to the Commissioner of Internal Revenue or have them forever barred.

It is a singular thing to apply the statute of limitations to cut off rights or remedies when they never existed. A party should at least have a short day in which to assert his rights if any he had. If we pay any of the tax on spirits wrongfully or unjustly collected, we should pay it all. It may be unwise to repay any of such tax.

PAY OF LETTER-CARRIERS.

June 7, 1878. The bill to fix the pay of letter-carriers being under consideration—

Mr. KEIFER said:

Mr. SPEAKER: I am in favor of the bill reported by the Committee on the Post-Office and Post-Roads to fix and regulate the pay of letter-carriers. It is not my design now to occupy the attention of the House by discussing in detail the several provisions of the bill; but I wish, in the first place, to call the attention of the committee reporting it to the fact that in the classification of letter-carriers in the second section of the bill they have made no provision for some offices which are at the present time free-delivery offices. The second section provides that in all cities containing a population of less than seventy-five thousand and not less than twenty thousand there shall be a class of letter-carriers who are to receive a salary of $850 per annum.

Now, I wish to call attention to the fact that there are quite a number of free-delivery offices in the United States where the population is less than twenty thousand. Thus it will be seen there is one class of letter-carriers not provided for.

I desire to put upon record for the examination of members some of the facts relating to these important offices in the United States. It is a singular anomaly that to-day under the laws of the United States there are free-delivery offices producing a gross revenue of less than $16,000 per annum and in some cases as low as $1,000 net revenue per annum, while there are other offices producing as much as $56,000 of gross annual revenue which under the law have not been made free-delivery offices. This is wrong. I shall publish with my remarks a complete list of all the free-delivery offices in the United States—eighty-seven in number. This list shows for the fiscal year ending June 30, 1877, the gross revenue, office expenses, free-delivery expenses, as well as the net revenue of all these offices.

   ❖   ❖   ❖   ❖   ❖

Now, sir, if this bill ever reaches a point where we can consider it, I propose to offer as an additional section the following:

Letter-carriers shall be employed for the free delivery of mail matter, as frequently as the public convenience may require, at every place containing a population of fifty thousand within the delivery of its post-office, and may be so employed at every place containing a population of not less than twenty thousand within its corporate limits, and at post-offices which produced a gross revenue for the preceding fiscal year of not less than $20,000: *Provided*, This act shall not affect the free delivery in towns and cities where it is now established.

Now, Mr. Speaker, originally the law on the subject of free-delivery offices provided that free delivery might be established at post-offices where the population within the delivery of the office reached twenty thousand. Subsequently, by an act passed in 1876, the law was changed so as to limit the establishment of free-delivery offices to cities having a population within their corporate limits of thirty thousand. Now, sir, neither test was proper. In the first place it is the business that ought to be the test in this matter of free delivery. Those who pay for the music ought to enjoy it. That is my proposition; and perhaps it is right to have this double test, population and revenue. To give a place free delivery of mail matter will add to the revenue in two ways at least: first by the payment of double postage on dropped letters, and second by the increase of letters written on account of the convenience of mailing and receiving letters through the establishment of letter-boxes at places remote from the post-office. In this way employment will be given to more worthy and needy men, and the people will be glad to pay for it. The general net post-office receipts will not be materially affected by a proper increase of free-delivery offices.

I suggest that we go back to a test which will allow towns or cities with a population of twenty thousand within their corporate limits, or cities or towns that produce from their post-offices a gross revenue in excess of $20,000, to have the free-delivery system.

I hold in my hand a list (furnished to me yesterday by the Sixth Auditor of the Treasury) of post-offices (exclusive of free-delivery offices) where the gross receipts for the fiscal year ending June 30, 1877, exceed $20,000. I find in this list Oakland, California, producing a gross revenue of over $20,000; Sacramento City, with a gross revenue of more than $33,000. Among the most remarkable instances in this list is Galveston, Texas, with a gross revenue of $56,181.99. Yet that city is not a free-delivery office under the present law. Its net revenue is $39,586.73, which is ten times as large as some of the offices that are free-delivery offices. Why this distinction? A gentleman suggests to me that it is about to be made a free-delivery office, but it is strange that it should not have been made one long ago.

Here is the list referred to:

List of post-offices (exclusive of free-delivery offices) where the gross receipts for the fiscal year ended June 30, 1877, exceeded $20,000.

Name.	State.	Gross revenue.	Expenses.	Net revenue.
Oakland	California	$20,588 30	$8,679 87	$11,908 43
Sacramento City	do	33,756 17	16,185 30	17,571 17
Denver	Colorado	43,825 55	17,266 09	26,559 46
Bridgeport	Connecticut	30,686 19	10,757 12	19,929 07
Norwich	do	20,886 25	8,292 06	12,594 19
Wilmington	Delaware	28,884 77	14,984 31	13,900 46
Augusta	Georgia	26,290 17	9,540 15	16,750 02
Rockford	Illinois	24,864 58	7,282 50	17,582 08
Terre Haute	Indiana	23,600 64	10,170 65	13,429 99
Keokuk	Iowa	22,455 57	7,355 55	15,100 02
Topeka	Kansas	21,840 92	7,672 81	14,168 11
Augusta	Maine	34,970 51	8,757 95	26,212 56
Concord	New Hampshire	21,515 34	6,839 75	14,675 59
Auburn	New York	28,874 02	8,826 21	20,047 81
Binghamton	do	21,262 03	8,074 77	16,187 26
Springfield	Ohio	28,355 90	7,912 92	20,442 98
Portland	Oregon	26,736 69	9,083 31	17,653 35
Austin	Texas	25,184 84	9,534 45	15,650 39
Dallas	do	22,860 29	10,819 10	12,041 19
Galveston	do	56,181 99	16,595 26	39,586 73
Houston	do	23,647 93	11,675 40	11,972 53
Madison	Wisconsin	23,887 81	7,993 71	15,894 10

The fact is, the law has always been defective in this respect. I live in a city, Springfield, Ohio, which for the year ending June 30, 1877, produced a gross revenue of $28,355.90, and a net revenue of $20,442.98, about five times as large as the net revenue of several free-delivery offices in the United States. Yet under the law as it exists now that city cannot be made a free-delivery office. By a recent statement furnished me from the Sixth Auditor's Office I learn that that city produced in round numbers for the year ending March 31, 1878, a gross revenue of $33,000 and a net revenue of about $26,000; yet under our present defective law there are offices with a gross revenue of less than $16,000 and a net revenue of less than $4,000 made free-delivery offices, and Springfield, Ohio, with its large business and great revenue cannot be made a free-delivery office. This wrong and injustice I propose to remedy.

Now, while we are willing to pay in accordance with our business, we want to have the privileges of the post-office system according to the amount we pay and the business we do.

Mr. HANNA. Before the gentleman takes his seat I would like to ask him one question. I observe that this bill makes a distinction as to the pay of carriers. In cities having a population of seventy-five thousand or less the highest salary allowed is $850.

Now, I would like to know why a letter-carrier in a city with seventy-five thousand or less population is not as justly entitled to a salary of $1,000 as a carrier in a city of larger population.

Mr. KEIFER. I think there are perhaps reasons why there should be a discrimination made. But I am not the author of the bill nor a member of the committee which reported it, and I ask the gentleman, in order that we may get a perfectly satisfactory answer, to call upon some member of the committee to answer his question.

I wish to say one word further in relation to letter-carriers. I know something about them. They are men who are required to go out in all kinds of weather. They are not permitted to neglect their duty either by day or by night. They are as hard-worked a class of men as there is in the United States. They suffer great hardships, and I think they are about the most poorly paid class of men in the country. The duties they perform are of a responsible nature, and they are required to be men of responsibility, of character, of faithfulness, of honesty in every sense of the word. I think that, while we have only about twenty-two hundred or twenty-three hundred of them in the United States, many of whom are maimed soldiers, they are very poorly paid. There are many thousands of petitioners appealing to Congress to increase the pay of the letter-carriers. This bill does not increase the pay very largely.

Mr. EAMES. I would like to ask the gentleman from Ohio a question: whether this letter-carrier system exists in any city or place in the country where the postal receipts do not exceed the postal expenditures?

Mr. KEIFER. I take pleasure in answering the gentleman's question. I think the gross receipts in all cases exceed the postal expenditures, and the lowest net revenue of any of the free-delivery offices of the United States is somewhere between $3,000 and $4,000. That will appear by the statement to be published in my remarks. But I submit, as I have already stated, that cannot be the test. I think cities at least that produce as much as $40,000 of net revenue should be made free-delivery offices.

Mr. EAMES. Is there any such city or place which is not now a free-delivery office?

Mr. KEIFER. Yes, sir; I know of one, lacking only a few dollars of $40,000.

Mr. EAMES. Are not all places having a population of twenty thousand free-delivery offices?

Mr. KEIFER. I live in a city, the population of which is perhaps over twenty thousand, which has not a free-delivery office.

Mr. EAMES. I understand places of that population are entitled to it by law.

Mr. KEIFER. Not at all. There are places having forty thousand inhabitants which do not have a free delivery. The test now by law is a population of thirty thousand within the corporate limits to be measured by the census of 1870. The law used to be twenty thousand within the delivery of the post-office.

    *   *   *   *   *   * .

Mr. KEIFER. Will the gentleman allow me to make a suggestion?

Mr. WILSON. Certainly.

Mr. KEIFER. I am not the champion of this bill, so far as regards the discrimination to which the gentleman refers, but I would suggest that one reason which influenced the mind of the one who drafted the bill, and of the committee which reported it, was that in the smaller cities of the country, in the smaller free-delivery offices, living usually is cheaper, and men can afford to work for a little less than in very many of the larger cities, such as New York and Philadelphia.

EMPLOYMENT OF DISCHARGED SOLDIERS.

On June 10, 1878, at an evening session, Mr. Butler, of Massachusetts, reported a bill "to enforce by appropriate legislation the will of the people in regard to disabled soldiers of the late war, with the recommendation that it do pass." It provided that whoever shall willfully violate or set at naught any of the provisions of section 1754 of the Revised Statutes shall be punished by a fine not less than one hundred nor exceeding five thousand dollars, and by imprisonment not less than one month nor exceeding two years.

After the reading of part of the report -

Mr. KEIFER said:

The report is a long one, and if we could have a word of explanation from the gentleman from Massachusetts, I am willing that the reading be dispensed with. I will say right here that I am not opposed to the principle which the bill seeks to carry out. The section of the statute that the bill now pending applies to is a very good one, and it is directory in its character perhaps more than mandatory. It was intended as an expression of the wish of the people of the whole country as to the matter of appointments, but it was not complete either in that sense. If it is literally carried out it will apply to but about one-third, and not more, of the disabled soldiers of this country. It would probably exclude two-thirds of the men who were disabled in the war: I mean all that class of men who went into the Veteran Reserve Corps: all that class of men who suffered disabilities and who were mustered out at the expiration of their term of enlistment or at the end of the war. Every one of these men is excluded from appointment under section 1754 of the Revised Statutes, and the only class included are those who were honorably discharged from the military or naval service by reason of disability resulting from wounds or sickness incurred in the line of duty, and it leaves all the others out.

The country is filled with thousands of men—officers, non-commissioned officers, and privates—who served until the war closed, or until the expiration of their term of enlistment, and were then mustered out by reason thereof, and not for physical disabilities, and many thousands of others in consequence of wounds or other physical disabilities were transferred to a certain kind of service in the Veteran Reserve Corps, for instance, and were never mustered out on account of wounds or sickness, and not one of them are included in this section. Now, there is another class of persons who may be regarded as worthy of appointment to office and positions of trust in this country in this latter day of progress and reform: a class of people now holding office under the Government of the United States, hundreds and thousands of them, and they also are excluded by this section 1754 of the Revised Statutes. I mean all the women of the country, including the widows and daughters of soldiers. If you are to treat this as mandatory, and fix a penalty and make it a high crime to violate it on the part of the Department, all the soldiers' widows, all these worthy ladies are excluded. If you are to give this section a literal interpretation then the gentleman [Mr. BUTLER] who champions this legislation and proposes to make the section mandatory by requiring the appointing power to give it a literal interpretation, advocates legislation that comes to nothing; it will prove to be legislation in vain.

I make these suggestions, at the same time saying that I will go as far as the gentleman from Massachusetts or any other gentleman upon this floor toward appointing these worthy and disabled soldiers, not only those who have been honorably discharged from the service by reason of physical disability or wounds, but all who have suffered by reason of the war and suffered physical disability, including the widows, daughters, and orphans of deceased soldiers and sailors. I hope this bill will not pass until it is amended so as to include all these worthy persons.

\#

Mr. KEIFER. I wish the gentleman would yield to me further.

Mr. BUTLER. Certainly I will, with pleasure.

Mr. KEIFER. I have given the gentleman from Massachusetts [Mr. BUTLER] a good opportunity to get in his speech on this bill. I will not be so unkind as to say that there was any buncombe in it: I will not even insinuate that, although he is not so particular about imputing motives to me for my opposition to this bill—not very delicate in reference to me. He seems to jump to the conclusion that the suggestion I made here was for the purpose of defeating his bill; he will not brook just criticism on his handiwork. Emanating from his pen, it must be regarded as sacred indeed.

And then he suggests that we ought to amend the bill. Why, sir, we men who are on the outside of his great Judiciary Committee are not supposed to be able to perfect things be moving amendments, when the gentleman is already on the floor calling for the previous question.

I suggested here what I can show to the gentleman is a defect in this measure, one that is radical. If he, a member of the Committee on the Judiciary, will suggest a new section here which covers the class of persons to which I refer, I will vote with him.

Mr. THORNBURGH. If the gentleman will yield to me, I will offer an amendment which I think will cover the case.

Mr. KEIFER. Wait a moment, until I am through. The gentleman from Massachusetts is utterly mistaken when he undertakes to say that the great mass of the veterans of the Veteran Reserve Corps are included under this section. I know hundreds of them who were discharged from their original regiments to enable them to enlist in the Veteran Reserve Corps; that was the mode of transfer from one volunteer regiment to another. They were not discharged, in the language of this section, "by reason of disability resulting from wounds or sickness incurred in the line of duty." They are excluded under this bill, and it has been the subject of complaint on the part of these men that they have not been included by these champions of the soldiers, these men who are always coming forward as champions of the soldiers, and who want "to do something" on the subject instead of simply "saying something."

I will enter the lists at any time with the gentleman from Massachusetts [Mr. BUTLER], or any other gentleman on this floor or elsewhere in advocating the claims, the rights, and the proper preferences of these soldiers; but I will not join with the Judiciary Committee of this House, led on by the gentleman from Massachusetts, in undertaking to impose a penalty upon the appointing power in behalf of a few of these worthy persons, leaving out the great majority of them. Why, sir, I know of men who served until the end of the war—officers who came out of the war with but one arm or one leg, who were never discharged by reason of their disabilities, but who served four years and more in the field, doing their duty to the end, though suffering, sadly maimed, and disabled. And to say these men, though indigent, could not be appointed under this section of the bill to any office within the gift of this Government, to appoint any one of them, should this bill pass not amended, would be to violate the law of the land, and the appointing power, the President of the United States if you please, would become liable to punishment as a felon. Has it come to this so soon after the great struggle for our nation's life.

The gentleman from Massachusetts must not cast upon me the imputation that I am simply opposing his bill. If he knows of cases such as he states here, they are great wrongs; and I am ready to join with him in endeavoring to have them redressed. But I do know that he is now advocating here a measure which is unjust to a very large class of worthy, disabled, honorably discharged soldiers of the Union; and this provision, if made mandatory, as it was never intended originally to be, would exclude the class of persons to whom I have referred, and all the soldiers' widows, their daughters, and other worthy ladies who hold office under this Government. Such was never the intention of the law. The original law was only intended, as it only could be, when read in the light of the Constitution of the United States, to be advisory; as expressing the views of the legislative branch of the Government to the Chief Magistrate of the nation and to others who might chance to have the appointing power.

So far as this bill undertakes to affect the appointing power of the Chief Executive of the Government. I say with a knowledge that the gentleman will charge me with making this utterance simply to defeat his bill, I say that in my judgment as a matter of constitutional law we have no right thus to dictate by imperative legislation whom the President shall appoint among citizens eligible to appointment to office in this country.

One further remark: How are you to find out under this section as it stands whether different persons are "equally well qualified?" Would the gentleman have a jury to sit and determine whether Postmaster-General Key, or Secretary Sherman, or perhaps the President of the United States has exercised aright his discretion in reference to appointments; in determining whether A B, who had but one arm, possessed equal qualifications with C D, who had no disabilities. You propose to try the question of a proper exercise of the discretion of the appointing power; you are to determine by the verdict of a jury whether the officer invested with this discretion judged rightly or wrongly, without reference even to his capacity to judge. He might not be so astute, so smart, so keen, so ready to discern the qualities that go to make up a competent clerk or other officer, as the gentleman from Massachusetts. But a jury is to sit and take the gentleman's standard of judgment, the gentleman's opinion, if he is the prosecuting attorney, and the jury is to find out whether the law has been executed with proper discretion, and whether the parties who are thus charged with its execution should be condemned and punished as felons or not. It looks to me as if there was somewhere some buncombe in this matter. [Laughter.] Yet I certainly disclaim ever charging upon the gentleman from Massachusetts any buncombe at all. [Laughter.] I would not do that. People know him, his habits and instincts, too well in this country for that. [Laughter.]

Mr. BUTLER. * * * I am utterly indifferent to the fate of this bill. I have done my duty to it, and as it is late at night and I have no more to say I will demand the previous question.

Mr. KEIFER. Let me say a word.
Mr. BUTLER. I cannot.
Mr. KEIFER. I wish to say one or two words in reply to the gentleman.
Mr. BUTLER. I cannot.
Mr. KEIFER. Permit me to make a suggestion.
Mr. BUTLER. No, I have heard your suggestion. '
Mr. KEIFER. I am sorry that the gentleman lost his temper.
Mr. BUTLER. I have not had a bit of temper all my life.
Mr. KEIFER. I am sorry he will not hear anything to quality——
Mr. BUTLER. You cannot qualify.
Mr. KEIFER. Allow me five minutes.
Mr. BUTLER. I cannot.
Mr. KEIFER. Allow me five minutes.
Mr. BUTLER. I cannot.
Mr. THORNBURGH Allow me to suggest an amendment.
Mr. BUTLER. I will hear it read.

The Clerk read as follows:

Nothing in the first section of this act or in section 1751 of the Revised Statutes shall be so construed as to exclude from appointment to office any soldier who was disabled in the line of duty and honorably discharged, or the widow or daughters of killed or disabled soldiers.

Mr. BUTLER. I will agree to allow that amendment to be offered, and now demand the previous question on the bill and amendment.
Mr. KEIFER. Will you not permit me a moment?
Mr. BUTLER. I cannot.
Mr. JAMES. I move the House do now adjourn.
The House divided: and there were—ayes 46, noes 91.
So the House refused to adjourn.
The question recurred on seconding the demand for the previous question.
The House divided; and there were—ayes 61, noes 91.
Mr. BUTLER demanded tellers.
Tellers were not ordered.
So the House refused to second the demand for the previous question.

Mr. KEIFER. Mr. Speaker, I had no disposition to prolong this discussion. I desired that we should legislate in a cool, orderly, efficient, and substantial way so that we may legislate wisely. I am sorry the gentleman loses his temper a little about this, because I had in my feeble way attempted to point out the defects in the bill which he reports and champions.

Now he says to the House, and especially to me, that I ought to have read the report; that I would have learned something; but I remember very well that he told us in the beginning that the report was his own, and after I had heard his speech and heard the best reasons he possessed and could give in favor of this bill, I knew when I heard the report read I would not get anything new to aid my understanding. I was advised in advance that the report did not contain any of the combined and concentrated wisdom of the Judiciary Committee of this House if I listened to it. The report contained only the gentleman's own statement of the case. That was all there was in it. I soon found I could not rely on that; and he himself in the beginning declined to have it read, did not want it read, and, as far as it was read, it was read at my instance.

Yet he charges upon me ignorance of the proposed legislation. I am no more ignorant in that respect, admitting my ignorance compared to his in many things, for I am young and may not have had his opportunities, but I am no more ignorant, perhaps, of this measure than the man who will stand on the floor of this House and undertake to cite as an instance or example in favor of his proposed legislation that the Congress of the United States has regulated the appointing power of the President in the past by prohibiting him by law from appointing a disabled man to West Point.

There is no such thing in the law and never was in the history of the country. The President does not appoint persons to West Point either; he never appointed anybody, nor did the gentleman from Massachusetts, as a member of Congress, ever appoint anybody to West Point. West Point cadets are not officers. In his capacity as Congressman the gentleman may have nominated somebody that was sent to West Point to appear before a board to be examined to see if he was eligible under the law of Congress to enter that public institution. Persons are not appointed when they go there to any office under the United States, constitutional or otherwise. They are nominated only by the President or by members of Congress, as the case may be. But the gentleman re-enforced all his argument in favor of this bill by that single illustration.

I am not so ignorant as to be unable to see that that is a mere scheme, far-fetched, to try to get up an analogy to his proposed legislation, and I am sorry the gentleman could not have found something more and something stronger. As he professes so much wisdom on his part, I am very sorry about it. I can see through that with all my defects.

I cannot allow the gentleman to escape from the erroneous statement he makes here in regard to discharged soldiers. He seems to have an idea that all men who were wounded in the war that went into the Veteran Reserve Corps were sent home. Three times in his statement he repeated that men who were wounded or disabled in the Army were mustered out of service by reason of their disabilities and sent home. That, sir, is not true. They were transferred from the Missouri, and beyond it, to the city of Washington to defend the very Capitol which we occupy to-night and to serve in the Veteran Reserve Corps of the Army. They brought here the wounded officers; they brought here the wounded and disabled soldiers, those who had broken down through sickness and disease, and in various ways, and they were brought here to defend the capital of the Republic. And they never were discharged from the Army by reason of disabilities; they were simply transferred from one regiment to another under a law of Congress, not discharged.

But, Mr. Speaker, there were many more that never were transferred. I know in this House to-night men who were in the service from the beginning of the war to the end and who were disabled, disabled in a material way, and yet they served until the last gun was fired, and witnessed at Appomattox the surrender of the great army of Northern Virginia under Lee, and were only discharged from the service when there was no longer any service to perform; and under this legislation, if it were to be carried out, those men could not be appointed to office under this Administration or any other without rendering the appointing officer liable to a criminal charge.

Now, Mr. Speaker, I do not intend to repeat what I have said, and will only refer to it again. I believe that this is intended to strike at the Executive, and if the Executive has erred in this respect, as the gentleman seems to think he has erred, I hope he will correct his work in the future. I hope that all future Presidents will stand by the disabled soldiers and the families of deceased soldiers in making appointments to office. I can most freely vote for any provision that perfects the law so as to include all this class of persons.

Mr. KNOTT. I ask the gentleman to yield to me for a moment.

Mr. KEIFER. How much time do you want?

Mr. KNOTT. Only a minute.

Mr. KEIFER. Certainly; two of them if you want them.

The SPEAKER. The gentleman from Ohio yields two minutes to the gentleman from Kentucky.

Mr. KEIFER. I yield him five minutes if he wants them.

Mr. KNOTT. I regret, in view of the large amount of unfinished business of my committee, so much time has been taken up in the discussion of this question already. I therefore asked my friend from Ohio to yield to me that I might say, simply in justice to myself, that I have not favored the passage of this bill for the reasons so forcibly urged by the gentleman from Ohio. I considered it an unnecessary restriction upon the appointing power to say the least of it, of doubtful constitutionality, that might be very difficult of enforcement, and that might make an unjust and invidious discrimination against those equally worthy with the class sought to be favored by this bill.

Mr. KEIFER. I now move the previous question on the bill and amendment.

The previous question was seconded and the main question ordered; and under the operation thereof the amendment of Mr. THORNBURGH was agreed to.

The bill, as amended, was ordered to be engrossed and read a third time; and being engrossed, it was accordingly read the third time, and passed.

Mr. KEIFER moved to reconsider the vote by which the bill was passed; and also moved that the motion to reconsider be laid on the table.

The latter motion was agreed to.

90 A—K——3

34

WILLIAM AND MARY COLLEGE.

A WAR CLAIM.

December 13, 1878. The House having under consideration in Committee of the Whole on the Private Calendar the bill (H. R. No. 189) to reimburse the College of William and Mary for property destroyed during the late war—

Mr. KEIFER said:

Mr. CHAIRMAN: The friends of this bill press it from one Congress to another with a pertinacity that challenges admiration. The many speeches made in this and former Congresses in favor of the payment of the claim of William and Mary College would make a large volume. The two eloquent appeals for the passage of this bill made at the last session of this Congress by the member from Virginia [Mr. GOODE] and the member from Massachusetts [Mr. LORING] were based chiefly upon sentiment. The same remark will apply to the speeches made in favor of similar bills in former Congresses.

As a matter of sentiment I too could vote for the bill if I did not take an entirely different view of my duty. The public funds should only be voted away upon sound principles of law, public duty, or policy. I regard this as a war claim, and as such to be tested by the known and well-established rules of international law, founded long since upon principles of public policy.

I may be charged because of my opposition to this bill with keeping the fires of passion engendered by the war still blazing. I disclaim any desire or purpose of doing so. Neither hatred nor ill-will toward the South or any southern man has an abiding place in my heart. Whatever the North suffered during the war has been more than requited by the losses and suffering of the South. Whatever of blood has been shed in the cause of universal constitutional liberty and for the preservation of the Union has been more than compensated for by the grand results attained. I welcome the era of reconciliation and good feeling between all sections of the country. I hope not to be behind any man, North or South, in efforts to secure universal good feeling, harmony of sentiments and purposes, provided at all times security is given for the full, complete, and final protection of all citizens of the Republic in all sections of the country in the exercise of their rights and privileges.

This bill is such that, to vote intelligently on it, will require the facts to be carefully and plainly set forth. The bill provides for the payment to William and Mary College, in Virginia, of $65,000 "to reimburse said college for the destruction of its buildings and other property, destroyed without authority by disorderly soldiers of the United States during the late war." I dislike to oppose the bill as it is in the interest of learning. The institution is an ancient one. It was chartered under the name of William and Mary in 1693, (fourth year of the joint reign of William and Mary,) and it is said to have had an existence as far back as 1660. It was originally founded and fostered as an aristocratic institution, in opposition to free schools and popular education. As early as 1671, Sir William Berkeley, the royal colonial governor in Virginia, a patron of this college, answered the following question from the lords commissioners of foreign plantations:

What course is taken about instructing the people within your government in the Christian religion? And what provision is there made for paying of your ministry?

Answer:

The same course that is taken in England out of towns; every man, according to his ability, instructing his children.

We have forty-eight parishes, and our ministry are well paid, and by my consent should be better, if they would pray oftener and preach less. But of all other commodities, so of this; the worst are sent us, and we had few that we could boast of since the persecution in Cromwell's tyranny drove divers worthy men hither. But I thank God there are no free schools nor printing, and I hope we shall not have these hundred years; for learning has brought disobedience and heresy and sects into the world, and printing has divulged them, and libels against the best government. God keep us from both.

This royal governor may have entertained the views, at least as applied to the common people, expressed by the poet Pope, that—

A little learning is a dangerous thing;
Drink deep, or taste not the Pierian spring:
These shallow draughts intoxicate the brain,
And drinking largely sobers us again.

This college, somewhat amply endowed, held its course in the heart of a State for two centuries where free schools were unknown until since the late war. It was regarded with favor in the South; was patronized by the South; propagated southern views; was hardly open to humble people, and has always excluded women from its benefits.

It is hoped that it has made some progress since the war. By the report of the Committee on Education and Labor we learn that patriotic considerations are relied on to induce Congress to vote for this bill. I quote from that report:

Every civilized nation has its hallowed spots about which its patriotic memories cluster, and whose names rise before the imagination whenever these memories are stirred.

* * * * * *

Under our form of government these hallowed spots are in the custody of States. But they hold them as trustees for the whole people and the gratitude and affection which surround and hallow them are the gratitude and affection of the whole people.

* * * * * *

Unless this be true, the American people alone among civilized nations are without any common objects of national reverence.

And further:

We doubt if any college in America or Europe can, in proportion to the whole number borne on its catalogue, show so large a list of names famous for conspicuous patriotic service.

These considerations being pressed on this House justifies me in looking more closely into the history of this college. I do this in no spirit of recrimination. That this college was the *alma mater* of Jefferson and Marshall and a long list of eminent statesmen, jurists, and lawyers is true. On account of its great age, and the fact that there were for a long time but few contemporaries of this college, it may truthfully be said that her graduates of distinguished men are comparatively large. Admitting the fact that "her list of names famous for conspicuous patriotic service" is large, how does the case stand when we look to the history of the college and its graduates immediately before and during the late war—the country's second baptism of blood for universal freedom in America?

It is safe to say, for the number of its students and graduates, the College of William and Mary furnished more men than any other institution of learning in the land, who favored secession, rebellion, and war.

Before we vote money to this college on the ground of its patriotic services to the country, we should not lose sight of the fact that it was destroyed by the inexorable events of war, brought on in part through its own teachings.

This college now appeals to the Treasury of the very Government which it, through its students and graduates, sought to destroy ; to restore and rebuild its burned and blackened walls within which in later days were taught lessons which denied the fundamental principle " that all men were created equal," and which would lead inevitably to perpetuate human slavery and to the overthrow of constitutional liberty.

Its board of visitors and its faculty were disloyal. Its teachings in later years were unpatriotic to the Union, as I shall be able to show. Its president, (B. S. Ewell,) prior to and during the war, was disloyal; and he is still its president, I believe. He left his high and honorable position as president of a college which boasted one hundred years ago of its patriotism in the cause of liberty, and took up the sword to destroy the country founded by Washington, Jefferson, the Adamses, Franklin, and their co-patriots, and to establish a new nation in which human slavery would be co-extensive with its boundaries. The teachings of the college led its students to indorse the constitution of the so-called Confederate States, which contained a section as follows :

No bill of attainder, or *ex post facto* law, or law denying or impairing the right of property in negro slaves shall be passed. (Art. 1, sec. 9.)

I shall not trace the individual history of the many confederate heroes this college gave to the late war. The history of the students and graduates of a college lead us unmistakably to know what principles and doctrines were taught therein.

As a mother who rears her child impresses indelibly upon it her character, which is not effaced during life, so a great institution of learning impresses on its young and susceptible students its true character. If this were not so, then indeed is education in vain.

'Tis education forms the common mind ;
Just as the twig is bent the tree's inclined.

Let us look to the annals of this college a little. In 1871 a history of the college was published by its faculty. At that late day the desire uppermost in the minds of the members of the faculty was "to get a perfect war record of its students."

I read a note from that history :

All students who are known to have been in the Confederate army have the letters C. S. A., with known rank, attached to their names. Some, or any in fact, are omitted, and as it is the desire of the faculty to get a perfect war record of all students, additional information is solicited from all concerned.

To begin with the class of 1857-'58—what was "the perfect war record of its students?"

In the class of 1857-'58, the alumni were thirty-two in number; twenty-two of these went into the Confederate States army; the other ten seem to have no history worth recording.

The class of 1858–'59 consisted of thirty-nine in number, thirty-three of whom went into the Confederate States army: six have no history.

The class of 1859–'60 consisted of thirty-four in number, thirty-two of whom went into the Confederate States army, one became an Episcopal minister, and one a Methodist minister.

The class of 1860–'61 consisted of thirty-eight in number, thirty-four of whom went into the Confederate States army—four are without history. From 1861 to 1865 the college was closed because of the war.

The history of this college I believe does not record one of its students as going into the Union Army during the late war. The committee's report is more remarkable for what it does not contain than for what it does. It seems clear that on account of the patriotic services of this college we cannot safely vote to pay this large sum of money. If, then, we cannot, on the ground that we owe as a nation a bounty to this college because its graduates have been "famous for conspicuous patriotic service" vote for this bill, can we do so on any other sound principle? Is it a war claim that should be paid on any principle of law, justice, public policy, or duty? The committee find some other and minor grounds upon which it believes this claim should be paid. Let me say here, I regret that this claim was not referred to the Committee on War Claims, where it appropriately belonged. (Several times before, however, this bill has been referred to the Committee on Education and Labor.)

Under the rules of this House it no more belonged to the Committee on Education and Labor than a claim for injury in the war to a bank building to the Committee on Banking and Currency; a claim for injury by the war to a ship, to the Committee on Naval Affairs or Commerce; a claim for injury in the war to private lands, to the Committee on Private Land Claims; a claim for injury or destruction in the war to a manufacturing establishment, to the Committee on Manufactures; a claim for the taking by the Army of products of the soil, to the Committee on Agriculture; a claim for destruction of a library or a botanical garden, to the Committee on the Library; over which my friend from New York [Mr. Cox] so gracefully presides.

The propriety of the reference is hardly strengthened by the fact that the author of the bill [Mr. Goode] is chairman of the Committee on Education and Labor and is interested in the appropriation of this large sum of money, he being one of the visitors or trustees of the college. He is at least the nominal author of the report which recommends the payment to himself and other cotrustees of $65,000. The report further finds as reasons why the claim should be paid, in addition to the one that the college is a "hallowed spot about which patriotic memories cluster," that Union soldiers, "provoked by defeat and under the influence of drink, set fire to the building and prevented the residents of the neighborhood from extinguishing the flames till it was wholly consumed"; that "the Government had taken possession of the property for its own purposes, excluding the owners and preventing them from taking any measures to secure its protection"; that "by the law of nations institutions of learning are exempted by all civilized nations from the hostilities of war."

Assuming the facts to be as stated in the first two of these reasons, nothing is better settled than that there is no legal ground, in the light of the judicial precedents, for the payment of this claim.

It is not true that by the law of nations colleges are exempted from the hostilities of war, and if such were the law it does not follow that when they are destroyed by a hostile army, either with or without the direction of those in authority, there is necessarily any legal liability resting on the Government to make restitution.

Let us consider these grounds in their order.

The bill recites that the college "was destroyed without authority by disorderly soldiers of the United States during the late war."

In other words, it is claimed that this property was destroyed by the wrongful and tortious act of the United States soldiers.

No case can be found where a sovereign or a government has ever been held liable for the torts of its officers even, let alone its humbler servants.

That the Government is not liable for the torts of its officers or agents has been repeatedly and repeatedly held by the Supreme Court of the United States. I quote from the *syllabi* of a case decided in 1868:

The Government is not liable on an implied assumpsit for the torts of its officers committed while in its service, and apparently for its benefit.

To admit such liability would involve the Government in all its operations in embarrassments, losses, and difficulties subversive of the public interest.—8 *Wallace*, 269.

Also, from the opinion of Justice Miller in the same case:

But it is not to be disguised that this case is an attempt, under the assumption of an implied contract, to make the Government responsible for the unauthorized acts of its officers, those acts being in themselves torts. No government has ever held itself liable to individuals for the misfeasance, laches, or unauthorized exercise of power by its officers and agents.

In the language of Judge Story, it does not undertake to guarantee to any person the fidelity of any of the officers or agents whom it employs, since that would involve it in all operations in endless embarrassments, and difficulties, and losses, which would be subversive of the public interest.

And further from the same opinion:

In a few adjudged cases where the United States was plaintiff, the defendants have been permitted to assert demands of various kinds by way of set-off, and these cases may afford useful guidance where they are in point. The cases of this class establish the principle that even in regard to matters connected with the cause of action relied on by the United States the Government is not responsible for the laches, however gross, of its officers.

The language of the statutes which confer jurisdiction upon the Court of Claims excludes by the strongest implication demands against the Government founded on torts. The general principle which we have already stated as applicable to all governments forbids, on a policy imposed by necessity, that they should hold themselves liable for unauthorized wrongs inflicted by their officers on the citizen, though occurring while engaged in the discharge of official duties.

It was sought in the case just cited to hold the Government liable to loyal parties because of the tort of a quartermaster. The books abound in cases to the same effect: United States *vs.* Kirkpatrick, 9 Wheat., 720 ; Dox *vs.* Paymaster-General, 1 Peters, 318 ; Connell *vs.* Voorhees, 13 Ohio, 523 ; Nichols *vs.* The United States, 7 Wall., 122 ; Flushing Ferry Co. case, 6 Ct. of Cl. 1.

If, for torts committed by high officers the Government is not liable, much less will it be liable for the unauthorized acts of private soldiers. The maximum *respondeat superior* does not apply between the General Government and its agents who are guilty of torts. I am not, however, satisfied that this college was burned by Union soldiers. There was no reason why they should do so. There were Army stores in the building. The United States forces expected to permanently occupy it. The Confederates had just been driven from it. The Union officers would have protected it if only to save the stores. It is more probable that the Confederate soldiers fired it, on their retreat, to destroy the stores in it, and to prevent its further occupancy by Union troops, &c. In a report made by Alexander Hamilton, Secretary of the Treasury, to the House of Representatives, November 19, 1792, he stated the laws and usages of nations in relation to the payment of certain claims thus:

That according to the laws and usages of nations a State is not obliged to make compensation for damages done to its citizens by an enemy, *or wantonly or unauthorized by its troops.*

This rule is based upon sound principles and authority, and has borne the test of time.

It will be remembered that by the twelfth article of the treaty of May 8, 1871, a commission upon the claims of Her Britannic Majesty against the United States, and of the citizens of the United States against Great Britain, was constituted.

Count Louis Corti, of Italy, was made president of that commission. Right Honorable Russell Gurney, member of Parliament, member of Her Majesty's privy council and recorder of London, was appointed commissioner on behalf of Great Britain. Hon. James S. Frazer, formerly justice of the supreme court of the State of Indiana, was the commissioner for the United States.

This commission began its session in Washington in September, 1871, and during its two years' sessions passed upon four hundred and ninety-seven claims, involving war claims of every conceivable character. Counsel of the highest talent and ability appeared before it. The most of the claims filed were of British subjects residing or owning property in the United States for damages caused by the Union Army. That commission uniformly and by unanimous vote disallowed all claims against the United States for unauthorized destruction of property by soldiers, and even when works of art were involved.

I read a paragraph or two from the report of Robert S. Hale, esq., the agent on the part of the United States, to Secretary Fish, of date of November 30, 1873, and from page 50 of volume 3, Foreign Relations, United States:

In several cases there were allegations of the wanton destruction of property by United States troops, and in some cases satisfactory proof was made of the fact of such destruction by soldiers without command or authority of their commanding officers and in defiance of orders.

In the case of Anthony Barclay (No. 5) allegations were made of wanton destruction of property, including valuable furniture, china, pictures, and other works of art, books, &c. The proof was conflicting as to whether the injuries alleged were committed by soldiers or not, but if committed by soldiers it was plainly not only without authority but in direct violation of the order of General Sherman. In the award made in favor of Mr. Barclay nothing was included for property alleged to have been destroyed.

Several claims were brought for property alleged to have been destroyed by the burning of Columbia on the allegation that the city was wantonly fired by the army of General Sherman, either under his orders or with his consent and permission. A large amount of testimony was taken upon this subject, including that of General Hampton and other Confederate officers on the part of the claimants, and of Generals Sherman, Logan, Howard, Woods, and other Federal officers on the part of the United States. The claims were all disallowed, all the commissioners agreeing.

Thus it appears that even the commissioner on the part of the British Government did not even claim that the United States were liable for the tortious acts of their unauthorized agents, though conceded to be liable for the necessary destruction of property of British subjects as incident to the war.

We come now to the question of the liability of the Government for the alleged reason that it took possession of the college for its own purposes, excluding the owners, &c.

The fact is, when the war came the owners—or rather the custodians of the college, its president and faculty—abandoned it and joined the insurgent army.

When this college was taken possession of by the United States forces it had been abandoned as a college, and was being used as barracks, and, by the Confederate forces. (Report, 1872, Globe, volume 88, page 939.) Finding it abandoned, the officers had a right to occupy it. It was in a hostile country that had to be held and occupied by Union forces.

It is further said that it was within territory excepted from Lincoln's emancipation proclamation.

This exception was not because it was in loyal territory, but because it was on January 1, 1863, held and occupied permanently by loyal forces and was within the Union lines. (It is not certain that the territory occupied by the college was excepted from the operation of the proclamation.)

By the custom, rules, and laws of war, unoccupied public buildings, of whatever character, are to be used for public purposes, such as shelter for stores and material of war, hospitals, &c., in preference to driving inhabitants from their dwellings.

Being rightly, under an appropriation to military use, in possession of the Union Army, (for if wrongfully in possession of that Army, then, as has been shown, no liability whatever attaches,) does it follow that its destruction raises an obligation to pay for it?

It is expressly held that the Government is not liable for the burning of a building which it has seized for its use. (Lagow's case, 10 Court of Claims, 266; Green's case, 10 Court of Claims, 466.)

In Lagow's case the court say in the syllabus:

The Government is not liable for the burning of a building which it has seized and used as a small-pox hospital, and it is immaterial whether it has given up possession or whether it remains constructively in possession.

To the same effect is Filor's case, 9 Wall., 45.

By the law of nations it is said that property of institutions of learning should be preserved and protected.

Grant this to be true, and it doubtless is true, yet it does not follow that in case of the willful destruction of such an institution by a conquering army that any legal or moral obligation arises as against the government to which that army belongs to pay for such destruction.

The committee have labored in vain to find instances or precedents for such an obligation. Not one has been found. None are given in the report and none are referred to in the speeches made during this or any preceding Congress. None exists.

Let us give attention to the cases cited in the report. It is said Washington made the trustees of Princeton College a present of fifty guineas as restitution for damage it sustained from the fire of the Americans at the battle of Princeton, and that after the close of the war Louis XVI, the ally of America, caused the college buildings in the United States accidentally destroyed by the fire of his troops to be replaced and every injury to be repaired. These are the only instances found where restitution has been made for an injury to an institution of learning. Both of these were in the nature of a gratuity to loyal institutions within friendly territory. In neither case was any legal liability as against a sovereign government admitted or recognized, but the contrary. As precedents these two instances are against the legal liability of the Government in any such case.

The committee also say:

In the bloodiest and angriest civil strifes England has respected her schools and colleges.

Grant this to be true, and it may truthfully be said that the United States to a remarkable extent "has respected her schools and colleges." The accidental or wanton destruction in the furnace of war of a school or college building under loyal or disloyal control raises no obligation on the part of the Government to pay for it. There are, it s true, some legislative precedents for reimbursing institutions of learning for damages caused by ravages of war. And here I adopt the language of Senator Sumner in a speech made January 12, 1869, in the Senate. (71 Globe, 301.)

From the beginning of our national life Congress has been called to deal with claims for losses by war. Though new in form the present case belongs to a long list whose beginning is hidden in Revolutionary history. The folio of State papers now before me, entitled "Claims," attest the mber and variety. From amid the struggles of the war, as early as 1779, Rev. Dr. Witherspoon was allowed $19,000 for repairs of the college at Princeton, damaged by troops. There was afterward a similar allowance to the academy at Wilmington, in Delaware, and also to the college in Rhode Island. These latter were recommended by Mr. Hamilton, while Secretary of the Treasury, as "affecting the interest of literature." On this account they were treated as exceptional. It will also be observed that they concerned claimants within our own jurisdiction.

These claims were paid in the interest of literature alone, and the institutions were at ll times loyal to the Government. I do not deny but that it is a paramount duty of an army to protect colleges, school-houses, churches, works of art, &c., belonging to the enemy. But it does not follow that in case such property is destroyed or injured that payment therefor must be made.

There is probably no instance where such property held or owned by an enemy has ever been paid for, though destroyed in violation of the usages of war. As a matter of discipline and wise policy, as well as humanity toward citizens of the country through which an army is being marched, the commanding general very often insists upon paying for all supplies taken for consumption by the army. The most rigid orders are often issued and enforced to prevent marauding upon the inhabitants.

The Duke of Wellington when he entered France with his victorious army from Spain, in pursuit of Marshal Soult in 1814, near the close of the final struggle of the Emperor Napoleon, punished pillage and foraging upon the French people with death, to preserve the perfect discipline of his army; and he required his officers to pay for all supplies taken from the country. But no rule of international law ever required a nation to pay for property of any kind belonging to the enemy taken or destroyed in violation of orders.

The committee quote in its report parts of paragraphs 31 to 36, section 2, of General Orders No. 100, giving instructions to the armies of the United States in the field. (This order was prepared by Dr. Lieber and approved by President Lincoln.) These paragraphs do not deny the right to take and use for military purposes colleges and other public buildings. Paragraph 34 expressly recognizes the right to seize universities, churches, &c., and it also asserts that they "may be taxed or used when the public service may require it." ●

The last clause of paragraph 37 (not quoted in the report) is as follows:

This rule does not interfere with the right of the victorious invader to tax the people or their property, to levy forced loans, to billet soldiers, or to appropriate property, especially houses, land, boats, or ships, and churches, for temporary and military uses.

Halleck on the laws of war says:

War * * * makes legal enemies of all the individual members of the hostile States; * * it also extends to property, and gives to one belligerent the right to deprive the other of everything which might add to his strength and enable him to carry on hostilities.

The people in the late war were divided territorially.

Our own Supreme Court has given us the rule of international law applied directly to our civil war.

I quote from the famous prize cases:

All persons residing within this territory, whose property may be used to increase the revenues of the hostile power, are in this contest, liable to be treated as enemies, though not foreigners. 2 Black, 696.

See to same effect Alexandria cotton case, 2 Wall., 404.

It has already been shown that the College of William and Mary was actually used, prior to its seizure by the United States forces, by the Confederate army.

In Jefferson's celebrated letter of May 12, 1793, to Minister Hammond, of Great Britain, on the subject of the liability of a nation to pay for losses sustained by the enemy in war, he says:

Since it is a condition of war that enemies may be deprived of all their rights, it is reasonable that everything of an enemy's found among his enemies should change its owner, and go to the treasury. It is, moreover, usually directed in all declarations of war that the goods of enemies, as well as those found among us as those taken in war, shall be confiscated. If we follow the mere right of war, even immovable property may be sold, and its price carried into the treasury, as is the custom of movable property. But in almost all Europe, it is only notified that their profits during the war shall be received by the treasury, and the war being ended, the immovable property itself is restored, by agreement, to the former owner. (Hynk.) Ques. Jur. Pub., l. 1, c. 7.

This states as a sound rule as to the status of all property of belligerents during a war. It is then perfectly clear that the occupancy of this property was not in any sense wrongful.

There was no attempt by its destruction to appropriate it to a public use. The Grant case, decided by the Court of Claims, (1 Court of Claims Rep., p. 41,) now so much celebrated and so often cited, does not furnish a precedent for the payment of this claim.

The court in that case found that a United States officer during the rebellion burned a mill of a loyal man, situate on loyal territory (Arizona), which had prior thereto been held and used by the Government of the United States for military uses, and that the mill was burned for the sole purpose of preventing it from falling into the hands of Confederate forces and being used by them in aid of insurrection, &c. On this state of facts the court found, as a matter of law, the destruction was an appropriation to a public use and the owner was entitled to be paid for his mill.

The facts of this college case are widely different from those in the Grant case. There was in no sense by the destruction of the college buildings an appropriation of the same to the public use within the meaning of the Constitution.

As has already been shown many losses occur in war which cannot be compensated for to the loyal or disloyal.

The hardships and devastations of war fall unequally. Individual losses are manifold. Hopes are forever blasted and homes made desolate through death and destruction incident to war. Affection and mercy are not attributes of war gods. The great Napoleon said "red-hot shot could not be fired into a populous city with affection." General Sherman said at Atlanta, "War is cruelty and you cannot refine it." For the blood and tears shed in war there is no adequate compensation. A full summary of wrongs growing out of a great war can never be made. The full account of these on either side will never be stated. Reconciliation must come without pecuniary compensation. Purification to all concerned, always incident to the triumph of a holy cause, must be accepted in lieu of the latter. Free schools, a necessary incident of perfect freedom, given to Virginia as a result of the war, must be accepted as ample compensation for the loss of the William and Mary College buildings. Examples of the utter futility of casting up accounts of alleged national wrongs and injuries and demanding their payment are not wanting. There is a notable one of very early origin. Jewish profane and traditionary history informs us that centuries after Moses led the children of Israel out of Egypt across the Red Sea, and thence to Mount Sinai and through the wilderness to the "promised land," the King of Egypt made and presented for payment to the Israelitish nation an account of the damages and losses sustained by Egypt and the Egyptian people, caused by the plagues sent by the Lord to soften the heart of Pharaoh, and also an account of the "jewels of silver and jewels of gold and raiment" borrowed of the Egyptians by the Jews at the command of the Lord immediately prior to their exodus.

The claim was stated on the part of Egypt about thus: To loss and damages caused by the river of blood; by the plague of frogs; by the plague of flies; by the murrain of beasts; by the plague of hail; by the plague of locusts, and by the smiting unto death of the "first born of Pharaoh that sat on the throne, unto the first born of the captive that was in the dungeon, and all the first born of cattle"; also for the value of the loaned "jewels of silver and jewels of gold and raiment" never returned. To this was superadded a claim for interest.

The prospect of having to pay so large a claim would appall the people of a rich nation of the present day. Not so the Hebrew people. They regarded the enormous claim with complacency. The Jews were then no special pleaders. They did not seek to cast the responsibility on their Lord. They did not demur because the claim was too remote or stale, nor because Egypt had slept too long on her pretended rights and thereby forfeited them; nor did they traverse the particular charges made or plead the general issue.

Moses had written the book of Exodus, and it had the divine sanction. Its record, to the Jews, imported absolute verity; and thereto turned the confident Egyptians for the proof of their claim. God's "chosen and peculiar people" did not, however, despair. The learned Levites went to work to state an account of offsets. Generally it included but one item, stated about thus: To work and labor performed, and services rendered by the twelve tribes of Israel, during four hundred and thirty years of unrequited Egyptian bondage in the land of Goshen, in Egypt, with all the attendant burdens, sufferings, stripes, tears, sorrows, wrongs, and deaths incident to oriental slavery. The learned ministry of Egypt, on receipt of this account, stood aghast and said, "'T is enough!" and the claim of the "Land of the Pharaohs" was not further pressed.

This exemplifies the vanity of trying to take an account of great national wrongs, &c. The recording angel only will sum them up at the judgment day; and the Lord of Hosts will wield the divine scepter of justice.

The further application of the illustration I must leave, for want of time, to reflecting minds.

The committee further insist that:

The colleges of the period preceding the war of the Revolution were among the most potent forces in accomplishing our independence and founding our Constitution.

And they say:

Among them none can claim precedence over William and Mary.

It is sufficient to say, in answer to this, as has already been shown, that in advancing the cause of rebellion "none can claim precedence over William and Mary."

The committee also express the opinion:

That if the accidents of war had led to the injury of Mount Vernon, of the house or the tomb of Washington, or of Independence Hall, in Philadelphia, we should have hastened to repair the injury.

These cases are widely different from the one under consideration. These are ancient—I might say sacred—places belonging to the nation, and they have no history around which treason to constitutional liberty ever clustered.

I make a quotation here from the remarks of President Ewell, of the college, before the Committee on Education and Labor:

Grant the prayers of petitions like this, and no more ever will the Union need arms to save people or their families, or their schools, or their houses of charity and learning, or their houses of God from ravages of civil war. This mode of treating the wounds of the past would be a salve indeed and heal them.

This contains an appeal and a promise that could be made on behalf of every weak and crippled institution of learning in the land, of which there are many North and South.

I hope no threat is to be implied from this language in case we fail to pass this bill. I have no time to speak of the propriety or constitutionality of Congress healing the wounds of the South by voting away the money of the people under the name of "a healing salve."

As a benefaction in the cause of education we might, possibly, be justified in passing this bill, but that would be of doubtful constitutionality. My friend [Mr. TUCKER] from Virginia could hardly vote for this bill, with his views of the constitutional powers of Congress, if it is not to be regarded as a "war claim" resting upon some legal or constitutional grounds. Too many benefactions are now pressing upon us to make an exception of William and Mary College.

We should apply the bounty of the nation as a "salve" toward healing the yet open wounds of the living bodies possessed of souls before we can be magnanimous to the soulless corporate bodies. There are yet throughout this land many sorrowing, suffering, and bleeding hearts of widows and orphans of dead soldiers, and they are not confined to the North.

Another matter contained in the committee's report deserves mention. I read from the report :

We believe that to follow the example of Washington, of Louis XVI, of Judge Cooke, of Tryon will make every college in America safer if civil strife or foreign war should ever hereafter disturb our peace.

It must be again noted in passing that these are not examples in favor of paying for injury or destruction of institutions of learning in an enemy's country, but noble examples in favor of protecting them in war. Washington and Louis XVI only made private donations to repair damages done by their troops to colleges loyal to the cause in which they fought. There are those who believe that to refuse to pass this bill "will make every college in America safer," because its fate will be pointed to as a warning to other colleges not to encourage civil strife, insurrection, and war, much less to teach the divinity of human slavery. The committee are equally unfortunate in saying that "no gentleman need fear that a vote for this bill will furnish a dangerous precedent for large claims against the Treasury," and that "a careful inquiry has failed to develop evidence of injuries sustained in the late rebellion by endowed institutions of learning, exceeding in all the amount of $100,000.

A full list of such institutions, with the amount of claims for damages caused by the late war, would be very large. Claims of this character have been presented to Congress for payment at different times since the late war, of which I give here only a partial list:

Alabama University	$250,000
William and Mary College, Virginia	65,000
Richmond Female Institute, Virginia	1,935
East Tennessee University	18,500
Jackson College, Tennessee	11,000
Alleghany College, West Virginia	8,000
Madison Female Academy, Richmond, Virginia	10,000
Male Academy, Athens, Georgia	5,000
Strawberry Plains High School, Tennessee	8,650
Protestant Episcopal Seminary, Virginia	20,000
Newberry College, South Carolina	15,000
La Grange College, Tennessee	31,300
Howard College, Alabama	8,000
Stewart College, Tennessee	1,000
Holstein College, Tennessee	6,250
Cane Hill College, Arkansas	10,000
Total	190,635

Most of these claims are now pending in this Congress. I am informed that members on this floor say they have been resisting the presentation of a flood of claims from their respective districts of kindred character to the above, which they will be no longer able to resist successfully if this bill passes. The Committee on Education and Labor of this House have already this Congress reported in favor of paying $85,000 of the above claims from Virginia alone, namely, the claims of William and Mary College and of the Protestant Episcopal Seminary. The claims in behalf of churches South are certainly more meritorious than the one under consideration. We are bound to presume that these churches of God upheld the banner of the Prince of Peace, and not of the demon of war.

There is a single claim in favor of the Book Agents' Publishing House, Methodist Episcopal Church, South, now pending in the Senate, which amounts to $458,400. The claims on behalf of churches which have been presented to Congress exceed already $1,500,000. The committee's facts and law are equally bad.

The report is a "comedy of errors." Take another instance. The committee say, as a reason why members should vote for this bill, that—

A bill like the present passed the Forty-second Congress, but was not reached in the Senate for want of time. It was received with expressions of approbation by the press of all parties, &c.

Certainly the draughtsman of the report did not intend to deceive or mislead any person by this statement. A bill such as the one under consideration, after amendment, was defeated in the Forty-second Congress by the House overwhelmingly. On the yeas and nays the vote stood—yeas 36, nays 127, not voting 78. (Globe, volume 92, page 188, December 13, 1872.) Nor did the bill receive the approbation of the press of all parties. In February, 1873, a bill similar to this one did pass the House by a small majority.

I conclude that on neither of the grounds set forth by the Committee on Education and Labor in their report can this House properly vote to pay this claim; nor can its payment be justified on any sound principle of law or true ground of national public policy or duty.

GENEVA AWARD.

December 17, 1878. The House having resumed the consideration of the bill (H. R. No. 4553) to provide for the further distribution of the moneys received under the Geneva award—

Mr. KEIFER said:

Mr. SPEAKER: I can hardly hope to say, in the very few moments I am permitted by the favor of the member from Pennsylvania [Mr. STENGER] to occupy the attention of the House, anything new on this momentous question. The millions of dollars—about $10,000,000—involved in the issue of this bill demands of each member his best judgment. The wide difference among the distinguished members of the Judiciary Committee at least warns those of us who are not able to say we have spent years in investigating the questions involved that there is room for honest differences of opinion. Principles, however, do not change on account of the importance or insignificance of cases. As to the details of the bills of the majority and minority of the Committee on the Judiciary I am forbidden for want of time to speak. The bill of the majority of the committee proposes to have the claims to the fund of all parties adjudicated by the Court of Claims, with a right of appeal to the Supreme Court of the United States; the bill of the minority proposes to revive the court of commissioners of Alabama claims, and submit the claims of some of the claimants to the fund to it, to the exclusion of other of the claimants, and to make the decision of such commissioners final. Stripped of all details and circumlocution, the two propositions coming from the Judiciary Committee may be fairly stated thus:

A majority of the committee, as set forth in the bill reported by the chairman, [Mr. KNOTT,] favors the granting to all claimants to any portion of the Geneva award fund or the interest thereon remaining undistributed a day in court, with a limitation of one year in which to file the claims, with the right of appeal given to each claimant or the United States to the Supreme Court of the United States, these claims to be, in the same manner, prosecuted as other claims in the Court of Claims. All persons are to be deemed claimants and have judgments rendered in their favor who were actual sufferers "by the violation of the laws of neutrality of Great Britain" for such amount as in the opinion of the court they shall severally be "justly entitled to recover under said treaty and award according to the principles of justice, equity, and the law of nations, without regard to any rule or principle of allowance, exclusion, inclusion, or distribution heretofore adopted by Congress," or by the Alabama claims commissioners; all payments hitherto made to be deducted from the judgments to be rendered by said court. The judgments so rendered are to be paid ratably if in the aggregate they exceed the total amount of the said fund and the interest thereon still under the control of the United States; all expenses incident to the hearing of said claims to be first paid out of said moneys; and if any part of the same shall still remain it shall be subject to the further action of Congress.

A minority of the committee (as set forth in the bill reported by the member from Ohio, Mr. McMAHON) favors the recreation of a court of commissioners of three persons, whose judgments shall be final, before whom certain designated claimants shall be granted the right to go, within six months from the organization of such court, and prove their claims, without regard to the "principles of justice, equity, and the law of nations," as the court might find and apply them. In its consideration of the designated claims referred to in the bill of the minority of the committee, the court will have no power in its rule of allowance to exclude or include any claim save as the proposed law directs.

No general principle is to be given to such court to guide it. The fiat of the law, arbitrarily applied, is to be the only guide of the court in making its final decrees. There is to be an utter disregard of the rights of all claimants whose claims were adjudged to be valid within the three rules laid down in article 6 of the treaty of Washington (May 8, 1871) as interpreted by the distinguished members of the tribunal of arbitration at Geneva. By section 4 of the bill of the minority the claims suffered to be presented to such court of commissioners are divided into three classes, namely:

First. Claims described in section 11 of the act of 1874 relating to the distribution of this fund so far as they are not adjudicated, and, to quote from the bill—

Claims directly resulting from damage done on the high seas by Confederate cruisers during the late rebellion, including vessels and cargoes attacked and taken on the high seas or pursued by them therefrom, although the loss or damage occurred within four miles of the shore.

Also:

In cases of the loss of a whaling-vessel and outfit the court shall allow, in addition to the compensation provided for in the said original act, the sum of 10 per cent. in lieu of freight upon the value of said vessel and outfit as found by said court.

And upon all judgments heretofore rendered under said act for the loss of a whaling-vessel and outfit there shall be allowed the said sum of 10 per cent. upon the awards as made by the court, with 6 per cent. interest thereon from the day from which said original award bore interest until the date of payment.

Second. Claims for additional interest upon judgments of the court of Alabama claims awarded under the act named, on which the new court is to award 2 per cent. additional interest from the time interest was allowed to the time of payment.

Third—

The third class shall be for claims for the payment of premiums for war risks, whether paid to the corporations, agents, or individuals after the sailing of any Confederate cruiser, in determining which it shall be the duty of the court to deduct any sum in any way received by or paid to the claimant in diminution of the amount paid for any such premium, so that the actual loss only shall be allowed.

Judgments on claims of the first class are to be first paid out of the fund; judgments on claims of the second class are next to be paid in full, or *pro rata* if the remaining fund is insufficient; and so of the claims of the third class.

Let us analyze these classes of claims a little.

The first class includes claims and pretended claims resting on various grounds.

Section 11 of the original act provided for the adjustment of claims for direct losses caused by the inculpated cruisers Alabama and Florida and their tenders, and all claims admissible under that act directly resulting from damage caused by the inculpated cruiser Shenandoah after her departure from Melbourne, (February 18, 1865.) These claims all ought to agree should be paid, but they are to be coupled in the same class with all claims for direct losses on the high seas during the rebellion caused by exculpated Confederate cruisers, of which there were a large number, and without regard to time or circumstances of the loss. The bill under the first classification directs the court to award 10 per cent. upon the value of whaling-vessels and outfit, as found by the old court, in lieu of freights; and the further sum of 10 per cent. upon prior awards for value of whaling-vessels and outfits, with 6 per cent. interest from the date the original award bore interest until payment. The second classification seems to be only for the purpose of fixing 6 per cent. as the uniform rate of interest to be allowed.

The third is for "premiums for war risks," or rather indirect losses, excluded from consideration wholly by the Geneva tribunal, and withdrawn by the United States without reservation from the "case" before that tribunal.

Nothing illustrates more sharply the absolute inequity and injustice of this classification for payment than the fact that nothing is to be included for national losses, damages, or injuries caused by a prolongation of the war, by a transfer of commerce to the British flag on account of the action of the Confederate cruisers, and for expenses in the pursuit of such cruisers, &c.; also excluded and withdrawn from the case of the United States before the Geneva tribunal. These national claims, and all private claims for indirect losses, including war premiums, were unanimously rejected by the judgment of that tribunal before the final submission of the case. They should all stand or fall together.

The tribunal, through its president, Count Sclopis, (June 19, 1872,) in deciding against such claims, said:

The arbitrators think it right to state that, after the most careful perusal of all that has been urged on the part of the Government of the United States in respect to these claims, they have arrived, individually and collectively, at the conclusion that the claims do not constitute, upon the principles of international law applicable to such cases, good foundation for an award of compensation or computation of damages between nations, and should upon such principles be wholly excluded from the consideration of the tribunal in making its award, even if there were no disagreement between the governments as to the competency of the tribunal to decide thereon.

The arbitrators being governed by the three rules provided for their guidance in article 6 of said treaty, and as also set forth in said article, "by such principles of international law not inconsistent therewith as the arbitrators shall determine to have been applicable to the case," in their final award also found as follows:

So far as it relates to particulars of indemnity claimed by the United States, the costs of pursuit of the Confederate cruisers are not, in the judgment of the tribunal, properly distinguishable from the general expenses of the war carried on by the United States. The tribunal is therefore of the opinion, by a majority of 3 to 2 votes, that there is no ground for awarding to the United States any sum by way of indemnity under this head.

And whereas prospective earnings cannot properly be made the subject of compensation, inasmuch as they depend in their nature upon future and uncertain contingencies.

The tribunal is unanimously of opinion that there is no ground for awarding to the United States any sum by way of indemnity under this head. And whereas, in order to arrive at an equitable compensation for the damages which have been sustained, it is necessary to set aside all double claims for the same losses, and all claims for "gross freights" so far as they exceed "net freights"; and whereas it is just and reasonable to allow interest at a reasonable rate; and whereas, in accordance with the spirit and letter of the treaty of Washington, it is preferable to adopt the form of adjudication of a sum in gross, rather than to refer the subject of compensation for further discussion and deliberation to a board of assessors, as provided by article 10 of the said treaty.

The tribunal, making use of the authority conferred upon it by article 7 of the said treaty, by a majority of 4 voices to 1, awards to the United States the sum of $15,500,000 in gold as the indemnity to be paid by Great Britain to the United States for the satisfaction of all the claims referred to the consideration of the tribunal, conformably to the provisions contained in article 7 of the aforesaid treaty; and in accordance with the terms of article 11 of the said treaty, the tribunal declares that all the claims referred to in the treaty as submitted to the tribunal are hereby fully, perfectly, and finally settled.

Furthermore, it is declared that each and every one of the said claims, whether the same may or may not have been presented to the notice of, made, preferred, or laid before the tribunal, shall henceforth be considered and treated as finally settled, barred, and inadmissible.

The finding and award of the august tribunal is thus set forth at length to enable members to comprehend the completeness with which the arbitrators disposed of possible questions coming within the scope of the treaty of Washington.

On what principles of law and justice the private claims rejected by the tribunal are to be admitted and the claim for national losses (also rejected) is to be excluded we are not advised. In the designation of "claims on the part of the United States" national and individual claims were confounded and were all comprehended together, without making separate mention of individual claims. The General Government, for itself and its citizens, as it was bound by usage and national honor, pressed a general claim for all injuries, damages, and losses against Great Britain. The result was an award in gross of a large sum of money, based on valid claims, found to be such by the rules and principles of international law which a great and wise tribunal found should govern it.

It is wholly immaterial whether it was, as is claimed by some members, the paramount purpose of the United States to have certain great principles of international law settled authoritatively or not by the treaty of Washington and the tribunal that met thereunder at Geneva. It is unquestionably true that so far as the proper disposition of the money award goes it should at least be first applied to the payment of the claims of parties for such losses as were, under the rules which governed the arbitrators, considered in making the award.

There are those who pretend to believe that the award made of $15,500,000 was made to the United States on account of all claims presented by the United States of every kind, name, and nature, and that the arbitrators, in assuming, as they had a right to do under article 7 of the treaty, to make an award in gross to the United States, utterly disregarded the rules which they held applied to claims and included damages for all losses sustained by the United States and all its citizens by reason of exculpated and inculpated cruisers during the whole war.

This is so violent a conclusion that it is hard to conceive how it can be calmly entertained. To reach such a conclusion is to impeach the integrity of all the distinguished arbitrators save Sir Alexander Cockburn, the arbitrator on the part of Great Britain. It is, in the absence of conclusive proof, a most violent assumption to say that these arbitrators laid down with great care rules for the exclusion and inclusion of claims presented, and then in making up an award in gross willfully violated and disregarded them. Had the rules established been allowed to be applied by a board of assessors, under article 10 of said treaty, it is conceded that only such claims as would have been valid under them would have been allowed. In a certain sense it is undoubtedly true, as shown by the award already quoted and as required by article 11 of said treaty, that all claims against Great Britain were finally settled by the award. That article is as follows:

The high contracting parties engage to consider the result of the proceedings of the tribunal of arbitration of the board of assessors, should such board be appointed, as a full, perfect, and final settlement of all the claims hereinbefore referred to; and further engage that every such claim, whether the same may or may not have been presented to the notice of, made, perfected, or laid before, the tribunal or board, shall, from and after the conclusion of the proceedings of the tribunal or board, be considered and treated as finally settled, barred, and henceforth inadmissible.

It will be observed that if the tribunal had left to a board of assessors to make up an award on each valid claim in detail, all other claims would still have been finally settled. But it does not follow that an award in gross was to be held to be paid on account of invalid and unpresented claims, as well as on account of recognized and valid ones. The reasoning in favor of such a view may possibly be called specious, yet it may lead to absurdity, injustice, and wrong. If only one valid claim had been presented and considered in making up the award together with an hundred wholly groundless ones, the holder of the valid claim, if this view is to prevail, would have to share the sum awarded with the holders of such other claims, even though they were grossly fraudulent. The statement of such a proposition is its own refutation. The bill, Mr. Speaker, of the minority of the committee has no better or broader foundation than can rest upon such an inequitable view. The proposition is captivating, that those who lost their vessels and cargoes on the high seas by all the confederate cruisers, and all those who had to pay war premiums by reason of such cruisers, should be reimbursed, whether the loss resulted or payments were made by reason of exculpated or inculpated confederate cruisers. But it is unsound. It is only because Great Britain was held liable according to international law for the payment of certain private claims for direct losses that any of the claims can be paid at all. It follows irresistibly that only such claims as formed the basis of the award against Great Britain should be paid.

Losses of any kind occasioned on the high seas by confederate cruisers put afloat through no fault of Great Britain stand on the same footing as all other losses or damages by the enemy, whether on sea or on land. Untold millions of dollars' worth of property have been destroyed by the enemy on land belonging to loyal parties North and South that have as much right in law and equity to the Geneva award fund as the holders of rejected or unpresented "Alabama claims." No person or party, I believe, has yet proposed to pay claims for losses occasioned by the acts of the enemy on land. They are included under the head of "ravages of war," the payment of which is always refused. There were also billions upon billions of dollars' worth of property destroyed by the Union Army which it is not pretended can be paid even where the parties are of undoubted loyalty and resided in the North. The sympathetic argument is not broad enough. The cloth will not cover all who are naked. It is specially pressed that those who paid war premiums to insurance companies should be reimbursed. It may be that many of them were reimbursed, and more too, by the war freights collected of the shipper, and hence suffered no loss.

The bill of the minority of the committee is on its face a confession of the inequity of many of the claims included in its provisions. All the claimants to this fund either stand abreast in point of right, or they have no proper standing at all. If the fund was awarded for all the claimants regardless of the merits of their claims, then all should be paid in full or suffer a reduction ratably. The bill itself discriminates not only against the second and third classes named, but may operate, yes, its friends admit it will operate, to exclude certain claimants who would be "justly entitled to recover under said treaty and award according to the principles of justice, equity, and the law of nations." By the bill of the majority, all persons and corporations claiming on account of losses during the late war a share in the Geneva award fund, no matter how or when such losses occurred, are permitted to have their claims tested finally by the highest judicial tribunal in our Republic, and by the principles of justice, equity, and the law of nations. This privilege the bill of the minority denies them. It has been said on this floor that to permit this to be done would give to certain insurance companies a portion, if not all, of the fund. This, as a member of this House, I need not decide; nor have I decided it. The highest court in the land is eminently qualified to determine, judicially, who is in equity and justice entitled to receive the fund.

If those who argue so strenuously that the award was made to reimburse all claimants for losses, whether their claims were considered by the tribunal good, bad, or fraudulent, then the court may under the bill of the majority of the committee be bound to include and pay them.

If the award was made to pay all claims, why not use the fund to pay all of them? The bill of the minority refuses to do this, and excludes absolutely the claims of parties known to have been regarded by the tribunal as valid.

It is a suspicious circumstance that great confidence is expressed in certain things connected with this grave question, and yet there is such bitter opposition made to permitting the highest judicial tribunal in the land to determine them.

Legislative adjudication is almost invariably unwise where great principles of law and equity are to be applied among a large number of parties, and it is always a doubtful expedient. The insurance companies, who it is said may have some claims in equity and justice, are so reviled and abused as to put some men in awe and cause them to hesitate to do their duty even here.

It has been vehemently asserted that these companies will, under the bill of the majority, get the fund "under the doctrine of subrogation by technical rules of the law," or that by invoking the application of such doctrine they will be admitted to receive a portion of the fund. Is the invocation of the doctrine of subrogation (or substitution) an appeal to the law's technicalities? If so, then the terms of the bill of the majority will rule out these companies. Technical rules are set aside by such bill. But subrogation, if not a head in equity, is a rule of equity, and it has no connection with the law's arbitrary and technical rules. Equity may be invoked where the law fails to do justice: it commences where the law leaves off. Subrogation as a rule in equity, where only it has application, had its origin in and was transferred from the Roman or civil law, and was founded, as says Judge Story, "in principles of natural justice." Thus it is made clear that the bill of the minority of the committee proposes to override the principles of natural justice in the distribution of this large sum of money.

The assault upon the insurance companies must not be mistaken for sound logic or argument in favor of a vicious proposition sought to be applied in support of pretended claims of parties who may have no higher rights, though sufferers, than thousands of others who were crushed under the car of Juggernaut, drawn along by the cruelty and fanaticism of war. The eagerness and zeal of a lawyer, sometimes, on account of the extreme exigency of his case, leads him to assail the real or supposed faults of his adversary in person, in lieu of the ability to successfully assail the grounds of his adversary's case. Though some of us may be lawyers, we are called on to do our duty as legislators. Let us try to perform that duty impartially. I am led to the conclusion I have arrived at by my conviction of what is right in the light of what I deem to be the natural justice and equity of the whole question.

In conclusion, let me say again that the distribution of this fund, it being the fruits of a treaty between this and a foreign government, comes strictly within the judicial power of the United States, vested under the Constitution in the Supreme Court and in such inferior courts as the Congress may from time to time ordain and establish. (Constitution, section 1, article 3.) This judicial power extends to all cases in law and equity arising under the Constitution, the laws of the United States, and all treaties made under their authority. (Constitution, section 2, article 3.) Shall Congress, as is intended by the proposition of the minority of the Judiciary Committee of this House, usurp to itself that power, or shall we relegate the whole question from Congress and send it for decision where under the Constitution it appropriately belongs, laying down no principles for the guidance of the court save those founded on the broad and comprehensive basis—justice, equity, and the law of nations?

SOUTHERN CLAIMS.

January 21, 1879. On bill involving the payment of Southern claims—

Mr. KEIFER said:

Mr. SPEAKER: I understand the distinguished gentleman from New York to have been in favor of a bill that would pay all these claims in some form or other through the interposition of a court; but as he could not pay them all, he would not now pay any of them.

Mr. POTTER. Oh, no.

Mr. KEIFER. That is the gentleman's proposition as I gathered it from his bill, which passed by so large a vote at a former session of this Congress.

Mr. POTTER. That did not provide for the payment of any one of these claims.

Mr. KEIFER. It looked to the payment of all of this class of claims. I of course yield to the gentleman when he insists, but I do insist my statement is correct. He is, however, mistaken about this bill, for it does not provide anywhere for a payment of this claim.

Mr. POTTER. But it provides for the adjudication of the claim in the Court of Claims and for a recovery, a judgment there, if established.

Mr. KEIFER. It provides for adjudication by the Court of Claims, applying to it the law which has been made applicable to cases of like character before the southern claims commission. The effect of the adjudication of this claim by the Court of Claims under this bill, should it become a law, will be the same as under the omnibus bill of the gentleman from New York. The latter clause of this bill has been carefully drawn. It was so drawn in order that the Court of Claims should not take the report of this committee as conclusive of the question of loyalty or of the question of the taking or conversion of the property for which the claim is made. The latter clause of the bill was intended to entirely free that court from any action of the committee or Congress, and it was put there for the purpose of guarding against the very thing which the gentleman says we are in danger of doing. I am not satisfied by the *ex parte* testimony which was before the committee that these parties were loyal during the war. I am satisfied so far as there was any evidence, or what possibly might be called evidence, before the committee, that it showed they were loyal, but I am not certain that it is true, and I will not accept it, it being *ex parte* testimony, as conclusive of that question. It frequently turns out when questions of this kind are judicially investigated, when testimony is taken properly, that the parties were not loyal. I know a very noted case. A very distinguished gentleman had a claim before the commissioners of claims ——

Mr. BRAGG. If this bill revives the law and the rule of evidence established for the claims commission in this particular case, does it not in fact revive that legislation and make it applicable to one case, whereas all other cases will be excluded from the benefit of it?

Mr. KEIFER. That is coming back to the same thing I understood my friend from New York to favor; that is, he would not pay one claim, however just, that may come within our consideration here because we could not pay them all. Let me say, Mr. Speaker, we have paid millions upon millions of dollars under the general law

and through the interposition of the commissioners of claims, called improperly
southern claims commissioners; we have paid, I have said, through their interposition millions upon millions of dollars of claims of like character to this one, assuming
these parties to have been loyal and that these goods were taken and used by the
United States authorities for the benefit of the Government.

Let me say, sir, that it is not proposed to enter upon the payment of claims generally for property taken or destroyed in the South either to loyal or disloyal parties.
That is not the proposition; but if these goods were commissary stores or quartermaster stores which were taken from or furnished by loyal parties to the United
States Army, of which the Army had the benefit—used for the benefit of the United
States—then we propose to pay for them as we have been paying millions of dollars
for like property, even though the claimants happened to live in the South, if we
find they were loyal.

Now that is a policy which was entered upon long ago; but there we have stopped,
and there I propose to stand so far as I am concerned.

Mr. POTTER. Then I understand the gentleman to say if these parties were loyal,
and if the goods which were taken were goods of the class he speaks of, then they
ought to be paid, notwithstanding the expiration of the law establishing the southern
claims commission.

Mr. KEIFER. The gentleman states one of the troubles I have had some difficulty
with myself all through. There are, however, a great many people, unfortunately,
who come here with claims having never heard of this limitation. Some were minors
and could not have known or understood the application of the law. It may be we
are opening up a statute in this case, possibly, which we ought not to do, but on rep-
resentations made to us and on the evidence before the committee it thought this was
a proper case to open a statute and let in these parties. That is one reason why we
should not like to pass a general law to apply to all cases. If a man knowingly slept
on his rights when the statute gave him a remedy he should be permitted to sleep on.
Statutes of limitation are for repose as well as in the interest of peace.

I know with what approval members upon this floor may receive remarks made
against paying southern claims. The position taken by the gentleman from New
York [Mr. POTTER] is a popular one, perhaps, before the country. But before this
debate closes to-day, I desire to say that I believe, limited as I have already stated to
the payment for property taken from loyal persons by the United States officers or
furnished by such persons to the United States officers for the express use of the Army
in suppressing the rebellion in the South, the policy of paying these claims is a wise
one. I believe it is wise because we will not say to these people down South who
were loyal throughout the war, loyal when it cost something to be loyal—we will not
say to them that what they furnished to the Army freely, in order that the war might
be carried on, they shall now be robbed of. This would be saying to the people down
South who had their property there, and tendered it freely to the United States to aid
in putting down the rebellion, and who were loyal throughout the entire war, "We
will not pay you because you were so unfortunate as to live in a country that was disloyal." Many members fail to distinguish between claims of southern loyal men and
what are generally called "rebel claims."

I stand upon the doctrine that was long ago announced in the other end of this
Capitol by the distinguished Senator from Indiana, Senator Morton, by Senator Sumner of Massachusetts, and others, that it was a wise policy to pay certain claims presented by loyal men from whatever section of the country they came. If we fail to
do this we put the loyal men in disloyal districts exactly upon a par with the disloyal
people in disloyal districts. That is a position which I do not desire to take, popular
or unpopular.

For the sake of the future of this country, if even we are to forget the past, I am in
favor, in proper cases, of distinguishing between the loyal and the disloyal, and always in favor of the former.

Rebel claims should never be paid. All claims arising out of the general ravages of
war should not be paid to loyal or disloyal persons. Supplies furnished by or taken
from loyal parties North and South should be paid for as a matter of right, and such
has been the policy of this Government from the beginning, and I trust it may ever
continue to be.

PROCEEDS OF PUBLIC LANDS FOR EDUCATIONAL PURPOSES.

January 23, 1879. Pending consideration of the bill to apply the proceeds of the public lands for educational purposes—

Mr. KEIFER said:

Mr. CHAIRMAN: I move to strike out the last word.

I understood the distinguished gentleman from Illinois [Mr. HARRISON] to say that it was the policy of the Democratic party to favor the preservation of the public lands for the people of the country. Let me say that I congratulate that party and the country if that is now its policy, for when we remember the history of our country we know that among the last acts of the last Democratic President of the United States (Buchanan)—and I trust he will ever be the last—was the veto of a homestead bill. He vetoed the bill because, as he said, "the granting of homesteads was a boon exclusively conferred upon the cultivators of the soil" that ought not to be granted. He vetoed the bill because, as he said, it would "prove unequal and unjust in its operation, because from its very nature it is confined to one class of persons;" and that in his opinion it was not expedient to proclaim to all nations of the earth that all foreigners "shall receive a farm of one hundred and sixty acres of land;" and that it is agrarian in principle. He did it because he said it was a charity to the poor that he did not favor. The gentleman will find that memorable veto message dated the 22d of June, 1860.

I rose for the purpose of stating and putting in the RECORD as a part of my remarks the great things that have grown out of the Republican homestead law, a law passed by a Republican Congress; a law which had the approval of Abraham Lincoln, a republican President. It was passed upon the 20th of May, 1862, and under that law there have been 384,848 homestead entries made, covering a territory in extent, if you deduct 10 per cent. of the whole number for canceled and abandoned entries, exceeding the whole of England, Scotland, and Wales. It exceeds by 10,000,000 of acres the whole of the territory of the New England States. The area in acres of New England is 43,742,720; the area of land taken up by actual settlers under a Republican homestead law, after making the deduction mentioned, is 55,418,112 acres.

It exceeds more than twice the area of my own State, the State of Ohio. The area of Ohio is 25,576,960 acres. After due allowance for canceled and abandoned entries, under the homestead law 350,000 heads of families have acquired homes. Such are the fruits of the policy of the Republican party in relation to the public domain, and in spite of the policy of the Democratic party of old. I congratulate that party that it has been educated up to-day by the Republican party, though it has taken nearly twenty years to do it, to a point where it is in favor of homesteads.

Mr. HARRISON. I want to ask the gentleman what bill did any Republican President ever veto granting millions upon millions of acres of the public lands to private corporations?

Mr. KEIFER. I am frank to say that the great champion of Democracy in the State of Illinois initiated the policy of granting public lands to railroad corporations. I refer to Stephen Arnold Douglas, of Illinois.

Mr. HARRISON. I would like to have the gentleman answer my question. And then I would like to have him answer the question whether Mr. Douglas did not have these lands given to the State of Illinois and not to a corporation? Read history and you will find that the Democratic party has not been the one to set the example of giving the public lands to private corporations.

Mr. KEIFER. The gentleman is entirely wrong in his statement. The land was granted to the State of Illinois in trust for railroad purposes.

Mr. SPARKS. Still it was granted to the State and not to a corporation.

Mr. KEIFER. It was granted to the State of Illinois for the benefit of the Illinois Central Railroad; there is where it went.

The CHAIRMAN. The time of the gentleman has expired.

Mr. KEIFER. The following is the table to which I referred:

Statement showing the number of homestead entries made in each State and Territory from the passage of the original homestead act, May 20, 1862, to June 30, 1878, inclusive.

States and Territories	1863	1864	1865	1866	1867	1868	1869	1870	1871	1872	1873	1874	1875	1876	1877	*1878	Total
Alabama				29	1,436	1,769	2,779	1,709	1,590	1,552	1,723	1,527	1,505	1,266	1,532	825	19,222
Arkansas				164	1,578	2,355	3,326	4,030	4,258	3,395	4,984	1,754	1,345	1,523	2,345	2,351	33,660
Arizona									4	4	5	21	23		32	26	147
California		269	390	204	508	460	376	944	1,127	906	1,521	1,572	3,400	1,995	1,746	923	17,146
Colorado		252	172	290	85	36	445	567	605	342	568	524	429	371	413	330	5,453
Dakota		100	76	299	255	677	363	635	900	1,022	1,819	1,470	835	1,554	1,184	4,128	15,513
Florida				828	1,217	1,603	728	539	379	321	439	541	1,766	1,855	1,612	564	12,623
Indiana							2		2						3		19
Illinois	3		1	1								3	6			4	63
Iowa	302	463	765	1,084	521	855	2,396	1,963	2,364	1,760	635	471	180	146	70	21	13,796
Idaho						53	81	87	90	61	91	130	72	137	232	59	1,161
Kansas	1,619	366	717	1,435	1,175	1,695	2,593	6,530	11,165	5,809	7,586	4,721	2,356	3,192	4,185	5,320	61,034
Louisiana					260	255	729	740	1,381	1,000	854	427	583	531	508	170	7,438
Missouri	84	271	2,026	2,899	1,871	2,612	3,264	3,376	2,177	1,442	925	529	506	454	490	398	23,327
Michigan	2,336	934	1,355	2,051	1,716	1,739	1,573	1,412	1,456	1,430	1,206	1,235	1,746	984	996	640	27,821
Minnesota	3,644	3,364	4,726	3,139	1,915	3,146	3,278	1,915	4,165	3,850	3,229	3,754	3,034	2,419	2,465	3,562	53,575
Mississippi					1,652	948	1,047	958	1,095	928	923	494	503	430	484	294	9,596
Montana				3	12	21	126	240	292	202	19	404	36	81	41	204	1,160
Nevada		44				18	15	51	70	74	12	41	55	61	41	72	632
New Mexico					5	5	13	94	61	19	19	70	50	27	20	25	319
Nebraska	796	621	1,123	1,463	2,178	2,895	4,083	4,678	6,866	6,164	5,309	4,106	1,700	1,851	1,375	2,279	47,962
Ohio	58	8		9	6				12	17		9	15	1		1	167
Oregon	271	175	333	509	512	501	497	688	783	714	442	436	592	526	649	357	8,025
Utah									252	529	130	200	341	356	561	461	3,575
Wisconsin	2,316	332	1,049	1,404	2,272	1,493	1,460	1,244	1,302	1,385	1,503	1,639	1,707	1,924	1,057	530	21,437
Washington	742	165	227	162	207	194	395	542	460	538	422	365	309	473	672	542	6,473
Wyoming							2	2	18	3	14	25	29	33	28	12	164
Grand totals	13,356	7,921	12,968	15,973	19,369	23,542	30,054	34,443	42,694	33,514	34,670	25,179	21,230	21,886	23,026	24,013	374,749

* Fractional.

J. A. WILLIAMSON, *Commissioner.*

CLASSIFICATION OF MAIL MATTER.

January 23, 1879. Mr. Keifer offered the following proviso to the bill providing for the classification of mail matter : "*Provided, however*, that nothing herein contained shall be so construed as to admit to the second-class regular publications specially designed for advertising purposes and not for dissemination to regular paying subscribers."

Mr. KEIFER said :

I do not wish to delay the progress of this bill, but it is perhaps proper that I should state very briefly why I offered this amendment. I believe it is reported that under a clause similar to that contained in this section a man who was so unfortunate as to be at the same time the regular publisher of a paper and also the owner of a saw-mill in the same county, inserted in one corner of his paper a notice in regard to sawing logs at his saw-mill, whereupon the Post-Office Department decided that his paper, although published regularly in all other respects, was primarily an advertising sheet and therefore could not be circulated at the ordinary rates of second-class mail matter.

The object of my amendment is not to get into the law a provision which will allow any kind of publication merely for the purpose of advertising sent out under any guise whatever, to advertise the business or occupation of the men publishing it. I have drawn my amendment to guard this from any evil of that kind. I know of many publications, and other members tell me the same thing, I know notably of one publication, I have the copy of the paper here before me, that has over fifty thousand subscribers, I am told over two thousand in the State of Texas alone, which has very little advertising patronage, paid or unpaid, very little indeed as compared with another paper I have in my hand, and I am told the Department is disposed to rule this paper with regular subscribers does not come within the rule of second-class mail matter because it happens the publishers of the paper have another occupation if you please. They are manufacturers; but if you will read the paper you will hardly find I think—it is impossible to find a reference to their own manufacturing business in it anywhere, and there are ninth-tenths of the entire print of general news for the people. If they should happen to get in a reference to the business of their own, according to the present law it will be held that it should be paid at the rate of third-class matter, as I read it.

I hold in my hand what I picked up this evening, what I would call an advertising sheet; it is called the New York Daily Commercial Bulletin. There are two or three columns that might be called general news matter; all the rest, with the exception of some little commercial quotations, is advertising matter. I have seen the Commercial Advertiser of New York with less than a column of general news in it and all the rest paid matter that may go all over the country as second-class mail matter, while another paper is to be excluded on a simple technicality. The word "primarily" is in this bill, and I do not wish to mislead anybody, but I understand it is substantially the language of the present law which is unjustly applied to publishers.

Mr. WADDELL. If my friend will allow me to interrupt him I will call his attention to the broad distinction between the paper from which he has read and a paper like Baldwin's Monthly, of New York.

Mr. KEIFER. If this is published for the purpose of circulating with a regular list of subscribers my amendment excludes it.

Mr. WADDELL. Baldwin's Monthly has a large amount of really interesting literary matter.

Mr. KEIFER. If it is merely to cover up, if the gentleman will pardon me, general advertising business to be advertised by sending this out to persons not regular subscribers, then it is excluded in the mails as second-class matter under the amendment I propose.

Mr. WADDELL. It is excluded under the amendment we propose.

Mr. KEIFER. I want to still exclude it.

Mr. WADDELL. Publications of that kind which contain a great deal of valuable literary matter, but which are sheets published for advertising purposes, are excluded under our bill from the privileges of this rate.

Mr. KEIFER. My amendment excludes all publications specially designed for advertising purposes and not for dissemination of news to regular paying subscribers.

REDUCTION OF THE ARMY.

February 4, 1879. An amendment was offered to reduce the number of enlisted men in the Army.

Mr. KEIFER said:

Mr. CHAIRMAN: I do not desire to interfere particularly with this family quarrel which has so suddenly broken out on the other side of the House, for those who come in as interlopers sometimes do themselves no credit. If I could pour a little oil upon the troubled waters, I should be glad to do so. I wish, however, to say in opening that the gentleman from Maryland [Mr. KIMMEL] who talks so vigorously against the dangers of a standing army forgets that only a short time since, July 20, 1877, the governor (Mr. Carroll) of his own State appealed almost piteously to the President of the United States to send to the city of Baltimore troops from the regular Army in order to put down a riot that could not be controlled by the militia and by the good citizens of the State of Maryland, and to this appeal the President responded. So much, then, for that.

I desire, sir, also to state what I understand to have been a high compliment passed upon President Grant by the distinguished gentleman from New York [Mr. COX]. I understand, stripped of the somewhat beautiful language in which he put it, that if it had not been for General Grant in the Presidential chair with the few troops gathered about the Capitol here, the decision of the Electoral Commission, approved and affirmed in this House and in the Senate, would have been overturned by violence and revolution. That is the way I understood the gentleman. In effect he said that but for a man in the Presidential chair who wielded the power and had the will to execute the Constitution and the laws as he was sworn to do we should have had revolution, violence, and everything else running riot in March, 1877, in this country; and we should have had a man put in the Presidential chair who was elected not by the people, not according to law and the Constitution, but put there and chosen after the regular election by organizations which would have come here, as threatened by the distinguished gentleman from Ohio in his 8th of January speech, 1877—put in the Presidential chair, perhaps, by that threatened hundred thousand men who were to come up here, inaugurate revolution, and overthrow the action of the duly constituted authorities of the Congress of the United States and of the Electoral Commission acting under law and by authority, and foist on this country a man defeated at the polls and also defeated in his attempt through bribery and corruption to buy the Presidency.

I am in favor of twenty five thousand men or more in the regular Army. Personally, and not speaking for my party or party friends around me now, I am in favor of a larger army than this bill provides for. I believe it would be economy for this Government to have an army that would stand guard, if you please, upon the borders of Texas and upon the borders of the Western frontier, and when we have that serenity there my friend from New York [Mr. COX] speaks of, we would have an army to keep all things serene. It is bad policy to wait until blood has flowed, until the pioneer of the West has been driven from his home or murdered, and his property stolen or destroyed by the Indians, and until the Mexicans have crossed the Rio Grande and performed their work also of desolation and death among our citizens. It is our duty to prevent and not alone to punish outrages against our people. I have much sympathy for the frontiersmen. A sufficient army at all points will prevent outbreaks of all kinds, Mexican marauding and Indian wars. The experiences of the summer of 1877 prove that many of the States—not Ohio—had to appeal to the regular Army to put down riots.

The thieving and cowardly Mexican will not invade our borders if it is suitably guarded by regular troops. We owe to our citizens of the Texas-Mexican border ample protection. Everywhere else than within the geographical limits of the United States our Government makes haste to protect her citizens. It is time we were beginning to do it at home.

Indian outbreaks will not take place if our frontier has upon it a proper complement of soldiers. No increase of the number of officers of the Army is needed; but the ranks should be filled up.

[Here the hammer fell.]

Mr. COX, of New York. I beg to correct the gentleman from Ohio [Mr. KEIFER] in some respects. I do not remember to have made the speech from which he quotes, on the 7th of January, about the one hundred thousand men.

Mr. KEIFER. The gentleman misunderstood me. I spoke of the gentleman from Ohio, [Mr. EWING]. I spoke of the 8th of January speech.

Mr. COX, of New York. I think the gentleman has in his mind some little loose talk about what was said about a gentleman from Kentucky at that time.

Mr. KEIFER. No, sir; it was borrowed perhaps from that gentleman, but it was reiterated in the capitol at Columbus.

WAR CLAIMS.

February 14, 1879. The bill for the relief of John T. Armstrong was under discussion.

Mr. KEIFER said:

I do not rise at this late hour of the day for the purpose of going generally into the question of war claims. We can hang as many speeches as we choose on that question; and it seems to me each succeeding day this question is up we get some new views. In this we are either taking better or worse ground than we have held to in the past. But let me say, if I understood the gentleman from Massachusetts rightly (and I tried to listen to him carefully) we are to understand his position to be this; that notwithstanding the fact a loyal claimant may come here from the South with a meritorious claim he is not to be paid, and a disloyal claimant is also not to be paid; and that if we will enter into some sort of arrangement of that kind, drawing no distinctions between loyalty and disloyalty on this floor, there may be such a change of sentiment in the North that before a great while the country will be prepared to pension the confederate soldier. If that is the position of the gentleman, and if it is not the gentleman is certainly entitled to correct it now——

Mr. BUTLER. I never require, if my friend will allow me, necessity for the correction of what I have said. I repeat that, whenever the question of the depletion of the Treasury by claims of anybody is put, I think the pity or the humanity of the North will take care of the maimed men of the war; and if you want to know, I say that I see no more reason why a confederate soldier, maimed and crippled in the honest discharge of what he considered to be his duty, should not be pensioned than why a confederate soldier who honestly believed he was doing his duty should be put into a Republican Cabinet.

Mr. KEIFER. I invited the gentleman from Massachusetts, in order that there should be no mistake about his position, to restate his position; and I was successful in getting him to restate it. We all understand him now. I invited the distinguished gentleman to restate his case, although in the first place it was very well stated. Now, as the gentleman from Massachusetts is in favor of pensioning the confederate soldier, he is therefore, according to his reasoning, taking the antithesis of all he had to say, in favor of putting a confederate into a Republican Cabinet.

Mr. BUTLER. I have never said that.

Mr. KEIFER. But that must follow. He is in favor of both, as he puts them exactly on a par; when he is in favor of one, he must be in favor of the other.

Mr. BUTLER. No, sir.

Mr. KEIFER. I should be, at least if I were in favor of pensioning the rebel so'dier.

Mr. BUTLER. But I have not said so. Will the gentleman allow me?

Mr. KEIFER. Oh, yes; I always try to be polite to the gentleman.

Mr. BUTLER. I have not said I am now in favor of it, nor do I think the country has yet come up to it; but when we have withdrawn all causes of difficulty, so that nobody from the North will object to a confederate soldier being in the Cabinet, then I say humanity will bring——

Mr. KEIFER. The gentleman has already stated his proposition. The gentleman undertakes by fair inference to say the present Administration is only a short step in advance of him; he has not yet come to the time when he is in favor of putting confederates into the Cabinet and pensioning confederate soldiers, but he thinks he will soon reach a point where he will favor both.

Mr. BUTLER. Neither one nor the other now.

Mr. KEIFER. Not yet; but he thinks he is very nearly there; "almost persuaded."

Now, Mr. Chairman, I do not want to misrepresent anybody; I have been one of those upon this floor from the beginning who have insisted steadily, persistently, and, as nearly as I could, consistently, upon making a distinction between loyal and disloyal claimants so far, and so far only, as loyal claimants have come here and presented claims well proved for supplies furnished to the army and which were used by the army. All other classes of claims for damages growing out of the general ravages of war, and all other claims of a kindred character we alike strike down, whether presented by the loyal or the disloyal men. But I want to enter my protest again here against the idea of voting money to rebuild, to reconstruct, and to carry on educational institutions where treason has been steadily fostered and where it may yet be fostered in the future. The gentleman from Massachusetts favors the payment of such claims, I believe.

Mr. AIKEN. Will the gentleman allow me to interrupt him?

Mr. KEIFER. I will in a moment. I am opposed to an institution of learning, destroyed by the accidents of war, being rebuilt out of the public Treasury in which the doctrine, the fundamental doctrine taught in it was against that principle of the Declaration of Independence which held that "all men were created equal," and where also the doctrine was inculcated in all the students of the institution that slavery was a divine institution, and wherein was indorsed and taught the principle which I once before quoted on this floor and found in the constitution of the Confederate States. I refer to the clause prohibiting any law ever being made that would in any way impair the right to hold human beings as slaves. Now I will yield to the gentleman from South Carolina, [Mr. AIKEN].

Mr. AIKEN. I would ask the gentleman this question : On his reasoning, if he is opposed to giving appropriations or help to institutions which have sent abroad men who favored the rebellion in this Government, how can he conscientiously vote for appropriations to West Point? How can he defend Northern institutions at which Southern men have graduated? Why vote for West Point appropriations when the leading men of the Confederate army all graduated there?

Mr. KEIFER. The gentleman has put a very fine question, a very refined one. If it happened in the past that students who came to the North from the South, where they had drunk in at the fountain-head and been taught in the cradle the doctrine of State rights, and that slavery was a divine institution, attended a Northern institution, then went back to their own people and still in some cases concurred in their early views, the gentleman says my reasoning would have us destroy that institution or never rebuild it if destroyed. My reasoning does not go to any such extent as that. But I do not object to the gentleman asking the question. He refers also to West Point. We hope and expect now that only loyal sentiments, true patriotism, and that this Republic is a nation not a mere league, will be taught at West Point to military cadets, and hence I am willing to vote appropriations to carry it on. Southern men have learned much by the lesson of the war.

I have some other suggestions I desire to make. It has been very common on this floor for those who take great pains always to oppose the payment of the claim of a loyal man to say that there were no loyal men down South during the war. I want to call attention to the fact that the records of the War Department, and I say it to the credit of the Southern States, will show that above seventy thousand white men from the seceded States entered the Union Army. I here give them to you by States. The number of men sent from those States is as follows: Virginia, 85; North Carolina, 3,575; Georgia, 152; Alabama, 2,471; Florida, 1,286; Mississippi, 681; Louisiana, 5,357; Texas, 2,444; Arkansas, 8,627; and Tennessee, 27,637, making a total of of 52,715. In addition to this number about twenty thousand white troops from these States (mostly from Tennessee and Alabama) were enlisted as refugees in organizations not embraced in the foregoing, making a grand total of over seventy thousand white loyalists who stood by the Government in its hour of danger. And even this does not include several thousand whose actual presence swelled the ranks of the Army of the Republic but whose real numbers cannot be known.

It is to be presumed that some of the loyal men South did not go into the Union Army. I know instances of men from Mississippi, Georgia, and other Southern States, for I have had occasion to examine into their history, who stood out against their States when they seceded, against their friends, their brothers, and fought the doctrine of secession and upheld the flag of the Union to the end, and who were trampled into the dust in every conceivable way during the war. We prohibited them, and rightfully perhaps, from coming here or going to the courts and having their claims adjusted and paid because they do not consist solely of claims for supplies.

But I am not here to go into that question. I have another purpose in view. When gentlemen have suddenly become converted to some new doctrine we are naturally suspicious and cast about for the reason why. I witnessed some of the same gentlemen seated here now, within the last ten days allowing a bill to go through this House by unanimous consent, reported by the gentleman from Illinois [Mr. EDEN], the chairman of the Committee on War Claims, appropriating half a million of dollars for just that class of claims that gentlemen are constantly, when a special claim comes up, declaiming against.

Mr. FINLEY. Why did not the gentleman object?

Mr. KEIFER. I did not object because I believed it was right. But gentlemen who want to make cheap capital when they have a special case to deal with, and a loyal man's case is up and not the case of a disloyal man, did not rise to oppose that bill. Their object is to make capital before the country. I did not rise because it has been the policy of the Government to pay these claims, and it was right to pay them. I will state further that within the next two weeks there will be another bill of the same character passed by the House appropriating over $200,000 for claims mostly from the State of Tennessee and Kentucky of loyal men for supplies furnished the Army during the war, based on claims examined by the Quartermaster's Department and the department of the Commissary of Subsistence, and allowed by the proper accounting officers. It is said we have voted away to this class of claimants $100,000,000. Well, now, was that right? If it was not, then gentlemen took a long time in learning whether it was right or not. It has been the policy of the Government for many years, if not from the beginning, and it is too late to turn round upon it now.

If we will go back a little further to the time when the war raged, even to the period when the first army crossed into Virginia, from Ohio, led by McClellan, and when we had some gold in the Army chests, we paid loyal and disloyal men alike for the supplies that we took. When the United States was fortunate enough to have money in many of the campaigns, for good reasons and wise purposes, perhaps, loyal and disloyal alike were paid for supplies for the Army.

But when we got through the war, and when we had come to the end of it, we established a principle that cut off all disloyal persons' claims, even for supplies; but we said that we would pay loyal men for supplies, and we have continued to act upon that principle up to the present time. And now let me say, as I conclude, that any loyal man who has not been guilty of some sort of laches in presenting his claim when the Court of Claims had jurisdiction I would still be in favor of paying; all others I would reject. I am not prepared to say that the claim now under consideration should be paid.

It is proposed by the Committee on War Claims to report a bill fixing a limit within which parties must present their claims to the Quartermaster and Commissary departments, or have them forever barred.

I want to say further, in conclusion, that I would not surrender at any time the just claims of loyal men, North or South, in order that by so doing it might have some effect in softening the hearts of the people, as the gentleman from Massachusetts hopes, to the point of pensioning Confederate soldiers.

THE COAST AND INTERIOR SURVEYS.

February 18, 1879. Pending consideration of the legislative, &c., appropriation bill, various provisions regarding public surveys were discussed.

Mr. KEIFER said:

Mr. CHAIRMAN: There is some difficulty in understanding clearly what is intended in this bill. One thing is perfectly clear, that a system which has worked well in this country for a great many years is to be struck down and a system established which is to depend wholly upon the discretion of a single man. It is an anomaly in our legislation to say that we shall by law strike down a well-established system, carried on for many years successfully, and establish another one which will be utterly in conflict with all our laws in relation to the public land. By this bill it is provided that the Superintendent of the Coast and Interior Surveys shall establish such a system as he pleases and change it from time to time as he pleases.

A gentleman upon this side of the House, the other day, seemed to think that we had arrived at a time when it was absolutely necessary to change the system of surveys. He said that in our surveys, going westward, we had arrived, to use his own language, at the "foot-hills of the Rocky Mountain chain," and our present system of surveys are no longer applicable.

Now let me call the attention of the committee to one fact, that so far as the surveys in the Rocky Mountains and mining regions generally are concerned this bill has upon its face the confession that the new system or any new system would be an utter failure. It provides that in the future all the surveys of the mineral lands shall be done by deputy surveyors, according to the present law. It is proposed under the provisions of this bill which we are about to pass to survey from the foot of the Rocky Mountains up to their top, and across them, and divide them into sections and quarter sections, or other divisions. This new system, whatever it is to be, if it is a radical change from the old one, will be a total failure in every sense, and all we shall have done will be to derange the well-established system for dividing the public lands into townships, sections, and quarter-sections; a system perfectly familiar to all the people of the Western country, as is evidenced by the strenuous opposition that is made here by almost every person representing the Western States. There may be an exception or two to this. These men, representing their constituents, who are so deeply interested in this question, should be heard. They are properly alarmed at the threatened legislation. Why was not the subject brought up as a separate bill and not hitched on an appropriation bill? In this way we are forced to take much of our vicious legislation.

It is proposed to force upon a people who well know their wants and needs in this regard a system that is to derange everything. The gentleman said our surveys are inaccurate, and this was said by a gentleman who ought to have known how these surveys are carried on. If lines are under our present system run so as not to meet exactly, they are adjusted from time to time. The fortieth parallel is a base-line extending west from the Missouri River. It is the boundary-line between Kansas and Nebraska. From this base-line township-lines are run off, numbering north and south. There are also established principal-meridian lines running north and south, from which ranges are numbered east and west. By this system some inaccuracies are possible, but they cannot be very great. A township of land is quite easily designated by the numbers of the township and range, and it is easily found. The whole system is very simple and well understood. Almost every man who is in any way interested in the agricultural lands of our country can himself find a quarter section of land after he has the section, township, and range. All this it is now proposed to change, and allow one officer to at his own will substitute some other. We are to embark upon an open field of experiment. This I am opposed to.

Sir, we cannot change the system without great public injury. We have sold our lands and granted them to railroad companies, and if we change the system, in the future we are to have nothing but confusion among the people familiar with the present system. Many of our laws would have to be materially changed, and especially our pre-emption and homestead laws. Some gentlemen say on this floor there will be no material change. I do not choose to trust any one man or a board of men on so important a subject.

I have said all I desire to say, and I ask no man to vote for this part of this bill upon the idea or mistaken belief that we have arrived at the point when we must from necessity change our entire land system.

Now as to these mineral lands in the mountain regions, nobody ever thought that we would want to divide them into townships, sections, and quarter sections. They are only valuable for mineral lands, and I trust the Government will not indulge in the great folly of surveying its mountain lands and laying them off under any system of survey into sections or other land divisions for any purpose in the world.

THE ELECTION LAWS.

February 19, 1879. The legislative, &c., appropriation bill was again under consideration, and it was proposed to repeal the election laws.

Mr. KEIFER said:

Mr. CHAIRMAN: During this entire Congress the majority on the floor of this House have not been found in any single instance in favor of a law that would put an end to fraud, violence, and intimidation in connection with our elections. Not one member of that side of the House has ever suggested or done by word or vote anything that would put an end to the fraud, violence, intimidation, and murders that are known to exist all over the South at each recurring election. Not one man on that side of the House has sought in any way to do anything to purify the ballot-box, but all have favored free fraud in our elections. By a free election is meant in Democratic eyes full freedom in the work of ballot-box stuffing, intimidation, bulldozing, and whatever else will prevent a full, fair, and honest expression of the will of all persons who have under our Constitution and laws the right to exercise the elective franchise.

The gentleman who offered this amendment [Mr. SOUTHARD] states in commendation of it (and he limits it there) that it is in the interest of economy—as though dollars and cents were to be measured here against fraud, violence, and murder. Another gentleman, who represents the State of Maryland [Mr. HENKLE], tells us to-day (and perhaps he is a prophet) that history repeats itself. Yea, it will repeat itself unless we call a halt soon. We will go back to everything that is terrible and awful in the history of this Republic if we do not put a stop to the fraud and violence sought to be forced upon the people of this country. At this very moment we are engaged as political iconoclasts in tearing down that which stands here as a protection to American liberty.

Talk about history repeating itself! Why, sir, the great raper of the ballot-box (Mr. Tilden) in 1868 was indorsed in 1876 by the Democratic party. He was convicted in 1868 by Horace Greeley as the head and front of all the promoters of fraud upon the ballot-box in the State of New York; and after his full conviction, and after the Democratic party indorsed Mr. Greeley in 1872, they then turned around, history repeating itself, and indorsed Mr. Tilden again by giving him their vote for President of the United States.

If we go on tearing down all the barriers of this Government we may come again to what we have seen in the past—red-handed war.

I beg you, gentlemen on the other side, to pause in your career before it is too late. And the gentleman from Mississippi [Mr. HOOKER] to-day cries "unconstitutional" as against these election laws. That is the cry raised by the Democrats when we sought to put down the rebellion. Democrats said it was unconstitutional to save this fair Republic of ours. It has been the cry of the Democratic party ever since I knew it. That party, through its leaders, said it was unconstitutional when war was waged against the Union to preserve any Constitution at all.

Now let me say in conclusion to the Democrats North that all the recruits they have which to-day make them strong on this floor come from the success of the Republican party in taking the bayonet, sword, and musket from the great body of the Democrats South and rehabilitating them again with the rights of the ballot, and the Republican party has never been thanked for all this. [Laughter and applause.]

58

GOVERNMENT CONTRACTS.

February 21, 1879. A bill involving the validity of certain contracts was up.

Mr. KEIFER said:

Mr. CHAIRMAN: I do not rise to discuss this bill. The gentleman in charge of the bill, who is familiar with all the evidence, has stated all that is necessary to be stated in reference to it, except what the report shows. I do not rise to say that the authority read by the gentleman from Wisconsin [Mr. BRAGG] is anything else than sound law. I want it distinctly understood, so far as the Committee on War Claims are concerned, that that decision is quite familiar to its members. But the trouble is it does not go far enough.

I admit that the Supreme Court of the United States has held that under a statute contracts made by quartermasters and commissaries of subsistence must have the approval of the Quartermaster-General and the Chief Commissary of Subsistence before they can be binding. In a much more recent case decided by the unanimous voice of the Supreme Court of the United States that very question has been reviewed, and the case cited by the gentleman from Wisconsin has been affirmed in a case where a quartermaster made a contract for the use of a steamboat which was used for Government purposes. In that case, after affirming fully the doctrine of the case read by the gentleman, which is known commonly as the Filor case, the Supreme Court went further and decided that the mere fact of making a contract which was not binding did not cut off the rights of the party who furnished the property which the Government had the benefit of.

Mr. BRAGG. Will the gentleman allow me to put a question?

Mr. KEIFER. Certainly.

Mr. BRAGG. I ask the gentleman whether that decision was not the result of an advantage gained by the plaintiff upon an issue made on a plea that had not been properly replied to?

Mr. KEIFER. No, sir; it was not. It was the result of the party claiming not only that the contract made was valid, but upon another count of the pleadings claiming that he was entitled to recover upon the *quantum meruit*. Now to give a full answer to the gentleman I will ask the Clerk to read a single paragraph from the opinion of the court in the case of Clark *vs.* The United States, decided at the October term, 1877.

The Clerk read as follows:

We do not mean to say that where a parol contract has been wholly or partially executed or performed on one side the party performing will not be entitled to recover the fair value of his property or services. On the contrary, we think that he will be entitled to recover such value as upon an implied contract. In the present case the implied contract is such as arises from a simple bailment for hire; and the obligations of the parties are those which are incidental to such a bailment. The special contract being void, the claimant is thrown back upon the rights which result from the implied contract. This will cast the loss of the vessel upon him. A bailee for hire is only responsible for ordinary diligence and liable for ordinary negligence in the care of the property bailed. This is not only the common law but the general law on the subject.

Mr. KEIFER. In this case it was sought to recover the value of the vessel destroyed while under the control of the Government. Of course the Supreme Court declared there was no question of negligence involved, and the real owners of the vessel must suffer that loss; but the court goes on to say that, notwithstanding the contract under which the vessel was taken was void, the Government of the United States had the use of it and was bound to pay a full and fair equivalent for such use during the time the Government used it prior to its destruction. In other words, the Supreme Court of the United States recognized the principle that the Government of the United States has no higher rights as between itself and an individual than an individual would have as between himself and another individual. The United States Government has no right with reference to its own citizens to turn round and say, "We took your property; we have used it; we have had the benefit of it; but we did this through officers who technically did not make a good contract, and therefore we will not pay anything for the use or occupation of such property. In other words, we have had and used the means that enabled us to get the benefit of property without paying for it; and now before the people of this country and before the world we will justify ourselves by standing on a technicality and robbing our own citizens."

Mr. BRAGG. Was there a single question involved in the Clark case that was involved in the case which I read? Did it turn upon a single question——

Mr. KEIFER. Exactly the same question—permit me to answer as you go along—exactly the same question was involved in the Clark case as in the Filor case, so far as regards the validity of the contract under which the steamboat was taken possession of.

Mr. BRAGG. No, sir.

Mr. KEIFER. And the Supreme Court expressly affirm the doctrine of the Filor case in saying that the contract was void, and on that contract, as alleged in one count of the pleadings, there could be no recovery whatever; but upon the doctrine of the *quantum meruit* the court say that the United States are liable for the use of the vessel during the time it was used by the Government.

Mr. BRAGG. Now will the gentleman let me finish my question?

Mr. KEIFER. I have answered one, I hope.

Mr. BRAGG. You have only answered part of it. You put this on the question of *quantum meruit*. The question I desired you to answer was whether in the Clark case it was the exercise of the sovereign power of the Government against the people who were in insurrection, where by the powers given the Government under the laws of nations they had the right to seize and take, and did seize and take—whether the Supreme Court of the United States said a *quantum meruit* would lie?

Mr. KEIFER. Now, Mr. Chairman, the United States in this case—in the Clark case—assumed that a contract, where a vessel is in the Southern waters——

Mr. BRAGG. I want the facts.

Mr. KEIFER. I have the printed opinion here of Judge Bradley, but my opinion is——

Mr. BRAGG. I want the facts, and not opinion.

Mr. KEIFER. I do not know whether this discussion has much to do with the merits or principles of this bill, but I had it read in answer to the argument of the gentleman, in which he claims that where technically a contract is void it is the duty of members of Congress to stand up and say the United States shall not deal justly with its own loyal citizens. That is the only question, I believe, that is left in this case.

Some gentlemen have inquired where the ship was taken possession of. I think somewhere in the Gulf of Mexico; I am not certain. But I remember another question spoken of in the Clark case. It was a vessel purchased by Clark of the confederacy, and the question was raised whether Clark could recover on that account. The Supreme Court held that it was unimportant. As a matter of right Clark was entitled to recover, notwithstanding he bought the vessel originally from the Southern Confederacy.

YELLOW FEVER EPIDEMIC.

March 1, 1879. Pending consideration of bill to prevent the introduction of contagious diseases.

Mr. KEIFER said:

I do not think that we should draw any very fine sight when we are dealing with this question. I have no disposition to speak here as if I were prepared to lecture members of this Congress for the levity that has been exhibited in relation to this most important question.

I have felt this afternoon and this evening as though this country, the people of the North as well as of the South, would not excuse this House if we went home without passing some thoroughly efficient law looking to a prevention, as far as possible, of this dread disease in our country.

Some men talk here as though we were legislating only for Louisiana or Mississippi, or some of the extreme Southern States, where this disease was at its worst. I remember that the disease invaded my own State, and the most healthful portion of it. My colleague [Mr. EWING] will remember that in portions of his district the yellow fever appeared and swept off the citizens without regard to their station in life. It was not confined to those who live in hovels, but it attacked the very best of our citizens.

There is another consideration. If this disease is not likely to reach the North at all, if it is never to invade Ohio, Pennsylvania, New York, or any of the Northern States, we should remember that when last year it was spreading through the Southern States and depopulating towns and cities almost, we in the North heard the cry for relief, and there was hardly a village, city, or hamlet that did not pour out from its means what could be spared for the purpose of alleviating the suffering people of the South. Should that time again come, we in the North will feel that we are interested in our fellow-citizens of the South, and will again assist so far as is in our power.

We have already had to-day a vote upon the question whether we shall inject into this most important national measure the question of State rights. I wish there were not so many patents on our Constitution. We get out one every few days. This House has spoken on that question and said that we will not legislate or attempt to carry this principle of State rights into so important a question as this. Now let us go back upon our steps, and if possible get at the Senate bill and pass it. If there are any amendments needed to it, as suggested by the committee, let us make those amendments and then pass the bill, so that when your gavel falls, Mr. Speaker, at twelve o'clock on Tuesday next, we can say that we have passed at least one law looking to the prevention of the plague in our country.

•

(Forty-sixth Congress.)

REPRESENTATIVES FROM CINCINNATI, OHIO.

March 18, 1879. On the petition of citizens of Cincinnati in regard to Congressional elections held in that city.

Mr. KEIFER said:

I understood the gentleman to state that he was presenting a petition from twenty-three citizens of Cincinnati—"prominent citizens," as he calls them—a petition affecting the seats of two members of this House now sworn in.

Now, I say that under the statute there could be no contest, and we could not take cognizance in any way of this petition so far as it asks action at our hands. If it is a mere petition, which the Constitution gives to every citizen of the United States the right to present, then it ought to go to the petition box; or the gentleman presenting it, if he desires it to be read and printed in the RECORD, should ask unanimous consent for that purpose. His object now, I suppose—I may be mistaken—is to have this paper read before the Congress of the United States and published in the RECORD to-morrow morning, and beyond that nothing; for nothing can come of it beyond the mere publication to the country.

Mr. CARLISLE. Do I understand the gentleman to say that it is incompetent for this House, under that provision of the Constitution which authorizes it to judge of the elections, returns, and qualifications of its own members, to take cognizance of this matter unless there are regular contests by some other persons claiming the seats?

Mr. KEIFER. I have said nothing of the kind. I am very much pleased to answer the question and to say that under the Constitution of the United States Congress has seen fit to provide by law a method of attacking the right of any person claiming a seat in this House, and under that legislation we have been professing to proceed for a great many years, if not throughout the entire history of the Government. Now it is proposed, I suppose, if the gentleman means anything by his question, to override the law and adopt a new method without first providing a new law.

The gentleman from Kentucky [Mr. CARLISLE] and the gentleman from Ohio [Mr. McMAHON], my colleague, both seem to understand the Constitution of the United States very well; but they seem to think, for the first time at least expressed upon this floor, that the Constitution executes itself, and that a law which has been passed to carry out that provision of the Constitution is utterly nugatory. I know the Constitution provides that this House shall be the judge of the qualification and election of its members. Suppose, if they carry that out, they should say this House has power to vote out any member sworn in and to vote in any person they find anywhere outside, as a mere matter of power. But the law undertakes to direct here what we shall do and how we shall proceed; and it is a matter of procedure or practice, if gentlemen choose to call it so—it is a matter of procedure. We find here a petition offered for the sole purpose of getting it into the RECORD, so far as we are able to learn from the gentleman presenting it. Do these twenty-three persons intend to prosecute the inquiry? Have they any standing upon which to do it either under the law or Constitution?

I wish to state that this attack is the only step which it is professed these men can take, and therefore they have no standing here except as mere petitioners, such as they may have under the Constitution, but not for the purpose of putting into the RECORD a long charge against a member; and I trust the Speaker will make himself quite familiar with this petition before passing upon it. He will find they are attacking members of this House who have already been sworn in, who have rights, and it is proper we should know how they are doing it.

ARMY AT THE POLLS.

Mar 28, 1879. Pending the Army appropriation bill, which contained a section relating to the use of troops at places of elections. A point of order was raised against the section.

Mr. KEIFER said :

I understood the gentleman in charge of this bill [Mr. SPARKS] to say in discussing this point of order that we are now engaged simply in an effort to repeal a law, and as that was all the work we were now engaged in, and as it related to the use of the Army, it was therefore germane to this bill to attach to it the class of legislation contained in section 6 of the bill. He also stated that it might be or was in the interest of economy to repeal the sections of our statutes relating to the use of the Army at the polls.

I also understood the distinguished gentleman from Texas [Mr. REAGAN] to state that because the bill under consideration related to the Army we had a particular right to legislate upon it in any way we choose on any matter that appertained to the Army, and that it would be germane to the bill to put on any such legislation. Now I think both of those gentlemen have spoken inconsiderately and inadvertently, and that neither of them will upon due reflection undertake to stand upon their statements.

In the first place, this is not a work of repeal which we are engaged in. It is a work of making that which was hitherto a duty, made so by law, a crime—a crime entirely new, wholly new, in connection with officers of the Army and officers of the Navy and the civil officers of this Government. Never before, I believe, in the history of this country has it been attempted to make it a crime for an officer of the Army or an officer of the Navy or a marshal of the United States or a deputy marshal of the United States to keep the peace. This proposed legislation is intended to do that. Then I say to the gentleman from Texas, this is not legislation that pertains to the Army alone. It undertakes to make it a high crime, punishable by fine and imprisonment, for any civil officer of the United States to appear on election day at the polls with an armed body of men, not troops, not United States soldiers, but to go with an armed body of men to the polls to quell a riot. That will be the express effect of this proposed legislation.

It does not change the old section altogether, but it re-enacts the section in such form as to make for the first time a civil officer guilty of a crime if he carries out existing law. Under the present law, by the statutes of the United States and at common law, it is made the imperative duty of marshals, deputy marshals, and all the constabulary force of the United States to put down riots and to suppress all kinds of disorder everywhere in the United States within their respective districts when such riots and disorders come under their observation and personal notice. This legislation undertakes to make it a crime for those officers to do this if they go with armed men to do it—not soldiers, but armed men. They may go with feathers in their hands without violating the law; but when armed force is to be resisted, when it becomes necessary to quell rioters with arms in their hands, persons gathered together for the purpose of murder, intimidation, or whatever else it may be, the marshals and their deputies, whose duty it is now by law to quell such disturbances and restore and preserve peace, must go without any armed men with them; otherwise under this proposed legislation they will be guilty of a high crime.

Mr. KNOTT. Will my friend allow me to call his attention to section 5528 ?

Mr. KEIFER. Yes, sir; that is one of the sections we are now dealing with, in which we propose to strike out the words "to keep the peace at the polls." That is all we propose to do, so as to make the penalties provided by these sections when re-enacted apply first to military officers, second to naval officers, third to civil officers of the United States when they come with troops or armed men to suppress a riot or any other kind of disorderly and illegal organization of men at the polls. Now, when the marshal or deputy marshal comes, as it is his duty to come, to quell a riot, he has the right to summon the law-abiding citizens of the community to obey his orders, to go if you please armed—to become his *posse comitatus* in quelling such disturbances. But this proposed legislation takes away from the marshals and other civil officers of the United States who are charged with similar duties the power of putting down a riot on election day at the polls and makes it a high crime punishable by fine and imprisonment if such an officer undertakes to do it. This does not relate to the Army and Navy alone, but to the civil side of the Government. This is the work we are engaged in.

Hence I insist that this proposed legislation is not germane to the Army appropriation bill. It is not germane because it affects officers of the Navy; and this is not a naval bill. It is not germane because it affects civil officers of the Government. It is not germane in any sense. If the legislation proposed as a whole includes anything not within the rule it must all fall together.

Mr. CHALMERS. The gentleman speaks of this being a new crime. Will he tell me when it was first allowed by law that the Army should be used at the polls to keep the peace?

Mr. KEIFER. When the Government was organized, when we first had an army of the United States, it became the duty of that army under certain circumstances to quell riots, to put down men engaged in any sort of disorderly conduct, whether at the polls or at church or wherever else in the country; and this has always been the law up to the present hour.

Mr. CHALMERS. The gentleman will permit me to correct him.

Mr. KEIFER. I will not permit the gentleman to make a speech in the middle of mine; I will permit him to put a question.

Mr. CHALMERS. Then I ask the gentleman whether he does not know that this law was enacted in 1865 for the first time?

Mr. KEIFER. Ah, Mr. Chairman, the gentleman entirely misunderstands the legislation on this subject, although he is a very excellent lawyer. For the first time, in 1865, there was enacted a statute making it a crime for any officer of the Army or the Navy or any civil officer of the Government to interfere on election day for any purpose except in repelling the armed enemies of the United States or in keeping the peace. But from the beginning of the Government to the present hour it has always been the right and the duty of the officers of the Army and the Navy, as well as certain civil officers of the United States, to keep the peace everywhere

Mr. SPARKS. The gentleman will allow me to ask him whether there is any statute to that effect enacted prior to 1865; and, if so, where is it?

Mr. KEIFER. The gentleman from Illinois [Mr. SPARKS], as I understood him, asked whether prior to the act of February 25, 1865, there was any law on the subject of the use of troops at the polls. That is the way I understood him. Now let me say to him and to other members, that was the first time in the history of the country, so far as I know, that there was any restraining statute upon our statute-books at all in relation to the use of troops at the polls or anywhere else in the United States, and that legislation prohibited the use of troops and armed men at the polls by military, naval, or civil officers in the service of the Government, except for the purpose of repelling armed enemies of the United States or to keep the peace at the polls. Those two cases were excepted in this legislation passed by a Republican Congress, and we propose that this legislation shall remain as it now is, so that it shall not be said, as a reproach and a stigma upon this country, that we have officers, military, naval, and civil, whose duty it is by law, under penalties, to keep the peace everywhere, save and except on one day at least in each year these officers shall be required to fold their arms and look on and witness riot, murder, intimidation, or anything else of an unlawful character going on before their eyes, or be subject to severe penalties.

Now, Mr. Chairman, I understand the distinguished gentleman from Maryland [Mr. McLANE] to say that he did not agree with my friend on the right [Mr. FRYE] in his statement in regard to the power and duty of the President of the United States in relation to the movement of troops. I understood him to state as a reason why he did not concur in my friend's statement that we had the power to regulate the President of the United States in his government of the Army. I understood the logic of that to be that it is the duty of Congress, and its right whenever we have a war, or that which is akin to it, insurrection, riots, or domestic violence, or whatever else arises in the country to put down which the Army is required—that it is the right and the duty of Congress, in the first instance, as each impending battle or engagement comes on, to meet in debate and consider just how the President shall order his troops to go into battle. I understood that to be the entire logic of the gentleman's position. He believes that the President must withhold his orders and act as the mere mouth-piece of Congress. In his view the President of the United States must wait until Congress has said, "Move your troops to the right or the left; charge upon the right, or the left, or the center, and so on." I do not understand that to be any part of the duty of Congress; and let me say I think perhaps it is the first time it was ever stated upon the floor of Congress that Congress had any such extraordinary right. The Constitution gives to the President as Commander-in-Chief the absolute right and the power to move the Army or Navy when raised as he pleases, when an emergency has arisen or war has been declared. By the second section of the second article of the Constitution of the United States the President is made the Commander-in-Chief of the Army and Navy of the United States, and of the militia of the several States when called into the actual service of the United States; and together with other powers given to him he has the right to move the Army whenever and wherever it is necessary to move it. The President is by the Constitution clothed with all the powers incident to a commander-in-chief, and such power cannot be taken away by law. We may pass laws for the government of the Army, but not to restrict and restrain the President's constitutional power so he cannot use it effectually and efficiently in time of war or any other time when it is necessary to call that strong arm of the Government into requisition.

SOUTHERN CLAIMS COMMISSION.

April 15, 1879. Pending the consideration of the legislative, &c., appropriation bill, an amendment was offered to repeal the law under which the Southern Claims Commission was organized.

Mr. KEIFER said:

I had expected to hear some argument offered by the gentleman who submits this amendment for the repeal of the law creating the Southern Claims Commission that went to the merits of the case. For a great many years this House has been entirely silent on the subject of laying down rules of practice for this court. To-day, after this committee has carefully prepared a rule to govern the court in future that takes away all the objections that are now urged by the gentleman from Wisconsin, we hear a ten-minute speech against the court because it has had in the past some agents who are said to have acted under rules that some of us thought were unwise.

Let us go to the merits of this question. The legislation which was postponed by action of the committee a few days ago will correct all of the evils that are now spoken of by the gentleman from Wisconsin; and when we were attempting to amend this bill so as to correct those evils the gentleman himself was silent, reserving his speech until after we had made the amendment. Now, Mr. Chairman, in the future there will be very little of importance in this matter of the rules for the conduct of cases before the Commissioners of Southern Claims. On the 10th day of March last, under the present law, the time for taking testimony by the claimants in all cases expired. The term of the Commissioners will expire on the 10th day of March, 1880, about eleven months hence.

The whole number of claims originally before the Commissioners was 22,298. Of these claims over fourteen thousand have been reported upon and finally disposed of, leaving about eight thousand unreported and now in the hands of the Commissioners, and of these eight thousand unreported claims about three thousand of the claimants have taken their testimony under the rules of the law and submitted their cases for decision to the Commissioners, and the expenses of these claimants of taking their testimony under this law of Congress has averaged in each case about $30, making an outlay of $90,000 at least for all these claimants, expended in getting their cases ready for decision by the Commissioners, who are now examining the claims and will be ready, as I am informed by one of the members of the Commission, to finally report the claims on the 10th day of March, 1880.

Now let me say that there are five thousand of these claims as to which not one particle of testimony has been taken at all. These claims now, under the statute passed by the last Congress, are absolutely barred unless we repeal these sections that the gentleman from Wisconsin [Mr. BRAGG] proposes to repeal, and the effect of that repeal would be to revive five thousand claims now barred by the statute. They ought to be barred. Under an amendment which was put on a bill of this House in the Senate in the last Congress, and adopted in this House, the Commission was required to report to the next regular session of this Congress the names of all of these claimants with their claims, so that we will have a record here of five thousand of these barred claims.

Mr. BRAGG. I desire to ask the gentleman if he thinks that this court should always live, because if we revive the act authorizing their appointment we shall revive barred claims, barred by lapse of time.

Mr. KEIFER. We do not propose to let the court live a single hour beyond the 10th day of March, 1880.

Mr. BRAGG. Will not these claims revive then?

Mr. KEIFER. These five thousand claims are absolutely barred unless we by legislation revive them and dump them into this Congress. If we do that, no less than five thousand claimants would come with claims, and with some equity, telling us, "You passed a law authorizing us to prepare and present our claims, and we have spent thousands and thousands of dollars in preparing our claims, and we have done it upon the faith of a law of the United States; we were ready to submit them when the court was wiped out."

[Here the hammer fell.]

Mr. HAWK obtained the floor and yielded his time to Mr. KEIFER.

Mr. KEIFER. I am much obliged to the gentleman.

So much for that part of the case.

Mr. BRAGG. Will the gentleman allow me to ask him another question?

Mr. KEIFER. Certainly; I shall be very glad to hear it.

Mr. BRAGG. The repeal of the provisions of the act which I propose to repeal would not repeal any statute of limitation at all.

Mr. KEIFER. It would repeal all this legislation and the legislation which would affect these claims. All I desire to say here upon that branch is, that we are ready to have a final adjudication, favorable or unfavorable, of three thousand claims with the testimony taken. Is it wise for Congress now to repeal these sections of the statute and wipe out this Commission? It is no argument against this Commission to say that they have had at some time or other in t e past what the gentleman chooses to denominate "detectives." Whatever I may have said the other day—and the gentleman admitted that he did not quote me correctly, and I will not stop to correct him—I wish to add that these detectives, or, more properly speaking, agents, have uniformly acted in the interest of the Government. If they have erred, it was against the claimant and not against the Government.

Now, upon the question as to whether these claims should be paid, I have heard nothing on the other side, and from the large number of claimants who have had their claims allowed, small and great, there are less than seven thousand out of twenty thousand odd presented to the Commissioners, and the record shows that about 10 per cent. of the number of claims allowed were the claims of Union soldiers. The court records show that not one of the —unless the Commissioners were cheated, or some fraud was perpetrated upon it—was disloyal in any way during the entire war.

The law is not now and never has been so that these Commissioners could allow and pay for damages caused by the war to loyal or disloyal claimants, but to pay for supplies furnished and which the Government had the benefit of, quartermaster and commissary stores, those things that the Government received when the war was going on and used for the purpose of carrying on the war.

We have thought it wise in the past to provide a law to pay them all, and for my part I have always believed that it was honest in the Government to do it ; honest to pay Union men and loyal men for that which they furnished to carry on the war to a successful issue. Further than that I have never been willing to go. Even though the law may have been originally an unwise one, still it would be exceedingly unjust, it would be an outrage, if I may use the term, to now say to these claimants, after they have prepared their cases under a law that has been on the statute-book for eight years, and by which they have been invited to prepare their cases and bring them to the court—it would be unjust to say to them that the court is to be wiped out, and the law that gave them the right to go before that tribunal and have their claims adjudicated there was also to be wiped out. That would be unjust ; it would be inviting them to a feast and then not giving it to them.

In regard to the three thousand claimants whose claims are now ready to be adjudicated, in which cases by an absolute statute the testimony on behalf of the claimants has been closed, if you wipe out this law those claimants will come here to Congress, for it would be the only place where they could come, and they will come here with an equity and say to us that we passed a law which authorized them to prepare their cases and present their claims, and then we took away the law before they could obtain a final adjudication of their claims.

I am in favor of a good statute of limitation to put an end to all this matter of Southern claims ; but I do not believe in the Government being unjust and entrapping any claimant.

(April 16, 1879.)

Mr. KEIFER said:
Mr. CHAIRMAN : We have presented here under a restriction as to debate one of the most remarkable and startling propositions which has come before Congress since I have had any knowledge of its proceedings. The proposition is to repeal all the provisions of law relating to the Southern Claims Commission, and to substitute for those provisions a law allowing any person, loyal or disloyal, who may have a claim against the United States founded upon equity and justice, and not barred by any statutes of limitations, to go into the Court of Claims with his claim and have it adjudicated.

It is proposed to say to all persons, whether they were loyal or disloyal during the war, that if they have any claims that they think are founded on "equity and justice" they may go into the Court of Claims and prove them and have them adjudicated and paid out of the United States Treasury. To do this may cost this Government over $100,000,000, perhaps $500,000,000. The law that it is sought to have repealed merely allows the Commissioners of Claims to consider claims for supplies, quartermaster and commissary stores, furnished for the use of the Army, and presented by persons who are shown to have been loyal throughout the war. The proposition of the gentleman from Tennessee [Mr. ATKINS] and the gentleman from Illinois [Mr. SPRINGER] is to allow all sorts of claimants, disloyal parties as well as loyal ones, to come into court with claims of all kinds, including damages caused by the war, not hitherto paid for to loyal or disloyal persons. If we do this let us do it with our eyes wide open.

The gentleman from Illinois [Mr. SPRINGER] stands up and delivers a lecture to this side of the House about war claims, while he is accepting from the hands of the gentleman from Tennessee [Mr. ATKINS] a proposition to open the Court of Claims for the first time in the history of the country to all disloyal claimants, so that they may have their claims examined and paid. I warn this House and the country of this covert attempt to provide for paying rebel claims.

Mr. SPRINGER. Does the gentleman distrust the Court of Claims on this subject?

Mr. KEIFER. I cannot yield to the gentleman. I would not give any court the right to adjudicate claims of persons who were disloyal. I want no lecture from him on this subject. We on this side of the House propose to stand by the loyal claimants of this country; I mean those who were loyal throughout the entire war, whether they lived in the North or in the South. But the gentleman's proposition is to strike down the provision of law relating to the Southern Claims Commission, and substitute a provision that lets in all persons, whether they were loyal or disloyal throughout the war.

Mr. SPRINGER. I submit, Mr. Chairman, that that is not the fact, and the record does not show it.

Mr. KEIFER. I do not yield to the gentleman. The proposition shows clearly that what I state is true. A new class of claimants, as to whom there is no legislation putting a bar on their right to go into court, are to be recognized by law for the first time if we adopt the substitute offered by the chairman of the Committee on Appropriations and accepted by the gentleman from Illinois [Mr. SPRINGER].

90 A—K——5

REPEAL OF ELECTION LAWS.

Friday, April 25, 1879. The House being in Committee of the Whole on the state of the Union, and having under consideration the bill (H. R. No. 2) making appropriations for the legislative, executive, and judicial expenses of the Government for the fiscal year ending June 30, 1880, and for other purposes.

Mr. KEIFER said:

Mr. CHAIRMAN: The reapers over this broad field of debate have had no Boaz to command them to purposely let fall handsful of the ripe harvest for gleaners who should come after them. I may be permitted, however, to glean among the sheaves. In what I have to say to-day I shall attempt no display of wit, rhetoric, or eloquence. We are called on to deal with a matter of supreme national importance: it behooves us to talk and act with propriety and sobriety.

If it were proposed to go forward promptly and provide the necessary appropriations to carry on the legislative and judicial branches of this Government, also for the necessary expenses of the several Executive Departments, and for the maintenance and support of the Army, I think no acceptable apology could be offered by me for occupying the time of this House in debate. Other things are proposed, however. At the last session of the Forty-fifth Congress there was abundant time to have made these appropriations, but the House of Representatives refused, and persisted in an effort to coerce a co-ordinate legislative branch of the Government into the repeal of certain laws (of which I shall speak as I proceed) in no way connected with the appropriations. Failing in that attempt, the last Congress adjourned without having performed one of its first and highest constitutional duties.

Both of the legislative branches of the United States being now Democratic, it is proposed to persist in passing the requisite appropriation bills coupled with other legislation foreign to the subject of appropriations and radically changing existing laws. By threats, boasts, and defiance we are given to understand the President will be coerced to surrender his constitutional prerogative and to approve any legislation, however much against his judgment or vicious it may be, or no further appropriations for the purposes named will be made. With a bare majority in this House and only a small majority in the Senate, the Democratic party threatens (for the first time in the history of the Government) to annul the veto power of the President by, if possible, intimidating him to approve such bills as it may pass. This high prerogative, wisely reposed in him by the Constitution, that party, in its mad and revolutionary career, says shall be rendered a nullity, or this Government shall have withheld from it the sustenance that gives it life.

The Constitution (second paragraph, seventh section, article 1) invests the President with a legislative power equal to one-sixth of each branch of Congress. He cannot refuse to exercise this grant of power, if in his judgment the rights of the people are about to be struck down through unwise legislation, without being recreant to his august trust. This power cannot be taken from the President in the manner proposed without making a long stride in revolution. Let us pause on the brink of so fearful an abyss!

It is vain to argue and read portions only of the Constitution to prove that all legislative power is vested in Congress. To the astonishment of many of us who know so well the legal attainments of two of my colleagues [Mr. McMahon and Mr. Hurd], we have heard them read portions of the Constitution, with an air of satisfaction, to try to show that the President has nothing to do with legislation, and while still panting for breath after having announced so utterly untenable a position, turn upon the President and warn and threaten him and the country with the direst consequences if he does not lay at the feet of the Democratic party a constitutional power they so vehemently deny he possesses. We have listened in vain for their reference to and comments on the seventh section, article 1 of the Constitution, which gives the President the veto power. They and others pass it by as though it was not to be found in the instrument. I would do my colleagues injustice to suppose they had never read or heard of it. I do them ample justice when I say their ripe judgments taught them that no subtle reasoning would convince anybody, not even their Democratic brethren, that its plain terms were meaningless.

It is true that all legislation originates with Congress, as all bills for raising revenue must originate in this House. (Section 7, article 1, Constitution.) If Congress should refuse to pass any bills we would have no legislation; if this House would originate no revenue bills there would be no new revenue laws; but this does not prove that Congress alone can make a law or that this House can alone provide for raising revenue. In the cases given these bodies can alone prevent legislation but cannot alone create it.

The President is given the sole appointing power under the Constitution (save as to certain officers), yet the Senate must advise and consent, or his appointments fall. The reasoning of gentlemen would authorize the President to say to the Senate that it should advise and consent at his dictation. The Constitution is wisely made up of "checks and balances." We cannot too clearly understand the momentous question, the final issue of which now engages the anxious attention of above forty-five million of people, who are just emerging from an era of long suffering and distress, connected with, growing out of, and incident to our recent great and bloody war, and entering upon a new era of comparative prosperity and happiness. The party now in possession of both branches of Congress, in its initial proclamation of ascendancy to legislative power, notifies the country that it will leave the legislative and executive branches of the Government unprovided for; that the administration of justice in the courts of the United States shall stop—"the wheels of justice" shall no longer revolve; and that the Army shall be disbanded and our frontiers be left unguarded, our forts and arsenals unmanned and unprotected, and the peaceable and law-abiding people and their property be left without security against domestic violence too great to be controlled by State and other authorities; or otherwise the officers and men of the Army shall go unpaid, unclothed, and unfed; and all this unless the minority in Congress and the chief executive head of the Government will assent to the repeal of all United States laws affording protection to citizens at the ballot-box from intimidation, murder, and violence, and which may prevent ballot-box stuffing, repeating, and other election frauds.

More briefly put, the Democratic party now says through its members here that all United States laws shall be repealed which stand in the way of free frauds and open intimidation and violence at the polls, or it will withhold the necessary means to longer carry on the Government. This is the issue and this is the stake. If that party cannot be allowed to hold and control this nation through a violation of the purity and freedom of the ballot-box, then this Union shall no longer live. Is this the height, breadth, and depth of the patriotism of that party or the strength of the tenure of its love for this country? One member [Mr. BLACKBURN] goes even further, and in his candor and frankness tells us his party does not intend to stop with what is now proposed. In his speech of the 3d instant he said:

For the first time in eighteen years past the Democracy are back in power in both branches of this Legislature, and she proposes to signalize her return to power; she proposes to celebrate her recovery of her long-lost heritage by tearing off these degrading badges of servitude and destroying the machinery of a corrupt and partisan legislation. We do not intend to stop until we have stricken the last vestige of your war measures from the statute-book, which, like these, were born of the passions incident to civil strife and looked to the abridgment of the liberty of the citizen.

This should be a timely warning, but warnings are seldom heeded. Eleven years and more have rolled by since a national Democratic convention, in 1868, declared all the reconstruction acts of Congress "unconstitutional, revolutionary, and void." The next step may be to repeal all laws for the punishment of treason or the suppression of rebellion; they are also of our war measures.

My friend from Virginia [Mr. TUCKER] and many on the other side of this House speak of their return to the Union, to the "long-lost heritage" of which the gentleman from Kentucky speaks. Their forced return was welcomed with a patriotic joy unspeakable. At their coming there were bonfires, illuminations, shouts, prayers, praises, and invocations all over the loyal North. The gates of the Union were set wide ajar that their coming might not be obstructed. If their return was voluntary the inducement to return was involuntary. The only condition of their return was that they should remain and be good citizens. Southern Democrats were forced at cannon's mouth and bayonet-point to take the ballot in the Union. When General Lee's army surrendered at Appomattox, Va., and General Johnston's at Greensborough, N. C. long steps toward giving the South a free ballot were taken.

Generals Grant and Sherman with their armies made a free ballot in the Union and under the Constitution for Democrats in the South possible. And still the Army is abused and maligned.

Paradoxical as it may seem, the Democratic party can now boast of nothing good in it (if it really possesses any merit) that it does not owe to defeat in peace or war.

The Republican party blazed the way for the Democratic party South to return to the Union, and on its return led its members up to the ballot-box, rebaptized them with American citizenship, reclothed many of them with justly forfeited civil rights, among which is the right to hold office, and rehabilitated many of them with the right to again gather around the sacred shrine of constitutional liberty and worship at its purified altar, on which, for its preservation and perpetuation and for the benefit and glory of all mankind, there was immolated half a million of patriots.

It is my purpose and design to briefly discuss the nature of the legislation proposed to be forced on this country, but before proceeding to do so I desire to notice the so often cited supposed precedent, drawn from English history, as a justification of the revolutionary course now entered upon by the dominant party here.

The distinguished gentleman from Connecticut [Mr. HAWLEY] in his recent able speech has fully shown that in two hundred years of constitutional government no such attempt as this has been made in monarchical England, where originally all power was vested in the Crown. I wish to add that from the days when a House of Commons was first formed and made the depository of legislative power; from the reign of Charles I—1625 to 1639—through all the long, bloody, and angry civil strifes in England, neither the House of Commons nor any other organized power contending with the King for concessions made a proposition even to take the life of the kingdom unless concessions were granted by the Crown. It is true subsidies for the Crown, the princes, and for the elevation and maintenance of royalty have been refused, also money to carry on a foreign war not approved of by the Commons has been withheld, and only granted as an equivalent for regal concessions to an oppressed people. But in vain will search be made in the history of England for a precedent for the action now proposed. When, in the history of Great Britain or any other country before this, has a legislative body ever said to the chief ruler, "Give us a law such as we demand, surrender to us a section of your arch of power, or we will destroy our own nation"? It is reserved to an American Congress controlled by a revolutionary Democracy to first enter upon any such suicidal policy. The proposition is not to withhold power or appropriations from the Chief Executive of the nation, but to destroy the Government by a failure to perform a sworn constitutional duty necessary to the Republic's life.

I crave your attention while I review, briefly as possible, the objectionable features of the proposed legislation.

THE TEST OATH.

It is proposed to repeal certain provisions of the statute known as the jury law, fixing the qualifications of jurors, the substantive part of which is found in sections 820 and 821 of the Revised Statutes of the United States. There is, I believe, a general acquiescence in the repeal of section 820, which makes acts of insurrection or rebellion causes of disqualification and challenge of jurors in the United States courts. This section was, doubtless, wisely enacted, but its repeal can do no great harm at this day.

Section 821 should not be repealed, in my opinion, though perhaps no great public injury would result. It only gives the attorney for the United States the right to move, and the court, in its discretion, the power to tender to persons summoned as jurors an oath or affirmation to support the Constitution, and that they have been guilty of no act of insurrection or rebellion against the United States, and, on their declining to take such oath or affirmation, discharge them from serving as jurors. There may still be cases where persons once engaged in rebellion should not sit in judgment upon acts of others involving the same elements of guilt. Under this section the whole matter is in the discretion of the court.

But we are not permitted to vote alone for the repeal of the test-oath laws. The proposition comes coupled with one requiring the whole plan of selecting jurors to be overturned. I believe for the first time in the history of the United States, or any of the States, so far as I can learn, party politics is to be forced by law into the jury-box. In addition to the repeal of certain sections of the law relating to jurors we are asked to vote for a provision which requires the clerk and a commissioner appointed by the court of the "principal political party opposing that to which the clerk may belong" to select one name, alternately, until the required number of jurors is obtained; they, of course, to select from their political party friends. Should a political millennium be found in any United States court district where all should see eye to eye in politics, no jurors could be selected at all. (Just now it does not look like we are approaching a political millennium.) Such a law can only be properly characterized as infamous. Jurors selected for party reasons would feel that the law justified them in standing by their respective party friends. Verdicts would be in many cases, both civil and criminal, impossible, and such is the avowed purpose of the proposed legislation. Such a law would be unconstitutional. It certainly violates the spirit if not the letter of the first section of the fourteenth amendment to the Constitution. It would abridge the privileges and immunities of citizens of the United States. Greenbackers, Nationals, Socialists, Independents, and non-partisans are to have no officer to put them on juries; they are practically denied, if not rendered ineligible by law, to sit upon a jury in the United States courts.

Mr. LOWE. Swallow both parties. We will take the whole jury.

Mr. KEIFER. I understand that you are capable of swallowing far more than you can digest. [Laughter.]

Mr. LOWE. There is no Republican party in Alabama. They met in State convention and there committed political hari-kari, and refused to nominate a ticket or arrange a platform.

Mr. KEIFER. Taken together the proposition is to qualify those recently engaged in rebellion, and to disqualify those who (as Greenbackers, &c.) do not belong to one of the two principal parties of the country from sitting as jurors. I protest against the insult and outrage.

This proposition comes, like the others, after mature gestation, from the womb of a Democratic caucus, although the member from Illinois [Mr. SPRINGER] appears as the putative father of it.

SUPERVISORS. MARSHALS, ETC.. AT THE POLLS.

This bill contains provisions for repealing all of substance of the present law authorizing chief supervisors and supervisors of elections chosen from different political parties to be appointed by a United States court, to see that there is an honest registration of voters in States where registration is required; to scrutinize, count, and canvass the ballots, &c., to the end that an honest, free, and fair election and count of ballots cast for Representatives and Delegates in Congress may be had; also for the repeal of the law authorizing the appointment to keep the peace by United States marshals of special deputies in cities of twenty thousand inhabitants or upward; and also the law defining the duties on election days of the marshal, his general and special deputies; also the only section of the statute providing a punishment for interfering with the discharge of the duties of such supervisors, marshals, &c.; also to modify the law so as in no case to require (only authorize) supervisors of election to attend at the polls on election days, and to prohibit them from canvassing the ballots cast.

The sections of the Revised Statutes sought to be repealed are 2016, 2018, 2020 to 2027, inclusive, and 5522; and section 2017 is to be modified by striking out of the first line the words "are required," and section 2019 by striking out all relating to canvassing ballots, and section 2028 by striking out all relating to "a deputy marshal," and the words "city, town, and parish."

If this bill passes in its present form it will take away all laws requiring marshals and their deputies to attend on election days and keep the peace and protect the supervisors of election. Supervisors (not chief supervisors) of election may still be appointed, clothed with authority (not required) to go to the polls and stand around with their hands in their pockets, at the risk of their lives, so they may have the sweet boon of informing on and swearing against violators of the law. What a glorious privilege granted to an American citizen! And herein lies all the boasted merit of the retained portion of the law authorizing the appointment of supervisors of election—the privilege (not duty) granted by law of watching their neighbors, and then swearing against them at some future time! The only section (5522) of the statute which would afford such supervisors the slightest protection while enjoying this privilege is to be repealed in such way as to indicate that while the law does not make it a crime for supervisors of elections to be at the polls, it is perfectly proper to break their heads while there. Their own hands are to be tied against resistance, and there is to be no law allowing any interference on election days to prevent breaches of the peace, murder, &c., at the polls. There is to be at the polls free frauds and free crimes, unrestrained by law.

It is not necessary to have a law to grant the privilege to become an informer and a witness where a crime is committed. That is a privilege belonging to every man's "heritage." The Democratic party (should their bills now pending become laws) can go to the country and say "it has considerately permitted free swearing after elections as well as free fraud in their conduct."

The section especially objectionable to Democrats is the one (2022) authorizing the United States marshal, his general and special deputies, to keep the peace and to protect the supervisors of election in the discharge of their duties, and which authorizes all these officers to arrest at the polls, without warrant, persons who in their presence commit crimes against the election and other laws of the United States.

It should be specially noted that at the polls on election days, under the proposed law, all persons are to be held sacred and free from arrest for offenses against the laws of the United States, although committed in the presence of officers of the law.

The power and right of marshals and their deputies in discharging their duties to call to their aid bystanders or a *posse comitatus* are to be taken away by the repeal of section 2024.

Is the power to make arrests without warrant an extraordinary one?

My colleague [Mr. HURD] said these "supervising officers are armed with authority unknown in the history of the common law or State laws. They have authority at the day of election to make arrests without warrants," &c.

With due deference I insist that he is grossly in error both as to the common law and State laws. At common law, high sheriffs, constables, marshals, and all other like officers are authorized to make arrests on view and hold the accused until a legal warrant can be obtained. This right is supposed to belong to any citizen.

In my State (Ohio), where the shackles of the law sit easy on the good citizens, all the constabulary force of the State is required by statute to arrest and detain all persons "found violating any law of the State," &c., "until a legal warrant can be obtained." (Section 21, criminal code, 1869.) Another section (22) of Ohio's criminal code is as follows:

Any person not an officer may, without warrant, arrest any person if a petit larceny or a felony has been committed and there has been reasonable ground to believe the person arrested guilty of such an offense, and may detain him until a legal warrant can be obtained.

Mr. HURD. May I ask the gentleman a question?

Mr. KEIFER. Certainly.

Mr. HURD. Will the gentleman read the section of the Ohio statute to which he refers?

Mr. KEIFER. I have just read one and have accurately quoted the substance of the other.

Mr. HURD. Which section has the gentleman read?

Mr. KEIFER. I read section 22 and quoted section 21.

Mr. HURD. What was the section the gentleman has just read?

Mr. KEIFER. Section 22 of the code which you drafted.

Mr. HURD. Will you please read it again, so that I may call the attention of the House to it?

Mr. KEIFER. I have not time to do it now, but I will send it to the gentleman and he can read it.

Mr. HURD. I will state that the provision of the Ohio code to which my colleague refers authorizes the arrest of private persons only in cases where petit larceny or felony has been committed.

Mr. KEIFER. All that is stated in the law, but I cannot yield longer to my colleague. I will send the provision to the gentleman, so that he can read it at his leisure. He wrote it, and he ought to know all about it.

Mr. HURD. I will state that it contains the well-established principle of the common law that no citizen can be arrested except for felony or breach of the peace.

Mr. KEIFER. My colleague is in error; it authorizes arrests by private persons without warrant.

Mr. GEDDES. Will the gentleman allow me to ask him a question?

Mr. KEIFER. Certainly.

Mr. GEDDES. Will the gentleman explain the meaning of that clause in section 2022 of the supervisors act which provides that a Federal officer may arrest a party who attempts or offers to commit one of the offenses named in the statute?

Mr. KEIFER. I will say to the gentleman that I will do that when I have more time than I have now, and as I proceed.

My colleague [Mr. HURD] will allow me to do him an honor by saying that he drafted these sections of Ohio statutes which so properly arms both officers and citizens with what he now calls extraordinary power. Many of the States have the same wise provisions in their statutes. It is a felony in Ohio to cast a fraudulent vote, and to commit other offenses against her election laws; and hence by law any officer or private citizen may arrest at the polls without warrant all such offenders.

The law now sought to be repealed does not authorize arrests to be made "without process for any offense not committed in the presence of the marshal," his deputies, or of the supervisors of election. With these limitations the statute confers no unusual or extraordinary powers, but very necessary and salutary ones. Only those desiring to offend against the election laws, or to abet offenders against them, or to gather the fruits of election frauds would be expected to complain of the present statutes.

There may be imperfections in the law or wrong done sometimes in its execution, yet not such as to afford a good reason for blotting it out. The sun, the center and source of all light and heat, has its dark spots. Who would for that reason favor striking it from the firmament of the heavens?

SHALL PEACE BE PRESERVED AT THE POLLS?

There is danger that some gentlemen may be deceived at the adroitness in which the proposed legislation on the Army bill is stated in debate. My friend from Virginia [Mr. TUCKER] and other distinguished members hardly want to deceive themselves in this way.

The question is not, shall troops or armed men be used at the polls to prevent a free and fair election? but it is this: shall peace be preserved at the polls to secure a free and fair election? No person favors the use of the military or civil power to prevent a free, fair ballot, but the Democratic party says, in effect, we shall not use the military or civil power to secure a free, fair ballot. The words "or to keep the peace at the polls" are to be stricken out of sections 2002 and 5528 of the statutes, thereby making it a high crime for any military, naval, or civil officer of the United States to put down violence or suppress open crime at the polls on election days. It is now by law a high crime for any of these officers to in any way hinder or prevent any person from voting. (Revised Statutes, section 2009.)

Existing law also prohibits officers or other persons in the Army or Navy from interfering with the right of a person to vote at any election (Revised Statutes, sections 2003, 5529–5532.) A violation of these sections subjects the guilty to a fine of not exceeding $5,000 and imprisonment at hard labor not more than five years, and also perpetual disqualification from holding any office under the United States. (Section 5532.) These extraordinary penalties having been affixed to any violation of the rights of a voter by United States officers, it remains to be determined whether their use to suppress riots purposely gotten up to prevent a full, free, and fair vote should be made a crime.

The proposition on the majority of this floor is to, by law, countenance and promote violence and disorders by lawless persons at the polls on elections days. Failing in this, the Democratic party say the Union is not worth supporting. It values free fraud and unrestrained violence more than the country.

To amend the law as now proposed will paralyze the officers of the United States, so that at least on one day and at one place in each year the shield of the laws of this country will be thrown around those who may engage in any kind of violence which will prevent a full, fair, and honest expression of the will of the voters.

In all this long debate not one word has escaped the lips of any Democrat in condemnation of the bands of lawless persons who are to be permitted to invade the polls. Nothing has been brought to the notice of Congress or the country during this long debate which tends to prove that the officers of the Government have ever prevented a single man from voting, and as he wished. The polls on election days should be a place of absolute peace. Disorders and violence are the forerunners of an incident to election frauds. What is the objection to peace at the polls?

It must be kept in mind that the legislation proposed makes it a crime for marshals and other officers in the civil service of the United States to suppress riots, &c., by the aid of an armed posse comitatus at the polls. It is not the employment of troops alone that is to be prohibited at the polls, but the civil power of the Government is to be suspended there. On a former occasion I said the Democratic party favored free francs at elections. From the legislation now proposed that conclusion is irresistible.

By statute (Revised Statutes, section 788) the duties of marshals and their deputies in executing United States laws are the same as sheriffs and other like officers in executing State laws. These officers have always been charged with the public duty of keeping the peace. They have been at common law and by statute authorized and required not only to suppress riots, &c., but to make arrests without warrant and detain persons found violating any criminal law or ordinance until a legal warrant could be obtained. Under this legislation the functions of all this class of officers are to be suspended at elections of members of Congress.

The real cause of complaint is not that officers charged with the duty under the present law of keeping the peace have failed to do their duty, or that they have prevented legal voters from voting, but that they have overawed, or are likely to overawe, disturbers of the peace at the polls who engage in preventing, by intimidation or otherwise, the legal voter from voting, or who engage in promoting fraud by repeating and ballot-box stuffing. To accomplish this end the Democratic party threaten, on failure, to stop the wheels of the Government and initiate revolution. The people will stand amazed in the presence of such a threat, but they will meet it with patriotism and their sovereign power.

Again and again during this discussion of the Army bill has it been said these two sections are unconstitutional. My colleague from Ohio [Mr. HURD] and my friend from Virginia [Mr, TUCKER], both justly distinguished for their legal learning, reiterate this view. I must be pardoned for differing with them. The sections, taken alone or separately, do not undertake to authorize anything to be done by any person; they are wholly prohibitory and restraining, not permissive, statutes; they make the use of troops or armed men at the polls a crime on the part of any United States military, naval, or civil officer; they only limit a power which may exist under the Constitution and laws. As has been so often said, these sections are not to be repealed, but only re-enacted so as to make it a crime (hitherto unknown) to keep the peace at the polls.

The claim of gentlemen, then, is this: that it is unconstitutional not to make it a penal offense to keep the peace where elections are being held. By necessary implication the proper officers should, as a matter of duty, keep the peace everywhere else.

During this debate it has often been stated that the legislation proposed on the Army bill is similar to English law. This is wholly untrue. The honorable gentlemen from Kentucky [Mr. KNOTT] and from Mississippi [Mr. MULDROW] somewhat astonished us by the confident manner in which they read English statutes to justify this legislation. I need hardly do more than invite attention to the laws quoted by them to convince every person that there is no possible similarity between the two.

The English statutes read are mere police regulations for the government of soldiers (not officers) when not on duty; no reference is even made to the duty of officers or the powers of the Crown. The English statutes require soldiers quartered within two miles of election polls to remain in barracks, &c., when not on duty during an election. The proposed law would apply only to officers, military, naval, or civil. There is not even an inference to be drawn from the English statute that the Government designed to limit its power through its officers to keep the peace at the polls or anywhere else. These English laws do not undertake even to regulate the conduct of all the soldiery, but only such as are quartered within two miles of a nominating or voting place; there is nothing prescribed as to the conduct of all other British soldiers at the polls English statesmen do not make and keep for one hundred years a defective law on the statute-books.

The statute of George II was passed when England had quartered all over it troops, who often made election days an occasion for riotous and disorderly conduct. The statute was then and is still a wise one, and would be utterly unobjectionable in this country.

I give here the section of the statute of George II so often cited:

SEC. 2. *And be it enacted,* That on every day appointed for the nomination or for the election or for taking the poll for the election of a member or members to serve in the Commons House of Parliament no soldier within two miles of any city, borough, town, or place where such nomination or election shall be declared or poll taken shall be allowed to go out of the barrack or quarters in which he is stationed, unless for the purpose of mounting or relieving guard, or for giving his vote at such election; and that every soldier allowed to go out for any such purpose within the limits aforesaid shall return to his barrack or quarters with all convenient speed as soon as his guard shall have been relieved or vote tendered.

The Government of England has frequently used its army to suppress election riots in London and other large cities; notably at elections held during the exciting times pending the repeal of the corn laws, and also when financial relief was demanded. In Scotland and Ireland the army has always been used to keep the peace when election riots have occurred. Pending the struggle which resulted in the passage of the reform bill (in 1831) the election riots in Belfast and other places in Ireland were put down by the British army, and it alone could keep the peace at the polls. Recently as 1872, during election and other riots in principal cities of Ireland growing out of the deadly strife between Catholics and Orangemen, English soldiers were used to keep the peace. By law also all the police and constabulary force of the kingdom are specially enjoined to keep the peace at elections.

It will be found that it was left to the Democratic party of this country to attempt to legalize fraud, outrage, and violence at elections.

My friend from Virginia [Mr. TUCKER] gave an instance where in 1741 an English officer was, "on bended knee," reprimanded by the speaker of the House of Commons for, my friend says, "using troops at the polls." Not so; but for, under a pretense of quelling an "alleged riot at Westminster," assuming to control the election of a member of Parliament.

Under our law a similar offense would not be punished by a parliamentary reprimand, but the offender would suffer fine, imprisonment, and total disqualification from holding an office under the United States. (Revised Statutes, section 5532.)

WHAT ARE FREE SOUTHERN ELECTIONS?

It is now alleged that recently peaceful, free, and fair elections have been held in the Southern States under Democratic rule, and Mississippi, Georgia, and other States are given as instances to prove the good effects of the "liberty of the citizen" at elections uninfluenced by troops or United States officers. We are often told that the colored men when left free vote of their own volition the Democratic ticket. Peace and order are now said to reign at the polls in Democratic Southern States.

An examination of election returns reveals to us some startling facts. If Democratic claims were true we would expect to find a largely increased vote in these States, especially Democratic vote. At the risk of being tedious I give here some figures showing the vote in years when it is alleged the bayonet and carpet-bag rule held sway, in comparison with more recent elections, held wholly free from such rule and conducted on the broader principles of "Democratic liberty." A few examples must suffice for the whole Southern vote where the same conditions exist.

In the second district of Georgia the Democratic vote in 1872 was 9,530, the Republican 9,616; in the sixth district the Democratic vote was 9,093, and Republican 6,196; and in the eighth district the Democratic vote was 7,437, and the Republican 6,230. In 1878 the vote in the same Georgia districts was, second district (Mr. COOK'S), Democratic 2,628, Republican 6; sixth district (Mr. BLOUNT'S), Democratic 3,192, Republican 18; and in the eighth district (Mr. STEPHENS'S), Democratic 3,673, and the Republican 54.

In these three districts of Georgia the aggregate vote on Congressmen in 1872 was, Democratic 26,060, and Republican 22,042, and with a Democratic "free election" in

1878 the total in the same districts was, Democratic 9,439, and Republican 78. The Democratic vote fell off from 1872 to 1878 over 60 per cent. (17,521) and the Republican vote all vanished save 78.

The Mississippi election statistics are, if possible, more significant. The vote given is on Congressmen.

In the third Mississippi district in 1872 the vote was, Democratic 6,440, and the Republican 15,047; in 1878 it was, Democratic (for Mr. MONEY) 4,025, and Republican 686.

In the fourth district in 1872 the vote was, Democratic 6,870, Republican 15,595; in 1878 it was, Democratic (for Mr. Singleton) 4,025, Republican 0.

In the fifth district in 1872 the vote was, Democratic 8,073 and Republican 14,847; in 1878 it was, Democratic (Mr. Hooker) 4,846 and Republican 686.

In the sixth district in 1872 the vote was, Democratic 8,569, Republican 15,101; and in 1878 it was, Democratic (Mr. Chalmers) 6,663 and Republican 1,370.

The total vote on Congressmen in these four Mississippi districts in 1872 was 29,892 Democratic and 60,560 Republican; in 1878 it was 20,154 Democratic and 2,050 Republican.

In 1872 the Republicans, by large majorities, carried each of these four Mississippi districts, but in 1878, when the Democratic vote had fallen off 33 per cent. (or 7,738), Democrats were elected in each nearly unanimously. The Republican vote went down from 60,560 in 1872 to 2,050 in 1878. The total vote fell off from 90,452 in 1872 to 22,240 in 1878. This is the fruit of a Democratic "free" election in the South.

The member from the third district of Mississippi in 1878 received 2,295 less votes than Mr. Chisholm received in 1876, when he was returned as beaten. The gallant Chisholm and his heroic son and daughter, with many of his political friends, had met violent deaths for their temerity in 1876.

Democrats boast that in the elections in Mississippi and other of the Southern States in 1878 peace reigned; it was the peace and serenity which succeeds death. The work of the kuklux, white-liners, rifle clubs, Democratic regulators, through intimidation, assassination, and crime unparalleled in barbarity, bore its fruits and established the rule of an armed and lawless minority over the timid majority, and the elective franchise was trampled in the dust. To an implacable and merciless opposition the people surrendered their political rights. When the people no longer struggle for their rights against lawlessness, then Democrats cry "peace reigns." The Czar Nicholas of Russia, after exterminating all the inhabitants of certain districts in poor, unfortunate Poland and making a wilderness of the country, called it "peace." By the proposed legislation these lawless Democratic bands are in effect to be legalized. The figures given show that the colored men did not vote the Democratic ticket, but did not vote at all.

The honorable gentleman [Mr. STEELE] of the sixth North Carolina district, who did me the honor in February last of answering with some feeling a five-minute speech of mine, then assured the House that I was in error when I charged fraud, intimidation, violence, and murder to be in election matters the allies of the Democratic party; and he also then, and in his recent speech, assured us of the utterly peaceful character of elections in his State, and especially in his own district. I need not furnish any evidence to the contrary. He did not, however, tell us why the vote in his district dwindled down from 23,261 in 1872 and 27,539 in 1876 to 5,328 in 1878; and he did not stop to explain why the Democratic vote (as reported) went down from 17,256 in 1876 to 4,908 in 1878, or why the Republican vote of 10,561 in 1872 and 10,282 in 1876 all vanished in 1878 but 254 votes. These figures are at least suggestive of a great controlling cause which compelled the people of his district to forego the privilege of voting. People do not voluntarily surrender this high privilege.

I make no charge against the honorable gentleman, but I assure him that the figures make out a case of wrong somewhere. He compared his district for fairness in the election with my own (fourth Ohio). My Democratic opponent received about the same number of votes in 1878 cast in the same year for the three Democratic members from the sixth [Mr. STEELE'S], the seventh [Mr. ARMFIELD'S], and the eighth [Mr. VANCE'S] North Carolina districts, and he was still beaten by 5,100 votes in a district below the average of Ohio districts in population, and in which no suggestion of fraud was made by any person. My opponent received in 1878 about 1,000 more votes than were cast in that year in the second, sixth, and eighth Georgia districts, and he was overwhelmingly defeated, while the three honorable gentlemen from that State [Mr. BLOUNT, Mr. COOK, and Mr. STEPHENS] are now chairmen of important committees of this House. With more votes than it takes to elect three of the most distinguished Southern Democratic members of this House, a single Northern Democrat is left at home. Other examples equally strong could be given to show the result of such Democratic rule.

It does not come with good grace from gentlemen to assail my party with the charge of preventing the people from voting. No case has been cited to prove that any voter has been prevented by the use of the Army under Republican rule from voting. The most that can be said is that in some instances lawless Democratic bands may have been prevented from taking possession of the polls. It is not for the mass of the people of the South for whom the Democratic party pleads. That party never did plead for their rights in times past. Is legalized riots one of the methods by which "property, intelligence, and education will rule the land?" as says a distinguished Senator [Mr. THURMAN]. Prior to the war, when there was so much eloquence expended over the rights and wrongs of the South by Democratic orators, nothing was said by them of the rights and against the wrongs of any persons, white or black, save those interested in slavery.

The census of 1860 showed 12,240,000 population in the fifteen Southern States, 8,039,000 of whom were white, 251,000 free colored, and 3,950,000 were slaves. The same census showed there were 384,884 slave-holders in the United States, less than 5 per cent. of the total white population of the South. Only about 20 per cent., as statistics show, of the total white population of the South in 1860 were, through family relationship or otherwise, interested in slaves or slave labor directly or indirectly. It is still over the supposed wrongs of this one-fifth of the white population (or their immediate descendants) of the South that the Democratic party had so long mourned and still mourn, utterly forgetting that the 4,000,000 colored people once held in slavery and the 80 per cent. of white people of the South, many of whom through the curse of slavery, socially and otherwise, were once worse off than the black slaves, possessed any rights to be guarded. The word "liberty" had no meaning for them. The Democratic party now, as in the past, in mockery cry out for liberty and the people's rights.

That party precipitated this nation into a civil war in which blood flowed in torrents for above four years to secure the supposed rights of one-fifth of the white people of the South, and to enable that few to forge new fetters for the feet of 4,000,000 of God's people. And now that the Democratic rebellion has failed, that old party, before the sulphurous smoke and fumes of a hell-born war have quite blown away, proclaims itself the champion of the people's liberties.

When we have that freedom of the ballot desired by Democrats it will be when and only when that sacred few of the South alone shall be suffered to vote, to the exclusion of the great mass of the white voters and all the colored. Unless a speedy remedy is applied the figures given warn us the day is near when this so much desired object of the Democratic party will be attained.

CONCILIATION.

It is also said that all these election laws should be amended or repealed in the interests of conciliation. What is conciliation, so much talked about on the other side of this Chamber? Webster says it is "to win over; to gain from a state of hostility." Are the gentlemen on the other side of the House and their constituents in a state of hostility? We are told the war and the rebellion have been at an end for above fourteen years, and yet daily and hourly here conciliation is demanded.

This demand is sometimes made to ring in our ears coupled with a threat that without it the nation is still imperiled. The thing demanded is concession (not conciliation) of the great fundamental principles of a free government, those for which the best blood of the land was shed. Are we never to be through conciliating those who tried to take the Republic's life? It is unworthy of a patriotic people to be constantly crying "Conciliate us!" "Conciliate us!" lest we do not become or remain good and patriotic citizens. Those who laid down their treason with their arms should ask no conciliation and they need no forgiveness. Out of the goodness and abundant thankfulness of the hearts of the loyal, patriotic people of this Union all this class of persons were forgiven when the bells rang out and the cannon pealed forth the joyful sounds of peace; that slavery was dead; that America's proud banner waved over none but the free; and that the Union was vouchsafed to us in all its integrity. Is conciliation all on one side? The North and my party demand nothing of the South but that her people, possessed of equal rights before the law, stand by the Republic now and for the future.

When, unwillingly, the South laid down its arms, the Republican party handed her hitherto rebellious people the ballot, granted them amnesty and pardon, rehabilitated them with full and complete citizenship, and without ample guarantees for the future made them the peers in political rights and privileges of those who, under God, saved through blood and tears, at the cost of untold millions, the Union. This was conciliation superadded to high magnanimity and grace. The North may yet tire of Southern Democratic demands. If, however, conciliation can be made still more complete by the continued exercise of grace and forgiveness, I am most sincerely and heartily in favor of it. But if concessions of cardinal principles are still further demanded, with no arrogance I hope, and without threat, speaking, as I believe, not only for my party but the truly patriotic people of this whole country, I warn those who make such demands that they will be successfully opposed not only in debate and by vote here and elsewhere, but should the final arbiter be appealed to, on the bloody theater of war.

Mr. Chairman, many of us have been surprised to hear advocates of this legislation against the purity of the ballot-box demand it in the name of

LIBERTY.

In February last, Mr. Hewitt, of New York, made a speech here favoring this legislation and headed it "personal liberty of the citizen." Others have said they favored such legislation because they desired "the subordination of the military to the civil power." My colleague [Mr. Hurd] says he is filled with joy to recollect "that the party of the Army is not in power in this Congress." Has it come to pass that the "personal liberty of the citizen" hangs on his power to perpetrate fraud and violence on election days? Does it not absolutely depend on his amenity to law in case he engages in either of those things? Is the "subordination of the military to the civil power" secured by protecting by law open violence at election polls? Would this not be under sanction of law the subordination of both the military and civil power to the licentious mob? Would it not be the enthronement of lawlessness and the overthrow of the highest and dearest rights of an American citizen?

It is true the Republican party "is the party of the Army." I hope it will, in the future as in the past, invoke that strong arm of this Government as a last resort to save endangered constitutional liberty. What is liberty, civil liberty? The nature of true liberty ought in this country to be understood. Liberty and authority go hand in hand in a republic. Liberty unrestrained by authority is license. Authority unmitigated by liberty is tyranny. The instructed eye can see no liberty where there is no restraint. Liberty and law sternly confront each other: if the latter is withheld the former falls. Law is the fly-wheel to the great mechanism of constitutional liberty. It is our proudest boast to-day that events of the last score of years have demonstrated that our Government is strong enough to maintain itself against foreign or domestic foes, yet shorn by its organic act of all power to oppress or degrade its most humble citizen. None now are so high as to be above the law and none so low as to be beneath the protection of the law. Liberty teaches us to reverence and support authority as well as to withstand tyranny. The love of liberty which does not produce these effects is as hollow and hypocritical as a religion which is productive of immorality and an evil life. Seldom have the rights of the people been assailed or cloven down that it was not done in the name of "liberty" or "religion," as though a great wrong could be sanctified by a name.

In the language of the heroic Madame Roland, as she bowed reverently before a statue of liberty at her execution: "O Liberty! what crimes are committed in thy name!"

Secession, rebellion, and treason invoked the sacred name of liberty to shield from the broad glare of the civilized and Christianized world the shame, the infamy, and colossal crime of attempting to perpetually enthrone human slavery! In this country, under the disgraced mantle of the Constitution of our fathers, slavery in its direst form was long protected and perpetuated. War was the only remedy for the eradication of such national sins. The sacrifices of that war, manifold and terrible as they were, are more than compensated for by the result attained. Let not licentiousness be mistaken for liberty. Licentiousness is a lawless power too often indulged in under a pretense of liberty.

The poet Milton fitly characterized a class of persons, all of whom are not yet dead. He said they were those—

> That bawl for freedom in their senseless moods,
> And still revolt, when truth would set them free;
> License they mean when they cry—liberty.

Let us cease this mockery in the name of liberty.

In conclusion, Mr. Chairman, I beg to say this Government would rightfully spring to arms to redress a wrong done to one of its citizens in a foreign land. Let it not be said that the broad shield of the Constitution and laws of the United States shall not be thrown over and around an American citizen at home.

I hope the Stars and Stripes shall ever be an emblem of liberty and protection for all citizens of this Republic on land and sea, at home as well as abroad. [Great applause on the Republican side of the House.]

PEACE AT THE POLLS.

June 11, 1879. Against the sixth section of the Army Appropriation bill, which read: "That no money appropriated in this act is appropriated or shall be paid for the subsistence, equipment, transportation, or compensation of any portion of the Army of the United States to be used as a police force to keep the peace at the polls at any election held within any State."

Mr. KEIFER spoke as follows:

I cannot enter upon any proper discussion of this important measure in four minutes, or even in five minutes. I simply wish to say that I am one of those who do not indorse all that has been said to-day upon the floor of the House. I apply this remark to the speeches made on both sides of the House. I am now forbidden the privilege of giving my views on the effect of this bill, and especially the sixth section of it.

One hour's time was given for the purpose of general debate for and against the sixth section of this bill, and all of that time has been used in debate by Democrats and Republicans in favor of it. I have asked time to-day to speak against this bill, which has been refused. Those of us who desire to utter our views in full on this floor against the bill and the objectionable legislation contained in it have been gagged, and we are not allowed to be heard. Gentlemen on this side of the House who favor the bill have all the time they desire.

That is all I need say, except that I wish to emphasize what I have before stated here by saying that I agree with those who claim they are opposed to using troops at the polls as a police force to keep the peace at elections, in so far and only in so far as their use may interfere with the conduct of elections. But I am in favor of using the troops, the Army of the United States if you please, to keep the peace at the polls by driving from the polls the irregular armed bands of men who may be there breaking the peace and interfering with elections. [Applause on the Republican side.]

I have never favored the use of troops as an ordinary police force, or as a substitute for the civil police, but only as an aid to the police when there were brought to the polls irregular and unauthorized troops of armed men, such as the ku-klux and white-liners, and others of like character, to drive away the police, overawe the honest voters, and control the elections and stuff the ballot-boxes. In that case I say it is time for the Government to come in and protect its citizens at home and at the polls.

I have on this floor and elsewhere deprecated the use of soldiers at the polls to intimidate the voter or in any way to interfere with the elector or the elections. I still deprecate such use. The United States troops have never been, as has often been shown, used for such purpose. They have never prevented a voter from voting at any election. But while I would not favor such use of United States troops, I am equally opposed to the use of lawless bands of armed men—call them what you may, ku-klux, regulators, white-liners, &c.—to drive from the polls, overawe, and intimidate voters and otherwise take control and conduct of elections. The Democratic party never has condemned the use of lawless bands of armed men at the polls, and it has, through many years, favored and justified the use there of such bands. Lawlessness is preferred to lawfulness by that party in the conduct of elections.

Arms at the polls are not objectionable to that party so long as they are not used to keep the peace. If they are to be used at the polls to promote riots, to commit murder, &c., in short, to prevent a full, free, and fair election, as in many instances in South Carolina and Louisiana, they are unobjectionable in the eyes of Democrats and should be countenanced and encouraged. Now, I am only in favor of using United States troops at the polls when and where, and only when and where, irregular and unauthorized bands of armed men are first used to interfere with elections and with the right of the peaceable and honest voter to go freely to the polls and peaceably vote for members of Congress, and then only for the purpose of putting down such bands. I would only use United States troops to prevent interference with elections and to protect United States officers, as now authorized by expressed provision of law—section 2024, Revised Statutes—when necessary and required, whose duties require them to see that free, fair, honest, and peaceful elections are held for members of Congress.

I cannot surrender these views by voting for this bill. While the sixth section of the bill repeals no law in force and does not affirmatively prohibit any act to be done which may be done under the Constitution or existing laws, it, fairly construed, denies the right to use any of the money appropriated, to be used to feed, equip, transport, or pay any portion of the Army, if it is at any time to be used to keep the peace at the polls in any emergency. To vote for this bill is to surrender, in principle, all we have so long contended for, in my judgment. The words in the section, "to be used as a police force," have no special meaning in the connection in which they are used. Whenever United States troops are used to aid the civil power to *keep the peace* they are used as a police force. In no case have United States troops been used in this country to keep the peace at elections or anywhere else in aid of the civil power save as a *police force*.

While the appropriation made in this bill may be made available, I cannot assent to the terms on which it is made as set forth in the sixth section of it, and hence I must vote against it.

LETTER CARRIER SERVICE.

June 6, 1879. On a Post-Office appropriation bill, which contained a clause repealing a recent law to extend the letter-carrier system.

Mr. KEIFER said:

Mr. CHAIRMAN: There ought to be no discussion relative to the merits of this bill, considering its origin. It ought to be borne in mind that the law which is sought to be repealed was passed after petitions had come to this House from one hundred thousand persons. And in connection with that we must bear in mind this measure which we are now considering was reported from a committee which did not have a single petition before it asking it to report any such proposition. Indeed, Mr. Chairman, the Committee on Appropriations never has had up to the present moment, as I am informed, the subject referred to it at all—never; and this is pure voluntary action on the part of a committee which, strictly speaking, under the rules has no right to deal with the matter at all. They have the right to provide appropriations to execute the existing laws——

Mr. CANNON, of Illinois. There was an estimate asking for this appropriation submitted to the House and referred to the Committee on Appropriations.

Mr. KEIFER. Nobody disputes that; all understand that; and it was the duty of that committee to come forward and make the appropriation and not undertake to pass a new law on the subject.

Mr. CANNON, of Illinois. This one hundred and twentieth rule not only permits but under the practice of the majority of this House commands legislation.

Mr. KEIFER. There is undoubtedly some vile practice in this House, if I may be allowed to use the expression, which permits this committee, and only this Committee on Appropriations, to report any legislation it pleases on an appropriation bill. And, I repeat, this comes alone from that committee without ever having been referred to it so far as the subject-matter of legislation here is concerned.

Now, there is that objection to it, and we ought to consider that this subject was fully debated in this House and in the Senate, for the gentlemen who opposed it took the pains to follow it with their opposition to the other end of the Capitol.

It has been stated by the gentleman from Illinois [Mr. CANNON] that the bill passed without debate. I have not time to go over the whole history of that, but at least thirty speeches were made in the last Congress on this very subject. How many did the gentleman from Illinois himself make against it? Can he tell.

Mr. CANNON, of Illinois. This bill was never considered in a single instance.

Mr. KEIFER. Now, Mr. Chairman, if that is all that is desired I will call the gentleman's attention to the proceedings in this House on the 7th day of June, 1878, when speech after speech was made. I know a great many speeches on this subject were made, printed, and circulated all over the country. I know my friends on my right made speeches and gentlemen all around me made speeches pro and con; and yet we are now told that the bill was not debated. It was debated on every hand, and every feature of the bill was debated. One feature was not in the bill as originally reported, and I took the pains from my place on this floor to have read as part of my speech, as the RECORD of the 7th of June, 1878, will show, the section of the law which I proposed to have the committee add and which it did add to the bill, and it is there in that speech exactly as it appears in the existing law. I took the pains in my speech then to say that under the old law we had made eighty-seven free-delivery cities in this country, many of them having a gross revenue of less than $12,000, and many having a net revenue of less than $4,000, and yet there were cities in this country under that law with a gross revenue of over $50,000 which could not have free-delivery offices. My own city—and the gentleman thinks I ought not to vote against his bill because of that fact—which had a gross revenue of $34,700, could not under the old law get a free mail delivery, while other cities of ten or eleven thousand gross revenue came in under the old law. Those were the subjects of discussion, and three-fourths of the members of the House, after they had been fully informed, voted to pass the law. So the objection of the gentleman falls that it never was discussed, for it did have discussion on every hand.

As a partial answer, Mr. Chairman, to the gentleman's sweeping statement that we are liable to have a very large number of cities in this country that will become free-delivery offices I will say that I hold in my hand a statement made yesterday at the Post-Office Department, showing thirty-four cities that would probably come under the present law and be made free-delivery offices. Every one of them, if they were made free-delivery offices, would have from $15,000 to $40,000 net revenue to go somewhere else to be expended after having paid all their own expenses, and all the expenses of a free-delivery office. Not one of them would fall below from $13,000 to

$15,000 of net revenue and some would range as high as $40,000, after having paid all expenses. I find one city, not a free-delivery office, the city of Denver, Colorado, produces a gross revenue of $53,491. That is among the very highest. The city of Galveston, Texas, has a gross revenue of $54,677 and it is not a free-delivery office.

Mr. CANNON, of Illinois. It has more than thirty thousand inhabitants.

Mr. KEIFER. I do not know but the gentleman may be right when he suggests that under the law which he proposes here to-day that city could be made a free-delivery office. There are five cities in the State of Texas that under the existing law would be entitled to become free-delivery offices, but under the proposed law would be excluded. You, Mr Chairman [Mr REAGAN in the chair], ought to take notice of this because you might be called upon here to vote in favor of some city in your State, and the gentleman from Illinois would have it thrown up to the country that a man had given a vote in the interest of his constituents in some way or other. I suppose that is the extent of the argument. You have five such cities in Texas, and there are nineteen States that would be affected in some way or other by the law if the Appropriations Committee would do its duty and report a proper appropriation to carry it out. I shall take pleasure in furnishing, as a part of my remarks, these lists to be printed in the RECORD, to which I suppose there will be no objection.

Now, I do not want to go into this discussion further. It is not necessary to prolong it. It ought to be borne in mind, however, as has been stated by my friend who has just taken his seat, that there are two causes that always increase the revenue at free-delivery offices. One is, in consequence of the additional convenience. Many persons write letters and have mail matter to send out who would not otherwise send it. That is the testimony and the experience not alone in this country but in Europe. If convenient boxes are furnished where a person can, without going a long distance to a post-office, mail his letters, more letters will be written. Many people write letters if they can mail them at a box near at hand when they would not otherwise do it if they had to carry them a mile or two to the post-office to mail them.

But that is not the principal reason why the revenue is increased. It grows out of the fact that in the case of all drop-letters there is paid double postage at free-delivery offices, and in that way this system becomes self-supporting in the main. I think it is reported in some of the former reports of the Postmaster-General, if not a recent one—I am not a member either of the Appropriations Committee, which usurps everything, or of the Post-Office Committee, and I may not be exactly accurate—but I think it has been reported that with the exception of four or five of the free-delivery offices in the United States they have been self-supporting on account of the increase of mail matter and also the increase of postage paid in consequence of it. What the last report may show upon this head I cannot say. Taken all together, the increased revenue at free-delivery offices is many thousands of dollars in excess of the increase of the expense incident to the free-delivery system.

Therefore, when we deal with this question, we come back to the fact that we are simply asking to give these flourishing places mail facilities where they pay for them themselves. Now I want to say one word further in relation to the matter of giving further mail facilities to cities that pay for them, and furnish a large net revenue in addition. I think in round numbers the net postal revenue from my city (Springfield, Ohio)—and it is no better than others—is $28,000. The amount of gross revenue is nearly $35,000. Therefore we pay in that little city toward carrying the mails and toward keeping up the mail system in other places $28,000 annually. Is it unreasonable to ask to have extended to us the free-delivery system which will enable us to furnish more revenue—perhaps a sufficient increase to pay the whole of the expenses? If we should take $3,000 more from the net revenue of the Springfield office to establish the free-delivery system we should still have $25,000 left to contribute annually to carry the mails over the prairies in Illinois, and to other places throughout the country. Are we to be told that we are greedy because we do not give you more money? Places that do not pay enough money to pay the expenses of the mail facilities furnished them complain that we want to spend more of our own money. That is the effect of the argument on the other side. My city is prosperous. We do a large amount of business there. I am proud to say that through manufacturing industries and otherwise we have built up a flourishing city. We now furnish and are willing to furnish much more than our own share of the revenue to carry the mails. We are quite willing to continue to do so. In my city we make 33 per cent. of all the reapers and mowers that are manufactured or used on the continent of America. We make, also, a large part of the machinery that plows up and cultivates your prairies of the West. We carry on an extensive business of that kind. And we think while we pay a large sum of money for the conducting of the postal service outside of our own place we ought to have all the benefits which can be furnished under the postal laws of this country.

I am not making any argument for my own city that I would not make for any other similarly situated; but I am not ashamed to say one of the things that operates on my mind is the fact that I live in a city that would be entitled to have this increase of mail facilities.

There is just one other city in the State of Ohio which under the present law would be entitled to this service, and that is the city of Akron. Unfortunately (according to the gentleman from Illinois), I suppose, for my colleague from Ohio [Mr. MONROE], it is in his district. There are also several cities in the State of Illinois, Rockford I recollect is one, that might be entitled to the free-delivery system, but the list I furnish will show all these places.

The gentleman from Illinois [Mr. CANNON] undertakes to state in his argument in explanation of the revenue of the city of New York that it is a great distributing office, and that is the reason why they have such a large revenue. My understanding of the matter is, and I am willing to be corrected by any gentleman who knows more about it than I do, that where you have a principal distributing office you have to have a great many more clerks, while there is nothing that adds to the revenue of the office. You have in New York and in the principal distributing offices of the country a large increase in the number of clerks merely for the purpose of distributing the mails over the country. But that adds nothing to the revenue of the office. The revenue of the office is derived principally from the sale of postage-stamps; and the fact of the office being a distributing office makes the expenditures far larger than they otherwise would be. I trust that when we come to consider the details of this bill we shall by a proper amendment strike out all this proposed and objectionable legislation.

Mr. KEIFER offered the following substitute for the bill:

"A bill making additional appropriations for the services of the Post-Office Department for the fiscal years ending June 30, 1879, and June 30, 1880, and for other purposes.

" *Be it enacted, &c.*, That in addition to the amounts heretofore appropriated, the following sums be, and the same are hereby, appropriated, out of any money in the Treasury not otherwise appropriated, namely :

" For payment to letter-carriers for the fiscal year ending June 30, 1880, and to extend the service of such carriers for said year under the provisions of the act approved February 21, 1879, entitled 'An act to fix the pay of letter-carriers,' in addition to the sum heretofore appropriated, $353,000. For payment of increased salary to letter-carriers under provisions of existing law for the fiscal year ending June 30, 1879, $71,000.''

Mr. KEIFER. I desire to say, Mr. Chairman, that the substitute is intended to make the appropriations necessary to carry out existing laws; it leaves out all of the general legislation proposed in this bill. Now, the statement made by the Post-master-General in a communication which be sent to the Senate some time ago in relation to the letter-carrier law which was approved by the President February 21, 1879, makes the various estimates necessary to carry out that law. The substitute is a mere appropriation bill which I have offered. It undertakes no legislation at all, it leaves out all the legislation contained in the pending bill. In the estimate of the Postmaster-General he states that there will be required for the remainder of the fiscal year, 1879, $71,000 to pay increased salaries and $21,000 to extend the service, making $92,000. In the appropriation as provided by my substitute I put in this $71,000, omitting the $21,000 for extending the services in the fiscal year ending June 30, 1879, for the reason that I am informed at the Post Office Department that in the remainder of this year it will be impossible to extend the service, so that the $21,000 is omitted in the appropriation.

The Postmaster-General states that for the next fiscal year, that is, the year ending June 30, 1880, there will be required, in order to extend the service and for the increased pay of carriers, the sum of $353,000 in addition to the $2,000,000 already appropriated, if one-half of the carriers in cities of the first-class are paid an annual salary of $1,000 each, and $415,000 if two-thirds of them are paid $1,000 each, as provided in section 4 of the law of last session. In my substitute I have included the smaller sum of $353,000 which, according to the estimate of the Postmaster-General, will enable him to pay only one-half of the carriers in cities of the first class at the rate of $1,000 a year each.

I understand that there are many members on this floor who think we should make provision for the maximum number of two-thirds of the carriers at $1,000 a year each, as provided for in section 4 of the act of February 21, 1879. That section provides that at no time shall the number of carriers in the first-class cities receiving the maximum salary of $1,000 be more than two-thirds or less than one-half of the whole number of carriers actually in service in the cities in which they are employed. For my part, I do not think these letter-carriers are overpaid. I would not, personally, object to paying two-thirds of them at the rate of $1,000 per annum. I have, however, offered my substitute so as to provide for paying one-half only at that rate, and I trust the substitute will be adopted.

Mr. BAKER. I rise to oppose the amendment.

Mr. KEIFER. I have not yet yielded the floor. I desire to say that the gentleman from New York [Mr. COX] made a suggestion to me to change the sum appropriated by my substitute from $353,000 to $415,000. If he desires to move such an amendment I will yield to him for that purpose.

(Mr. KEIFER's substitute was agreed to.)

POLITICS IN THE JURY BOX.

June 10, 1879. On the bill making appropriations for judicial expenses, and the section providing that the names of three hundred persons shall be placed in the jury-box, from which shall be drawn grand and petit jurors, "which names shall have been placed therein by the clerk of such court and a commissioner, to be appointed by the judge thereof, which commissioner shall be a citizen residing in the district in which such court is held, of good standing and a well-known *member of the principal political party opposing* that to which the clerk may belong, the clerk and said commissioner each to place one name in said box alternately until the whole number required shall be placed therein."

Mr. KEIFER said :

I do not desire, Mr. Chairman, to take up the time of the committee if gentlemen desire to vote on this extraordinary measure. I believe until near the close of the Forty-fifth Congress no such astounding proposition as is contained in this bill was ever made in the Congress of the United States, or so far as I can learn in any legislative body in any of the States of the United States. I believe, sir, that so infamous a proposition has never crept into any law of any State of this Union, and I beg gentlemen on the other side of the House, especially from the Southern States, to rise and say whether in any one of their States they have ever advocated the policy of legislating in this manner politics into the jury-box, or whether in any of their States now such a proposition in principle has ever been carried out or enacted into law? I hear no man respond to that inquiry. Then I may truthfully say, for one hundred years, for a whole century, we have gone along with no such proposition as this in any law of a State or in the United States.

Now, Mr. Chairman, what is the object of this law in relation to jurors? The object is perfectly obvious. There have been violations of the United States laws in the South, the stealing of the timber belonging to the Government, the violation of the revenue laws throughout certain districts of the South, and when gentlemen found, after attempting legislation, that they could not get these matters determined in the State courts where they had juries, all of whom are Democrats, then they say, we will legislate into the jury-box in the United States courts enough partisan Democrats to prevent the Government from ever convicting any person charged with such crimes or recovering a verdict for anything in any case. And there is the foundation for the whole of it. When this proposition was first made in the last Congress its real purpose was no secret. My colleague from Ohio [Mr. McMAHON] says there is something to be learned from looking to the Electoral Commission. I think there is where we are to learn a very bad lesson. We found that gentlemen of the Electoral Commission voted according to their politics.

Nay, we have, Mr. Chairman, this extraordinary instance in relation to that commission : A gentleman who was appointed by the Forty-fourth Congress on a committee to investigate the elections in the State of South Carolina, to take testimony and report who carried that State in 1876, and whether the electors in favor of Tilden or Hayes carried that State (I refer to Judge Abbott, of Massachusetts), went there, and after the testimony was taken and he had it all before him, came back to the Forty-fourth Congress with other Democratic members of the committee, reported that the Hayes electors had carried the State of South Carolina, and then he was put on the Electoral Commission; and when he had no testimony before him he voted in effect that the Tilden electors had carried the State of South Carolina and that the Hayes electors had not.

Now, do you want to carry that out as a precedent? You want to carry politics into the jury-box. In Ohio we have no such law, and there is no complaint. We do not legislate men into the jury-box with a view of their voting for their own party in rendering verdicts. We have not had any trouble there, and gentlemen from the South do not complain in their own States where the jurors are now all Democrats.

My objections are numerous. I have stated them in a former speech I made on this floor, and I wish it distinctly understood I put my objection on the ground that men must not be told they are put in the jury-box expressly to stand by their party friends, for that is the effect of the proposition in this bill. We have had one hundred years' experience under our present law, and it has worked well. It is because we have fallen on strange times in the history of our country and because we have peculiar ends to accomplish that this proposition is now brought forward.

*   *   *   *   *

Mr. Chairman, I did not desire to prolong this discussion, especially on the point which the gentleman from New York [Mr. Cox] seems to be so much agitated about, as neither he nor I were prepared to go fully into all these reports. I stated the result, I stated the fact, I stated the effect, and I reiterate it. The gentleman has undertaken to read here a portion of a report not at all responsive to what I stated, and only of the report signed by Mr. Abbott, of Massachusetts. He attempted to evade the point, and then to beg me to withdraw my statement in the face of the report, and I declined to do so.

I wish to say, Mr. Chairman, that the great question before the Electorial Commission at the time the case of the State of South Carolina was being considered, if it was not in all cases, was this: those claiming that Tilden was elected, or that Tilden electors were elected, claimed it on the ground that the returns showed the fact of their election on their face.

Now I repeat here that Mr. Abbott signed a report which contains a statement and summary of all the election returns in the State of South Carolina, wherein it is stated, among other things, after summing up the returns, that "the result by thus ascertaining the votes"—that is, by the returns, and that is what the Democrats stood on before the commission—"that the result by thus ascertaining the votes cast at the precincts and correcting the mistakes made by the managers in the returns is as follows;" and then follows a statement in summary. Then the report states "this gives Bowen, who received the smallest vote on the Republican ticket, 92,033 votes over McGowan, who received the largest vote on the Democratic ticket, 91,262 votes, a majority of 831." That was the report; and the question was what did the returns show, and the returns did show that the Hayes elector who received the lowest vote on his ticket had 831 more votes, according to Mr. Abbott's report, than the highest Tilden elector, and so they reported. I read farther from the same report:

Your committee believe they have obtained with substantial accuracy the number of votes cast, &c.

So much for that, then.

Then, considering the great question which was before the commission, which was, who was elected by the returns, and denying the right of returning boards to correct mistakes or to throw out returns or votes for fraud, Mr. Abbott in effect voted that the Hayes electors were not elected and the Tilden electors were.

There is a good deal in this report, Mr. Chairman. It is the most marvelous thing we have ever seen. It contains a great many things which gentlemen may speculate about outside of these figures, but the substance is what I have given you here. It contains that most extraordinary statement that comes to us twice in reports made by Democratic committees of the Forty-fourth Congress relating to the Presidential election in 1876, and on which the Democratic party proposes to throw out votes in certain districts. I give the statement in the language of this report now before me: "Women utterly refuse to have any intercourse with men of their own race who voted against the Republican ticket;" and that was adjudged by Democrats to be a fraud upon the Democratic party. [Laughter on the Republican side.]

90 A—K——6

THE TRADE DOLLAR.

June 18, 1879. The House having under consideration the bill (H. R. No. 931) to provide for the exchange of trade-dollars for legal-tender silver dollars—

Mr. KEIFER said:

Mr. SPEAKER: This bill, if enacted into a law, will compel the Secretary of the Treasury to exchange legal-tender silver dollars for trade-dollars at par, and to recoin the trade-dollars into legal-tender or standard silver dollars and to stop the further coinage of trade-dollars. I understand the Committee on Coinage, Weights, and Measures to recommend the passage of this bill.

Mr. FISHER. Do not say that the committee recommend this bill without amendments.

Mr. KEIFER. I understand them to report it back without amendment.

Mr. WARNER. The majority of the committee are in favor of amending the bill.

Mr. KEIFER. They have reported it without amendment, and I think my statement is correct.

I think the whole measure unwise, and if opportunity is afforded me I will move as a substitute for the bill the following:

That the silver coins of the United States known as the trade-dollars shall be a legal tender at their nominal value for any amount not exceeding $5 in any one payment.

The substitute proposed would restore the trade-dollar to the status it held in this country at the time it was first issued under the act of February 12, 1873, and which it held until totally demonetized by the act of July 22, 1876. This latter act was passed chiefly through the efforts of Democrats in the Forty-fourth Congress and when this House was overwhelmingly Democratic.

But for the demonetizing act of July 22, 1876, no trouble would ever have arisen in this country about the trade-dollar. But for that act no man in this country, rich or poor, would have suffered inconvenience or loss on account of the trade-dollars, and no banks or brokers would have attempted to speculate in them.

The trade-dollar, as well known, was coined for the Asiatic or Chinese trade, and this Government did not issue them on its own account, but only coined them under the act of 1873 for private parties (on their paying the actual expenses of coinage) from bullion deposited at the United States mints for that purpose.

These trade-dollars never were intended for circulation in the United States, but in various ways a portion of those coined came into general circulation. The Secretary of the Treasury possesses, under existing laws, the right and power to restrict the coinage of trade-dollars to the necessities of the actual export demand, and under this power he wholly suspended their coinage in April, 1878. The total coinage of trade-dollars since the passage of the act of 1873, which first authorized them, has been $35,959,360. Returns of customs collectors show that 25,703,950 of these dollars had been exported prior to November 1, 1878, in the Chinese trade alone, and after making a reasonable estimate of the number which have found their way out of this country through Chinese returning to their own country, and of the number smelted for manufacturing and other purposes, and as bullion at the mints ($106,000 have been melted at the mints), and making due allowance for those returned in various ways, there can hardly be found in this country five million of the trade-dollars.

Without making any allowance for those used for manufacturing purposes, the Director of the Mint in his report dated November 1, 1878, estimates the number of trade-dollars then in the United States at five and a quarter millions, and these were held principally by California banks. On the 13th of June, 1879, the trade-dollar, notwithstanding it had no legal-tender character, had a commercial value in New York City of ninety-nine cents, and the standard silver dollar then had with its legal-tender character a commercial value of ninety-nine and seven-eighth cents. On that day the bullion in a trade-dollar could have been purchased for ninety-one cents. In view of these and other facts I would not withdraw the trade-dollar from circulation abroad at so great a cost to our Government. We can purchase the amount of bullion (and there is plenty of it, the product of our mines) in a trade-dollar for ninety-one cents, if desirable to have a more rapid coinage of standard silver dollars. The silver in the trade dollar has already been utilized, and it would now be unwise to offer a premium for the return to this country of over thirty millions of the trade-dollars already absorbed in foreign commerce and not needed at home, and to take up and recoin at a loss to the United States of not less than nine cents on each of the five millions still in this country.

I appeal to those who favor a free coinage of silver dollars and to those who are interested in mineral districts not to favor this measure, as it will only tend to depreciate our own silver bullion and to widen the breach, at our present ratio, between the gold and the silver standard. It will also be ruinous, for a time at least, to our silver-mining interests in this country. There is plenty of bullion without melting the trade-dollar to occupy our mints indefinitely to their fullest capacity. There is no legal or moral obligation resting on this Government to take up these trade-dollars at above their value as bullion. The Chinese Government has no mint and is not likely to have, and the trade dollar is constantly increasing in favor there, hence I would not take away from the Secretary of the Treasury the right in his discretion to coin, under the original act, trade-dollars expressly to meet an export demand. Silver is the money standard of China and most of the oriental nations, and it will be largely to the interest of this country, as far as possible, from its inexhaustible silver mines to supply them with their coin or money.

Dr. Linderman, the late Director of the Mint, in his last report, speaking of the trade-dollar, very wisely says:

It will be to our advantage to furnish these coins, so far as we can without detriment to our own money system; and the trade-dollar having attained such a favorable position in China, it would not appear to be advisable to repeal the law authorizing its coinage.

No more trade-dollars will in any event be coined, unless it is to the interest of bullion-holders to have it done. They will not, with the approval of the Secretary of the Treasury, deposit at the United States mint bullion to be coined into trade-dollars, unless it will be more profitable than to sell it to the Government for coinage or to other parties. Why should this means of utilizing our silver productions be withdrawn, especially while silver bullion is so much depreciated in the markets of the world? No harm can come to anybody from the continued coinage of the trade-dollar under the restrictions stated already, provided my proposed substitute is adopted. As has already been stated, the trade-dollar never was intended to become one of the coins of our country to go into ordinary use; and notwithstanding the fact that it contains 6¼ grains more pure or 7¼ grains more standard silver than the now legal-tender silver dollar, I would not give it a full legal-tender character. To do the latter would destroy the original purposes of the act of 1873.

The limited legal-tender character of that act should, however, never have been taken away, and should now be restored so as to protect all persons, laborers, and others from inconvenience and loss on account of those now in or which may come into their hands. Brokers or large dealers in trade-dollars can protect themselves by disposing of what they now have on hand for the continuing Asiatic export trade. Persons holding a few trade-dollars who have received them for wages or otherwise can use them in small sums, if they are only given a legal-tender quality for $5, as I propose. If employers should use them to pay their employés, the latter could buy without discount any of the necessaries of life with them. To make them a legal tender for $5 will not injure the Government to any extent, but it will prevent loss to that class of persons who cannot always protect themselves. The bill of the committee is against the interests of the Government and in the interest of the banks and brokers who have hoarded the trade-dollar.

The bullion in all the trade-dollars could be purchased by the Government for $32,725,017 at the present advanced price of silver bullion, but under this bill the Government would be required to pay $3,234,343 more than they are worth as bullion, thus opening a means of speculation at the expense of the Government and offering an inducement to parties to gather up at home and abroad and send to the mints all the trade-dollars hitherto minted. This bill is in the interest of those who have already hoarded in large sums the trade-dollars, purchased at eighty-five and ninety cents apiece. It provides a means of robbing the United States Treasury to the extent of millions of dollars in the interest of speculators, and affords no sort of relief to persons who hold trade-dollars in small quantities and who have received them for wages, produce, &c. It must be noted that the passage of this bill will give no relief to holders of small sums of trade-dollars. Such holders can only sell at a discount to speculators, to be sent off to the Treasury or subtreasuries of the United States for exchange. To give such dollars a legal-tender quality only in sums not exceeding $5 will necessarily force those now in our country abroad, and will cause them not to circulate at home generally.

Let us coin our standard silver dollars to the extent of the capacity of our mints, if necessary; but out of fresh bullion, the product of our mines and the fruits of the toil and enterprise of our miners.

I am not speaking against the silver dollar or the silver standard, but I speak in favor of a silver dollar for our own home circulation which may never be dishonored, but held up abreast, for all purposes, of the gold or now paper dollar of this Government, and also in favor of finding an easy market and good price for a great and exhaustible product of our country.

We have coined, prior to June 1, 1879, under existing law, 33,187,̄ silver dollars, which are now ready for or in circulation. Who lars can get them in any sums desired. The *per capita* of silver dollars in this country is much greater than at any other time in its history.

The Democratic party were the pioneers in the work of destroying the "monetary power" of silver in the United States.

From the organization of the United States Mint (1793) to June 30, 1873, the total silver coinage was as follows:

Dollars	$8,045,838 00
Half dollars	99,845,235 50
Quarter dollars	22,001,218 50
Dimes	9,000,795 50
Half dimes	4,906,946 90
Three cents	1,281,850 20
Total silver coinage prior to 1873	145,141,884 60

On February 21, 1853, a Congress, Democratic in both branches by large majorities, by legal enactment took away the thitherto full legal-tender character of all subsidiary silver coin, except in payment of debts for sums under $5. Upon the principle of this Democratic law above $137,000,000 of our silver coinage were demonetized.

It is claimed that what remained at home and were not melted up for various uses of the $8,045,838 silver dollars coined prior to June 30, 1873, were by a Republican Congress demonetized by the act of February 12, 1873. If true, this would be a comparatively small matter. A very large share of the responsibility of that act also belongs to prominent Democrats in both the Senate and the House.

Until June 22, 1874 (the date of the taking effect of the Revised Statutes of the United States), all silver dollars coined by authority of the United States were a legal tender, equal with gold coin. Section 3586 of said statutes demonetized all United States silver coinage, and made it a legal tender for only $5.

The act of February 12, 1873, provided only for limiting the legal-tender character to $5 of the silver coins issued under its provisions, including the trade-dollar.

Now that members of all political parties are in favor of a coinage of legal-tender silver dollars, and some of each of the two principal political parties are in favor of a free coinage of silver on the same terms and on an equal footing with gold, let us do nothing to bring discredit on a policy which tends to make coinage of silver dollars desirable in our country.

Above all, let us not, under the pretense of legislating in the interest of more silver dollars, make a law to give banks, bankers, brokers, and speculators millions of dollars at the expense of the United States Treasury, and without giving relief to the only persons in this country who have suffered from a circulation of silver (trade) dollars.

By the adoption of my proposed substitute for this bill full relief will come to this last class of persons, and the Government and other parties will suffer no loss.

No money or representative of money or obligation of any character which this Government is or has been in any degree responsible for passing into common circulation among the people should be allowed to be made the instrument of injury or loss to any citizen. The remedy proposed, so far as the trade-dollar is concerned, is easy, simple, and efficient.

June 19, 1879. Remarks on the adoption of the substitute:

Mr. KEIFER. I have proposed this substitute for the purpose of bringing us back to the point from which we started. The trade-dollar was originally legal tender for $5. A Democratic House and a Republican Senate in 1876 demonetized the trade-dollar. We are now asked to enact a bill which provides that that trade-dollar, which only three years ago was supposed to be of a character that ought to pass for nothing in this country, must now be bought in at more than it is worth. The proposition is now that the trade-dollar is too good to circulate in this country, that it has too much bullion in it, and therefore the United States must pay nine cents on each dollar more than it is worth as bullion, and take it up at a cost of over $3,000,000, if all the trade-dollars issued by this Government shall be presented for redemption.

Already they are gathering up on the Asiatic coast and shipping these trade-dollars to New York City in order to speculate in view of the legislation proposed here to-day. I am opposed to such a policy as utterly unwise. Now, if you will simply make these trade-dollars legal tender in sums of $5 they will circulate everywhere. If we had not passed the act of 1876 demonetizing the trade-dollar we would not have heard on the political rostrum all this talk about the trade-dollars. Let us go back to where we were before the act of 1876 was passed, and the trade-dollar will then circulate everywhere throughout the country.

Mr. FORT. I would like to ask the gentleman a question.

Mr. KEIFER. Certainly.

Mr. FORT. Does the gentleman think that making the trade-dollar a legal tender will bring it up to par?

Mr. KEIFER. Undoubtedly it will, as the subsidiary silver coins which the gentleman uses every day are at par.

Mr. FORT. Then why should there not be the same inducement to send the trade-dollars back here from China and put them in circulation at par?

Mr. KEIFER. Because by this bill it is proposed to buy them up as bullion and pay nine cents on each dollar more than they are worth as bullion.

Mr. FORT. Your amendment would make them legal tender without recoinage.

Mr. KEIFER. Only for $5, and therefore they will not become current to any great amount.

BANK RESERVES.

January 22, 1880. On the bill requiring reserve of national banks to be kept in gold and silver coins of the United States.—

Mr. KEIFER said:

Mr. SPEAKER: Notwithstanding the painful regret expressed by the chairman of the Committee on Banking and Currency [Mr. BUCKNER] yesterday in reference to the matter of members indulging in irrelevant debate, we have been obliged to-day to listen to a great deal more of that kind of debate. But I wish to give a reason or two in the moment I have to occupy the floor why I shall vote against this bill. I shall not be in harmony with some gentlemen who have spoken against the bill here to-day.

First, let me say when this bill first came before the House for consideration the gentleman from Missouri [Mr. BUCKNER] having charge of it told us in substance that the bill was to have no effect at all upon the country. He took pains as long ago, I believe, as the 14th of January to demonstrate, by putting into the RECORD a table, that there was coin enough now in all the banks of this country to meet the requirements of this bill. We were then to be soothed with the idea that we were to make no draught upon the reserve coin in the Treasury except to secure resumption. He then assured the House we were engaged in harmless if not useless legislation. That was the burden of his speech, and he demonstrated then that there was more coin already in possession of the national banks than was essential for the coin reserve required by this bill. But yesterday, to our surprise, he told us that he introduced this bill at the extra session, or one very similar to it, and he further said:

But my purpose was to unload the Treasury of a portion of its immense hoards of gold and silver for the purpose of diffusing them among the banks and the people.

But, Mr. Speaker, when we read the bill, we find the sole effect of it is to put the padlock of the law on $50,000,000 of the coin of the United States, that the people cannot reach under any process known to the country. The effect of the bill is to lock up, in round numbers, $50,000,000 of coin that the people cannot reach under any circumstances. The coin reserve required to be kept in the sixteen principal cities of this country, where they are required to keep in "lawful money of the United States" a sum equal to 25 per cent. of their circulation and bank deposits, and in the other banks of the country, in like lawful money, 15 per cent. of their outstanding circulation and deposits, which reserves aggregate, in round numbers, $100,000,000—we are, then, Mr. Speaker, by this bill to say that one-half of that large aggregate is to be locked up in the banks, where it is not to be reached at all. It is to be absolutely withdrawn from circulation.

We are, it is true, to turn out instead $50,000,000 of greenbacks. What for? Do the people want them? I venture to say there has not been a petition presented to this House or to the Senate, asking that these greenbacks shall be turned out and taken from the reserves of the banks—not a single one.

We are here taking up time in trying to legislate upon a subject that is not demanded by the wants of the country or by the wishes of the country anywhere. And what is the real design and purpose of this bill? If not the design, what will be the real effect of it? Not to use up, as I understand it, for we ought not to do that, the amount of coin that is now in the banks for the use of the people whenever they go to the banks to get it; not to take up the coin in the pockets of the people, for they need that for their own uses, and will be likely to hold on to it, but to compel the banks to go to the Treasury of the United States and to draw from the fund now there $50,000,000 of the coin reserve, to lock it up so that it cannot be made available for securing permanent or continuing resumption. This is the whole scheme and design of this bill. It is unwise, and I trust no man who believes in the doctrine of having paper money and gold and silver coin abreast will vote for it. I also trust all those who believe resumption is right and will and should be maintained, will vote against this bill. Not only do you take by this $50,000,000 in coin from the Treasury vaults of the United States and lock it up, not permitting it to be used for the purposes of securing resumption—not only do you do that, but you turn out $50,000,000 of the paper money of the country now held in reserve by national banks, and make it available to be used in an emergency by opponents of resumption for presentation for redemption.

The bill enacted into a law withdraws $50,000,000 of coin necessary to be used for the purposes of resumption and substitutes therefor $50,000,000 of paper money to be presented everywhere and at any time for redemption.

Now, Mr. Speaker, that is not good financial policy in this country, or at least it is in the face of what is usually regarded as good financiering in any country. There should be a great center where coin is accumulated so as to strengthen the power which has the responsibility of carrying out the policy of resumption. It has been the policy of Great Britain and it has been the policy here when we acted wisely, and until very recently it has been the policy of the Democratic party also.

I remember very well in the last national campaign in this country the gentleman who had the distinguished honor of being selected as the standard-bearer of Democracy arraigned the party in power, the Republican party, for not providing for a reserve of coin in order to procure resumption of specie payment upon the legal-tender notes issued by the Government. I have here his exact language:

The amount of the legal-tender notes of the United States now outstanding is less than $370,000,000, besides $24,000,000 of fractional currency. How shall the Government make these notes at all times as good as specie? It has to provide, in reference to the mass which would be kept in use by the wants of business, a central reservoir of coin, adequate to the adjustment of the temporary fluctuations of international balances, and as a guarantee against transient drains artificially created by panic or by speculation.

This I have read from Mr. Tilden's letter of acceptance. It lays down the true doctrine on this question, and the one the Republican party adopted when the time came to act in the matter of carrying out the resumption act of January 14, 1875.

Mr. Tilden complained that a "reservoir of coin" was not provided several years before the resumption law was to take effect. The Republican party was satisfied to provide one only when it was needed. Let us not destroy it, now that we have resumption with its good results in the revival of business, restoration of business confidence, &c.

I might read more from this letter of acceptance, but my time is too short. The proposed legislation is a direct thrust at the Treasury and at the power of the Government to maintain resumption, and we learned yesterday for the first time, from the distinguished gentleman who has charge of this bill, that it was so designed; for he then said it was to take the coin out of the Treasury of the United States, and for fear that the money should be used as we now use the reserve provided for the national banks, he then offered an amendment to the bill which requires the money to be locked up in the vaults of the several national banks in the country. As the law is now, three-fifths of the reserve of the country banks may be kept in the cities which are selected as depositories for the redemption of the circulating notes of the banks. That is no longer to be done, so far as the coin reserve, which will be required to be kept by this proposed legislation, is concerned. It changes and alters the entire national banking system, so far as the reserves are concerned. We shall no longer keep any portion of this one-half coin in any of the cities selected for the purpose of deposits in order to secure the redemption of the circulating notes of the banks. There are eighteen of these cities in this country. Of these eighteen, seventeen may, under certain circumstances, select banks in the city of New York where they may keep a portion of their reserves, and thus make available for business purposes a large amount of money as required now to be kept under the present law.

Let me say in conclusion, Mr. Speaker, as the law now stands every bank, if it is wise, or if necessary, will keep coin as a part of its reserves. These banks are required to keep their reserves in lawful money of the United States. The lawful money of this country is defined by the statutes to be gold and silver coin, United States Treasury notes, and demand Treasury notes for the purpose of the banking law of the country. I think that the passage of this bill would be the first great blow at the established policy of this country, that policy that has been so wisely undertaken and so successfully maintained, namely, the policy of resumption of specie payment after it had been so long suspended.

(The bill was lost.)

DEATH OF HON. ZACHARIAH CHANDLER.

January 28, 1880. A message from the Senate, by Mr. BURCH, its Secretary, communicated the reso lutions of that body upon the announcement of the death of Hon. ZACHARIAH CHANDLER, late a Senator of the United States from the State of Michigan.

Mr. CONGER offered the following resolutions:

Resolved, That the House of Representatives has received with profound sorrow the announcement of the death of Hon. ZACHARIAH CHANDLER, late a United States Senator from the State of Michigan.

Resolved, That business be now suspended to allow fitting tributes to be paid to his public and private virtues; and that, as a further mark of respect to the memory of the deceased, the House at the close of such remarks shall adjourn.

Mr. KEIFER said:

Mr. SPEAKER: If we were to call the roll of the dead who have fallen from the ranks of those who have mustered in this our country's Capitol, we should hear the names of many historic souls familiar to the ears of the people of all lands, and not among the least of those would be found the name of him on whose account we meet here to-day to pay a last tribute of respect.

My personal relations with the late Senator Zachariah Chandler were limited to occasional and incidental meetings during the last two years of his life. To those who knew him well and intimately during many years of his long, eventful, and useful life it must be left to speak of him in his social and family relations. But his public life and acts belong to the whole country; and in so far as he was the instrument of good to mankind; in so far as his life was exemplary and worthy of imitation; in so far as he was a type of American manhood and an honor to his country and race, he belongs to history.

While his life and public services may not have been singularly grand, they were transcendently great. It has often been said with a view of detracting from individual greatness that men only become great because they have lived and been called on to grapple with great events. It is not to be denied that great occasions develop great intellects and great men. It is also true that men who have high and responsible public duties cast on them as a rule meet and discharge them often to the surprise of their friends, with singular faithfulness and ability. But in the long and eventful period in our country's history through which the lamented Senator lived many strong men faltered, hesitated, and fell.

The differences in men are rarely to be measured by their difference in natural and purely intellectual endowments; they consist more commonly in the differences in zeal, energy—physical energy—perseverance, devotion to duty, to friends, and country, pride of success, love of honor, self-respect, high resolve, dauntless spirit, and, above all, a desire to do good.

Senator Chandler possessed most if not all of these endowments, and more largely than most of the great and good men of the world.

If I were compelled to name the one leading characteristic which he was endowed with in a higher degree than another, and which ruled him in private and public affairs throughout his useful life, I should say it was *heroism*. Though not a warrior in the period of war, his whole life was a heroic one. Heroes are not found alone in the fiery furnace of war; they are common to the paths of peace. He possessed true heroism, "the self-devotion of genius manifesting itself in action." He was not only of that kind of heroism denoting fearlessness of danger, passive courage, ability to bear up under trials amid dangers and sufferings; nor was it only that fortitude, bravery, and valor which is essential to those who go forth to conflicts with living opponents in personal mortal combat as duelists or in battle; it was made up of that intrepidity and courage which shrink not in the presence of appalling danger. Senator Chandler was unpretentious, and as a husband, father, and friend, was kind, patronizing, and gentle; but when stormy times came his brow seemed to darken, and that great body of his, which appeared to the beholder to be one of the motive forces of creation, strode fearlessly to the front, and there, by common consent held sway until all danger was passed.

Many courageous men, not truly heroic, falter and fail to enter the lists when a conflict is imminent. Not so the deceased Senator. He was a leader when the times or occasions demanded true valor. It is in the lead where men fall or are sacrificed. The leaders in charging a foe are the most conspicuous marks, and they are the first to receive the manly fire of bold enemies and often the cowardly arrows of hiding foes in the rear, not unfrequently springing from the bow of envy or jealousy.

He escaped in a singular degree, and died in old age with his armor on. In a successful civil as in a successful military life—and in the eyes of an often undiscriminating public success in either is the only test of true greatness—it is easier to be led to scenes where honor and glory are won than to be one of the few who lead there.

In the bloody conflicts of war the percentage of those who cannot, if well commanded, meet the actual conflict of battle with a good show of courage is very small indeed; yet the large mass of men are physical cowards. Mr. Chandler had no element of cowardice in him. He was always a natural leader.

As a business man he sought out a comparatively new State, and attained success by foresight, energy, and enterprise. He left a large fortune. This same foresight, energy, and enterprise he carried with him throughout his public life. He was devoted to his friends and magnanimous to his foes, but not to the latter until he was sure they were conquered.

As a political leader he was known to be a violent partisan. This came from his having no half-way convictions of duty and right. When he had work to do he struck heavy blows. He did not lightly tap a nail on the head to start it on its course, but drove it home at a single blow. He was said to be uncompromising in his character. This was unjust to him, save in all matters where his country or principle was involved. He was honest, and integrity in private and public affairs was a pole star for his guidance. He may have erred, and doubtless did, in many things. It is only human to err. His impetuous and fiery nature may have sometimes caused him to go astray, but he was willing to make amends for any wrong he had to another when in his power.

Like all positive men who come prominently upon the stage of life, he had not friends alone, but violent enemies. But, like a giant oak that withstands the tornadoes as well as the gentler winds for a century, and grows stronger and firmer in its fiber, Senator Chandler grew in mental and moral stature by reason of the violence of his foes. He, like the oak, could not have flourished alone in the sunshine of life. He needed, if he did not deserve, its stormy days to prepare him for his high destiny. It has been said by another who had to bear more than seemed to be his share of violent opposition, "that he could as little afford to spare his enemies as his friends." They fitted and qualified him for better and nobler duties. Mr. Chandler's body and mind were alike, of the rugged not to say rough, cast.

His light, though not such as would be called in high literary circles as brilliant, yet it burned fiercely, reaching on occasions a white heat, in the presence of which his opponents withered. In debate he was fearlessly outspoken. He could take as well as give herculean blows. Better men may have lived than plain old Zachariah Chandler, but none excelled him in love of country or of his fellow-men. For subterfuge and dodging he had a brave man's scorn. He always spoke his mind and acted boldly up to his convictions. He was for war when peace no longer seemed possible. As early as 1860 he gave it as his opinion that "*a little blood-letting would be good for the body politic.*" He was then for war. And in the national halls of legislation he gave his voice and votes for its rigorous prosecution.

He believed in the fiat of the emancipation which made plain Abe Lincoln's name immortal. It has been said that he was indiscreet, boisterous, and headstrong. So far as this may have been true it was because he had in great affairs absolutely no nonsense about him.

As a political enemy of his has said: "He went straight for the thing in sight, and generally came off with it."

His warm and generous nature would not allow him to betray a friend or thrust an enemy in the back. If throughout his whole career his life was not one in all respects to be imitated by the young men of the country, it cannot be said that he corrupted them.

It was my fortune to meet him for a day near the close of his life. He was then on duty for a cause in which his heart and soul were enlisted, and in that cause he died. He had then entered upon his last campaign. It was bounded by no State lines. He addressed the people in Ohio on the political issues which he deemed vital to them; he flew from place to place rapidly, and was gone, and the "*talking lightning*" told us he was in the distant State of Massachusetts, and thundering his plain but convincing speech in Faneuil Hall to the learned men of Boston. We heard of him elsewhere in that State and in the State of New York; then came the news that he was in the far Northwest—the State of Wisconsin—pouring livid, convincing arguments out to her people. The morning papers announced that he was to address the assembled multitudes in that magic, wondrous city of Chicago on the night of October 31, 1879.

The early papers on the next day gave us his speech, but with it came the startling announcement—Zach. Chandler is dead. Strong men and women mourned. His friends and foes stood dazed in the presence of the sad tidings. They did not know how to contemplate him from the stand-point of death. He died as a hero might wish to die—like a plumed knight, "booted and spurred." It is fitting that here in these halls that knew him so long we should pay him a last tribute, and shed copious tears to his memory. As we contemplate him dead, in his final chamber of repose, in the poet's language we may truthfully say:

Here lurks no treason, here no envy swells,
Here grow no damned grudges, here are no storms,
No noise; but silence and eternal sleep.

RULE XXI.

Mr. KEIFER said:

This seems to be a good time, Mr. Chairman, while considering this subject, to express our opinions generally on a clause in Rule XXI of the new rules reported.

I wish to say that I am opposed to the pending amendment in relation to the transfer of the Post-Office appropriation bill from the Committee on Appropriations to the Committee on the Post-Office and Post-Roads; that is, I am opposed to it provided Rule XXI shall be amended as I think it ought to amended. I desire to say that in my judgment it is better to have one common appropriation committee, whose duties shall be confined entirely to the preparation of appropriation bills in accordance with existing law.

I believe, Mr. Chairman, that if you transfer to the various committees of this House the duties of preparing the several appropriation bills there will be a strife between those committees, the Committee on Military Affairs, the Committee on Naval Affairs, the Committee on the Post-Office and Post-Roads, and so on through, each striving to obtain the most appropriations for the Department of the Government directly under its charge, and in that way we will necessarily augment the annual appropriations beyond the ordinary revenues of the Government.

While, however, that in my mind would be a great evil, it would be simple and insignificant in comparison with the evils that would result from the operation of clause 3 in Rule XXI as now reported, and which have resulted from the rule as it now exists. That clause is a mere trap. It has been claimed by our distinguished Speaker that it furnishes the great means of reducing appropriations and saving money to the people. But I have observed in this Congress, I observed in the last session, that the sole purpose of that clause was to enable the Committee on Appropriations to hang political legislation on appropriation bills. Under the guise of that clause of our rule we were here during the last session for more than three months, standing face to face and eye to eye, fighting over the question as to whether we should repeal our election laws, and whether we should by a law of this Government make it a crime to keep the peace at the polls on election days. There is no such thing as retrenchment intended. All that was intended was to coerce the minority of this House and to coerce the Executive of this Government to submit legislation dictated by the majority of this House on the other side. That is what is meant by this clause under the guise of retrenchment to force legislation upon appropriation bills.

Let me give you an example that is not political. I remember that in the Forty-fifth Congress, by more than a two-thirds vote of the House and by a unanimous vote of the Senate, regardless of party, we passed what was known as the letter-carrier bill; yet when this same Appropriations Committee came to deal with that matter they said in substance that the House and the Senate had passed the letter-carrier bill and the Executive who approved of it did not understand the subject. They said they would cut that bill to pieces or they would make no appropriations at all for the purpose. That committee came in here with an appropriation bill containing a very small sum of money for the letter-carrier branch of the service, and with new legislation, proposing altogether to repeal and overthrow the action of the House and the Senate. We fought that committee here for a whole day to compel it to make appropriations in accordance with existing law. That committee did not report those provisions under any guise of retrenchment.

SPECIAL DEPUTY MARSHALS.

March 18, 1880. To the deficiency appropriation bill an amendment was offered, providing: "That hereafter special deputy marshals of elections and general deputy marshals, for performing any duties in reference to any election, shall receive the sum of $2 per day in full for their compensation; and that all appointments of such special deputy marshals or of general deputy marshals having any duty to perform in respect to any election shall be made by the judge of the circuit court of the United States for the district in which such marshals are to perform their duties, or by the district judge, in the absence of the circuit judge, and not less than two nor more than three appointments shall be made for any voting precinct where such appointments are required to be made, and the persons so appointed shall each be of different political parties, of good character, and able to read and write the English language, and shall be well-known residents of the voting precincts in which their duties are to be performed."

Points of order were raised against it.

Mr. KEIFER said:

The points of order have been well stated by the gentleman from New York [Mr. HISCOCK]. I wish to call attention to a bill introduced by the gentleman from Illinois [Mr. SPRINGER] and referred to the Committee on Elections, and I will say that this amendment is in substance that bill. I agree that it is not in precisely the same language, but in every sense it is in substance that bill. I take pleasure in sending a copy of the bill to the Chair.

Now I wish to say if this be not true—if it be controverted by the gentleman from Illinois—if he claims that this proposed amendment is not in substance the bill now before the Committee of Elections, then the point made by the gentleman from New York is sound—that this subject-matter referred to in the amendment was never before the Committee on Elections. It was never referred to that committee if it did not get there by virtue of the reference of the bill of the gentleman from Illinois.

In terms the proposed amendment contains more than the bill that was referred. It contains in addition an appropriation, but in its subject-matter it proposes to change existing law in relation to the special deputy marshals and their mode of appointment. The objection must go, of course, to the whole amendment. If the amendment simply proposed to pay these special deputy marshals in the State of California the objection would not be good, and I think I am safe in saying that no objection would be made, at least on this side of the House, to such an amendment. That amendment would be entirely in order, because this is a deficiency made in accordance with law. I know it is that sort of deficiency that my colleague [Mr. McMAHON] undertakes to say the Congress of the United States ought not to make good. But, Mr. Chairman, while I do not characterize that utterance of my colleague, I wish to characterize the conduct of the Congress of the United States in refusing to make appropriations which are in exact accordance with the mandates of law. It is not cowardly to refuse, but it is doing that which will be denominated before the country and the world dishonest not to appropriate money to pay a debt which has been contracted in exact accordance with law.

I understand, Mr. Chairman, that my point of order must go to the whole of this proposed amendment; and I wish to have it distinctly understood the gentleman can make proper appropriations but in this way. He cannot change existing laws. We do not wish either to have a repetition of what we have had in the early days of this Congress.

Mr. SPRINGER. The gentleman from Ohio, who has just taken his seat, makes the point of order, first, that the subject-matter of this amendment has not been before the Committee on Elections; and secondly, that the subject-matter of it is before the Committee on Elections, and for that reason is not in order.

Mr. KEIFER. The gentleman will understand me: I say that it is not before the Committee on Elections unless it gets there by virtue of a bill which the gentleman has introduced; and if it does get there by virtue of that bill then he can only report in accordance with the subject-matter contained in that bill. If it is not in accordance with that then it should be ruled out upon that ground.

I simply wish to add a word or two to what I have already stated. I am induced to do it by the intimation of the Chair that on one point I suggested the Chair differed from me. As has already been said, I regard the ruling on this question as a very important one, not for to-day or perhaps for this session or for this Congress, but for the future Congresses. I wish to state again what I tried to state in the first instance: that is, if the Committee on Elections had the subject-matter of this amendment referred to it by reason of the reference of the bill offered by the gentleman from Illinois [Mr. SPRINGER], and if we gave that committee jurisdiction to report upon this question at all, or jurisdiction to consider the question at all, then it was because the amendment itself was in substance the same as the bill.

I have invited the attention of the Chair to the consideration of the bill. The analysis of the amendment will show that it pertains generally to an alteration of an existing law relating to the appointment of special deputy marshals. Is not that the substance of the bill of the gentleman from Illinois [Mr. SPRINGER]? If it is not then the committee which this morning undertook to instruct its chairman to report an amendment to this House was doing a vain thing and one outside of its jurisdiction.

Let me repeat, if that bill gave jurisdiction to the Committee on Elections over this matter, then it was because it contained the substance of this amendment. If the amendment contained the substance of the bill, then we can come logically, I think, to the conclusion, that it is not in order under the fourth clause of Rule XXI, which prohibits the introduction by way of amendment of "the substance of any other bill, or resolution pending before the House." That is all I desire to say on this point of order.

(The points of order were overruled, and debate followed.)

Mr. KEIFER. Mr. Chairman, on the merits of this bill which we have been considering for many days I have not undertaken to occupy a moment's time. I would not take the short time allotted to me under the rules but for the fact that I think we are again launching ourselves upon the issue which divided this House and divided the country and concentrated the interests of this country all through the extra session of this Congress.

The amendment proposed to the substitute by my distinguished colleague from Ohio [Mr. GARFIELD] may be entirely unobjectionable in form and in terms, but, Mr. Chairman, to me it is wholly objectionable, because it comes here in the form of a rider to an appropriation bill, and a mere deficiency bill at that. While I may feel bound to vote for it if I think it is the best we can get, especially after the Chair has ruled such an amendment is in order, yet I wish here distinctly to protest against it.

I am not particularly surprised that the gentleman from New York [Mr. COX] undertook to set himself up against the Supreme Court of the United States and at his undertaking, by his *ipse dixit*, to say, that a solemn, well, and carefully considered decision of that most august body of this country is wrong. I was not surprised to hear him say that. Mr. Chairman, I was not surprised to hear the general applause coming from that side of the House when they responded to that statement. The decision of the Supreme Court remains, however, the supreme law of the land under the Constitution.

That Supreme Court of ours he says is partisan in its character: *packed* is the word he uses. Who packed that court? Turn to the character of those men; read it; read the record they have made in all their life-time—each one of them—and you will see how utterly reckless and false this statement was. I might say their lives would give the lie to such a charge as that. The source of the charge need not be considered.

I desire, Mr. Chairman, to say one thing further, in reference to a remark made by my colleague from Ohio [Mr. McMAHON] who has charge of this bill on the floor. He undertook to state to the committee a day or two ago that while the Supreme Court decided these election laws were constitutional, yet that court did not decide the law was a good one. Of course he made that statement without having read the opinion of the court. I have not time here, in the limit allowed me, to go into that opinion. I hold it in my hand. There are some grand views stated there in the opinion of Justice Bradley, who spoke for the majority of the court. Unless there is objection, I will insert an extract or two as part of my remarks.

The court say in the recent case of *Ex parte Siebold et al.*, in speaking of governmental power, that—

In exercising the power, however, we are bound to presume that Congress has done so in a judicious manner; that it has endeavored to guard as far as possible against any unnecessary interference with State laws and regulations with the duties of State officers, or with local prejudices. It could not act at all so as to accomplish any beneficial object in preventing frauds and violence, and securing the faithful performance of duty at the elections, without providing for the presence of officers and agents to carry its regulations into effect. It is also difficult to see how it could attain these objects without imposing proper sanctions and penalties against offenders.

And in another place Justice Bradley, in the opinion, says:

Without the concurrent sovereignty referred to, the National Government would be nothing but an advisory Government. Its executive power would be absolutely nullified. Why do we have marshals at all if they cannot physically lay their hands on persons and things in the performance of their proper duties? What functions can they perform if they cannot use force? In executing the process of the courts must they call on the nearest constable for protection, must they rely on him to use the requisite compulsion and to keep the peace while they are soliciting and entreating the parties and bystanders to allow the law to take its course? This is the necessary consequence of the positions that are assumed. If we indulge in such impracticable views as these, and keep on refining and refining, we shall drive the National Government out of the United States, and relegate it to the District of Columbia, or perhaps to some foreign soil. We shall bring it back to a condition of greater helplessness than that of the old confederation. The argument is based on a strained and impracticable view of the nature and powers of the National Government. It must execute its powers or it is no Government. It must execute them on the land as well as on the sea, on things as well as on persons. And to do this it must necessarily have power to command obedience, preserve order, and keep the peace; and no person or power in this land has the right to resist or question its authority so long as it keeps within the bounds of its jurisdiction. Without specifying other instances in which this power to preserve order and keep the peace unquestionably exists, take the very case in hand.

Let me read a single extract more on the power of the Government and its duty:

It is argued that the preservation of peace and good order in society is not within the powers confided to the Government of the United States, but belongs exclusively to the States. Here again we are met by the theory that the Government of the United States does not rest upon the soil and territory of the country. We think that this theory is founded on an entire misconception of the nature and powers of that Government. We hold it to be an incontrovertible principle that the Government of the United States may, by means of physical force—

Note the words, gentlemen—

by means of physical force exercised through its official agents, execute on every foot of American soil the powers and functions that belong to it. This necessarily involves the power to command obedience to its laws, and hence the power to keep the peace to that extent.

A power that gentlemen on the other side deny—the power to keep the peace at elections, if you please, the places of all others where it should be maintained.

I might pursue this further, but I will not. It is sufficient for me to say the Supreme Court of the United States has not only said this legislation which has proved good whenever executed was constitutional, but it has in effect pronounced it a good, wise, and wholesome law. This law ought to have been executed with a stronger arm and firmer hand than it has been. Now that the Supreme Court has held all these election laws to be clearly within the purview of the Constitution of the United States and that it is right in principle, it becomes our duty to appropriate money to pay for its execution, and especially is this so since a debt has been contracted on the faith of the law. The Democratic party can hardly afford to persist in refusing to pay officers chosen under a constitutional act of Congress, and who have in good faith performed their duty on the faith of it. No party can afford to be thus faithless to its duty.

April 23, 1880. Pending a proposition to regulate the appointment of special deputy marshals.

Mr. KEIFER said:

I have but a word or two, Mr. Chairman. I regard this clause relating to the mode of appointing special deputy marshals as a piece of the proposed legislation which we have had pending along through the entire life-time of this Congress, all of which tends, and was so intended, to hedge about the powers of the Government and to so provide when wrong is threatened or actually exists at the polls on the part of those who are anxious to destroy the purity of the ballot-box, the Government should stand there mute and powerless.

This is a piece of it. It is intended to break down the power of the Government at the very fountain-head and at the very source of all our strength.

I do not agree with the remark made by my colleague [Mr. GARFIELD] who has just taken his seat, that because this amendment may be by implication a repeal of a portion of the election laws now on the statute-books on the subject of special deputy marshals, that it necessarily provides a mode of executing itself. It may be by implication a repeal and a total destruction of that part of our law which I regard wise and necessary, and yet in and of itself not make provision for a peaceful election or the appointment of these special deputy marshals at all. It may be, in other words, a repeal without adding anything or putting anything into the law which can take the place of what is repealed. I think this House already understands my views on this subject of the right and duty and the constitutional power of this Government to execute all its laws and especially election laws. I intended when I rose to make a remark in reply to a reference of the honorable gentleman from Maine [Mr. REED] which I thought was possibly, by implication at least, a little unkind to my distinguished colleague from Ohio [Mr. EWING], who spoke the other day after the previous question had been ordered. We had the benefit of hearing what he had to say, but not the pleasure yet of reading what he said.

The honorable gentleman from Maine incidentally referred to a recent election in Ohio in which my colleague was prominent, intending, I presume, to refer to the fact that he was recently the standard-bearer of the Democratic party in Ohio in the election for governor. Now, in his defense, and I may add he can defend himself, I wish to say he went into that campaign with a high character, not only as a civilian, but as a statesman and a soldier. He went there embodying all that was good, if there be any good, in the Democratic party. He had it all with him, and he had clinging to his skirts some of the good things gathered when he trained in the gallant, chivalrous, patriotic, and progressive Republican party. He also had embodied in himself everything good that belonged to the national Greenback party. With all these things emblazoned on his banner, he went into that campaign under apparently favorable circumstances; but, Mr. Chairman, he and his party were damned at the polls by the patriotic people of Ohio because of the conduct of the Forty-sixth Congress in the extra session, in which the Democratic party proclaimed that we had a Government of so little value to the people of this country that it should be starved to death, by withholding appropriations unless the President laid his constitutional powers at the feet of the Democratic party and allowed it to pass into laws the most vicious things ever proposed by a legislative body in any civilized country.

A continuation of this evil and dangerous course here will cause more men to be led to the sacrifice. Their political blood will be on the heads of their own political friends.

We are on the eve of the time when the national political ax will fall.

PATENT EXTENSIONS.

March 26, 1880. Pending consideration of a bill to extend a patent.

Mr. KEIFER said:

I offer an amendment to the bill which I understand is not objected to by the friends of the measure.

The Clerk read as follows:

Add to the bill the following:

And provided further, That no prior assignee or purchaser of an interest, legal or equitable, in said patented invention shall acquire any interest therein by virtue of an extension of said patent under this act.

Mr. KEIFER. A single word, Mr. Speaker. It is rarely proper to extend a patent or to pass a bill authorizing the extension of a patent which has run for the period of seventeen years, as this patent has. It was originally patented in 1863, to date from some period in 1862. I am informed in this case, however, this man claims still to be the owner of that patented interest; that he never parted with it. Yet men are often mistaken; and it turns out after we pass a bill here through grace, and not because of any right, in order to reward some person who has shown great genius in inventing something that is valuable to the general public or something that is useful, it turns out, I say, that assignees who have acquired interest under that patent when the extension has been granted have acquired the entire interest, and the man in whose favor the bill has been passed is a mere name under which the extension has been obtained and under the law has no interest in it whatever.

The records of the Patent Office will show that almost all these patents, where extensions have been granted, do not, at the time, belong to the patentees; and when we have gotten through with the bill in favor of the original inventor we find that we have passed a law simply for the purpose of benefiting those who control monopolies and control patents—persons who are entitled to no grace at our hands at all. I do not concede we do anything on this question as a matter of right; but with this amendment which I have proposed I shall be satisfied with the passage of this bill.

BRADLEY VS. SLEMONS.

March 30, 1880. On this contested election case—

Mr. KEIFER said:

Mr. Speaker, I shall occupy but a few moments in the consideration of this case. It was not my purpose to say a word upon it. With a great deal of reluctance I came to the conclusion that the sitting member, Mr. Slemons, upon the testimony found in the record, was entitled to hold his seat in this House. I came to hat conclusion following the precedents which make the law for the government of this body.

There are many things in and about this case not in the record, and there are some things thrown into the record which excite a very considerable amount of suspicion that the contestee was not entirely free from very bad conduct in the course of the election in his district in 1878. But, Mr. Speaker, one thing is true—and upon that my distinguished friend from Iowa [Mr. WEAVER] will agree with me—that the testimony here which attacks a portion of the majority of the contestee obtained in election is sufficient to overthrow his entire majority.

In all kindness to the gentleman from Iowa, without desiring to detract at all from the glory he may take in attempting to assume here to be the champion of free elections, let me say that in his report he did not find that any such thing had happened as would suffice to overthrow the entire majority returned for the sitting member. The gentleman's very short report is not quite up to his boldness on the floor of the House, for it simply suggests that there may be something in this case tending to show that Mr. Slemons was not elected. In the discharge of our duty here toward a fellow-member, are we called upon on such a finding as that to oust a sitting member? I wish to observe here that I do not deny the right of the House to reject the entire vote of a voting precinct where it is shown that intimidation, fraud, or bribery so far entered into the election as to render it impossible to eliminate it from the honest vote cast. But in such case the unlawful means used in a particular voting place would not vitiate the election held in other voting places in the district.

Mr. Speaker, there is one question which may arise, and doubtless has arisen, in the minds of many gentlemen around me. Suppose it appears by the proof that the sitting member's majority as returned is 2,827 ; suppose it appears that of this majority 2,000 votes were obtained through intimidation, fraud, or other improper means; suppose it appears that these 2,000 votes ought to be struck off of the contestee's majority, because the proof shows that he was guilty of fraud and violence; suppose his majority is thus reduced to about 800. Now, are we upon that sort of finding called upon to say that this gentleman was not elected. Let it be understood that we give to the contestant the benefit of every claim, every shadow of claim, that he submits; yet in the case I put it leaves the contestee with a majority of 800 unattacked. Upon such a case are you prepared to find that the contestee, as a matter of law, was not elected? That would be equivalent to saying that because he claims 2,800 majority and was entitled to claim only 800, therefore he is not elected at all. This is a proposition which the gentleman from Iowa does not meet, and cannot meet. In his report he does not undertake to say that the majority of the contestee was overcome. He does suggest that if the House would find certain things which he does not undertake to say were proved by the evidence, then he is in favor of the resolution which he submits. The gentleman was a member of the sub-committee that examined this case, and if he had been able to point the committee or the House to any evidence showing that the majority of the contestee was overcome by reason of improper conduct on his part or on the part of his political friends, I would have been willing to respond to his appeal to vindicate the purity of the ballot-box. I would not draw fine legal distinctions to save the contestee or any person who might be guilty of polluting the ballot-box. But the gentleman does not make such a case. In his report he utterly fails to do so.

Now let us go one step further. If the case which I put be true—that the contestee has an untainted, unpolluted majority of 800—are we to declare the seat vacant because he has been guilty of intimidation or fraud in the course of that election ?

Mr. HAZELTON. I would like to ask the gentleman how the aggregate number of votes as counted compares with the census or registry of voters?

Mr. KEIFER. I am unable to answer that question; there may be other gentlemen who can answer it.

Mr. CALKINS. There was a very light vote throughout the district.

Mr. KEIFER. Now, Mr. Speaker, I desire to call attention again to this proposition whether it is within the power of the House, properly exercised, to say to a man who has been guilty of fraud in the conduct of his election which did not affect the result of the election, whether it is in the constitutional power of Congress to declare the election was void. I undertake to say, Mr. Speaker, in the hundred years of our constitutional history, you cannot find a case where that position has been taken. I have examined the strongest case pointed out in the history of the country, the case of Abbott vs. Frost, which arose in the State of Massachusetts, on which the committee reported, and the House stood by the report, and held where the charge was one of bribery by one of the parties, and they could purge and purify the ballot-box by throwing out the bribed votes, that it was the duty of the House to do it. We have the more recent case of Platte against Goode, from Virginia, where the minority of the committee reported to the Forty-fourth Congress in favor of the sitting member, and reported that there had been bribery at a certain place, I think in Norfolk, Va., and they held it was their duty to come forward and purge that election of all bribery and count the unbribed votes. A different rule, Mr. Speaker, is claimed to exist in England.

Mr. BAKER. I have some familiarity with the two cases alluded to by the gentleman from Ohio, and I ask him to yield to me for a moment.

Mr. KEIFER. Certainly; but do not make a speech. If you wish to contradict this I will hear it.

Mr. BAKER. The question I wanted to submit was this: Whether, in either of those cases, there was any evidence adduced or any fact found by the committee that connected the sitting member, or the member who was adjudged entitled to the seat, with the fraud which was found to exist in the election; and whether or not the gentleman can point out a case where the party who claimed to be entitled to a seat upon the floor of this House is connected with fraud, you are to carefully tear off the fraud, so far as you can discover it, on the assumption he has done nothing but what you have been able to unearth? The rule is, where a man claims to be entitled to a seat on the floor of the House and has been connected with fraud, he is the man who is to come forward and show that all the votes he claims are fair and honest.

Mr. KEIFER. I have no objection to a question, but I do object to a speech. I take it the gentleman's position would be this, if he means to take any position at all, and I give it as an illustration, and that is in the case the return of a majority for a man was 3,000, and it was shown the man had bribed three voters only, then the burden was upon him to prove he was elected. That is the gentleman's position.

Now take the first case, of Abbott against Frost, where the committee, without deciding whether or not the sitting member had been shown to have been guilty of bribery, but going on to state the law, say that the votes are to be thrown out, not that the sitting member is to be ousted from his seat; not that, but they say that ballots obtained through bribery ought to be disregarded. Then, to quote:

To count them in a general canvass is to place them on the same footing with the votes cast by the honest, free, and independent voter. To seat a member upon majorities obtained through such influences is to defeat the proper object for which the statute was created.

No, Mr. Speaker, the language here is "to seat a member upon majorities obtained through such influences." That leaves out of view the question, where a member does not obtain his majority through such means are we to say we would not seat him? If I understand the proposition of the gentleman from Indiana, it is to the effect that where a man has been guilty of bribery which does not affect the majority, we are to resort to an absurdity and to stultify ourselves by saying still the man was not elected. It is a question of election, Mr. Speaker, we are trying now. We are inquiring as to the fact of election, not the fitness of a member to his seat.

Just one word further. It may occur to gentlemen that there would be some remedy for a case where a man has been guilty of fraud or violence, intimidation, bribery, or whatever else you choose to call it, and through that means does not secure his seat, but through that means taints himself and renders himself impure and unfit to hold a seat on this floor. If a case can be made—and I am not required to find that for the present—if a case is made against the sitting member, and it is shown he was guilty of gross fraud and violence, or of bribery or anything of that kind, the Constitution of the United States has probably pointed out to us our only remedy, and that is by expulsion.

It is said that in England they hold to the rule that where it is found a man has been guilty of bribery in his election to a seat in the House of Commons the election must be declared void, although the bribery did not affect the result, or, in other words, did not produce his majority. I do not think from an examination of parliamentary authorities that will be found to be true even in that country; but if it is, it is a rule which has grown up there where they have no written constitution to guide them in such cases. Then the rule might obtain in that country upon the theory that the man was elected, but still is unworthy to hold a seat, and, therefore, by means of an election contest he should be expelled. What we deal with here is a pure matter of election contest, and it is unfair to the sitting member to treat him as though he were on trial, with a view to his expulsion, when he should be entitled to a trial in a wholly different way for an offense which would justify his expulsion. In such case before he loses his seat here there must be a two-thirds vote against him, as provided in the fifth section, article I of the Constitution of the United States.

I do not find from the testimony in this case that Mr. Slemons has secured a majority of the votes for him by any of the means it is said were resorted to by him and his friends; and I undertake to say that no member of the committee found any such thing. I do undertake to say, though, Mr. Speaker, that the majority of the committee—those that signed the report proper without any qualification—did give to the contestant all that he could claim under his testimony, and then they found that if they did give him all the votes which he claimed he would still be defeated by over 800 majority. It is fair to say for the committee that they did not absolutely reject the testimony that was taken out of rule and out of time under the law. They did not reject that testimony, but they considered it in cutting down the returned majority from 2,800 votes to about 800. For my own part I wish to say that under all the circumstances I was in favor of considering that testimony, and it resulted in the entire testimony being considered by the whole committee, as will appear by looking at page 17 of the report.

Mr. BOWMAN. Will the gentleman permit me to ask him a question? I understand that his argument is based upon this proposition, and I wish to ask whether he is willing to state that this proposition is applicable to all such cases, namely: if there was intimidation and fraud in the election, it must nevertheless be shown affirmatively by competent evidence that enough votes were changed to affect the result.

Mr. KEIFER. Sufficient unto the day is the evil thereof.

Mr. BOWMAN. But I wish to understand the gentleman's proposition. If I have understood his argument it is that no matter if there was intimidation and violence in the election, that unless you can identify the votes cast under intimidation, and unless you prove that the result of the election was changed by these frauds, it must stand as a valid election.

Mr. KEIFER. No, sir; I stated no such proposition. I submitted no general proposition of that kind. I did say that if the proof showed, after giving to the contestant everything he claimed on every hand and every vote he could claim was affected by his testimony, and then it appeared that the sitting member still had an untainted majority outside of that, it was not our duty—nay, our right—to vote the sitting member out of his seat. Now, if you undertake to infer a different proposition from what I have said, and state it as the distinguished gentleman has stated it, then I do not indorse it. I do not claim it is necessary to deal with anything beyond the testimony in this case. If from all the testimony in this case it is clear that the sitting member had an untainted majority, it is not our duty to oust him from his seat. I do regard it as absurd in the highest degree to say that a man has a majority rejecting everything to which he is not entitled, and yet at the same time resolve that that man was not elected. I say that is absurd.

As my colleague [Mr. CAMP] states here on my right, if he has committed that sort of flagrant crime which renders him unfit to hold a seat in this body, then the question may come up on a motion for expulsion under the Constitution of the United States. One gentleman asks if a man is responsible for the deeds of his party—during elections I suppose he means. To a certain extent he is; but if we are trying to see if he is guilty of the crimes which would render him unfit to hold a seat here as a member of this body, then we should have to go still further and prove by clear and satisfactory evidence that he was himself cognizant of the crimes which had been committed by his friends. Otherwise we cannot hold him responsible at all for it.

THE ARMY AT THE POLLS.

April 8, 1880. Pending the Army appropriation bill, the following amendment was read by the Clerk:

SEC. 2. That no money appropriated in this act is appropriated, or shall be paid, for the subsistence, equipment, transportation, or compensation of any portion of the Army of the United States to be used as a police force to keep the peace at the polls at any election held within any State.

The CHAIRMAN. On this amendment the gentleman from Ohio [Mr. KEIFER] raises the point of order.

Mr. KEIFER. Mr. Chairman, I regard this point of order as of very great importance. While I will not occupy many moments in attempting to have the Chair understand the precise questions of order which can or ought to be made against this amendment, in my judgment, I shall have to ask the Chair to indulge me for a little while.

The proposed amendment has just been read. I shall claim under the rule that it is not in order because it, at least for the coming fiscal year, changes existing law. I shall claim also it does not retrench expenditure. I shall claim it was not reported at all, as a matter of fact, and properly considered under our rules, from the Committee on Military Affairs. I shall also claim, assuming I am wrong in that point, that the Committee on Military Affairs have no jurisdiction on the subject-matter of this proposed amendment to the Army appropriation bill.

And now, sir, before I proceed to take these points up and discuss them in detail, in order that I may demonstrate the first point if possible, I ask the Clerk to read section 2002 of the Revised Statutes.

The Clerk read as follows:

SEC. 2002. No military or naval officer, or other person engaged in the civil, military, or naval service of the United States, shall order, bring, keep or have under his authority or control, any troops or armed men at the place where any general or special election is held in any State, unless it be necessary to repel the armed enemies of the United States, or to keep the peace at the polls.

Mr. KEIFER. I ask the Clerk also to read sections 2004 and 2005, to show the present condition of the law.

The Clerk read as follows:

SEC. 2004. All citizens of the United States who are otherwise qualified by law to vote at any election by the people in any State, Territory, district, county, city, parish, township, school district, municipality, or other territorial subdivision, shall be entitled and allowed to vote at all such elections, without distinction of race, color, or previous condition of servitude; any constitution, law, custom, usage, or regulation of any State or Territory, or by or under its authority to the contrary notwithstanding.

SEC. 2005. When, under the authority of the constitution or laws of any State, or the laws of any Territory, any act is required to be done as a prerequisite or qualification for voting, and by such constitution or laws persons or officers are charged with the duty of furnishing to citizens an opportunity to perform such prerequisite, or to become qualified to vote, every such person and officer shall give to all citizens of the United States the same and equal opportunity to perform such prerequisite, and to become qualified to vote.

Mr. KEIFER. Let the Clerk read next sections 5298, 5299, and 5528.

The Clerk read as follows:

SEC. 5298. Whenever, by reason of unlawful obstructions, combinations, or assemblages of persons, or rebellion against the authority of the Government of the United States, it shall become impracticable, in the judgment of the President, to enforce, by the ordinary course of judicial proceedings, the laws of the United States within any State or Territory, it shall be lawful for the President to call forth the militia of any or all the States, and to employ such parts of the land and naval forces of the United States as he may deem necessary to enforce the faithful execution of the laws of the United States, or to suppress such rebellion, in whatever State or Territory thereof the laws of the United States may be forcibly opposed, or the execution thereof forcibly obstructed.

SEC. 5299. Whenever insurrection, domestic violence, unlawful combinations, or conspiracies in any State so obstructs or hinders the execution of the laws thereof, and of the United States, as to deprive any portion or class of the people of such State of any of the rights, privileges, or immunities, or protection, named in the Constitution and secured by the laws for the protection of such rights, privileges, or immunities, and the constituted authorities of such State are unable to protect, or, from any cause, fail in or refuse protection of the people in such rights, such facts shall be deemed a denial by such State of the equal protection of the laws to which they are entitled under the Constitution of the United States; and in all such cases, or whenever any such insurrection, violence, unlawful combination, or conspiracy, opposes or obstructs the laws of the United States, or the due execution thereof, or impedes or obstructs the due course of justice under the same, it shall be lawful for the President, and it shall be his duty, to take such measures, by the employment of the militia or the land and naval forces of the United States, or of either, or by other means, as he may deem necessary, for the suppression of such insurrections, domestic violence, or combinations.

SEC. 5528. Every officer of the Army or Navy, or other person in the civil, military, or naval service of the United States, who orders, brings, keeps, or has under his authority or control, any troops or armed men at any place where a general or special election is held in any State, unless such force be necessary to repel armed enemies of the United States, or to keep the peace at the polls, shall be fined not more than $5,000, and suffer imprisonment at hard labor not less than three months nor more than five years.

Mr. KEIFER. Mr. Chairman, I have caused to be read these sections of the United States statutes which are in force for the purpose of making clear this one point, to wit, that the proposed amendment would change existing law for and during the ensuing fiscal year. I may say, Mr. Chairman, that I am not prepared to concede now that it is within the power of Congress through any sort of legislation to take away from the President of the United States his power under the Constitution to execute the laws of the United States. And, sir, while I state that proposition I doubt further very seriously whether or not by any legislation which we may put upon the statute-books we can take away from the President the power to execute all of the laws of the United States which he is sworn when he enters upon the duties of his office to execute. While I say this I am bound to assume that this proposed amendment is offered for the purpose of annulling that presidential power, or, in other words, changing existing law. Under section 2002 of the Revised Statutes we find that the military, naval, and civil officers of the Government are to be punished if they, in any improper way, interfere with elections; but we also find by the clearest sort of implication that it is regarded under our law eminently right and proper, indeed absolutely lawful, for these military, naval, and civil officers of the Government to keep the peace at the polls under certain conditions. Now, so far as this section can apply at all, it is intended to prohibit the President of the United States from using the military power of this Government to keep the peace at the polls on election days, and to that extent, Mr. Chairman, I hold that it would change existing law.

Mr. TOWNSHEND, of Illinois. I rise to a point of order.

The CHAIRMAN. The gentleman will state it.

Mr. TOWNSHEND, of Illinois. My point of order is that the gentleman is not confining himself to the point made against the amendment, but is making an *ad captandum* speech.

The CHAIRMAN. The gentleman will confine himself to the point of order.

Mr. KEIFER. With all deference to the Chair, I desire to state that I am proceeding to do that, as I understand it, and I trust that I will not be under the censorship of a man who is used to making *ad captandum* speeches, for which purpose he takes wide latitude. I am trying to demonstrate as briefly as I can that this amendment is out of order on the ground that it changes existing law, first, because it takes away from the President of the United States the power to use, when necessary, the military force of the Government to keep the peace at the polls. I might extend it by running over each of the several sections of the statutes which I have caused to be read. But it will be apparent to every person who reads the sections or who has read them and examines this proposed amendment that if it passes all the power expressly given under these several sections to the President of the United States to use the military officers of this Government to execute the laws on certain occasions and to execute the laws of the land where there has been a breach of the peace, or where riot reigns, or where violence is controlling the peaceable action of the people—I say that this amendment is offered here for the purpose of saying to the President he shall not use these officers or any part of the Army for the purpose of preserving the peace. That is the effect of it.

Now, it is true this amendment does not say that the Army shall not be used for the purpose of preserving the peace at the polls or for the purpose of executing the laws of the United States, the duty of executing which is intrusted to the President of the United States under certain circumstances, but it does say that no money appropriated in this act, referring to the appropriation bill which is supposed to contain all appropriations for the Army—that no money in this act is appropriated or shall be paid for the subsistence; that is, to feed the soldiers—for the equipment or transportation or the compensation of any portion of the Army of the United States to be used as a police force to keep the peace at the polls at any election held within any State. This amendment, if adopted, would amount to an absolute inhibition on the President in the use of the Army for any of the purposes contemplated under the existing laws to which I have referred.

Mr. FRYE. Will the gentleman allow me to interrupt him a moment?

Mr. KEIFER. Certainly.

Mr. FRYE. I wish to state that the gentleman has inadvertently said that if this amendment is enacted into a law it would take away from the President the power to use the troops for the purposes which he has enumerated. I say the gentleman has inadvertently made this statement. I do not understand he means that. But I understand from a former statement that he means to say it is an attempt to take away this power. I hope no Republican, at all events, will admit, even if this amendment does becomes a law, that it will take away from the President that power.

Mr. McMILLIN. If the proposed amendment does not change existing law, then why does the gentleman make the point of order against it?

Mr. KEIFER. I cannot qualify every portion of my remarks. I opened by saying that I did not concede that Congress had the right to take away from the President the power to execute the laws of the United States, but I was bound here to treat the proposed amendment as if that was its scope and design——

Mr. TOWNSHEND, of Illinois. I rise to a point of order. It is evident that the gentleman from Ohio has prepared an elaborate speech upon this amendment——

Mr. KEIFER. The gentleman is very much mistaken.

Mr. TOWNSHEND, of Illinois. And I make the point of order that he must confine himself to the point made against the proposed amendment, and not enter into a discussion of the merits of the amendment itself.

Mr. KEIFER. I do not expect to convert the gentleman.

Mr. TOWNSHEND, of Illinois. If the gentleman has any desire to print his speech on this amendment I have no objection to that, but I make the point of order that he cannot debate the merits of the amendment on the point made against it.

The CHAIRMAN. The Chair has already admonished the gentleman from Ohio to confine his remarks to the point of order. There is a limitation on the debate as to points of order.

Mr. FRYE. The gentleman from Ohio has not in the slightest degree transgressed that limitation.

The CHAIRMAN. The gentleman from Ohio will proceed in order.

Mr. TOWNSHEND, of Illinois. I ask the Chair to decide whether the gentleman from Ohio is confining himself to the point of order.

Mr. KEIFER. I will be obliged to the gentleman from Illinois if he will not listen to my argument to keep still.

Mr. TOWNSHEND, of Illinois, rose.

The CHAIRMAN. This is a matter for the Chair to decide. It is sometimes very hard to prescribe the precise limits to be observed in an argument of this nature. The gentleman from Ohio will proceed in order.

Mr. KEIFER. I have, Mr. Chairman, concluded for the present and perhaps for all time all I desire to say on the first proposition. I desired to make it clear to the House that this amendment was designed to take from the President all his power in the coming fiscal year to use the troops at the polls to keep the peace. It will hardly be claimed on the other side that the President could use the troops at the polls to keep the peace when he was forbidden by this proposed new section to feed them while there; forbidden to equip them while there; forbidden to transport them there; forbidden to pay them there while they were engaged in this duty, so that it amounts to an absolute prohibition against his right to use them during the coming fiscal year at all to keep the peace at the polls.

When we come to the merits of the proposition, if we should be so unfortunate as ever to do so, then I may perhaps have something further to say. I now submit that the amendment is not in order under paragraph 3 of Rule XXI, a part of which I desire now to read. Perhaps I might as well read it all:

3. No appropriation shall be reported in any general appropriation bill, or be in order as an amendment thereto, for any expenditure not previously authorized by law unless in continuation of appropriations for such public works and objects as are already in progress. Nor shall any provision in any such bill or amendment thereto changing existing law be in order, except such as, being germane to the subject-matter of the bill, shall retrench expenditures by the reduction of the number and salary of the officers of the United States, by the reduction of the compensation of any person paid out of the Treasury of the United States, or by the reduction of amounts of money covered by the bill: *Provided*, That it shall be in order further to amend such bill upon the report of the committee having jurisdiction of the subject-matter of such amendment, which amendment, being germane to the subject-matter of the bill, shall retrench expenditures.

It already appears the amendment will change existing law. It is clear that the proposed amendment does not retrench expenditures. All the money, Mr. Chairman—and I beg your careful attention to this—all the money appropriated by this bill will be appropriated and expended whether the amendment becomes a part of the bill or not. If that proposition is disputed I should be very glad to yield to some gentleman who would be able to enlighten me or the Chair on that subject. The amendment does not propose in any feature of it to cut down the expenditures of the Government. It leaves the appropriation complete in every respect. It leaves the money to be expended, every dime of it, all the same whether this second section is added to the bill or not. So that we may say with perfect safety that the amendment does not, and will not, if it should become part of the law retrench expenditures.

The amendment applies to the proposed appropriation for the Army for the fiscal year ending June 30, 1881. The whole sum, I repeat, appropriated by the bill if it becomes a law will be expended even though the amendment should become a part of it. The proposed new section does not reduce " the number and salary of the officers of the United States;" nor does it reduce "the compensation of any person paid out of the Treasury of the United States;" nor does it reduce " the amounts of money covered by the bill." This is necessary under the rule before the amendment could be in order.

Nor is the amendment in order under the proviso of the third paragraph of the rule just read. I call attention specially again to that in order that the Chair may have it fresh in his mind:

Provided, That it shall be in order further to amend such bill upon the report of the committee having jurisdiction of the subject matter of such amendment; which amendment, being germane to the subject-matter of the bill, shall retrench expenditures.

Having already shown that the amendment will not retrench expenditures if ruled in order, and if as a part of this bill it is enacted into law, it is scarcely necessary for me to pursue the subject much further. Under this proviso just read, though an amendment may be reported from a committee having jurisdiction of the subject-matter of the amendment, still it will not be in order unless it shall retrench expenditures.

Then, if I am right, Mr. Chairman, in the proposition that this amendment does not retrench expenditures, it is quite immaterial whether or not this amendment was reported from the Committee on Military Affairs or not; but I further insist, Mr. Chairman, that the amendment within the true meaning of the rule was never reported from the Committee on Military Affairs. The rule requires the amendment before it is in order to be "upon the report"—for that is the word—"the report of the committee having jurisdiction," &c. Mr. Chairman, no report has been made from that committee. I wait for a reply from the gentleman who offers this amendment, if he desires to state whether or not there has ever been a report made from the Committee on Military Affairs on this subject.

Mr. HASKELL. I desire to call the attention of the gentleman from Ohio to the fact that every report to this House from any committee must be in writing under the rules.

Mr. KEIFER. I think the gentleman from Kansas [Mr. HASKELL] is right in his suggestion. I wish to say, Mr. Chairman, I listened with care——

Mr. SPARKS rose.

Mr. KEIFER. I will hear the gentleman from Illinois in a moment. I listened with care to learn—for I wanted to be accurate in any statement I might make—I listened to learn whether or not the gentleman from Illinois came here clothed with the power to make a report from the Committee on Military Affairs, and I learned no such thing. I now yield to him to make any statement he desires, even stronger than he made on yesterday.

Mr. SPARKS. Are you through; or do you just want me to answer a question?

Mr. KEIFER. I am not through.

Mr. SPARKS. I presume the gentleman certainly understood me to report this proposition from the Committee on Military Affairs. I certainly was explicitly instructed by that committee to do so.

Now, the point the gentleman seems to be making—I presume he alludes to that—is whether or not any proposition was sent by this House to that committee, and the committee acted upon any proposition pending before it having come from the House, to wit, a bill to that effect. I state to the gentleman that I do not remember whether there was any such proposition sent to the committee or not by the House. I will assume that there is not any. I will take it that such is the fact; at least that is my understanding. The Committee on Military Affairs considered this subject, and instructed me to report this proposition as an amendment to the Army appropriation bill. I presume that answers the gentleman. Does it?

Mr. FRYE. With the leave of the gentleman from Ohio [Mr. KEIFER] I will ask the gentleman from Illinois [Mr. SPARKS] a question.

Mr. KEIFER. Certainly.

Mr. SPARKS. I will answer it if I can.

Mr. FRYE. Was the subject-matter of this amendment ever referred by the House to the Committee on Military Affairs?

Mr. SPARKS. I have answered that by stating that to my knowledge it was not. I have not sent to the committee-room to ascertain; but I do not know that any such proposition was ever referred to the committee by the House.

Mr. FRYE. Does the gentleman know of any way in which the Committee on Military Affairs could get jurisdiction of a subject which has not been committed to it by the House?

Mr. SPARKS. I will answer that under the rules of the House it could do so by its own volition. If there is any point in that, make it. I will take it for granted that no bill or resolution upon this subject has been offered in the House and referred to that committee. I do not know that to be the fact, but I am willing to assume that to be the fact; I believe that to be so. I could learn, as a matter of course, by sending to my committee-room.

Mr. KEIFER. One thing at least is made clear, if not everything that I have spoken about: that is, that the gentleman never was authorized to make and in fact never did make a *report* to this House on the subject-matter of this proposed amendment.

Mr. SPARKS. How do I understand the gentleman?

Mr. KEIFER. I will try to state it as plainly as I can. The gentleman himself says that he never in fact and under the rules made any report to this House on the subject-matter of this proposed amendment.

Mr. SPARKS. I beg the gentleman's pardon; he entirely misunderstands me.

Mr. KEIFER. I put my own construction on the gentleman's language.

Mr. SPARKS. The gentleman certainly will allow me to put him right. He does not want to misrepresent me, does he?

Mr. KEIFER. No.

Mr. SPARKS. I will state the fact that the Committee on Military Affairs especially and positively instructed me to report this proposition to the House, and move it as an amendment to this appropriation bill. This identical amendment was acted upon by the committee, and I am instructed to move it as an amendment to this bill.

Mr. KEIFER. The gentleman has repeated that two or three times; but he never undertakes to tell us where his report is, when he made it, under what rule he made it to the Committee of the Whole, or in what morning hour he made it to the House. He leaves it perfectly clear, as I said before, that he never has made such a report.

Mr. GARFIELD. Has the gentleman a copy of that report ?

Mr. KEIFER. I would be glad to have it read. The gentleman stated yesterday what he has stated to-day. I will read his language :

Mr SPARKS. By instruction of the Committee on Military Affairs I offer as an additional section that which I send to the Clerk's desk.

That is, he was instructed by that committee, perhaps by only a majority of the members of the committee, to propose an amendment here to the Army appropriation bill. But that committee never authorized him to make a report to the House in favor of such an amendment, and the gentleman will not say so, for he never did in fact make such a report.

Mr. SPARKS. The gentleman is technical, I think. What I stated is critically correct.

Mr. KEIFER. Well, if it is "critically correct," I am satisfied with it if the gentleman is.

Mr. SPARKS. That is so.

Mr KEIFER. That is, in some sort of way, formally or informally, he got the consent of a majority of the members of the Committee on Military Affairs to come in here and offer an amendment to the Army appropriation bill, not to make a report to enlighten this House, not to make a report that would give us the reason for tacking such an important amendment on an appropriation bill. The gentleman still insists that what he stated on yesterday is exactly right.

Now, the second point I make here in this connection is this: I deny that this amendment comes from a committee having jurisdiction of the subject-matter of the proposed amendment. That is a part of the requirements of the proviso of the third paragraph of Rule XXI. I repeat that the committee did not have jurisdiction of the subject-matter of this proposed amendment.

Pray tell me how it acquired such jurisdiction. I am authorized to state that no bill of this character was ever referred by the House to the Committee on Military Affairs; that no measure of this character was ever referred to that committee. In the very nature of things, none could have been so referred. You could not refer a bill of this character to that committee, a bill that was intended to limit the use of money in an appropriation bill; that could not well have got before the Committee on Military Affairs.

Now, Mr. Chairman, this section analyzed amounts to nothing more than a direction as to how money appropriated in this Army appropriation bill shall be used. It has no connection with military affairs at all in that sense. But in other views it is perfectly clear that this committee could not have had jurisdiction of the subject-matter of it, and that the House, obeying its own rules, would never have dreamed of referring such an amendment to that committee. The subject-matter did not belong there. In what way did the committee get jurisdiction of regulating, not military affairs, but the powers of this nation in his constitutional duty to execute the laws of the United States? I might stop here and read the last paragraph of section 3, article 2, of the Constitution of the United States, which defines the powers that will be affected by the adoption of this amendment at least for the coming year. I call attention to this, in order that members generally as well as the Chair may bear it in mind. In speaking of the powers of the President the Constitution declares:

He shall take care that the laws be faithfully executed, and shall commission all the officers of the United States.

His oath of office requires him to faithfully execute the laws.

Here is an attempt by an amendment to take from the President his constitutional power to execute the laws. This committee had not jurisdiction of a subject-matter of that kind. When and in what manner was the subject-matter of this amendment referred ? I have made that point perfectly clear already. Under the new rules the subject matter of the amendment could not have been referred, as I have stated, to the Committee on Military Affairs. I read from Rule XI:

All proposed legislation shall be referred to the committees named in the preceding rule as follows, namely: Subjects relating—

10. To the military establishment and the public defense, other than the appropriations for its support; to the Committee on Military Affairs.

It is thus made clear under the rule that this committee had not jurisdiction of the subject-matter of this amendment, and the terms of the rule suggest an express exception of such a measure, because this amendment refers to the mode of applying money already appropriated.

In conclusion, I wish to say that the amendment if adopted——

Mr. McLANE. Will the gentleman from Ohio allow me a moment?

Mr. KEIFER. Certainly.

Mr. McLANE. I ask pardon of my friend from Illinois [Mr. SPARKS] for offering what I conceive to be a conclusive answer to the question addressed by the gentleman from Ohio to the gentleman from Illinois. I understood the gentleman from Ohio to inquire whether the gentleman from Illinois had moved this amendment as a report from a committee. The reply of the gentleman from Illinois was to call attention to the amendment. It is urged that this amendment is no report from a committee in the sense of the rules. The rules require a written report to accompany any bill, resolution, or petition reported by a committee. But the gentleman from Illinois introduced no bill, resolution, or petition. He did what he was authorized to do by the twenty-first rule, which has no relation at all to the rule requiring a report in writing to accompany a bill, resolution, or petition reported from a committee. The new rules of the House, it is true, require that a committee reporting a bill, resolution, or petition shall accompany it with a report in writing; but that requirement of the rules has no reference to an amendment which the twenty-first rule expressly authorizes a committee to move to an appropriation bill. There are two distinct rules—one requiring a report in writing to accompany a bill——

Mr. SPARKS. I would understand that technically any action of a committee——

Mr. KEIFER. I yielded to the gentleman from Maryland for a suggestion only.

Mr. McLANE. I am addressing myself to the gentleman from Ohio.

Mr. SPARKS. But right here I would like to interject the remark, of course with the leave of the gentleman from Ohio——

The CHAIRMAN. The Chair desires to say to the gentleman from Ohio that he had ten minutes to explain his point of order, and he has taken forty. The Chair has not, however, interrupted him, but he desires to say that on a point of order in Committee of the Whole there should be a limitation upon discussion, and the limit, in the opinion of the Chair, ought to be five minutes.

Mr. CONGER. Not by any rule.

The CHAIRMAN. The Chair has a discretion on the subject. He has allowed the gentleman to speak forty minutes instead of ten. He will proceed.

Mr. SPARKS. I hope the gentleman from Ohio will get through very soon.

Mr. McLANE. My inquiry of the gentleman from Ohio is whether he recognizes the distinction I have pointed out.

Mr. SPARKS. I will attend to that matter. Let the gentleman from Ohio finish.

Mr. KEIFER. I am unable to understand the meaning of language if the twenty-first rule does not require a report. I read again:

Provided, That it shall be in order further to amend such bill upon the report of the committee having jurisdiction of the subject-matter of such amendment.

That means a report because it says so. I cannot dwell longer on that, and will conclude.

Now, Mr. Chairman, I beg your attention further to this: that the amendment if adopted would have the effect to regulate the subject-matter of elections as well as the matter of the Presidential power to enforce the laws and put down violence and disorder. Section 2002, already read, which is specially aimed at, is part of the criminal and not a part of the military laws of the United States. It is the section making improper interference on the part of military, naval, or civil officers of the United States in elections a crime. It is the section of the United States statutes which recognizes the right of the President, Commander-in-Chief of the Army of the United States, to keep the peace at the polls when there is a breach of it. This section is found in the statutes under the title "*The elective franchise.*" It is the first section under that title in the Revised Statutes. I submit this amendment refers more to the manner of regulating elections, more to the manner of amending in some form or other, peculiar as it may be, the criminal statutes of the United States. It refers also to the manner of using appropriated money. It does not retrench expenditure. It could not come from the Committee on Military Affairs, because that committee has no jurisdiction over it. Indeed, in every possible view, it must, or at least ought to be, ruled out of order.

I need not say a word, Mr. Chairman, on the subject of the great impropriety and the very bad policy of this character of legislation.

(The point of order was overruled.)

EXECUTIVE POWER TO USE THE ARMY. &c.

April 10, 1880. The House having resolved itself into Committee of the Whole on the state of the Union, and having under consideration the bill (H. R. No. 5529) making appropriations for the support of the Army for the fiscal year ending June 30, 1881, and for other purposes—

Mr. KEIFER said :

Mr. CHAIRMAN : This Congress will be known in future history as the one in which it was proposed by the party in power to destroy the Government unless the minority of this House and the President of the United States would allow laws to be passed legalizing in effect fraud, violence, and crime ; and it will be known as the first Congress in the history of this country in which it was proposed in both branches to annul all the President's power to execute the laws of the United States authorizing the preservation of peace and order at the polls on election day.

In the course of the discussion of this question I propose very briefly to review the history of legislation in this Congress,

First, I may say that the Forty-fifth Congress adjourned without having performed its constitutional duty by appropriating the money necessary to carry on the legislative, executive, and judicial departments of the Government, and also without providing for the pay of the Army. The Democratic party then embarked upon the policy of coercing the minority of the House of Representatives and a Republican Senate and the President in the matter of important legislation. How far has it succeeded ? The first bill of this Congress proposed to appropriate for the Army, only on condition that a section in it should be allowed to become a law making it a high crime to keep the peace at the polls on election day. That section was notice to the country that the Democratic party, in the future as in the past, proposed, when necessary to accomplish its ends, to have riots and other breaches of the peace on election days at the polls. This legislation was shipwrecked by the veto of the President.

The second bill brought forward was designed to disarm the Executive and paralyze his power to enforce all laws of the United States even to the suppression of rebellion except on the motion first taken of the State authorities. This also signally failed. The third bill proposed to appropriate for the legislative, executive, and judicial branches of the Government, only on condition of the repeal of all United States election laws which secured the constitutional right through supervisors of elections, special deputy marshals, &c., to have free, and honest elections of members of Congress. This bill also was notice to the country that open fraud by means of violence, intimidation, repeating, tissue ballots, and other unlawful measures would be in the future as in the past the pernicious policy of the Democratic party. It met at the hands of the Executive the fate of the other two bills.

These misfortunes, Mr. Chairman, notwithstanding the defiant boasts of certain Democratic members, led the Democratic party to "dally" and "doubt" in the face of the authoritative statement [by Mr BLACKBURN] that "he who dallies is a dastard, and he who doubts is damned." Other direful threats came to us that certain members of the Democratic party would stand by the revolutionary policy entered on "until the marble of this Capitol crumbled into dust by the never-failing action of time." But, Mr. Chairman, time, aided by the firm stand of the Republican party here in Congress, and the vetoes of the President, acted with singular rapidity on the minds of Democrats and on their unwise policy here.

It is said that when disease seizes on the human body, it develops first in the weaker parts. Through the purse of Democrats the weakness in the first place cropped out. The remedy was applied. An old-fashioned appropriation bill, shorn of all extraneous matter or political legislation, was at the extra session promptly prepared one on which all parties struck hands, although it was an anomaly in form, omitting the usual appropriations for the judicial branch of the Government. It was hastily pushed through without a rider, and it received the Executive approval.

The pay of members for the fiscal year ending June 30, 1880, being made certain, the old policy of coercion of the Executive was promptly returned to ; a new Army appropriation bill was brought forward from the Democratic caucus which contained a section restricting the right to use any of the money appropriated to clothe, equip, or transport any portion of the Army to be used as a police force to keep the peace at the polls at any election. We have the same amendment now before us ; and I ask the Clerk to read it.

The Clerk read as follows:

SEC. 2. That no money appropriated in this act is appropriated or shall be paid for the subsistence, equipment, transportation or compensation of any portion of the Army of the United States to be used as a police force to keep the peace at the polls at any election held within any State

Mr. KEIFER. Mr. Chairman, this proposed amendment would, in my opinion, if literally carried out, have the effect to annul the appropriation for the Army to the extent that no part of it could be used to keep the peace at the polls. To use troops in aid of the civil power, all authorities concur in holding, is to use them as a police force. While troops of the United States are being so used, they may possibly be said to be used as an army, but they are none the less used as a police force. Ths very language, Mr. Chairman, of the proposed amendment indicates that the soldiere are not to be transformed into policemen, but that they are simply prohibited from being used as a police force in keeping the peace.

One of the early struggles in the history of this Government was during the administration of President Washington, about the right to maintain a navy; and also as to how that navy was to be used. Alexander Hamilton, who was the leader of the Federalists, maintained that it was the right and the duty of the Government to establish a strong navy; and, to use his own language, he said that "it ought to be established and maintained to be used on the high seas as a police force to protect our flag and our commerce." He did not mean that the seamen were to be turned into policemen, but that our ships, properly manned, should patrol the seas "as a police force," and there maintain the majesty of our Government, &c. That great controversy, which lasted for years, between Alexander Hamilton and the great Secretary of the Treasury, Albert Gallatin, the leader of the then Republican party, resulted in the question being settled (and since maintained) in favor of the United States having a Navy to be used on the high seas as a police force. In this amendment is found the precise language used in that controversy; it speaks of using the Army of the United States as a police force to keep the peace at the polls. But I will not dwell further on that point:

Let us analyze this amendment. I may say, Mr. Chairman, that it is exactly the sixth section of the Army appropriation bill which was passed at the extra session of this Congress, against which my friend here [Mr. WILLIAMS, of Wisconsin] and a few others with myself voted. A fair construction of this proposition drives us to the conclusion that it inhibits the use of the Army at the polls to keep the peace and quell election riots, and that it is purposely gotten up to prevent a quiet and an honest election. By the very terms of the amendment the President of the United States, if he feels bound by it if enacted into a law, and I think it is our duty to oppose it as though it was binding on him, although it might be regarded by him as a nullity, would not have for the ensuing fiscal year the right to use the Army in the discharge of his constitutional duty in enforcing all the laws. I maintain, if we enact this amendment into law it will have the moral force at least of saying that the Army of the United States shall not be used to put down riots on election day.

But let us analyze it a little further. Before troops could be used at the polls on election day they must be stripped of their Union blue. They are not to be clothed if they go to the polls when an election is being held during the coming fiscal year; they are to have no equipments; they are to have no subsistence; they are to have no ammunition or arms; in other words, they are to go naked and hungry and without arms to put down a riot if there be one at the polls on election day. That is what we propose to say if we adopt this amendment. I understand some gentlemen contend this does not prohibit the use of troops at the polls on election day, because it does not expressly repeal any law. I simply answer such persons by saying it prohibits their use at least to the extent that, if they are used, they are to go to the polls unclothed and unarmed by the Government of the United States, and they are not to eat at the Government expense while there, and while they perform that most important duty they are to be docked their pay.

It is claimed they are only prohibited from acting "as a police force." I repeat they cannot act in aid of the civil authorities at all unless they act as a police force. Some gentlemen claim that because men are soldiers they cannot act as a police force. The very terms of the amendment provide, not that they shall be changed from soldiers to police, but as soldiers they shall not act as police to keep the peace at the polls on election day.

Passing from that, this amendment, Mr. Chairman, has the merit of conveying to the country by irresistible implication the willingness to allow the President of the United States to use the Army of the United States "as a police force to keep the peace" at all other places within the States and Territories—at all other times and places save at such times and places when and where an election is being held for Delegates and Representatives in Congress.

Nothing short of free fraud, free riot, and free crimes at elections is to be regarded as constitutional, according to Democratic notions of constitutional law! Now, I do not propose to be misunderstood on this question. I have heard on both sides of this House the claim made that it was wrong to use the troops of the United States at the polls to regulate elections. I have heard gentlemen on both sides talk about this character of legislation as though it was intended to prevent interference in elections. On another occasion when I was permitted to have only about two minutes' time, I undertook to draw a distinction, which I beg leave to refer to again in this connection. I am opposed to the use of troops at the polls on election day to in any way interfere with the election officers or with the voters in the rightful exercise of their constitutional privilege.

But, Mr. Chairman, I am in favor of the use of troops at the polls, or the use of any other force under the command of the Government, to interfere with the bad men who arm themselves and go to the polls to get up riots and interfere with the election officers in the honest discharge of their duties and to interfere with the right of the citizen to cast his vote. That is the extent to which I would go in the use of physical force at the polls. What this legislation is aimed at is not to protect the voters or election officers on the day of election from being interfered with by the United States Army, but it is to prevent Ku-klux bands, White-liners, and armed bands of whatever name, who propose to interfere with elections, from being interfered with by the Army when they are too powerful to be controlled by the civil authorities. The men who engage in fraud, in intimidation, in high crimes, and in the work of driving the honest voter from the polls, are the only ones to be shielded by the proposed law. Such is its avowed purpose. A Republican Congress long since put upon the statute-books a law making it a crime for military, naval, or civil officers of the Government to in any manner by the use of troops interfere with elections. (Revised Statutes, sections 2002 and 5528.) The Democratic party now desire to make it a crime for those officers to interfere with those who do interfere with elections. I contend that the Government should execute its laws on the subject of elections and that it should have ample power to enable it to execute them. We ought no longer to hear doubts expressed about the constitutionality of laws designed to enable the United States authorities to preserve the national authority at elections. A recent decision of the Supreme Court of the United States has authoritatively settled this constitutional question of governmental power in that regard.

I hope the House will pardon me while I read an extract from the syllabi in the case of *Ex parte Seibold et al.*

I read:

The National Government has the right to use physical force in any part of the United States to compel obedience to its laws and to carry into execution the powers conferred upon it by the Constitution.

The concurrent jurisdiction of the National Government with that of the States, which it has in the exercise of its powers of sovereignty in every part of the United States, is distinct from that exclusive jurisdiction which it has by the Constitution in the District of Columbia, and in those places acquired for the erection of forts, magazines, arsenals, &c.

The provisions adopted for compelling the State officers of election to observe the State laws regulating elections of Representatives, not altered by Congress, are within the supervisory powers of Congress over such elections. The duties to be performed in this behalf are owed to the United States as well as to the State; and their violation is an offense against the United States which Congress may rightfully inhibit and punish. This necessarily follows from the direct interest which the National Government has in the due election of its Representatives and from the power which the Constitution gives to Congress over this particular subject.

The right to use physical force in any part of the United States to compel obedience to the laws is thus authoritatively settled. This right must now be regarded as the fixed law of the land.

From the exhaustive opinion of Justice Bradley, who spoke for the court, I read further:

The more general reason assigned, to wit, that the nature of sovereignty is such as to preclude the joint cooperation of two sovereigns, even in a matter in which they are mutually concerned, is not, in our judgment, of sufficient force to prevent concurrent and harmonious action on the part of the National and State Governments in the election of Representatives. It is at most an argument *ab inconvenienti.* There is nothing in the Constitution to forbid such cooperation in this case. On the contrary, as already said, we think it clear that the clause of the Constitution relating to the regulation of such elections contemplates such cooperation whenever Congress deems it expedient to interfere merely to alter or add to existing regulations of the State. If the two Governments had an entire equality of jurisdiction, there might be an intrinsic difficulty in such cooperation. Then the adoption by the State government of a system of regulations might exclude the action of Congress. By first taking jurisdiction of the subject, the State would acquire exclusive jurisdiction in virtue of a well known principle applicable to courts having coordinate jurisdiction over the same matter. But no such equality exists in the present case. The power of Congress, as we have seen, is paramount and may be exercised at any time, and to any extent which it deems expedient; and so far as it is exercised, and no further, the regulations effected supersede those of the State which are inconsistent therewith.

As a general rule it is no doubt expedient and wise that the operations of the State and National Governments should, as far as practicable, be conducted separately in order to avoid undue jealousies and jars and conflicts of jurisdiction and power. But there is no reason for laying this down as a rule of universal application. It should never be made to override the plain and manifest dictates of the Constitution itself. We cannot yield to such a transcendental view of State sovereignty. The Constitution and laws of the United States are the supreme law of the land and to these every citizen of every State owes obedience whether in his individual or official capacity.

And quoting further from this opinion:

In exercising the power, however, we are bound to presume that Congress has done so in a judicious manner; that it has endeavored to guard as far as possible against any unnecessary interference with State laws and regulations, with the duties of State officers, or with local prejudices. It could not act at all so as to accomplish any beneficial object in preventing frauds and violence and securing a faithful performance of duty at the elections, without providing for the presence of officers and agents to carry its regulations into effect. It is also difficult to see how it could attain these objects without imposing proper sanctions and penalties against offenders.

And in another place Justice Bradley, in the opinion, says:

Without the concurrent sovereignty referred to, the National Government would be nothing but an advisory government. Its executive power would be absolutely nullified.

In speaking of the fair and obvious interpretation of the Constitution and the mode of reaching it, the judge says:

We shall not have far to seek. We shall find it on the surface, and not in the profound depths of speculation.

The greatest difficulty in coming to a just conclusion arises from mistaken notions with regard to the relations which subsist between the State and National Governments. It seem to be often overlooked that a national Constitution has been adopted in this country, establishing a real Government therein, operating upon persons, and territory, and things; and which moreover is, or should be, as dear to every American citizen as his State government is. Whenever the true conception of the nature of this government is once conceded, no real difficulty will arise in the just interpretation of its powers. But if we allow ourselves to regard it as a hostile organization, opposed to the proper sovereignty and dignity of the State governments, we shall continue to be vexed with difficulties as to its jurisdiction and authority. No greater jealousy is required to be exercised toward this Government in reference to the preservation of our liberties than is proper to be exercised toward the State governments. Its powers are limited in number and clearly defined, and its action within the scope of those powers is restrained by a sufficiently rigid bill of rights for the protection of its citizens from oppression. The true interest of the people of this country requires that both the National and State Governments should be allowed, without jealous interference on either side, to exercise all the powers which respectively belong to them according to a fair and practical construction of the Constitution. State rights and the rights of the United States should be equally respected. Both are essential to the preservation of our liberties and the perpetuity of our institutions. But in endeavoring to vindicate the one, we should not allow our zeal to nullify or impair the other.

I am tempted to read another extract from this most admirable exposition of the constitutional powers of this Government:

It is argued that the preservation of peace and good order in society is not within the powers confided to the Government of the United States, but belongs exclusively to the States. Here, again, we are met with the theory that the Government of the United States does not rest upon the soil and territory of the country. We think that this theory is founded on an entire misconception of the nature and powers of that Government. We hold it to be an incontrovertible principle that the Government of the United States may, by means of physical force exercised through its official agents, execute on every foot of American soil the powers and functions that belong to it. This necessarily involves the power to command obedience to its laws, and hence the power to keep the peace to that extent.

This power to enforce its laws and to execute its functions in all places does not derogate from the power of the State to execute its laws at the same time and in the same places. The one does not exclude the other except where both cannot be executed at the same time. In that case the words of the Constitution itself shows which is to yield. "This Constitution and all laws which shall be made in pursuance thereof * * * shall be the supreme law of the land."

And still another:

Why do we have marshals at all if they cannot physically lay their hands on persons and things in the performance of their proper duties? What functions can they perform if they cannot use force? In executing the process of the courts must they call on the nearest constable for protection? must they rely on him to use the requisite compulsion and to keep the peace while they are soliciting and entreating the parties and by-standers to allow the law to take its course? This is the necessary consequence of the positions that are assumed. If we indulge in such impracticable views as these, and keep on refining and re-refining, we shall drive the National Government out of the United States, and relegate it to the District of Columbia, or perhaps to some foreign soil. We shall bring it back to a condition of greater helplessness than that of the old confederation.

The argument is based on a strained and impracticable view of the nature and powers of the National Government. It must execute its powers or it is no Government. It must execute them on the land as well as on the sea, on things as well as on persons. And to do this, it must necessarily have power to command obedience, preserve order, and keep the peace; and no person or power in this land has the right to resist or question its authority so long as it keeps within the bounds of its jurisdiction. Without specifying other instances in which this power to preserve order and keep the peace unquestionably exists, take the very case in hand.

There are other extracts which might be read to the same effect, but I will not stop to read them now.

The power to keep the peace at elections is here expressly recognized, and it is a necessary power; otherwise the foundations of our Republic would crumble away. A Government without power to protect all of its people from lawlessness and violence at all times and places is unworthy to exist, and of all other times and places it should have and exercise the power of preserving the peace on election day at the polls.

On the necessity of this Government having ample power and the right to exercise it in all fundamental matters which concern its life, I read a single extract further from Justice Bradley's opinion:

The true doctrine, as we conceive, is this, that while the States are really sovereign as to all matters which have not been granted to the jurisdiction and control of the United States, the Constitution and constitutional laws of the latter are, as we have already said, the supreme law of the land; and when they conflict with the laws of the States they are of paramount authority and obligation. This is the fundamental principle on which the authority of the Constitution is based, and unless it be conceded in practice, as well as theory, the fabric of our institutions, as it was contemplated by its founders, cannot stand. The questions involved have respect not more to the autonomy and existence of the States, than to the continued existence of the United States as a Government to which every American citizen may look for security and protection in every part of the land.

Mr. Chairman, I believe in State sovereignty in purely State matters. But I believe in United States sovereignty in all United States matters. I believe States to be creatures of the Constitution, and in all matters not reserved by the Constitution to the States they are subordinate to the United States. Some of these States the United States bought and paid for with both treasure and blood. We bought from the first Napoleon the territory comprised in the States of Louisiana, Arkansas, &c., and in due time we erected this once French territory into States. Later some of these States set up for themselves the pretense that the thing created was superior to their owner and creator. The Republic of Texas, not quite able to stand alone, knocked at the door of the United States, and it was admitted within the portals of the Union and habilitated with the garb of a State in the Union with a Republican form of government; and in a few years she, too, proposed to turn the United States out and set up a new government on the same mistaken notion that the created was superior to the creator.

Time, shot, shell, bullets, bayonets, powder, and spilled blood, in short, war, proved this a mistaken notion to eleven States in this Union that went into rebellion.

It should now be clear to the blindest of partisans, at least, that we have a nation. By stealth, or if I should not say that, under false colors, it is proposed fifteen years after the close of the war to accomplish by peaceable methods what the inexorable events of war failed to do. It is a marvelous and yet dangerous spectacle for the people of a great nation to look on and see a party which arrogates to itself the championship of liberty, struggling for the right to maintain violence and disorder on election days at the polls. If there is to be no disorder or no broken peace, what is the necessity of tying the hands of the General Government so that it cannot keep the peace or quell disorders at elections? The whole country is bound to judge the Democratic party for the future by its acts of preparation as well as its past deeds. The proposed action to-day is notice to the order-loving people of this country, North and South, that in the coming elections of members of the next Congress, and also in the election of the next President of the United States, it is essential to Democratic success that no force possessed of the requisite power shall be used to prevent the use of such violence as may be needed to secure Democratic success against the will of the people when fairly and peaceably expressed. There will be no mistake made by the people in this matter. The Republican party, a party of law and order, of course cannot fear the use of troops at the polls to keep the peace. The law is not a terror to those who do not expect to violate it. There would seem to be no necessity for struggling here from day to day and from month to month as we have been doing in this Congress to get an inhibition against the power of the Government to put down riots and disorder, if there were not a party somewhere in this Government that was in favor of organized riots and broken peace, especially on election day.

A little further review, Mr. Chairman, of the revolutionary legislation had and proposed may be valuable. I need hardly offer an excuse for reviewing the past. I think it throws light on the present. We find here that party that started off so defiantly in the latter days of February and the first days of March, 1879, claiming that this Government should not live, should not have the necessary sustenance, unless these vicious measures were allowed to be adopted. We find to-day in the presence of debate and in the presence of a shocked people the members of that party hesitating and sitting mute in their seats. They were warned before we entered upon this general debate—perhaps in pleasantry, but certainly none the less a warning—that if any one indulged in debate on that side of the House he should be shot. Their tongues cleave to the roots of their mouths in the presence of this combat. Why are they silent? Let it be noted in this land that they sit silent in their seats, unable if not unwilling to meet the contest.

Mr. ATKINS. The gentleman from Georgia [Mr. COOK], who made the remark the other day in the purest spirit of jest and pleasantry, to which the gentleman from Ohio has adverted, is not in his seat. I do not think it is worthy of the gentleman from Ohio to make use of that remark in the way he does in his speech.

Mr. KEIFER. I said the remark might have been made in pleasantry, but it was none the less a warning, as the gentleman from Tennessee would have understood if he had been listening carefully. But if that remark was uttered in pleasantry, it had also a well-understood meaning.

Gentlemen tried hard all through the extra session of Congress to convince the people of this country that it was the right of the majority in Congress, nay that it was patriotic to sit here and attempt to tear down the whole fabric of this Government, unless the President of the United States would lay at the feet of that party all his veto power and allow them to pass just such legislation as they deemed essential to their future success; and when their proposed legislation was spread out before the country, it was all found to be vicious and in opposition to good order.

Mr. CONGER. If the gentleman from Ohio will permit me I will call his attention to the fact that the gentleman from Georgia who said every one should be shot who spoke on this subject on the Democratic side is now in his seat.

Mr. KEIFER. If the gentleman from Georgia desires to rise and deny that statement, I will yield to him.

Mr. COOK. I will say that I had no thought of intimidating the gentlemen over there, not the least.

Mr. KEIFER. No, sir; the intimidation was meant for the gentlemen on the other side who thought they had not enough of idle debate. The threat was not to shoot us down, but to shoot down his own colleagues if they were so foolish as to attempt hereafter to enter upon debate on a subject that they had already heard debated to their utter overthrow and disgust.

Mr. SPARKS. Well, I suppose you would like to see some of us shot.

Mr. KEIFER. And then, Mr. Chairman [Mr. SPRINGER in the chair], I know you have been quite impartial to-day and willing to recognize gentlemen over there. But with the single exception of the gentleman from Illinois [Mr. SPARKS], who made a remark or two in explanation of his amendment, in which he did not enter upon the merits of this discussion, and who was so very clever as to yield fifty-five minutes of of his hour's time to a gentleman on this side of the House—with that single exception they have all been silent to-day, and we understand that they promise to remain so.

I might say that some of the distinguished gentlemen who were in the lead, who were in the van, who were early in the battle and sounded the charge in the extra session, are now out of their seats; they are otherwise engaged. Why are they away? Why do we not hear their clarion voices here? Has there been any edict of the Democratic caucus to seal their lips or keep them out of the House for fear that in listening to this debate they would become excited and rise to their feet and say foolish things in the estimation of the country, and thus jeopardize the coming Presidential election? [After a pause.] I have been a little deliberate, thinking that in the interval some of the leaders, some of those who with great readiness issue fiats to that side of the House, might rise and say that they would take off the gag; but they are still silent. There are deeds so dark or so grave that they can only be done in silence.

I speak now for myself if not for my party. I have referred to the action of the Democratic party to show that its members here do not desire to openly legislate on the merits of a measure. During the extra session the Democratic party tried to menace the Executive into approval of appropriation bills containing vicious amendments, and when failure after failure had come to that party it abandoned passing the usual bill making appropriations for the legislative, executive, and judicial departments of the Government. It might be unkind if not unfair to say that the Democrats of this Congress, who but a few months ago proposed to couple all kinds of extraneous legislation with appropriation bills, discovered their lack of ability to collect into one bill and intelligently act upon it the ordinary appropriations for the support of a single department of the Government. But time and Presidential vetoes have done much to demoralize the Democratic party in this Congress and I hope throughout the country.

At the revolutionary or extra session of this Congress the appropriations for the judicial department of this Government had to be dropped from what is known as the legislative appropriation bill. The appropriations for that department had to be segregated, seemingly to enable the Democratic mind to grasp and comprehend them.

It was of course reasonable to suppose at the close of the extra session that with the aid of numerous deficiency bills to be passed at future sessions the several departments of the Government would be provided for in some way in the ensuing fiscal year, save only the fees of United States marshals and their deputies, and also compensation for special deputy marshals provided for by statute, and whose duties are to aid supervisors of elections in the discharge of their duties under the United States election laws. We now know that these United States officers who performed their duties without pay are not to be paid unless the election laws of the United States are rendered wholly nugatory.

Mr. Chairman, it is always dangerous to prophesy; but it is generally safe to prophesy of the shortcomings of the Democratic party. In the face of the knowledge that the so-called legislative appropriation bill, which became a law at the extra session, was not understood in its full scope by its authors or supporters in either House of Congress—and I mean no reflection upon the capacity to understand of any Senator or member of this body, for the bill was simply incomprehensible—the Government would be under constant embarrassment until Congress should give construction to that measure. It was an anomaly in legislation.

The marshals bill vetoed at the extra session contained, as printed, five lines devoted to the appropriation of $600,000 for the payment of the fees of United States marshals and their general deputies for the fiscal year ending June 30, 1880. The remaining twenty-seven lines of the bill were devoted to vicious legislation, all of which has received the disapproval of the President. Some of this objectionable legislation is now abandoned in the face of the judgment of the people and the decision of the Supreme Court.

I have another purpose in view in speaking to-day, and I cannot review fully the effect of the proposed legislation at the last session in relation to United States marshals. If the marshals bill had become a law, however, the effect of it could have been summarized thus: First, no part of the money could have been used to pay any compensation or fees or expenses of any kind or character incurred under title 26 of the Revised Statutes of the United States relating to elections. Second, it was proposed to make it unlawful for any Department or officer of the Government to incur any liability for the payment of money under the provisions of said title 26 until an appropriation had first been made by law; notwithstanding the provisions of the said title are as imperative on the judges, supervisors, marshals, and other officers as any law on the statute-book.

On proper application of a court or judge, who is sworn to obey the laws, he must act and appoint supervisors of election, and thus necessarily incur a liability on the part of the United States for compensation, expenses, &c. That bill enacted into a law would have made it unlawful for a judge or court to obey an imperative statute.

Third, the penalty which would have been incurred by a judge for acting in obedience to a mandatory law was subjection to a fine of not exceeding $5,000, or by imprisonment for not exceeding five years, or by both fine and imprisonment, in the discretion of the court.

Gentlemen on the other side said at the last session of this Congress that the so-called marshals' appropriation bill should typify the "last ditch," in guarding which they resolved to die. It was quite fitting. The purpose of the Democratic party, so easily understood from the beginning, was quite prominently shown in that bill. The country noted it, and we had its verdict. It was then and still is proposed to withhold from the courts of the United States their sole executive arm in enforcing their judgments, orders, and decrees; it was proposed that the marshals and their general deputies should go without payment of their lawful fees and the expenses incident to the performance of their duties unless the minority in this Congress and the President would yield assent to the vicious legislation already referred to. The duties of marshals and their general deputies are many and of the highest importance. They constitute the physical arm of the United States courts in the arrest of all violators of the law and in the execution of all processes.

Mr. Chairman, I cannot refrain from occupying a few moments more, with the indulgence of the House, in making some observations suggested to my mind in the course of the debate on the marshals appropriation bill at the close of the extra session. The member from New York [Mr. Cox] then took pains to have read an old resolution of his and the vote thereon relating to the issues settled by the late war. My honorable friend from Michigan [Mr. Conger] had read in reply a like resolution of his and the vote thereon. It seems to me it is of more concern to know how members now stand on the issues made up and determined by the war. A close observer of the debate between my colleagues [Mr. Garfield and Mr. Hurd] at the last session, on this marshals bill, would have had no trouble in discovering, with unerring certainty, how members regarded the war issues and their settlement. When my colleague [Mr. Garfield] declared that the principle of national unity was perpetually and eternally settled by the war, free from the right of a State or any number of States ever to destroy it, applause went up in response from this side of the House; but gentlemen on the other side sat as mute and dumb as they do to-day. When my other colleague [Mr. Hurd] declared his belief in the superior sovereignty of a State under the Constitution, that heresy which brought this country to the court of war, before which the Union shook from foundation to turret for more than four years, a general and spontaneous cheer went up from the Democratic members of this House. My colleague [Mr. Hurd] undertook then to expound to us some other supposed constitutional law long since exploded. He then claimed that the Constitution and the Union were "the creature of the States," to use his own language, and he then read to us the tenth amendment of the Constitution. This amendment, Mr. Chairman, was found necessary to be adopted long after the Constitution went into operation, for the purpose of granting to the States or to the people such powers as they could not otherwise possess, and which were not expressly delegated to the United States by the Constitution nor prohibited by it to the States. Had the gentleman begun by reading the preamble of the Constitution of the United States, he would have found out whose instrument it was he was talking about so inconsiderately. I quote that preamble and commend it to the gentlemen on the other side:

We the people of the United States, in order to form a more perfect union, establish justice, insure domestic tranquillity, provide for the common defense, promote the general welfare, and secure the blessings of liberty to ourselves and our posterity, do ordain and establish this Constitution for the United States of America.

You will note the opening language, "We, the people of the United States." In the judgment of the framers of the Constitution, "the people of the United States" ordained and established this instrument. It was not ordained by the States. The framers of the Constitution understood that the sovereignty of the States was merged in the Federal Government under the Constitution. In the letter of the convention, bearing date September 17, 1787, the day of the signing of the Constitution by its framers, George Washington, speaking for the convention as its president, uses this language:

It is obviously impracticable in the Federal Government of these States to secure all rights of independent sovereignty to each, and yet provide for the individual safety of all. Individuals entering into society must give up a share of liberty to preserve the rest.

He further says in the same letter:

In all our deliberations on this subject, we kept steadily in our view that which appears to us the greatest interest of every true American, the consolidation of our Union, in which is involved our prosperity, felicity, safety, perhaps our national existence.

I have not time to follow my colleague through all his other propositions of bad constitutional law. He still reiterates in this session of Congress his old theory of the right of this House—because of its constitutional right to originate money bills—to have grievances redressed before making appropriations to carry on the Government and to execute existing law. This theory has been so thoroughly exploded both by speeches and by the recent back-downs of Democrats in both ends of the Capitol, that I need hardly comment on it now. When the cool judgments of men of both parties gain full sway, there will be no person found bold enough to announce the dread doctrine that it is the constitutional duty of this House of Representatives to destroy this nation's life by withholding needed appropriations, unless the party in the majority in the House for the time being, shall be allowed to dictate to the Senate and the President of the United States the passage of laws for the redress of real or supposed grievances. No legislative body of any country ever before undertook to destroy the nation which its members were sworn to support, unless some other branch of the government of the same nation would assent to its dictation.

My colleague still adheres with characteristic obstinacy to the view that the measures to which the Democratic party objected were unconstitutional. He still stands by his constitutional argument made early in the extra session to demonstrate that a law on the statute-book was unconstitutional because it did not make it a high crime for a civil, military, or naval officer of the United States to keep the peace at the polls. This was the doctrine announced by the gentleman in the extra session, and I understand him to adhere to it now as a constitutional proposition. Verily, we have developed strange expounders of constitutional law when it is declared that an act is inimical to the Constitution of the United States because it does not in terms make some act of the people a crime.

A confident appeal was made to English statutes to show that in Great Britain troops were not permitted to keep the peace at the polls. A statute which provided for the conduct of British soldiers not on duty was often read and referred to as proof of this. History, however, reveals to us the fact that at no time up to the present has the Government of Great Britain failed to use its military power to put down riots and to keep the peace at the polls in England as well as in Ireland and Scotland. Do gentlemen challenge that proposition? In the long and sometimes angry debates during the extra session of Congress, Democrats have gone down before facts, principles, and arguments, until there may be some excuse for their present silence.

I will notice another attempt at constitutional exposition by my colleague, [Mr. Herd]. I quote from a speech of his, made in the last expiring hours of the extra session:

Strange to say, the President and his advisers and the gentlemen on the other side to the House seem to have lost sight of the constitutional provision which gives the President the power to execute the laws. The language of that instrument is that the President of the United States may call upon the militia of the several States to execute the laws. There is the power given to him for the execution of the laws; not the Army, unless Congress say so, but the militia of the States, because the Constitution so provides.

Mr. Chairman, it must have distressed my friend's constituents when, after reading his speech they took down the old Constitution and read it through, and found it contained no such language as he attributed to it. The Constitution nowhere, in terms, authorizes or empowers the President to call out the militia of the United States. Section 8, article 1, which gives Congress power to raise and support armies, grants to it power "to provide for calling forth the militia to execute the laws of the Union, suppress insurrection, and repel invasion." The President, it is true, is the Commander-in-Chief of the Army and Navy of the United States, and of the militia of the several States when called into actual service of the United States; and Congress has the same power over the organization of the militia in actual service that it has over the creation of a regular Army, except the right is reserved by the Constitution to the States to appoint the officers and to raise and train the militia according to the discipline prescribed by Congress.

I commend, then, the rereading of the Constitution to my colleague. He, with others, still insists if Congress does take from the President his right to use the Army the duty still rests upon him to "take care that the laws are faithfully executed" as required by the Constitution and his oath of office.

The CHAIRMAN. The gentleman's time has expired.

Mr. BLACKBURN. Mr. Chairman, in order to promote the comfort of the gentleman from Ohio [Mr. KEIFER], and without the slightest fear of doing any detriment to free elections by the presence of troops at the polls, I move his time be indefinitely extended.

Mr. KEIFER. I am always thankful to my friend for any favors. I suggest, however, I only want a minute and a half.

Mr. BLACKBURN. This side is more than willing to give him an hour.

Mr. KEIFER. I only need a minute and a half.

Mr. TUCKER. I hope the gentleman's time will be extended.

The CHAIRMAN. There being no objection the time of the gentleman from Ohio is extended.

Mr. KEIFER. While I thank my honorable friend from Kentucky for his great consideration for me, I feel very glad that by anything I have said, whether it has been pleasing to his ears or otherwise, that I have at least brought him to his feet. [Laughter.]

Mr. BLACKBURN. Mr. Chairman, I must be frank enough to state that I have not been induced to listen to what the gentleman from Ohio has said; I am fortunate in having been absent from the House. [Laughter.]

Mr. KEIFER. I have in the course of my remarks included the gentleman from Kentucky among those who were absent, and one of those who may have been regarded on the other side as unsafe to have present.

Mr. BLACKBURN. The gentleman knew my good taste.

Mr. KEIFER. And your proneness to give utterance to your peculiar views.

Mr. BLACKBURN. Thank you.

Mr. KEIFER. I was referring when my time expired to some propositions which were maintained or insisted upon by my colleague from Ohio [Mr. HURD]. Let me add he, with others, still insists that if Congress does take from the President his right to use the Army, the duty still rests upon him to see that the laws are faithfully executed, as the executive power of the United States is by the Constitution of the United States vested in him.

We are cautioned to remember that to take away the right to use the Army does not withdraw any constitutional power or duty from the President. Granting this to be true, how will the President execute the law if the instrumentalities by which he may do it are taken from him, as is proposed by the present amendment? It is proposed to strip the President of all means with which to enforce the laws of the United States, and then in mockery point out to him his duties under the Constitution. The logic of the proposed amendment to this bill would require the President to go in person to execute the laws; require him to go on election day in person to keep the peace at all polls where riots raged or were threatened. We were told at the extra session that party issues were made up. I concur in this, and await complacently the verdict of the whole country. We have recently had the verdict of the people in my own State. Until the people have declared that civil liberty is endangered by not allowing fraud, intimidation, ballot-box stuffing, riots, and bloodshed at the polls, I shall have full faith in them and in my country's future. [Applause.]

COURT OF PENSIONS.

May 18, 1880. An amendment proposing to strike out a clause providing that from and after the passage of the act only pension cases certified by the court shall be passed upon by Congress was under discussion.

Mr. KEIFER said:

In addition to the objections which have been assigned to this clause that is proposed to be stricken out I wish first to say that it is flatly in the face of the Constitution of the United States. By enacting this clause in this section we undertake to say to the people and the soldiers of this country that they shall not petition Congress for the redress of grievances or for any relief whatever, and that is the proposition here: and when you turn over to the fifth section of this bill we find that all the pension cases now pending in this Congress are to be thrown out of Congress without consideration and remitted to this court. That includes ninety-nine cases out of every hundred of them that do not come within the provisions of the second section of this bill.

They are not cases where the Commissioner of Pensions had original jurisdiction at all over them. We are to say by the adoption of this clause proposed to be stricken out, that no person in this country, no matter who, whether the widow of a deceased soldier or a maimed and wounded soldier himself, no person, no matter what are his merits, no matter what are his deserts or what right he may have in the premises, is to be permitted to come here to apply as an original proposition for a pension.

Mr. BUTTERWORTH. Does the gentleman think that this law would have the power or the force to prevent that?

Mr. KEIFER. No, I do not; but we perpetrate the supreme folly of saying that we would not have the power to perform our constitutional duty if we pass this bill. It is the most supreme absurdity in the world for us to pass such a bill as this and say that we shall not have the power to perform our constitutional duties; in other words, to limit ourselves as to our future power. We cannot do it. Of course we can pass the bill, but the Constitution of the United States prohibits us from passing a law that will cut off the power of any citizen of the United States to petition us for relief. Yet this clause proposes to do it, and the fifth section of this bill proposes to wipe out all of the pension cases upon our calendars or pending here in Congress and transfer them to the court. This is a strange sort of legislation. I must confess I cannot understand it. I do not know what it means.

Mr. WHITE. Will the gentleman allow me to ask him a question?

Mr. KEIFER. I have very little time to answer questions.

Mr. WHITE. Will not the passage by Congress of any pension law repeal that portion of the law? It is nothing.

Mr. KEIFER. I suppose the gentleman is not in favor of it because it is nothing. I am in favor of striking it out. I am in favor of striking out the whole of the fifth section. I am in favor of some law that will give the pensioners the opportunity that they want to get their claims speedily acted upon; in other words, that will give them relief. But I am opposed to saying that they shall not come here to Congress for relief, and that is the purport of this section.

MANAGERS OF THE NATIONAL HOME FOR SOLDIERS.

May 27, 1880. The House having under discussion the sundry civil appropriation bill, a point of order was raised on the paragraph providing for the support of the National Home for Disabled Volunteer Soldiers and the appointment of managers therefor.

Mr. KEIFER said :

Mr. CHAIRMAN : I have to-day had the misfortune to hear points of order made from the other side against the provisions offered in the interest of science, and the Chair has been appealed to to apply the strictest possible construction of the rule in order to exclude provisions which we desired to incorporate into this bill and which were entirely germane to it. But up to the present moment I find the leaders of the other side and the men who have charge of this bill sitting silent here and allowing new legislation to be incorporated in this bill which has no sort of relation to or connection with an appropriation bill.

And I learn as a mode of arguing before the House of Representatives, that it is sufficient in the estimation of the gentleman from Wisconsin [Mr. BRAGG] to show that previous Congresses have violated the provisions of the charter under which this National Home was organized; and that is held up as a sufficient argument why the Chair should rule that this Congress should again violate the law. He gave you not one, but two and three instances where the original law, which provided that these men should be selected by joint resolution, had been disregarded. Hence he says that you are now bound to disregard that old act, that old charter, and to hold that this provision is not in violation of the law, and does not change the operation of that law. Some of us have never learned, even up to this time, with the aid of all the singular propositions submitted here, that that is sound logic.

The gentleman says that on a former occasion I made a point of order against a similar provision to this, which it was proposed to incorporate in an appropriation bill, and the point of order was ruled against me. And he now says that you, Mr. Chairman, ought to rule the same way, notwithstanding that the rule under which the point of order is now raised was not in existence at all at that time. He waives that all aside and says that the old ruling is sufficient for you.

Mr. BRAGG. While you are trying to make a distinction between a law which is a joint resolution and a law which is an act, are you not subjecting yourself to the criticism of my Lord Coke: *qui hæret in litera, hæret in cortice.*

Mr. KEIFER. The gentleman will draw his own conclusion about that ; he will arrive at his own conclusion in regard to that matter. I will say, in the first place, that I have not yet undertaken to show any such distinction ; but I will do so now.

The provision of the original charter which required the appointment of these trustees of the National Home was doubtless put in the form it was in order to exclude us from doing the very thing which it is proposed to do here to-day. And although the gentleman says there is no distinction between a joint resolution and an act of Congress—and I agree with him that after they are passed they are in effect the same—there is a vast distinction between a joint resolution and an act when we come to deal with the subject here in the form of legislation.

You cannot incorporate a joint resolution in an appropriation bill as a rider, even with all our strange rulings, up to this time. It is sufficient now to say that under the third clause of Rule XXI such a provision as this is expressly excluded. That has been read once, but I beg to call the attention of the Chair to it again:

Nor shall any provision in any such bill or amendment thereto changing existing law be in order except such as, being germane to the subject-matter of the bill, shall retrench expenditures

"Retrench expenditures" how ?

by the reduction of the number and salary of the officers of the United States, by the reduction of the compensation of any person paid out of the Treasury of the United States, or by the reduction of amounts of money covered by the bill.

Is this provision germane to the sundry civil appropriation bill ? Gentlemen on the other side say yes, because under a former rule of this House it was ruled to be in order ; not under the present rule, for they do not deign to read the present rule.

But last of all we get the most singular and strange declaration that comes from the examination by the gentleman from Wisconsin [Mr. BRAGG] of the joint resolution which was passed February 26, 1875. He reads the whole of that joint resolution which appointed three of these trustees, and says that, although the joint resolution says nothing about it, yet those three men were appointed for terms which began long before the joint resolution was passed. Now I beg of the gentlemen to point out where there is a syllable in that joint resolution of February 26, 1875, which indicates that the three persons there named, Martindale, Bond, and Wolcott, were appointed for terms of office which began at an earlier day than the one upon which that joint resolution was approved.

It is true, Mr. Chairman (and I beg your careful attention to this), the bill recites that the term of office of these three persons as originally fixed expired some time before. But the original act, which has been read by the gentleman from New York, provides, as the Chair will remember, that the term of office shall be for six years, and until their successors are appointed. Now, all that this bill undertakes to state is that their term (referring to their six years' term) had expired some time before. But their lawful terms would continue forever if Congress did not act. So we have here three persons whom it is proposed to appoint to take the place of persons who have been appointed and whose term does not expire until February 26, 1881. It is proposed by this very proviso to shorten the term of Martindale, Bond, and Wolcott.

Mr. BRIGGS. The Revised Statutes also provide that the term of office shall be for six years, and until their successors are appointed.

Mr. KEIFER. I am told that in the Revised Statutes the same language is used that was used in the original act when the national home was incorporated.

Now, to summarize my points briefly. This provision is not germane. It does not retrench expenditures. It has no reference to cutting down salaries or expenditures, or amounts of money appropriated by the bill. It undertakes to limit the terms (fixed by law or by joint resolution, as gentlemen prefer) of three of the present managers of the home. More than that, it undertakes in an appropriation bill to violate the terms of the original act and to appoint these persons. I have not claimed that if an act is passed making these appointments it will not have the same effect as a joint resolution; but I do claim that this is not a joint resolution, and hence is not in accordance with the existing law, and is in effect new legislation.

Mr. SPARKS. Mr. Chairman, it is a mistake when any gentleman asserts that the term of any one of these officers expires next February. Their terms all expire April 21, 1880.

Mr. VAN VOORHIS. Will the gentleman explain how he reaches that conclusion.

Mr. SPARKS. I will with the greatest pleasure. General John H. Martindale, whose term is the only one in question, was appointed a manager for the term beginning April 21, 1868, and has continued in office for that and a subsequent term, making twelve years from April 21, 1868, to April 21, 1880.

Mr. KEIFER. General Martindale was appointed February 26, 1875, by an act passed in the Forty-third Congress.

Mr. SPARKS. I am reading and make this statement from the joint resolution of March, 1868.

Mr. KEIFER. It does not make any difference what the gentleman is reading. Here is the law.

Mr. SPARKS. I have it before me.

Mr. KEIFER. No, sir, you have not.

Mr SPARKS. Yes, sir; I beg the gentleman's pardon. I have the joint resolution before me and from which I read that General Martindale was appointed at the time I have mentioned to fill a full term of six years. I read from the joint resolution—

That Erastus B. Wolcott, of Wisconsin, and John H. Martindale, of New York, be, and are hereby, appointed managers of the National Asylum for Disabled Soldiers, under the provisions and conditions of the third section of an act approved March 23, 1866, for six years, from the 21st day of April, 1868; and that Hugh L. Bond, of Maryland, be, and is hereby, appointed a manager to serve out the unexpired term of Horatio G. Stebbins, of California, resigned.

This act was approved March 12, 1868. You will perceive, Mr. Chairman, that the term commenced April 21, 1868. I have not the next act appointing General Martindale; but he could not have been appointed under any circumstances so that his two terms would extend beyond twelve years. By the act I have read he was appointed for six years; and I presume that at the end of six years he was again appointed.

Mr. VAN VOORHIS. That is where the gentleman makes his error.

Mr. SPARKS. His second term must have expired on the 21st of April last.

Mr. VAN VOORHIS. Not at all.

Mr. SPARKS. Why not?

Mr. VAN VOORHIS. His term began February 26 1875—his last term.

Mr. SPARKS. Oh, no! I have read the law showing that he was appointed for a full term of six years, beginning April 21, 1868.

Mr. KEIFER. Will the gentleman read the law of February 26, 1875, passed more than six years after the law which he has read?

Mr. SPARKS. He was appointed April 21, 1868, for six years, as the joint resolution says.

Mr. KEIFER. When I heard the opening remarks of the gentleman from Massachusetts I knew in advance where he was going to land, for a man always prepares himself by first speaking of his own supreme virtue before he makes a lunge in some strange direction. I would not make this remark of the gentleman if he had not chosen to lecture me and all on this side of the House before he undertook to lay down his strange position of law, to sustain which he stopped by reading only a part of a paragraph.

The law fixing the terms of managers of the National Military Asylum says that the term shall be for six years and until a successor is elected. When the gentleman stopped after reading simply the provision that the term should be for six years, of course we knew he was preparing to spring into some great field of virtue.

Except in case of death or resignation there cannot be a vacancy in the office of manager of the Soldiers' Home. I submit, Mr. Chairman, that when in your ruling you undertake to say that there are terms for less than six years you do it by interpolating in the law what is not there. All laws that provide for filling vacancies, where vacancies can possibly occur, speak in terms of the unexpired term. But in all these laws—the original act and all subsequent acts, whether in the form of joint resolution or specific acts of Congress—there is not a word about the unexpired term. No man since the original appointments could be appointed for less than an entire term.

Now let us suppose that General Martindale, instead of being appointed (if he was so appointed) as his own successor, had been appointed as the successor of some other person who had held the position for six years or longer. Do I understand the Chair to rule that this appointment, without anything said in the act about the term, would have been for a less period than six years? Of course that is what the Chair means to conclude, and that is what my distinguished friend from Illinois claims is the law. But we have decision after decision arising under State organic acts in this country all of them holding, in the absence of provision for filling unexpired terms, that the term means the time fixed in the organic act. And I venture here to say to the lawyers on this floor, at least to those who are not filled with partisanism or with supreme virtue, they cannot find a single law anywhere that has been construed otherwise, or a single constitution. There is not one which can be pointed out.

After appealing to my friends on this side of the House, simply as Republicans without claiming anything more than belongs to me as a partisan, I now appeal to lawyers on the other side not to vote alone as partisans, but to adopt and accept and carry out some of the plain virtue laid down by my distinguished friend from Massachusetts, who prefers some of these men in this bill to some who are to be legislated out.

DEPUTY MARSHALS AT ELECTIONS.

June 11, 1880.   Pending a bill on the subject of deputy marshals, at the polls.—

Mr. KEIFER said:

Mr. SPEAKER: Before entering upon a brief discussion of this measure I desire to have the Clerk read section 2021 of the Revised Statutes relating to the time and manner of appointment of special deputy marshals to assist the supervisors of elections.

The Clerk read as follows:

SEC. 2021. Whenever an election at which Representatives or Delegates in Congress are to be chosen is held in any city or town of twenty thousand inhabitants or upwards, the marshal for the district in which the city or town is situated shall, on the application, in writing, of at least two citizens residing in such city or town, appoint special deputy marshals, whose duty it shall be, when required thereto to aid and assist the supervisors of election in the verification of any list of persons who may have registered or voted; to attend in each election district or voting precinct at the times and places fixed for the registration of voters, and at all times and places when and where the registration may by law be scrutinized, and the names of registered voters be marked for challenge: and also to attend, at all times for holding elections, the polls in such district or precinct.

Mr. KEIFER. I desire the Clerk also to read the succeeding section of the Revised Statutes, which relates to the duty of the marshal and his general deputies and also such special deputies as may be appointed under section 2021.

The Clerk read as follows.

SEC. 2022. The marshal and his general deputies, and such special deputies, shall keep the peace, and support and protect the supervisors of election in the discharge of their duties, preserve order at such places of registration and at such polls, prevent fraudulent registration and fraudulent voting thereat, or fraudulent conduct on the part of any officer of election, and immediately, either at the place of registration or polling place, or elsewhere, and either before or after registering or voting, to arrest and take into custody, with or without process, any person who commits, or attempts or offers to commit, any of the acts or offenses prohibited herein, or who commits any offense against the laws of the United States; but no person shall be arrested without process for any offense not committed in the presence of the marshal, or his general or special deputies, or either of them, or of the supervisors of election, or either of them, and, for the purposes of arrest or the preservation of the peace, the supervisors of election shall, in the absence of the marshal's deputies, or if required to assist such deputies, have the same duties and powers as deputy marshals; nor shall any person, on the day of such election, be arrested without process for any offense committed on the day of registration.

Mr. KEIFER. Mr. Speaker, bad as this bill is, devoid as it is of anything which would be at all efficacious in the direction of enforcing the United States election laws, great sham as it is in merely pretending to be in favor of something which would be efficient in the direction of enforcing law and order at the polls, with all these defects in the bill, I consider it a matter of congratulation that we should now have it before us.   The Democratic party is especially to be congratulated that to-day, in the expiring hours of the first regular session of the Forty-sixth Congress, it should be pressing a bill which in name at least, if not in substance, recognizes the constitutional power of the United States to enforce its own laws and preserve order on election day at the polls wherever members of the House of Representatives are to be chosen.   To this extent I want to congratulate not only the Democratic party, but the whole country.

But this bill is a mere sheer deception, if I may be pardoned for using the expression.   It is intended to be passed for the purpose of annulling, instead of really improving, the statutes upon the subject of the use of special deputy marshals at the polls to aid the supervisors of elections in preserving peace and order when there is open disorder and violence.   Already it appears, by what has been read by the Clerk, that there are two classes of deputy marshals known to the law, to wit, general and special deputy marshals.   Each class has duties to perform under the law, as defined in section 2022 of the Revised Statutes, which duties relate to the conduct of elections on election day when a Member of the House of Representatives or a Delegate is to be chosen.

But the bill proposes to create a distinct class called "*deputy marshals for services in reference to any election.*"   In the original draught of the bill as offered by the distinguished Senator from Delaware [Mr. BAYARD] the word "special" preceded the word "deputy," and it was supposed it was the purpose to pass a law which referred to and regulated the appointment and conduct of special deputy marshals of elections as they were appointed under section 2021 of the Revised Statutes.   It was thought wise to strike out the word "special," and to define this class of deputies as "deputy marshals for services in reference to any election."   Such deputy marshals have always been unknown to the law, and they are still unknown to it.

In order that we may understand what this bill is, let us go through it and analyze it.   The bill provides that these deputy marshals for services in reference to any election shall be appointed by the circuit court of the United States at the next term preceding any election of Representatives or Delegates in Congress, and it further provides if there should be no session of the circuit court in the State or district where such marshals are to be appointed, then the appointment may be made by the district court.   Here we have a new class of deputy marshals appointed by the courts without suggestion from the executive power, without the cognizance, and against the will, if you please, of the marshal of the district where the deputies may be required to serve. In no event is this class of officers, if they may be dignified with the name of officers—in no event are these officers to be responsible to the executive power, that power which by the Constitution of the United States and by the laws of the United States is responsible for the execution of all the laws of the United States.

But if we look further we will see that under the very thinnest kind of gauze it is proposed to hide away the real purpose of the bill. I submit, Mr. Speaker, it is impossible for any gentleman to name a possible case where a district court of the United States could appoint under this bill, if it should become a law, a deputy marshal to serve in reference to an election—to appoint anybody under the bill. Before the exigency can arise where the district court of the United States may be invoked to make these appointments we will have to discover a district in the United States wherein there never has been or will not be before the coming election a term of the circuit court of the United States.

I repeat, Mr. Speaker, that before a district court can acquire jurisdiction under this bill to appoint a deputy marshal to serve at any election you must find a district wherein no circuit court has ever been held. If gentlemen on the other side desire to use any portion of my time for the purpose of telling me where and how a case can arise and the district court can ever make an appointment of any one of these deputies to serve at an election, I will yield with great pleasure. Mr. Speaker, I would like to know whether there is any gentleman here prepared to defend this scheme, if I may be pardoned for using the expression. Under the terms of the bill it is impossible for the district court to appoint one of these so-called officers in any place in the United States.

If that cannot be done, then what? Unless it happens between this and the coming election for members of the House of Representatives and Delegates to Congress that a circuit court is in session, and in such session that its power might be invoked for the purpose of making these appointments, then it will be impossible to have one of these deputy marshals at the succeeding election.

The bill does not propose to have the district court exercise this power in the absence of the circuit court that might be held after the passage of the act and before the election ; but if there ever has been a circuit court in session in any district, then the district court is not allowed to take jurisdiction for the purpose of making appointments under this proposed law. So it will be impossible, and I am quite warranted in saying it will be impossible in most if not all the cases, to have this class of officers should this bill become the law. By the terms of the bill it is not made the right or duty of any person to pray the court to appoint deputy marshals. The court must act, if at all, on its own motion.

The time I shall occupy will be for the purpose of trying, in my way, to develop what there is and what there is not in this proposed legislation. A provision of this bill is to the effect that the officers appointed shall be in equal numbers from the different political parties. Some persons misnamed this measure as non-partisan. I am not quite well enough advised to speak with confidence, but I believe that it is the only absolutely partisan measure pending before Congress. Under this bill every non-partisan in the United States is rendered ineligible to be appointed a deputy marshal to serve at an election. Under this bill it is proposed to make special partisans of the officers who execute the most delicate law of the land, to wit, the election law. We are to give power to the most vicious partisans, if you please, upon either side, amid the heat of political controversy, and send them to the polls armed with that power to stand face to face and eye to eye in opposition to each other on political grounds. They are to be specially chosen with reference to their partisan character. There may arise an emergency where one party, through its supporters, will try to overthrow the election officers, or may try to compel them to do what is not their duty under the law, or one party may engage in an effort to prevent honest voters from exercising their right of voting. In such an emergency there would be found a deputy marshal on one side who would be willing to see the law executed and the officers and voters protected, but the other deputy, denying the right to interfere, stands face to face with him, and says, " My duty here, is to see that you do not do your duty. I am appointed under the law of Congress because I am a partisan ; I represent my friends, the plug-uglies and the bulldozers here, the partisans on the other side. I am the chief captain of them all, and it is my purpose here to see that you do not interfere or perform your duty. I was appointed for that purpose. I was recommended to the judge of the court because I was a partisan, and I will do my duty to my party." And this is the kind of non-partisan legislation that you are proposing to write upon our statute-books.

I might elaborate this, but it is sufficient to cite the provisions of the law which it is proposed to enact, for all here at least can comprehend them and their real design.

In this connection, Mr. Speaker, it must be remembered that these so-called officers are in no sense responsible to the appointing power. No power by the provisions of the bill can remove them. The judge that appointed them has no power to remove them. They have, as I have already pointed out, no connection with the executive power of the Government. They are to receive no orders, no instructions, and are under no control by the marshal of the district. They give no bond, and it is fair to say that under the provisions of the law as it now stands they are not required to qualify at all, even by the taking of an oath of office. No qualifications, no bond; and nobody gives a bond for them, as in the case of the deputy marshals now provided for.

And further, Mr. Speaker, it will be observed by following the language of this bill that they have no jurisdiction outside of the immediate location of the election polls. If it should be thought by one of them that it was his duty to arrest a man at the polls who was committing or was proposing to commit some crime against the election law he could arrest him possibly, but the very moment he passed with his prisoner a rod beyond the immediate location of the polls he would be required to release him for want of jurisdiction to continue him under arrest. The jurisdiction of the proposed new class of deputies is not to extend beyond services at an election.

I have just called the attention of the House to the fact that the supposed officers, called deputy marshals for services in reference to any election, if they have any sort of power as officers can only exercise it in connection with the election; and if it should turn out that they were obliged to arrest a person who was guilty of repeating at the polls, guilty of any sort of crime against the United States election laws, guilty of a breach of the peace or any other offense known to the law, they might perhaps technically have the right to arrest the man and carry him a few feet from the place of election and let him go. Nobody pretends that this proposed law gives such deputy marshals jurisdiction to arrest an offender and hold him for trial and punishment, or that they can execute a warrant under the direction of a marshal of a district. By the terms of this bill—and I give the exact language as set forth in the proviso added to the second section—

The marshals of the United States for whom deputies shall be appointed by the court under this act shall not be liable for any of the acts of such deputies.

They are not to perform the duties of a general deputy marshal. They are not to perform the duties of a special deputy marshal of elections appointed under section 2021 of the Revised Statutes, and whose duties are defined by section 2022 of the Revised Statutes; but they are officers without duties save and except as they may be inferred from the use of the language in the first section of the bill, to wit:

Deputy marshals for services in reference to any election.

That is all. Then they are not to be responsible themselves; and I repeat they are not to qualify by the form of oath provided for deputy marshals appointed by the marshals themselves under section 780 of the Revised Statutes, and the form of oath given in section 782 of the Revised Statutes. These deputy marshals for services in reference to any election could not qualify at all. The bond of the marshal required to be given by the statute (section 783) for the purpose of securing the faithful conduct of the marshals covers the duties of his own deputies.

While the bill provides that there shall be such a singular and anomalous thing known to our statutes as a deputy marshal, who will himself be responsible to nobody for his acts, it was wisely thought by the draughtsmen of this bill that it would be well to make nobody responsible for him. Hence the bill says that the marshals of the United States shall not be liable for any of the acts of the deputy marshals which the court might appoint. He has no qualification under the law; he has a naked appointment, and is required to fight an adversary who is to be chosen because he is able to compete with him, and peculiarly because he is a partisan. He is not responsible for malfeasance or misfeasance, and he has no sort of duty to perform that anybody can hold him liable for failing to perform. He is to be called a deputy marshal for services at any election.

Now it is a grave question whether or not the general statute defining the duties of special deputy marshals or general deputy marshals under our election laws would apply to such officer at all. It is exceedingly doubtful whether they would apply to such deputies under any fair construction, and the bill, if it becomes a law, is not to have a liberal construction. When we are determining the powers of an officer who may arrest a man for crime we are not to construe his powers liberally but strictly as defined in the statutes. Strictly speaking, the statute laws of the United States could give and would give no sort of power to an officer called a deputy marshal for services at an election. The general statutes require duties of the marshal of the district and of his general deputies and his special deputies, as will appear by the sections of the Revised Statutes already read; but no provision of the general statute would reach these deputy marshals for services at any election. Therefore, when you strip this all down to the bare pole, you will find that it is a mere scheme to destroy our election laws, barely recognizing the right of Congress to uphold the power of the Government of the United States in the execution of such laws. The law, however, is to be so drawn that it cannot be executed, and that great power, the power which, wisely executed, preserves peace and order at the polls, where of all places in this country we should have peace and order, the entire machinery for that purpose is to be destroyed under the guise of a new and more perfect law.

This is the worst of the legislation proposed in this Congress and in the closing session of the Forty-fifth Congress. It was more manly to stand up openly and say that you wanted to and would repeal all the laws of the United States that gave to the Government of the United States the power to preserve peace at the polls on election day. The party that took that position, as did the Democratic party a few months ago, once stood upon a more heroic plane than now.

It is of necessity groveling now, coming down to an attempt to enact a law that is a mere pretense for a law and to say that by it the election laws of the United States to preserve peace at the polls are to be enforced, but really undertaking to put on the statute books a law that cannot be executed at all. If this bill should become a law the Democrats will at least be enabled to go before such of their people as will listen to them and say that while they could not repeal the election laws of the United States, while they could not repeal the laws that secured peace and order at the polls, they did succeed in getting through the Congress of the United States a bill that renders nugatory all those provisions, in so far at least as deputy marshals at the polls are concerned.

I like the Democratic party for some things. It is an obstinate party.

Mr. WILSON. And an honorable party.

Mr. KEIFER. The gentleman from West Virginia says that it is an honorable party. By that I suppose I am to infer that he means that when the Democratic party is whipped and overthrown in a fair fight it will attempt to accomplish its purpose in some other way.

We find that party here pressing for a vote on a bill entitled "An act regulating the pay and appointment of deputy marshals." A few months ago we were warned that we should have no appropriations to carry on this Government until we allowed all the laws relating to the appointment of deputy marshals and their use at the polls to be absolutely repealed. In the light of what has since taken place, especially in the Forty-sixth Congress, in the light of the overwhelming defeats of that party in this Congress and at the polls, in the broad glare of the light which comes to us from the Supreme Court of the United States through recent decisions, we are to-day witnessing the grand scene of that party bowing humbly to the powers that be and recognizing the Constitution of the United States as a Constitution conferring upon the Government of the United States power to preserve itself and to enforce its own laws.

Education comes slowly to that obstinate party. If I were to review its history I could find a vast number of things that it set out to oppose. Step by step it opposed all the grand measures that now stand forth as great monuments to the success of the Republican party, the party of progress.

When we proposed at the close of the war to amend the Constitution of the United States so far as to wipe out human slavery, Democrats stood up in this Hall in the Congress of the United States, and said that it was unconstitutional to amend the Constitution of the United States so far as human slavery was concerned. The Republican party, by its might and power, recognizing the right to amend the Constitution in every respect, wiped out human slavery by the adoption of the thirteenth amendment to the Constitution, and the Democratic party, after the fact was accomplished, in time bowed and said, "We, too, are in favor of destroying human slavery."

We tried them on the fourteenth amendment, that amendment which proposed to define citizenship, and which contains various other wise provisions. We found the Democratic party steadily against it, not only in the Halls of Congress, but in the halls of the State legislatures all over the country. By voice and vote they were against it, but they were defeated. After being defeated, as time rolled on, they again said, "We were wrong then, but now we are right."

We said, "We will enfranchise all American citizens by the adoption of the fifteenth amendment of the Constitution; and every Democrat, I believe, voted against that measure, and so far as the members of that party spoke they spoke against it all over the country, in Congress and out of it. But the Republican party erected another monument to its glory and adopted the fifteenth amendment. Then lagging along behind came the Democratic party, crying out that they, too, were in favor of the fifteenth amendment.

Everything that this party has learned in a score of years has been through its defeats; ay, a large part of its members learned patriotism through defeat, not only at the polls, but upon the field of battle. I do not doubt their patriotism now; but I do know that they learned it, many of them, before the months of cannon and amid the clash of arms in the field. I glory in this, for this was an heroic way of acquiring it when other methods failed. While speaking to this measure (and I do not intend to occupy any more time) I wish to say that as we close this session we add one thing more to the success of the Republican party the education of the Democratic party up to the idea that we have a Government strong enough to defend itself from foes within or without, and yet shorn of all power to oppress any of its citizens.

COUNTING THE ELECTORAL VOTE.

December 7, 1880. Against the concurrent resolution of the Senate in reference to counting the electoral vote for President and Vice-President, Mr. Keifer made the point of order that it was not a question of privilege.

He said:

Mr. SPEAKER: I do not desire to enter into any general discussion of the point of order; but I wish to say that, while it may be true that under the Constitution of the United States and the statutes, the counting of the electoral vote, when the time arrives, may become a question of privilege, I deny that a resolution (such as this at least) undertaking to regulate the manner of the count is a question of privilege. In other words, in my opinion the Constitution of the United States, together with the laws on the statute-book, regulates the whole subject of counting the electoral vote. I deny also that it is a matter of proceeding of the two Houses in joint session to count the electoral vote. The proceedings for the purpose of counting that vote, when the two Houses are assembled, are the proceedings of the President of the Senate in the presence of the Senate and the House of Representatives, and nothing is required to be done by the Senate and the House. I think the rule—if we were permitted to look at that; a rule that is to be established without having the force and effect of law, but a mere rule of the two Houses—cannot confer constitutional power such as is attempted to be conferred by this resolution on the two branches of Congress.

But I did not rise to elaborately argue this question. I repeat what I said before, that the manner of counting the electoral vote may be a question of privilege whenever it may come up in either branch of Congress; but the matter of a concurrent resolution which undertakes to confer extraordinary power on the Congress, or, as this resolution does, upon one branch of Congress, is not a question of privilege.

The point of order was overruled.

* * * * * * *

Mr. Speaker, this resolution passed the Senate at its last session, and this House was then, with great zeal, pressed to concur therein. Failing to force the resolution through the House before the last adjournment, it was made a special order for the opening day of this session. Its prompt passage was supposed to be important, because we were in a Presidential election year.

On every hand we were warned that under its provisions this Congress, with a Democratic majority in each House, would count in the Democratic candidates of 1880 for President and Vice-President of the United States. Leading Democrats outside of Congress openly proclaimed to the country such a purpose. But now, fortunately, the people of this country, having in their sovereign capacity given a judgment so unmistakable as to hush to silence all further talk of this kind, it seems as though wisdom would dictate that we should again plant ourselves on the plain provisions of the Constitution as interpreted in the light of the precedents of almost a century.

In the consideration of this question partisan spirit should be forgotten. A remembrance of the fact that after the presidential election of 1876, on account of a division of opinion on this question, not confined to party, this nation was brought to the brink of anarchy and civil strife, business was paralyzed, and faith in the perpetuity of the Government was shaken, should force us to a solemn realization of our duty as legislators and cause us to anxiously inquire what can be done to prevent a repetition of like scenes and events.

I propose now to give some reasons why I am unalterably opposed, not only to this proposed joint rule, but to legislation in every form which undertakes to withhold from the President of the Senate his constitutional powers and vest them in Congress, or one branch thereof, and which also proposes to provide a means by which the vote of the electors of a State may not be counted. I deny that the power not to count the electoral vote belongs anywhere.

I know the ground I purpose to tread has been trodden in recent years by some of the great statesmen and political giants of this country, and I am conscious that I shall be charged with attempting to parry with a rapier the broadsword cuts of political friends as well as political foes. I shall, however, endeavor to show, as an excuse for my temerity, that the construction of the Constitution which I maintain is the one given it by the convention that framed it, by individual members of that convention after its adjournment, by the almost uniform course pursued under the Constitution, and by statesmen who figured prominently in the political arena in the early days of the Republic.

PROPOSED JOINT RULE.

The first section of the resolution provides for the meeting of the two Houses to witness the count, which the Constitution and laws already provide for. Sections 4, 5, and 6 relate to wholly immaterial matters, such as the preservation of order, arrangement of seats, &c., in joint session. The material parts of the resolution are these:

Appointment of tellers.

SEC. 2. Two tellers shall be previously appointed on the part of the Senate and two on the part of the House of Representatives, to record and compute the votes of electors.

Opening the list of votes and receiving and counting them.

SEC. 3. The certified list of votes of electors shall be opened by the President of the Senate in the presence of the Senate and House of Representatives and, in the alphabetical order of the States, beginning with the letter A. He shall open all the certified lists of votes of electors, (or papers purporting to be such certified list of votes), of each State respectively, which shall have been delivered to him, in the order herein prescribed, and shall deliver them to the tellers, by whom they shall be read in the presence and hearing of the two Houses.

When the papers in one of such certified lists shall have been so read, and before another sealed package or list of votes of electors from the same or any other State has been opened, the President of the Senate shall call for objections to receiving such certified list of the votes of electors and to counting the votes therein certified, or any or either of them. If no objection is made, in the manner herein after provided, such list shall be received and the votes be counted, and no other package purporting to be a certified list of votes of electors from such State shall be opened.

If objection is made to receiving such certified list of the votes of electors or to the counting of any vote therein certified, such objection or objections, if more than one objection is made, shall each be submitted in writing and shall state the grounds of objection succinctly and without argument, and must be signed in duplicate by at least two Senators and three Members of the House of Representatives; and one of said duplicates shall be handed to the President of the Senate and the other to the Speaker of the House of Representatives; and the said objection shall be stated by the President of the Senate in the presence and hearing of the two Houses; whereupon he shall proceed to open another package, if there be any other, purporting to contain a certified list of votes of electors from said State. And the same proceedings shall be had, and in the same order, with reference to said list and any other certified list of votes of electors from said State, or papers purporting to be such lists, in succession, if two or more lists are opened and read in accordance with this rule.

If any list of votes from such State is so opened and read, and no objection is made to receiving such list, or to counting any vote therein certified, it shall be received as the valid and authentic list of votes of electors from such State, and the votes therein shall be counted, and the list or lists previously opened, read, and objected to shall be rejected.

If upon the reading of the certified list or lists of votes of electors from any State no list has been received without objection to the same or to any vote therein certified, the Senate shall withdraw to its Chamber and shall proceed to consider such objections as have been made as aforesaid. And thereupon the House of Representatives shall also proceed to consider said objections.

Senators and Representatives in their respective Houses may each speak upon such objections ten minutes and not longer, nor oftener than once (except by unanimous consent), and after one hour's debate on the objections the main question shall be put upon receiving each list of votes and counting the same. And when all objections so made are decided upon in either House, it shall communicate its decision to the other House; and when both Houses have disposed of such objections, they shall immediately again assemble in the Hall of the House of Representatives, and the President of the Senate shall state the decision of each House upon the questions so submitted to them.

And all objections so made to the receiving or counting the votes of electors from any State shall be disposed of before a list of votes of electors from any other State is opened.

If but one list of votes of electors from any State has been so submitted to each House for its decision, and it shall appear that the Houses have not concurred in rejecting said list, the same shall be received. But if both Houses shall have concurred in rejecting any vote contained in such list, such vote shall not be counted; otherwise all the votes therein shall be counted.

If more than one list of votes of electors from any State, or paper purporting to be such list, has been submitted to each House for its decision upon objections made thereto, and it shall appear that the Houses have not concurred in receiving either of said lists as the authentic and lawful list, they shall each be declared by the President of the Senate, in the presence of the Senate and House of Representatives, as being rejected; and no list of votes of electors so rejected shall be afterward read in the presence of the two Houses except for information.

The votes having been ascertained and counted in the manner provided in this rule, the result of the same shall be delivered by the tellers to the President of the Senate, who shall thereupon announce the state of the vote, and the names of the persons, if any, elected, which announcement shall be deemed a sufficient declaration of the persons elected President and Vice-President of the United States, and together with a list of the votes, be entered on the Journals of the two Houses.

An analysis of the proposed rule will show its startling character. It is sought by a concurrent, not a joint resolution, to adopt a *joint rule* that casts new and inconsistent duties on the President of the Senate—an officer whose duties are defined by the Constitution—by requiring him to open "*papers purporting to be certified lists of votes*" whether they are such or not, and this in the face of the constitutional provision only requiring him to open actual certificates of votes, all of which votes are required to be counted. It is proposed to give Congress the right not only to *count* the electoral votes for President and Vice-President, but also the power *not* to count them at all. To do this, would, by a concurrent resolution, confer extraordinary and dangerous powers on the bodies passing it, and without a reasonable pretense of constitutional warrant.

The last clause of section 8, article 2 of the Constitution authorizes Congress to make all necessary *laws* to carry into execution certain enumerated powers, "*and all other powers rested by the Constitution in the Government of the United States or in any department or officer thereof.*" The right of Congress to make laws to carry into effect every provision of the Constitution will not authorize it to confer power on itself. A joint rule adopted by a concurrent resolution, such as the one now being considered, and without the President's approval, could in no sense be regarded as a law. This is a bold scheme to enable Congress to select the President and Vice-President of the United States from the persons voted for, regardless of the one receiving the highest number of electoral votes.

I do not admit by any means that the foregoing or any clause of the Constitution gives the right to Congress to *by law* confer such high power on itself.

The grounds of objection (if indeed any are required under the rule) to the certified list of votes of electors are left to the whims and partisan views of members of Congress. Whatever the objection may be, the two Houses must separate and consider it; and if there be a genuine certificate from a State and a paper purporting to be a certificate from the same State, the electoral vote of such State cannot be counted at all, on objection being made to each, without the concurrent action of both Houses. Under the rule, then, either House of Congress could prevent the vote of a State from being counted. This would result in one House (not Congress) controlling by its negative action the election of President and Vice-President of the United States. Under such a rule the case could arise where by the Senate and House acting together, or separately, no electoral vote would be counted, and there would then be no power to elect a President or Vice-President, and the country would be without either.

The House cannot elect a President, or the Senate a Vice-President, except from persons who have received *counted* electoral votes.

The resolution then goes to the extent of giving to each House the right to *count or not to count* the electoral votes of any or all of the States; and I agree there is as much warrant in the Constitution for this as for the authority to give Congress such right, especially by a joint rule of the two Houses.

The member from Indiana [Mr. BICKNELL] in charge of this measure was once in a speech here (June 10, 1880,) candid enough to say:

In my [his] judgment no joint rule will meet the existing emergency. Where an obligation rests on Congress to provide the legislation necessary to carry into execution constitutional provisions, a joint rule is not legislation. A joint rule in such a case is a mere make-shift, a temporary expedient: it binds nobody. Either House adopting it to-day may abandon it to-morrow. It carries no moral force with it.

Still with these views the distinguished member presses this resolution as its chief advocate. Constitutional obligations at times are made to set easy.

I am surprised that the advocates of the right of Congress to *count* the electoral votes should be willing to support that part of this "make-shift" which allows electoral votes to be counted without the concurrence of both Houses of Congress. I refer to this language of the resolution:

If but one list of votes of electors from any State has been submitted to each House for its decision, and it shall appear that the Houses have not concurred in *rejecting* said list, the same shall be received.

In such case who will count the electoral vote? Will not the President of the Senate count it?

But the measure of this proposed usurpation of power is to be found in that clause of the resolution which gives to one branch only of Congress the power to reject, with or without grounds, any and all electoral votes.

Two sets of certificates can be furnished for any State. Any person can make and return "*papers purporting to be a certified list of votes,*" and then one House could throw out the entire vote of the State. A simple illustration of the workings of the rule in this respect may be given: Suppose a presidential candidate received 214 electoral votes including the States of New York and Pennsylvania, and another had 155, and two sets of certificates were placed in the hands of the President of the Senate for each of these States. On objection being made, if one House should vote not to count the votes as shown by either of the certificates, 64 (New York 35, Pennsylvania 29) votes of the leading candidate would be rejected, his remaining vote would be only 150, and the candidate having 155 votes would become President of the United States. A majority of one branch of Congress would thus make a President from those voted for by the electors. A Vice-President would be made in the same way.

Having indicated the design, scope, and workings of the proposed rule, and in some measure shown the want of power to adopt it, let us take a broader view and consider who has the right to appoint electors, determine the validity of their votes, and to count their votes.

THE APPOINTMENT OF ELECTORS

is a purely State matter. The language of the Constitution is:

Each State shall appoint, in such manner as the legislature thereof may direct, a number of electors, equal to the whole number of Senators and Representatives to which the State may be entitled in the Congress, &c.—*Section* 1, *article* 2.

The same section of the Constitution provides that—

The Congress may determine the time of choosing the electors, and the day on which they shall give their votes.

Here the power of Congress in relation to the electors begins and ends. It has nothing to do with the *manner* of appointing them, and it follows that it has no right to establish a mode of determining when the legislature of the State has appointed them if it has acted at all.

Nothing is clearer than the fact that if electors have been chosen as the Constitution provides, at the time and in the manner fixed by law, and they have cast their vote on the day prescribed by law, that it must be counted as cast; and every attempt to prevent its being counted would be a bold effort to rob the people of this country, in flagrant violation of the Constitution of the United States, of their choice for President and Vice-President.

The proposed joint rule can only be characterized as a measure of usurpation and fraud, the enforcement of which could hardly in the end lead to anything short of bloodshed and war. It proposes to vest Congress, through the rejection of electoral votes, with the prerogative of selecting the two highest officers of the Government from the persons voted for, no matter how clearly it may have been determined by State or other authority that the votes were duly cast. It occasionally happened in republican Rome that her senators, the lords, and aristocrats would appear in the Campus Martius, and, with the aid of their armed servants and a hired retinue, prevent on an election day the choice of a consul unfriendly to them. This at least had the merit of boldness compared to a subtle method of depriving the electors of their votes after they were cast. The barbaric methods of two thousand years ago have been adopted in elections in some places in our Republic; they now seem to be giving way to the more bloodless method of not counting the votes cast. In these Halls we should give no countenance to either method.

WHO TO COUNT THE VOTE.

If the right to count the electoral vote, or, rather, to decide what vote should be counted, is not given specifically by the Constitution to any authority, it does not follow that Congress can assume it. The debates on the adoption of the Constitution show that it was designed to remove as far as possible the choice of President and Vice-President from the control of Congress.

Charles Pinckney, of South Carolina, a member of the constitutional convention, January 23, 1800, when speaking on the subject of the election of President of the United States, said:

He remembered very well that, in the Federal convention, great care was used to provide for the election of the President of the United States, independently of Congress, and to take the business, as far as possible, out of their hands.—*Elliott's Debates*, volume 4, page 424.

It may be observed here that it is quite immaterial who counts the electoral vote. The addition of a few figures is an easy task for any person. It is purely a matter of computation. The privilege of counting the vote, however, carries with it no right to reject it. The uniform construction put upon the language of the Constitution by its framers when adopted and first put in practice justifies the claim that Congress has no duty to perform in relation to counting the electoral vote other than to witness its count.

PRECEDENTS OF CONSTRUCTION.

The Constitution was signed September 17, 1787, and on the same day a resolution passed the convention unanimously directing the mode of putting the constitutional government into operation; and on the matter of counting the electoral vote for the first President, it says:

That the Senators should convene at the time and place assigned; that the Senators should appoint a President of the Senate for the *sole purpose of receiving, opening, and counting the votes for President.*

Washington, the president of the convention, signed this resolution.

Here was a clear construction of the Constitution, before the ink used in writing and signing it was dry, and by the voice of all its framers, which should alone close the mouths of doubters and modern constitutional expounders.

In accordance with the resolution the first Senate chose John Langdon, one of its number, President of the Senate; and, as its order declared—

For the sole purpose of opening the certificates and counting the votes of electors of the several States in the choice of President and Vice President of the United States.

Accordingly, on April 6, 1789, John Langdon did open the certificates and *count* the electoral vote for President and Vice-President, and he then declared, and so certified, that George Washington and John Adams were elected, the former President and the latter Vice-President of the United States.

The certificates were prepared by a committee of the Senate, and they recited that—

> The underwritten, appointed President of the Senate for the sole purpose of receiving, opening, and *counting* the votes of the electors, did, in the presence of the said Senate and House of Representatives, open all the certificates and *count all the votes of the electors for a President and Vice-President,* &c.

An extract from the Journal of the House of the last-named date also conclusively shows that the President of the Senate declared what votes should be counted by the tellers. Here it is:

> Mr. Parker and Mr. Heister [House tellers] then delivered in at the clerk's table a list of votes of the electors * * * as the same were *declared by the President of the Senate* in the presence of the Senate and this House.

This is the highest evidence that the President of the Senate not only opened the certificates but declared the electoral votes to be counted.

In both branches of Congress there were then many members of the convention that had but recently framed the Constitution. None were found to protest against the action of the President of the Senate.

Members of Congress of this day who deny the right of the President of the Senate to declare what votes are to be counted must occupy the unenviable position of believing that the makers of the Constitution did not know the cunning of their own child; and, as we shall presently see, they must hold that Washington, John Adams, Jefferson, Madison, &c., were each declared elected President of the United States on a count of electoral votes made in violation of the Constitution.

While the champion of this resolution [Mr. BICKNELL] admits that Mr. Langdon did the counting which made George Washington and John Adams first President and first Vice-President, the member from Virginia [Mr. HUNTON], in the face of history, denies that fact; yet they, by some sort of Democratic reasoning, bring themselves into mutual embrace and agree that one branch of Congress alone may count or not count the electoral vote. After giving a construction to the Constitution in favor of the President of the Senate's right to count the electoral vote, Congress passed, March 1, 1792, a law regulating the election of President and Vice-President, and therein recognized such construction. The material part of a section relating to the ascertainment of the vote is this:

> That Congress shall be in session the second Wednesday in February * * succeeding every meeting of the electors, and the said certificates, or so many of them as shall have been received, shall then be opened, the votes counted, and the persons who shall fill the offices of President and Vice-President ascertained and declared agreeably to the Constitution.

In that act there is no intimation that Congress had any right to count or reject electoral votes. This law, hoary with age, but yet in force, it is now proposed to annul by a simple concurrent resolution of Congress. Under it John Adams opened the certificates, *counted* the votes (February 5, 1793), and declared Washington President, and himself Vice-President, to commence the 4th of March, 1793. Again, in February, 1797, John Adams discharged his duty as President of the Senate by opening the electoral certificates and counting the votes, at the conclusion of which he pronounced *himself* elected President and Thomas Jefferson Vice-President, and thereupon delivered himself of a beatitude, thus:

> And may the Sovereign of the universe, the Ordainer of civil government on earth, for the preservation of liberty, justice, and peace among men, enable both to discharge the duties of these offices conformably to the Constitution of the United States with consciencious diligence, punctuality, and perseverance.

Mason of Virginia then reported from a committee of the Senate a resolution, which was adopted, requiring a notification of election to be sent to Mr. Jefferson, from which I read an extract:

> The underwritten, Vice-President of the United States and President of the Senate, did, in the presence of the said Senate and House of Representatives, open all the certificates and *count all the votes of the electors* for a President and for a Vice-President.

No clearer evidence could have been preserved, not only of what John Adams did, but of the judgment of the then Congress as to the duty of the Vice-President to count the electoral vote. In the fourth presidential election Jefferson (February, 1801) as Vice-President discharged his duty in relation to the electoral vote, and signed a certificate in compliance with an order of the Senate from which this is an extract:

> The underwritten, Vice President of the United States and President of the Senate, did, in the presence of the said Senate and House of Representatives, open all the certificates and *count all the votes of the electors for President,* whereupon it appeared that Thomas Jefferson, of Virginia, and Aaron Burr, of New York, had a majority of votes as electors, and an equal number of votes.

Here is the most conclusive evidence of Mr. Jefferson's personal action under the Constitution. The distinguished member from Iowa [Mr. UPDEGRAFF], who in June last made an exhaustive argument on this subject, has shown that Mr. Jefferson was called on to count the vote of Georgia for himself on a certificate (if it could be so called) which was more than technically defective. An account of his conduct, showing that he directed without consultation with anybody the vote of that State to be counted for himself and Aaron Burr, will be found in Davis's Memoirs of Burr, volume 2, page 71.

The honorable member from Georgia [Mr. STEPHENS], who, as I understand from his public writings and speeches, wholly repudiates the principles of the proposed joint rule and favors both Houses of Congress, while in joint session, exercising the right to settle by a vote *per capita* all disputed votes, in a published article (International Review, January and February, 1878) says Mr. Jefferson favored legislation by Congress to regulate the electoral count, and he quotes from what is said to be Mr. Jefferson's draught of an amendment to a bill pending before the Senate while he was Vice-President. It is fair to say that Mr. Jefferson's subsequent open public act which resulted in making himself President of the United States is in opposition to such a construction of the Constitution. No public act or speech of his supports this posthumous claim as to his views. It is quite certain that after Mr. Jefferson had written the paper referred to by the honorable gentleman he did not think well enough of it to have it offered in the Senate or to otherwise give it publicity, and he entombed it so thoroughly that its resurrection day did not come for seventy-five years and until grass had grown over his grave above half a century.

In the draught he is made to say that it is to be inferred from the wording of the Constitution that the members of the Senate and House of Representatives are to do the counting, and that they are brought together "*for that office, no other being assigned them.*"

The views of the gentleman from Georgia [Mr. STEPHENS] and those of Mr. Jefferson are in harmony on the question of the right of the two Houses in joint session to count the electoral vote, if this paper of Mr. Jefferson can be accepted as his settled views, and both are against the usurpation sought to be worked out through the pending resolution.

If we take Mr. Jefferson's draught as a whole, we will find that he did not believe any authority could or should deprive any State of an electoral vote. I quote from it:

That whenever the vote of one or more of the electors of any State shall for any cause whatever be adjudged invalid it shall be lawful for the Senators and Representatives of the said State, either in the presence of the two Houses or separately and withdrawn from them, to decide by their own votes to which of the persons voted for by any of the electors of their State [or to what person] the invalid vote or votes shall be given, for which purpose they shall be allowed a term of [one hour], and no longer, during which no certificate shall be opened or proceeded on.

This, however, so flatly contravenes the Constitution, which gives to States the right to select the persons who shall cast the electoral votes, that Mr. Jefferson on reflection may well have consigned this fugitive paper to supposed oblivion.

Those who assume to be the guardians of his name and fame should not have disturbed its resting place or discovered it to the public eye.

My friend from Georgia, while he regards Mr. Jefferson as an apostle of strict construction to be followed in the matter of the authority of Congress to ascertain the vote to be counted, could not but repudiate his views set forth in the quotation just made. He does not think Mr. Jefferson should be followed so far outside of the pale of the Constitution as to favor the casting of rejected electoral votes by members of Congress from States having such votes. While some differences of opinion developed early, yet they, on discussion, were dropped, and the uniform course obtained for the Vice-President to count the vote, and this prevailed until modern expediency has found it necessary to try to change it.

I might take up, did time permit, each Presidential election succeeding those given, and show the method I now contend for was uniformly pursued. Apology may be necessary for having gone into the details of history at all. I should not have done so but for the fact that at a recent session at least one member [Mr. HUNTON, of Virginia] confidently claimed that (with a single exception) "*the two Houses of Congress have exercised the power of counting the electoral vote.*" It is a misfortune that we so often read history awry, or that we do not read it at all.

CONSTITUTION.

A recurrence to the language of the Constitution on this subject and the history of its enactment will confirm us in the belief that the early and uniform practice we have shown to have existed was in accordance with its letter and spirit. The language of that instrument (section 1, Article II) is this:

The President of the Senate shall, in the presence of the Senate and House of Representatives, open all the certificates, and the votes shall then be counted.

This same language is found in the twelfth amendment to the Constitution, which is now in force. That amendment was proposed at the first session of the Eighth

Congress (December 12, 1803), and it was adopted by the required number of States in 1804, after four Presidential elections had been held under the Constitution, in which the President of the Senate counted the vote in the presence of the two Houses of Congress. If, as has been claimed, there is a *casus omissus* in respect to the electoral count, those who set the Constitution in motion did not discern it. No amendment was deemed necessary to change the prevailing construction of the Constitution, or to inaugurate a new policy in the matter of counting the electoral vote. No fears were then felt that the prevailing practice would lead to serious trouble. Why should we now drift from the old moorings? What new light has poured upon us in respect to this question? To use the language of Mr. Dallas in its defense:

> The Constitution in its words is plain and intelligible, and it is meant for the home-bred, unsophisticated understandings of our fellow-citizens.

In the original draught of the Constitution, reported to the convention from a committee of eleven (September 4, 1787, Elliott's Debates, volume 1, page 283), the language used was:

> The President of the Senate shall, *in that House*, open all the certificates, and the votes shall then *and there* be counted.

Two days later, when the report was under consideration, the convention added to this clause, after the word *counted*, the words *in the presence of the Senate and House of Representatives*, thus showing it only intended these bodies to be auditors at the opening and counting of the vote. No vote or other act of the convention indicates any change of such intent on its face. All that appears is that in a reformation or revision of the language of the clause it was thought best, without any change of the sense, to transpose it and insert the words *in the presence of the Senate and House of Representatives*, in lieu of the words *in that House*, and also to strike out, as superfluous, the words *and there*. This left the clause as it now stands. From such revision no possible inference can reasonably be drawn that the convention intended to alter its previously expressed purpose of requiring the votes to *be counted in the presence of the Senate and House of Representatives*. The language of the clause was improved, the meaning was not changed. Eleven days after this clause was agreed upon the same convention by resolution, as already shown, gave construction to it in harmony with its plain words. The convention did not, by inference, confer powers on Congress. Its powers were all carefully enumerated. (Section 8, Article I.)

The language is imperative and requires the votes shown by the certificates opened by the Vice-President to *then be counted*. What votes are then to be counted? Only the certified votes, and all these are absolutely required to be *then* counted. If votes are not certified they cannot be counted: if they are, and the certificate is laid before the joint convention, they must be counted, and *then*, for the Constitution so says.

If all that were contended for here was the privilege to perform the mere ministerial act of *counting* the votes, as so evidenced, it might be conceded, as no possible harm could come from it. Any person learned in addition could be trusted to do that. There is no objection to tellers doing it, as has always been the practice. The material thing is the declaration of the vote *to be counted*, and this duty devolves on the President of the Senate. This resolution requires the tellers "*to record and compute the votes of electors*," and this is all the actual counting needed. What is proposed, I repeat, is, under cover of an alleged power to count the electoral votes, to give Congress, and in certain cases one branch thereof, the right *not to count* them.

Those who advocate this plan contend that the right to count (or not count) the vote is not expressly granted to the Vice-President, and hence Congress may assume it. No right is given to Congress to gather to itself all powers not elsewhere conferred. It is said it is dangerous for the power to count the vote to be vested solely in one man—the President of the Senate. Grant this; it is always dangerous to repose power anywhere. If such power must belong somewhere it will be as safe with him as with Congress. In nearly one hundred years of our constitutional existence no case of abuse of power (unless Mr. Jefferson's acts constitute one) can be or has been charged against a President of the Senate in respect to the counting of the electoral vote. We could not hope for as happy results if Congress were clothed with this important duty.

Large bodies are more tyrannical than individuals. Oppression, tyranny, usurpation, and injustice, as history teaches us, are the offspring of party factions in republics as well as the children of absolute monarchs. The Roman senate in the last two centuries of republican Rome incited, countenanced, justified, and condoned more wanton bloodshed than can be laid at the door of individual monarchy for the same period in the history of any so-called civilized nation. If we turn on the light of the present in our own Republic we are not reassured. We have recently seen, under the *dictum* of party caucus, crime, and fraud, in the presence of which civilized man stands appalled, justified—not only justified, but sought to be legalized. We have witnessed legislative bodies abuse as well as usurp power. We have seen members of both great parties at our recent Presidential electoral count united in a commission hermaphroditically organized, partaking of law judges and law makers, divide on every material question—8 to 7—according to party bias. This was not calculated to quiet the sensitive nerves of the Republic. The defeated party cried through the land that the result was a larceny, grand larceny, Presidential larceny, and that it would be vindicated. The vindication has not yet come, it is true, and it is not likely ever to come in that case. A bad cause can have no vindication.

It has frequently occurred that a President of the Senate has unflinchingly discharged his duty under the Constitution, by counting the electoral vote and declaring elected a President and Vice-President of the opposite political party. When the fires of civil war were already lighting, in 1861, John C. Breckinridge (shortly thereafter a leader in rebellion), himself a Presidential candidate, then Vice-President, opened the certificates and counted (with the aid of the usual tellers), and so certified, the electoral vote that made the now immortal Lincoln President of the United States.

It is conceded that the President of the Senate, and he only, has authority to "open all the certificates," showing the electoral votes. This is a more dangerous power than the right to count the votes thus shown. He is to judge of the genuineness of the certificates. Should he decide that a paper purporting to be a certificate of such votes was not what it purported to be he need not present it, and there would then be no opportunity to count the vote of a State. This has actually occurred. On February 8, 1865, Vice-President Hannibal Hamlin, of Maine, withheld certificates from the States of Louisiana and Tennessee; and when, during the joint session of the Houses, he was called on to submit them, he refused, and they were never submitted, nor the votes counted. It is true he had the authority of a joint resolution (approved by the President), which had the force of a law, for refusing " to receive or count" the votes of these or other States. I refer to the joint resolution President Lincoln approved (February 8, 1865), and then sent a protesting message to the Senate disclaiming all right of the Executive to interfere in the matter of counting the electoral vote.

My friend from Virginia [Mr. HUNTON], in a speech here, says President Lincoln approved the twenty-second joint rule, adopted in that year. It was adopted by a concurrent resolution (February 6, 1865), and it was never submitted to him for his action. Other members have fallen into the same error. I understood the honorable Speaker, to-day, to cite the message of President Lincoln on the "joint resolution declaring certain States not entitled to representation in the electoral college," in support of the power of Congress to count the vote. Errors of judgment track in the wake of errors of history.

I do not justify the long-since abrogated twenty-second joint rule.

The resolution which President Lincoln approved set forth in its preamble that eleven States, and named them, were then in rebellion and on that account declared that " no electoral votes shall be received or counted from said States." This went to the root of the case, and it was not a regulation of the conduct of the count in joint convention of the Houses. Then Democrats, South, were absent, claiming these eleven States were out of the Union for all purposes, and Democrats North were agreeing with them in the main; but some of them claimed they were still in the Union far enough to help elect a President of the United States. In that instance, if in no other, the Republican party sided with the Southern Democrats, and accepted their view of the case, to a certain extent.

I am aware that my opinions are not parallel with any party lines.

Some members say, in the cases where the President of the Senate has counted the vote, he has done so under the authority of Congress. This cannot be true. Congress cannot delegate the constitutional powers it possesses. John Langdon, the first President of the Senate, had no authority of Congress to count the vote, yet he counted the vote without objection.

The accountability to which a Vice-President would be held in case he should abuse his official power or fail to faithfully perform his duty is a sufficient guarantee that he will never attempt either—certainly not before his party friends in Congress would be ready to do likewise.

It may be going too far to hold that Congress has not power to, in the ordinary way, pass a law to guide the Vice-President in opening and counting the electoral vote, but any law or rule which would deprive him of the right to do either would be unconstitutional.

The opinion entertained by Mr. Jefferson, and which my friend from Georgia follows, that whatever is done having relation to the count must be while in joint convention, is undoubtedly sound. It harmonizes with the Constitution. The Constitution absolutely fixes two things: (1) the certificates shall be opened; (2) the votes shall then be counted, and all in the presence of the two Houses.

There can be no counting or agreement to count or not count the vote in separate sessions.

In the adoption of this resolution the text and spirit of the Constitution is to be ignored, the truth of history is to be denied, all good and safe precedents are to be disregarded, an a single doubtful, dangerous, and repudiated precedent which grew out of a wholly unanticipated state of affairs incident to a civil war is to be invoked as a justification of the act.

If the Constitution does charge Congress with the duty of counting the electoral vote, it will exist without the aid of a joint rule; and if it does not exist under that instrument, then Congress cannot by joint rule impose that duty on itself.

That it could not have been contemplated that Congress should have the right, by vote, to disfranchise a State in the choice of a President, is plain enough from the whole structure of the Constitution and the division of powers.

The duties of Congress are legislative, and it cannot change itself into a returning board any more than it can resolve itself into a court with jurisdiction to try causes.

What is required to be done is "*in* the presence of the Senate and House of Representatives," and not *by* these bodies acting jointly or separately.

A final count of the vote and announcement of the result is very commonly made in the presence of both houses of a State legislature, as required by statute or organic law. In Ohio this is done by constitutional requirement, by "*the president of the senate in the presence of a majority of the members of each house.*" No person in that State has yet been crazy enough to start a question of the right of the general assembly of the State to count the vote or, what is worse, to throw out by its own fiat such votes as it pleased. It is quite convenient and proper for a formal count of votes cast in the election of high officers to be made and the result announced in the presence of a State or national legislature. In the effort to find some justification for the proposed rule some members resort to the clause of the Constitution which says "*each House may determine the rules of its proceedings.*" (Section 5, article 2.) Just what ray of light is thrown on this question by that clause some of us cannot see. Not even the right to make joint rules is given by it, much less a warrant to Congress to impose duties upon and withhold others from the Vice-President of the United States and to confer extraordinary powers on itself.

The "*proceedings,*" when the Houses have met in joint session, are not those of either body, but rather of the President of the Senate in the presence of both bodies.

The supreme danger from such a rule can, however, only be seen when we look to the fact that no concurrent action of the Houses is required to reject the votes of a State. When objection is made the certificate is not even *prima facie* authority for counting the vote certified if there is another paper which purports to be a certificate from the same State. The Constitution charges States with the duty of appointing electors in such manner as their respective Legislatures may direct, thus making their appointment a State matter exclusively. It also defines their eligibility. It is binding on States and their legislatures as much as upon Congress, and we are not in this or any other matter to assume, as does the proposed rule, that they will not only obey it as faithfully as Congress. What authority is there in that great charter for making that body the judge of how others upon whom a constitutional duty devolves discharge it? It may be enough for us to be the keepers of our own conscience. If we are seeking for grounds of apprehension we can soon satiate ourselves. We can find many ways by which the electoral vote of a State may be prevented from being counted. This would result from a failure of electors to meet after they were chosen, or after meeting, if they refused or neglected to vote, or make a certificate of the vote, or to return it if made, &c.; or if the President of the Senate should suppress the certificate, &c.

This resolution, based as it is on the idea that members of Congress can do no wrong, is not broad enough to cover all possible cases of failure of officers to discharge their duty. Bribery, as has been attempted, of a single elector might alter the result of a Presidential election.

I do not say that the President of the Senate would not be bound by a law which gave him fixed rules by which to ascertain the genuineness of electoral certificates, and which otherwise directed him in the execution of his duty, but such a law is scarcely necessary. The Constitution requires him to open the certificates, genuine certificates only, of the votes cast, and the counting of them follows as a matter of course. No judgment or suggestion of judgment or discretion is enjoined on this officer or other person or body in this regard, but the power only is given to declare the result of the prior action of the electors for the several States.

Neither the President of the Senate nor other authority can constitutionally disfranchise, in whole or in part, a State by rejecting certified electoral votes. There are persons who assume that if Congress has not the right to count or reject the electoral votes, that right is left with the President of the Senate. It is a grave error to suppose such right rests anywhere. There are few, if any, boards that are authorized to count and make returns of votes cast at any ordinary election that have any power to reject them.

The count of the electoral vote everybody has the right to make when the certificates are open, but it must be made once before the joint convention. No formal declaration of the result need be made; the Constitution does not require it. If a majority of the votes are for one man his election follows; if no person has such majority then the House must immediately proceed to elect a President as the Constitution directs, and the Senate in like case a Vice-President. There may be a necessity for some authority to judge finally of the true result in all cases of dispute. This necessity will exist as much in case the Congress counts the vote and in cases where the House and Senate elect the President and Vice-President, where no election has taken place by the electors, as if the President of the Senate counted it.

With appropriate legislation the question might possibly be settled in the Supreme Court of the United States by proceedings in *quo warranto* or by some other form of contest. To its final judgment all patriotic people would bow in submission. We are forced by the very nature of our Government, free as it is, to have to submit at last to some final arbiter, and often suffer injustice if it is meted out to us; otherwise the pillars of our political structure would go down in the first storm. The judgment of a high court would be more freely acquiesced in than the action of a partisan Congress.

Let us abandon this attempt to exercise powers not granted in the Constitution; let us cling firmly, persistently, and to the end to all our constitutionally granted powers; let us guarantee to all authorities or officers in the Union their properly granted powers, and no more; let us encourage them to faithfully discharge all their duties; let us cease to set bad precedents to others in the matter of usurping powers belonging elsewhere; lastly, if we have been so unfortunate as to find a weak place in the great charter of our national existence, let us gather around it and devote ourselves to curing its weakness; stand close about it and guard it from attack, strain, or break, so that our Republic, which has already, in, as we hope, the youth of its existence, been compelled to withstand the shock of a political earthquake from which it barely escaped being rent in twain, may never again be rocked in the cradle of civil strife.

Greater devotion to purifying the political morals and to the education, civilization, and Christianization of our people, and less to expedients under the pretense of providing against apprehended wrong, will be more fruitful of happy results. If we find our organic law is defective, let us amend it agreeably to its own provisions. Such a policy will avert any possible danger and transform all our fears to hope and confidence.

This country should now only be in the blossoming period of its growth and greatness. The possibilities of the future we do not yet hope to compass, but we may do our duty by strengthening all weak places as they appear, and by not attempting legislation based on an assumption that fraud and wrong will exist generally throughout all the departments of our dual Government.

Time would be well spent here if we devoted ourselves to legislation that would condemn electoral frauds in every part of the Union, and set the seal of infamy upon all persons, whether in high or low places, who practiced, excused, or countenanced them, or accepted the fruits of them.

Political morality ingrained into our national existence will create strength as nothing else creates it. Without an improvement in this respect and an abandonment of expedients by which one or another party hopes to gain, against the expressed will of the people, some advantage over all others, the time may not be far distant when this American Republic, teeming as it already does with above fifty millions of the happiest and freest people of the earth, may be found ready for final judgment. This particular epoch in our history is an auspicious one to adjust persons and parties on a true and patriotic basis; and if it should be found that any party ship has sailed so far out of a true course as to be incapable of being brought back, it should be scuttled, abandoned, and consigned to a deep-sea burial. This Government will roll on in safety upon the old lines if those who control its destiny are content to steer it by the landmarks of the Constitution planted by the patriotic fathers who set it in motion.

February 9, 1881. On the resolutions providing for assembling the two Houses in joint session to count the votes of electors for President and Vice-President.

Mr. KEIFER said:

Mr. SPEAKER: I do not rise for the purpose of specially opposing these resolutions. The first resolution is in the usual form, and it is wholly unobjectionable. The second resolution provides the alternative of not counting the vote of any State about which there may be a question. Of course that is directed, in this particular case, against the State of Georgia. It is seemingly an innocent expedient. It has precedent for it; but it is objectionable because it assumes a direction by Congress in the counting of the electoral votes. It undertakes to direct by a mere resolution of the two Houses what the President of the Senate shall do in the performance of a constitutional duty specially cast on him.

I deny that any power, whether the Vice-President or the Congress of the United

States, has the right to say the counting of the vote of any State shall not take place, and I deny that there is any power anywhere to reject the vote of any State after it has been cast and properly certified and returned. I believe the election of President and Vice-President took place, in effect, at least, in November last. I believe that on the first Wednesday in December last the voice of the people was recorded through the electoral colleges over this country, and that the President and Vice-President of the United States were then elected, and that the forms we are about to go through here are mere forms provided and fixed by the Constitution. I believe that our action in the matter of counting electoral votes does not make or unmake the President or Vice-President.

In the presence of the two Houses the Constitution requires certain things to be done, which amounts only to a public declaration of an election of President and Vice-President which has already taken place.

After electoral votes are ascertained to have been cast, it would be high usurpation in any person, official, or body to reject them.

I wish to say a single word in reference to Georgia. If the question were presented here now, with the light I have upon that subject, I should, if I were to participate in determining it—and I do not see how that could possibly be under the Constitution—I should be in favor of counting the vote of Georgia, because I believe the people voted in November for electors for President and Vice-President. They then elected the electors of the State; and while those electors did not meet on the precise day fixed by the laws of the United States, still they seem to have in good faith met and cast their votes in accordance with the instructions and directions, so to speak, of the people of the State of Georgia. There was no fraud or intention to commit fraud or wrong. I do not hold that time can be the essence of that vote, although I admit if any fraud or any wrong were thereby committed, the State might be disfranchised for that reason.

Mr. COOK. I desire to ask the gentleman a question.

Mr. KEIFER. I will hear it.

Mr. COOK. Suppose the vote of Georgia changed the result of the Presidential election, would you then vote for counting it?

Mr. CALKINS. I would if there were no fraud.

Mr. KEIFER. I do not admit, in the first place, that I would have or could have, under the Constitution and laws of the United States, any right to decide that question; but if I had, as I now understand it, I should vote under such state of case to admit the votes of that State in the count.

FEES OF EXAMINING SURGEONS.

December 16, 1880. The House, in committee, had under consideration the pension appropriation bill, the pending clause was a provision fixing one dollar as the fee for the examining surgeon for each examination of a pensioner, as provided by law, "except when the examination is made by a board of surgeons, in which case the fees now allowed by law shall be paid."

Mr. KEIFER moved to strike out "one" and insert "two," making the fee two dollars, against which a point of order was made.

Mr. KEIFER said:

Mr. CHAIRMAN. If I understood the honorable gentleman aright in his answer a few moments ago, when I called his attention to this matter, he now makes a statement which is entirely the opposite of that. He then stated to us, and I thought he was right, that the law gave to each examining surgeon in these cases $2; but that under this new-fangled method—that is, the effect of what he said—of legislating upon appropriation bills, for a few years past, this has been ingrafted on the law and the fee thereby cut down to $1.

Is it not true that under existing law, without a provision in the appropriation bill and without a limiting clause in the bill, the allowance would be $2? From year to year for a few years past we have been changing existing law on our appropriation bills, and in this case we have cut down the sum allowed examining surgeons to $1. Now, if I understand the law aright, the amendment that I offer is not only in exact accordance with the existing law, but simply proposes to restore the law to what it was before this temporary change was made, and the point of order therefore ought to have been made that this, which in reality changes the law, is legislation on an appropriation bill. This provision in the bill, coming from this august Committee on Appropriations, is simply an undertaking to change existing law itself. My proposition is to restore the clause so that it will be entirely consistent with existing law. If the gentlemen on the Committee on Appropriations deem it possible that they can violate a rule by injecting into their bill or by undertaking to put into their bill a provision that changes existing law, I ought to be allowed by my motion at least to restore the law.

The CHAIRMAN. The Chair presumes, and it will not be controverted, that the appropriation made heretofore for the purpose of providing fees for surgeons in such cases has been at the rate of $1 for each examination.

Mr. KEIFER. Will the Chair allow me to suggest that that applied to the law regulating the distribution of the appropriations under that particular bill and for that fiscal year only, but it did not undertake to change existing laws permanently.

The CHAIRMAN. Be that as it may, the Chair is of opinion that the existing law provides that the fee shall be $1. It will not be denied that for this year at least the law has been $1. Then, if you hold that you do not repeal the present law you will have the absurdity of two laws existing at the same time directly the reverse of each other, which is an impossibility. The Chair is of opinion that this is the existing law, and therefore that the point of order is well taken.

Mr. KEIFER. Do I understand the Chair to say that if the law was modified for but one year, not by repealing the act, but modified simply for that year, that it would change it forever? I believe it is conceded that recent appropriation bills of like character to this have only undertaken to amend that law pro tanto in this respect, and for the fiscal year appropriated for only. But in the absence of any other legislation on the subject the old law would operate again. The existing law for the coming fiscal year, for which we are now appropriating, would be $2.

Mr. HISCOCK. I believe it is entirely right the House should have had a chance to express an opinion on this question. Therefore, I would suggest to the gentleman from Ohio that he modify his motion and move to strike out the proviso.

Mr. KEIFER. That I intend to do.

The point of order was sustained.

Mr. KEIFER. I will not appeal from the decision of the Chair, although I am inclined to think that my amendment does not change existing law for the year for which this bill proposes to make appropriation. But the point of order having been sustained, I move to strike out the proviso beginning on line 29, as follows:

Provided, That a fee of $1, and no more, shall be paid to the examining surgeon for each examination of a pensioner, as provided by law, except when the examination is made by a board of surgeons, in which case the fees now allowed by law shall be paid.

The object of my motion will be quite apparent to the committee. It is to get rid of the legislation proposed in this appropriation bill on the subject of regulating the fee to be paid to an examining surgeon for the examination of pensioners. I understand, and I believe it to be conceded all around, that in the absence of such a limitation as is found in this bill the fee of an examining surgeon, under existing law, would be $2. The last clause in the proviso that is proposed to be stricken out is simply in the nature of an exception in favor of paying the sum of $2 when there is an examination made of a pensioner by a board of surgeons. The proviso says that in such a case the fees now allowed by law shall be paid. So that if the committee and the House should decide to strike out all that I have called attention to and that is included within my motion, the law would operate and the sum of $2 would be paid, under the law as it now stands, to examining surgeons.

Mr. HUBBELL. As I understand, there is no general law as to that.

Mr. KEIFER. Gentlemen all around me say there is. And there is certainly a presumption there is a general law when we find the Appropriations Committee undertaking to do something in limitation of that general law. It is a very late day, it is true, to undertake to talk about legislation upon appropriation bills; but I may be permitted to say again that it is exceedingly unsatisfactory, not only to members of the House, but to the country. We have to get along with these appropriation bills rapidly. We are expected to appropriate the necessary money to carry on the different departments of the Government and to pay for the important services that are to be paid for by appropriations; and we very often find that in the appropriation bills we have struck out many provisions of law that are very wise for the country.

[Here the hammer fell.]

Mr. SAPP obtained the floor, and yield his time to Mr. KEIFER.

Mr. KEIFER. I am very much obliged to the gentleman from Iowa.

Now, a word as to the merits of this. In the first place, it is but simple justice to pay a skilled surgeon or physician what his services are worth. I need not add anything more than that. All over this country, when you employ a good surgeon or physician to do so important a thing as to examine the man who claims to be suffering from wounds or diseases contracted in the service of the United States, it will be agreed that $1 is too small a sum. For my part, I think the general judgment of the country would say that $2 was too low a fee for such a service. The corporations that are called upon to employ physicians to make examinations in reference to life-insurance I think in every case pay at least $3 for a single examination, and in many cases $5. But that is immaterial. It is but just that a physician who is fit to be selected for this duty should be paid what it is worth.

Without any reflection upon the physicians who accept this duty, I believe it is better for the Government to pay what the service is worth: it is in the line of economy to do it; and it will at least be some incentive to the physician to do his work well, and will protect the Government also against any mistakes or errors of his, and in some degree, however slight, will avert that great danger to which the distinguished gentleman from Michigan says we are constantly exposed in the matter of appropriations. I do not quite agree with that gentleman in the methods he would adopt to ferret out what he calls suspected cases of fraud. If we employ a good Commissioner of Pensions, if we employ good clerks, if we employ the best physicians of the land, and pay them, we are very likely to get rid of much of what the gentleman denominates and classifies generally as frauds upon the Government.

Now, I think it would be a wise thing to take the judgment of a Congress that has passed upon this question deliberately, not in an appropriation bill, but in a law, and that re-enacted that law in the Revised Statutes of the United States, and pay at least something that approximates the real value of this important service to the Government.

Mr. ROBINSON. I do not desire to speak upon the merits of the pending proposition, but I wish to suggest to the gentleman from Ohio [Mr. KEIFER] that he should consider what is the law now, for there is great doubt about his accomplishing with his amendment what he wishes.

Mr. KEIFER. I do not know but possibly there is something in the point made by the gentleman from Massachusetts [Mr. ROBINSON], though I am inclined to think there is not. I am obliged to him, however, for making the suggestion. I think the clause he has read from the last pension appropriation bill has reference to the payments for examinations of pensioners under that act.

Now let me submit a slight evidence at least in favor of that position. It is that our Committee on Appropriations in preparing this bill gave interpretation to their bill of last year and came to the conclusion that in order to prevent the operation of section 4777 of the Revised Statutes, which allows the payment of $2 for each examination, it was necessary to repeat this clause in this appropriation bill. If I am not mistaken, then under the law of last year, by a provision put into an appropriation bill—I will not say stolen into it—with the understanding that it applied only to the then coming fiscal year, gentlemen have accomplished a repeal of a general law. I do not think they intended to do that, and I do not think they did do it. I think if my motion to strike out this proviso shall prevail we will go back to the general law found in section 4777 of the Revised Statutes.

Before I close I desire to say one word in response to the argument, if I may so call it, which came from the gentleman from Georgia [Mr. BLOUNT] in favor of economy. As I understood it, amid the confusion around me, the gentleman was under the impression that distinguished physicians of the country ought to perform this work for less than it was worth because it might be an advertisement for them.

Now, I wonder if we here work on any such principle? I wonder if the gentleman himself takes his seat in Congress, draws his pay of $5,000 a year, and his mileage for coming here and returning, on the theory that his services are worth a vast deal more than that amount, but that the rest is paid him by a mere advertisement to the people of the country and to the world?

The humble physician in a remote village, wherever he may be, is to be annoyed by pensioners and called upon to perform a great and valuable service to the country merely as an advertisement! Sir, the people in my portion of the country do not accept such an advertisement. I am told by gentlemen around me that in the principal towns on the frontiers of Kansas, Nebraska, and other States physicians cannot possibly be found who will, for the miserable sum of $1, make this examination; and the poor pensioner is obliged in many instances to travel scores of miles to find some man who is willing to perform this service for the pitable sum of $1.

Now, if we are to protect the Government as we should protect it, we should employ the best men for the purpose and pay them for their services; we should secure the best skill of the country and pay for it as individuals are willing to pay for it and as large corporations pay for it.

The CHAIRMAN. The question is on the amendment of the gentleman from Ohio [Mr. KEIFER].

Mr. SPARKS. Has not a point of order been raised on that amendment?

The CHAIRMAN. No point of order has been made upon it.

Mr. KEIFER. None can be made.

Mr. SPARKS. Of course none can be made now.

The question being taken on agreeing to the amendment, there were—ayes 62, noes 62.

Mr. KEIFER. I call for tellers.

No quorum having voted, tellers were ordered; and Mr. KEIFER and Mr. HUBBELL were appointed.

The committee divided; and the tellers reported—ayes 80, noes 74.

So the amendment was agreed to.

BISBEE VS. HULL.

January 21, 1881. On this contested-election case of Bisbee against Hull—

Mr. KEIFER said:

Mr. SPEAKER: I propose to occupy the time of the House but a very few minutes. I was about saying, when interrupted, that the subcommittee of the Committee on Elections, consisting of five members, heard this case early in the extra session of this Congress. Counsel were heard orally before the committee. Printed briefs were furnished. And I may say that that subcommittee considered this case long and carefully before it was enabled to reach a unanimous conclusion. It then did reach a unanimous conclusion, which conclusion was affirmed unanimously by the full Committee on Elections, at least so far as its members were present at the time the case was considered.

Now, I will say, briefly, that when the State canvassing board of the State of Florida canvassed the votes of the second Congressional district of Florida it rejected the entire vote of one county of that district, Madison County. By the rejection of that vote a result was reached which gave to the sitting member [Mr. HULL] a majority of 12 only. That State canvassing board had before it the returns from Madison County, all regular in form, as shown in the record in this case, and all unassailed then and now. There never has been a word uttered or shown in the record against a single one of the returns from Madison County before that canvassing board. Up to the present time not a word has escaped the lips of the sitting member or his counsel in the form of an objection to any one of those returns that were before the State canvassing board. By canvassing those returns with the other counties canvassed by the State canvassing board, Horatio Bisbee, jr., was found to have received a majority of 201. The State canvassing board, it is fair to say, rejected the returned vote of Madison County because the return of one precinct of that county, precinct No. 4, was not there. Somebody had destroyed it or disposed of it, or it had been lost; so that it was not present. The contestant applied to the supreme court of the State of Florida and obtained a peremptory writ of mandamus directed to the State canvassing board which compelled that board to assemble again and canvass the returned vote of the county of Madison.

When it had been canvassed they found that the contestant, Mr. Bisbee, had a majority of 201. When that majority was ascertained the contestant appealed to the then governor of the State of Florida to issue to him a certificate, the governor having theretofore issued a certificate of election to the sitting member. The governor very politely referred that application of Mr. Bisbee to the attorney-general of the State, a distinguished lawyer and Democrat, asking his opinion as to whether he ought to annul his former certificate and issue a certificate to the man who, as shown by the canvass of the canvassing board, had been elected. The attorney-general with commendable promptness returned the application with a lengthy opinion, exhibiting great ability, and saying that it was the imperative duty of the governor to cancel his previous certificate and issue one to Mr. Bisbee. Thereupon the governor declined to do so.

The Committee on Elections, I will say, put no great stress on all this that I have stated about the supreme court, but finding the whole of the returns before the committee, together with the indisputable return from poll No. 4, Madison County, showing the precise vote in that precinct—the committee heard by all the returns before them, said unanimously, "It is immaterial what the supreme court did or what its powers were; here is the vote of the county all here; it is regular in form, unassailed in every respect." Hence the committee counted it, and by counting that vote the committee found that the majority for Mr. Bisbee, without taking anything else into consideration, was 258 instead of 201. We found that at poll No. 4, the poll unreturned to the canvassing board, the majority for Mr. Bisbee, undisputed by the contestee in his brief, was 57. There is no case where, with the vote all before the House and its committee, with the returns all regular, the votes undisputed, the House has ever undertaken to reject a claim to a seat because somebody failed to do his duty.

Now I turn to Marion County, and only to refer to what is very commendable in the sitting member. The contestee himself, after examining the vote in that county concedes openly and plainly in his brief that there was fraud in the Long Swamp or, Whiteville poll of that county—fraud committed by the judges of election, they taking 93 votes from those actually cast for Horatio Bisbee, jr., and transferring them to the vote actually cast for the sitting member, thereby making a change of 186 votes. The vote of that county was canvassed by the State canvassing board, giving to the sitting member in that precinct 131 votes and to the contestant 41, whereas it is admitted on all hands and abundantly proved that it should have been 134 votes for the contestant and 41 for the contestee. We have there a change of 186.

We find that in one precinct in Alachua County, Cow Creek poll, the vote was not returned, and that poll really gave to the sitting member 24 votes, and to the contestant 2 votes.

The county of Brevard I have not spoken of; and that is the only other part of the case to which I mean to refer. In that county the vote was returned in some form or other to the State canvassing board, but the board unanimously rejected the entire vote of that county—did not canvass it—for what particular reason we have been unable to ascertain. We do know from their return that they threw the whole vote aside for some reason which they deemed sufficient. The contestant, Mr. Bisbee, attacks the whole vote of this county. He thinks there were irregularities. It is shown in the case, it is true, that in one precinct, in the absence of a ballot-box such as is prescribed by the statute of the State of Florida, in the absence of a box or anything with which to make one, the vote was taken in a beer-bottle. It is shown that in another case a cigar-box was used, and so on. But we examined all these things carefully; and in view of an agreed statement of fact which we find in the case we have decided to count the vote of Brevard County, which gives to the contestee 116 votes and to the contestant, Mr. Bisbee, 41 votes.

In view of everything in the case we have concluded that it is our duty to canvass this vote. Canvassing all the votes in the light of the returns, in the light of agreements and everything that is before us, we find 350 majority for Horatio Bisbee, jr. This is subject to a very slight deduction. The contestee objects to 18 votes in certain counties—Duval, Putnam, Baker, Columbia, and Suwannee. He claims that those votes were cast by non-residents or non-registered voters. Without stating any reasons, I may say that the committee deduct 11 votes from the majority of 350, and find the majority of the contestant to be 339. Only 18 votes were attacked in that way.

Now, Mr. Speaker, I have occupied much more time than I intended. I demand the previous question on the resolution, and if, after that demand is seconded and the main question ordered, the gentleman desires a portion of the time accorded to me under the rules, I will be willing to yield it to him.

(Mr. Bisbee was seated.)

YEATES VS. MARTIN.

January 27, 1881. On the North Carolina contested-election case of Yeates against Martin—

Mr. KEIFER said:

Mr. SPEAKER. It has seemed to some gentlemen on this floor, as they indicated a few days ago, that we were considering two cases here as though each were a pure matter of favor. When we were considering the case of Mr. Bisbee of Florida *vs.* Mr. Hull some gentlemen thought we ought to comple it with this one, because in that case it was proposed to turn out a man who was a Democrat and put in a Republican, and that we ought as a matter of reparation and by courtesy all agree that we should now turn out a Republican and put in a Democrat. I wish to say that up to this moment, although I think I have given due consideration to the report of the committee, as well as to the argument of the distinguished gentleman from Georgia— and I will say for him that it is the best argument I think that side of the question is susceptible of—I have learned of no higher or better reason than that for unseating Mr. Martin, and that in my judgment it is proposed here to commit a great outrage upon the gentleman from North Carolina. I would not speak in this way if I did not feel that I was justified by the report of the majority in saying that in every case—every case I believe with the exception of the one where it is claimed that the gentleman from North Carolina himself was guilty of an act of indiscretion in regard to a certain voting precinct—all that is claimed here in effect is that the Democrats have contrived at the election held in the several precincts in North Carolina, over which a contest arises, a scheme by which they might fix up a plan for unseating this man and putting another one in his place. We will see if we do not show this as we go along.

I intend to consider this case, I think, as impassionately as possible. It ought to be kept in mind that the election held on the 5th day of November, 1878 was an election for members of Congress in the State of North Carolina, and that it was coupled with no election for any other officer whatever. It was a simple question as to who should be chosen for Representative in Congress, and was not complicated by any State, municipal, or township election. The returning board of North Carolina is composed of the governor, the secretary of state, the attorney-general, and two State senators, the latter appointed by the governor from each of the two parties. The canvass made by the State board gave Mr. Martin his seat by 51 majority. Now, it is conceded, I think, on all hands that the county canvassing board had no right to reject the vote of Providence Township, in Pasquotank County, North Carolina. In that township the contestant received a majority of 39 votes. I want to say, Mr. Speaker, that I have saved myself a very great deal of trouble in the consideration of this case over this question as to whose duty it was to bear the returns from the voting places to the county seat. It is claimed—and I do not care whether that is true or false—that a registrar of a voting precinct could not be chosen properly under the laws of the State of North Carolina to carry the returns to the county seat. There is some little difference of opinion on that point, but we bottomed a case a few days ago in which we all were happily united upon this principle, that it matters not what irregularities had taken place from the time the votes were put into the boxes up to the time they came to be considered and counted here in the House, that it matters not what irregularities were shown as to the returns if we had the vote or the returns before us here which would indisputably show the real vote cast, that it was our duty to count it. That is the law, and has never been disputed, so far as I know, unless in this present case. So it is unnecessary to write long reports or to make long speeches to show that A ought nor that B ought to have carried the returns, if we have the returns here. It is our duty, in fairness to the people and as an act of justice to the man elected, to give him the benefit of the votes cast.

I agree that it was not right to reject the vote of Providence Township, which gave to the contestant 39 majority, simply because the wrong man may have carried the returns to the county seat.

I find in the briefs of counsel for the contestant this same question discussed as to whether it is not the duty of the House, on the same ground that we admit this voting precinct, to reject Salem precinct, in the same county. It is not very clearly shown, I admit, in the certificate that was read by the gentleman from Georgia whether or not these two precincts were rejected by the county board solely on the ground that the right man did not carry up the returns. But it is argued all through the case, and the distinguished gentleman himself in preparing and presenting his report to this House assumes that was the state of things, and says we are not called on in this township to reject that vote—the vote of Salem Township—because he says it is already rejected. And that is the *summum bonum* of all his argument in the report against counting the vote in Salem Township, which was rejected on the ground that the right man did not carry the returns to the county seat.

The difficulty about counting that precinct was that it gave a majority of 135 for Mr. Martin, the sitting member. This was the trouble about its being counted. There was no trouble about counting 39 votes for the contestant; there was no difficulty, no legal trouble about that.

But I admit, and I shall come to that as I go along, that there is some question made on another ground as to counting the vote of Salem precinct. But I shall consider that when I consider the same question as applied to other precincts in other counties.

The contestant objects to counting the vote in several precincts because polls were not opened at the proper hour. This objection applies to precincts giving the contestee the majorities following: Salem precinct, Pasquotank County, 135; South Mills precinct, Camden County, 64; Vandemere precinct, Pamlico County, 10. The votes in South Mills and Vandemere were canvassed by the returning boards. The vote in Salem was not canvassed.

Now, Mr. Speaker, the registrar in each of these precincts, J. S. Lester in Salem, John E. Spence in South Mills, and H. C. Holton in Vandemere, were Democrats. I may say as a matter of fact that all the registrars in the State of North Carolina were Democrats. Now in these three precincts it is claimed that the contestee, the Republican, should not be entitled to have counted for him the majorities that were cast for him because, as the facts show, Democratic registrars connived, schemed, planned, and arranged so that the polls should not be opened until after the hour of seven o'clock in the morning. They planned it and arranged it and sent Democrats through the township saying that they would not open the polls, when in fact they did open the polls after the time fixed by law.

Mr. MANNING. You do not pretend to have any testimony for that?

Mr. KEIFER. Yes, sir; and it is Democratic testimony, too.

Mr. MANNING. I give notice to the gentleman that I will assert and undertake to maintain that there is not a syllable of proof to justify the criticism he is now pronouncing. And I will show that the gentleman in the statements he is now making is giving way too much to his passion instead of manifesting that impartiality which ought to characterize the discussion of a case like this.

Mr. KEIFER. I will say to the gentleman from Mississippi that I am the mildest mannered man, I trust, and the best tempered man in this House. [Laughter.]

Mr. MANNING. I hope when I take the floor I will not be so reckless of the testimony, as I understand it, as the gentleman from Ohio is now illustrating himself to be.

Mr. KEIFER. That which hurts gentlemen always makes them squeal.

Mr. MANNING. I give you notice that I will make good what I have just stated.

Mr. KEIFER. I have named the men who are the registrars. I am hardly required, in order to satisfy a gentleman who is possessed of an acute, reasoning, logical mind—I am hardly required to go and get some man to swear that these Democratic registrars got somebody else to perpetrate this outrage when it was their duty to prevent its being done. Do you want me to call a witness to swear that Holton did not manage Vandemere precinct, in Pamlico County, so that the polls were not opened until after seven o'clock? Why, he swears he did it himself, if you want that. The gentleman from Mississippi wants the proof. The fact is admitted that all these registrars were Democrats. They did call on some men to serve as inspectors, but took pains to call on men who would not serve when there were plenty around who would serve. It is shown that when Democrats found the polls were not opened at the hour fixed they scattered off like rats. That is not the language of the witnesses, but the effect of what some of them say. It seems that the Democrats only ran off for fear the polls would be opened and they might have a right to vote. Some of them hastened away, according to the proof, after the polls were just about being opened.

Now, who is to blame that these polls were not opened? Not the contestee, but the friends of the contestant. It is proved, I think, to the satisfaction of everybody that these precincts where they did not succeed in getting the polls opened at precisely seven o'clock in the morning were largely Republican precincts. No Democratic precinct suffered such a hardship. I say that impassionately.

Mr. MANNING. We prefer, I think, to take the conclusion that Mr. FIELD reached. I say that in reply to all which the gentleman states so impassionately.

Mr. KEIFER. There were a few Republicans who went away in one place where it was publicly stated that the polls would not be opened. I think gentlemen will want to rely on something more than Mr. FIELD if they expect to satisfy the judgment of this House. Mr. FIELD reaches a conclusion fairly. I wish they would take him in everything. Gentlemen must not assert that his conclusion is in opposition to what I am saying on this question, for it is not.

Mr. MANNING. I do assert it, and the testimony will show it.

Mr. KEIFER. Does the gentleman say that these registrars were not Democrats?

Mr. MANNING. That is begging the question ; you must live up to your sweeping charge.

Mr. KEIFER. I am willing to yield to any proper question without getting into a mere colloquy. I always yield to gentlemen for proper questions.

Mr. MANNING. I do not want to interrupt you any further.

Mr. KEIFER. I do not want to get into any colloquy about this matter of testimony. It is proper to say that there was a man by the name of Wilcox who was substituted along in the day in one of these precincts for registrar, and he was not a Democrat. He got the polls opened as quickly as he could after he was substituted.

Mr. MANNING. I do not want you to modify what you have said.

Mr. KEIFER. I do not modify it. I say that the registrars who had the duty of opening these polls in every instance were Democrats. It is said some of the election officers were not sworn, or if sworn, it was by persons not authorized to administer oaths. The authorities and the argument already made make it clear that this can make no difference. I will not stop to argue that, for if these officers performed their duty and committed no fraud or wrong, they became *de facto* inspectors and judges of elections, and the election under the law must stand just the same as if they had been *de jure* officers. In this the whole blame was on the Democratic registrars and other officers.

Now, no fraud is shown to have taken place in any of these precincts where they say the polls were not opened in time. None is charged, none is alleged. None of these persons had a right to leave the polls until the registrar and other officers whose duty it was to open the polls had left. And they have no right to complain now that they were not permitted to vote.

There is one of the polling precincts, that of South Mills, where the additional objection is made that a Democratic board and a Democratic registrar or judge of election by the name of Overton, when they went to dinner, took the ballot-box, locked it up in a room and kept it there, and after they got through dinner took the box back to the voting place and the election went on.

Now, we are asked to decide, and I believe some of the members of the Election Committee hold, that that act ought to destroy the majority which the sitting member received in that precinct. Saying nothing now about any scheme or contrivance, for it may not have been a scheme on the part of the officer in that case, the law is against throwing out that vote. There is a recent case in my own State precisely in point (19 Ohio St., 25), and the decision follows the uniform decisions all over the country. In those decisions it is held that unless there was fraud, unless somebody was wronged, unless somebody was prevented from voting, the election should not be declared void. There is no charge of fraud or wrong done in this case.

In Hamilton precinct, Martin County, 64 votes are to be excluded because Mr. Martin, the sitting member, in the presence of the Democratic registrar, assisted to check off some of the votes. I repeat that 64 votes are to be excluded from the vote of the sitting member because a Democratic registrar allowed or permitted or requested the sitting member to check off the list some few of the names of those who voted.

Now, the testimony shows that no person was harmed. The testimony affirmatively shows that there was no corruption in that case. The testimony clearly shows that no man was prevented from voting; that there was no harm done any one, and that there was nothing done by Mr. Martin as registrar at all, except in one or two instances to act as the hand in striking off votes of the Democratic registrar, who was there, and who himself swears that there was no corruption and no harm done.

I understand that only a minority of the Committee on Elections hold that the objection urged on that account is a valid objection. Perhaps it would be well, in order to make the point clear (for it is an important matter), to call attention to the testimony in this case upon that point.

I will read all the testimony that has any material bearing on the subject of the alleged misconduct of Mr. Martin. I read first from the testimony of Justus Everitt, who says he was present at the election in Hamilton precinct, Martin County. He further says:

I was there a part of the time, and Mr. Martin was also present, and had charge of the registration books, and had charge when I left, which was in a few minutes.

Q. What Mr. Martin did, was it done in the presence of the poll-holders ?
A. It was.
Q. Did Mr. Martin act corruptly ?
A. Not that I know of.

Now I read from the testimony of Jonathan G. Carroway, the Democratic registrar. In answer to a question he says :

I was present on the day of election spoken of ; Mr. Martin was present around the polls, and I saw him check off some of the registered names of voters as they voted ; and my impression is that at one time he came around the counter where the judges of election were, and while on the side of the counter where the judges of election were I think he did not check off any names while there ; and when he checked off names he was on the side of the counter where the people came up to vote.

I read further from his cross-examination:

Q. How many names did Mr. Martin check off the poll-book?
A. I can't say positively, but I think he checked off some forty or fifty.
Q. Was the checking off done in the presence of the poll-holders?
A. I think it was, or a majority of them.
Q. Did Mr. Martin act corruptly in checking off the names?
A. Not that I know of.
Q. Who received the votes?
A. W. K. Gladson.
Q. Was any man's name deposited in the box before his name was checked off of the poll-book?
A. None that I know of.
Q. Were you one of the judges at said election?
A. I was acting as registrar for Mr. Justus Everitt, who was the legally appointed registrar.
Q. Was the election conducted fairly?
A. So far as I know.
(The counsel for the contestant objects to the above upon the ground that it is going into new matter.)
Q. What party do you belong to?
A. To the national Democratic party.
Q. Who did you vote for?
A. I voted for Jesse J. Yeates.

That is all the testimony in the record, I think, bearing on this question. So I may leave that point.

Now, Mr. Speaker, if gentlemen feel that I have spoken with some earnestness or even passion on this subject of the exclusion of votes because Democratic registrars did not go to the polls in due time, let them reserve their feeling for this next point. In Merry Hill precinct, Bertie County, 108 votes cast for Mr. Martin where thrown out because of an alleged "device" upon the tickets. Now let me state the facts of this matter. A man, said to be a distinguished lawyer of the State of North Carolina, named J. B. Martin—(please do not confound him with J. J. Martin) J. B. Martin, a distinguished lawyer and the attorney in this case for Jesse J. Yeates, unblushingly swears that he hired a man by the name of Bond, a Democratic printer, to print these tickets which were thrown out, and which we are told are not to be counted. J. B. Martin had them printed with this so-called "device" upon them; he himself, according to his own testimony, distributed them to unsuspecting persons—colored persons and others—and this caused these tickets to be voted; and when he found they were being voted he went and appealed to the judges of election, a majority of them Democrats, to throw them out; and they did his bidding.

As soon as this contest came up we find J. B. Martin appearing as the counsel of Jesse J. Yeates in this case; and the majority of the committee say that it would be a righteous thing to purge the ballot-box in this precinct by not allowing these tickets to be counted for Mr. J. J. Martin. If anybody disputes the facts I will prove them from the record. The majority of the committee say that the purity of the ballot-box in North Carolina requires that these tickets with this wonderful "device" upon them should not be counted. Perhaps it would be a good thing to put into the RECORD the testimony of this most unsavory gentleman. It would take too much of my time to read it, but unless there is objection I will print as a part of my remarks the testimony of Mr. J. B. Martin himself upon this point, and also the testimony of Mr. Bond; Mr. J. B. Martin being the man who had the tickets printed, who distributed them, who then had them rejected, and Mr. Bond being the man who printed them. Here is the testimony of J. B. Martin:

Q. What is your age and occupation?
A. James B. Martin; age thirty-five, occupation attorney at law; resident of Bertie County.
Q. Just previous to the Congressional election in 1878 did you have printed some tickets, as follows: "Republican ticket: "For Congress, J. J. Martin?"" If so, who printed them, and how many of them were received by you?
A. I did. I did not receive to exceed one hundred and fifty. Wm. M. Bond, of Edenton, printed them.
Q. Were those received by you prior to the election?
A. I received them night before election.
Q. What did you do with them?
A. A part of them were put in an envelope and directed to Daniel Cooper, and deposited in Nicholls's store, at Merry Hill precinct, in a box, where the public got their mail. I think some of them were placed near the voting place in a box near the polls.
Q. Who directed the envelope?
A. I did.
Q. Who is Daniel Cooper?
A. A negro politician of the Republican party.
Q. Was he an active supporter of Mr. J. J. Martin at said election?
A. I presume so, from the fact that he distributed those tickets very rapidly.
Q. Who did you support?
A. Jesse J. Yeates.
Q. Did you and James B. Nicholls put up those tickets in packages at the time and place mentioned?
A. We put them up in one package and directed them to Daniel Cooper.
Q. Who requested you to have those tickets printed?
A. No one.
Q. Is Cooper an ignorant man?

A. I judge he could read from the fact that he examined those tickets and compared them with others.

Q. Was any representation made to Cooper that those tickets were sent by J. J. Martin?

A. No such representation made to him by myself, nor any other person to my knowledge.

Q. Was the envelope containing the tickets stamped with a United States postage-stamp?

A. It was not to the best of my knowledge and belief.

Q. Were any of these tickets voted at Merry Hill precinct at said election?

A. Tickets similar in appearance were voted at said election—about one hundred and nine, as I am informed. I am not positive as to the number.

Q. Were the said tickets so voted refused to be counted for J. J. Martin, candidate for Congress, at said November election held at Merry Hill precinct, Bertie County, in said Congressional election and State?

A. I do not know of my own knowledge.

Q. What is your best information and belief as to that?

A. Basing my answer on hearsay evidence, they were not counted.

Q. By whom were the said tickets thrown out and refused to be counted?

A. I do not know of my own knowledge.

Q. What is your best information and belief on that point?

A. From hearsay testimony, by the judges of election at said precinct, on the ground of device and voting more than one ticket; the device consisting in the words "Republican ticket' printed on the said ballot.

(Answer to the two preceding questions objected to on the ground of hearsay.)

Q. What was the political complexion of the board of judges of election?

A. My impression is that J. E. Nicholls, J. H. Brown, T. J. Webb, and James W. Smith were the judges of election, all of whom were Democrats, and supported J. J. Yeates for Congress.

Q. Did you not advise the judges of election that these tickets were illegal and should not be counted?

A. I did.

Q. Did you send or give any tickets to D. C. Winston, in form "Republican ticket. For Congress, J. J. Martin?"

A. I did.

Q. About how many?

A. About twenty-four.

Q. Is D. C. Winston a resident of Windsor, Bertie County, a lawyer, and a strong supporter of Joseph J. Yeates in said election?

A. He is and was.

Q. Do you know if D. C. Winston received said tickets?

A. I was informed by D. C. Winston that he received them.

Cross-examined:

Q. Did you see any official connected with said November election take any of those tickets, "Republican ticket—For Congress, J. J. Martin," and publicly exhibit them to Republican voters, and advise them that said tickets were illegal?

A. I did; Mr. J. C. Freeman, the registrar. My impression is they were so exhibited by him before any of them were voted.

Redirect by counsel of contestee:

Q. Did Mr. Freeman do this at your request?

A. He did not.

Further this deponent saith not.

J. B. MARTIN.

Deposition of William M. Bond.

WILLIAM M. BOND, a witness on part of the contestee, Joseph J. Martin, being duly sworn, deposes and says:

Q. What is your name, age, and occupation?

A. William M. Bond; age, twenty-one; occupation, newspaper man.

Q. In the fall of 1878 were you editor and manager of the Chowan Gazette, a Democratic newspaper published in Edenton, North Carolina?

A. I was.

Q. Do you know James B. Martin of Merry Hill precinct, Bertie County.

A. Yes.

Q. Was he then and is he now a leading Democratic politician in said county?

A. Yes. He was an active Democratic politician of that county.

Q. Did he hold any official position in said county at that time?

A. I think he was chief-justice of the inferior court of that county.

Q. Was he, in the Congressional election in November, 1878, an active supporter of Jesse J. Yeates?

A. I think he was.

Q. Who were candidates for Congress in the first Congressional district of North Carolina in November, 1878?

A. J. J. Yeates, J. J. Martin, J. B. Respass, and I. S. Chamberlain.

Q. Were you, just previous to said election, requested by any one, and, if so, by whom, to print several hundred tickets, of which the one attached is a copy? Please state if the said tickets were printed and delivered or received by any one; and, if so, by whom; and any other facts connected therewith.

A. I was requested by J. B. Martin to print said tickets for him, of which the attached is one. I printed several hundred of them, and sent them to Mr. J. B. Martin, and he stated afterward that he received them.

Q. Were they printed and received prior to the November election, 1878?

A. They were.

(Contestant's counsel declines to cross-examine.)

Further this deponent saith not.

W. M. BOND.

Witness: WM. P. GURLEY.

REPUBLICAN TICKET.

For Congress:

J. J. MARTIN.

The question presented here is whether you shall unseat J. J. Martin because the counsel for Jesse J. Yeates succeeded in getting these votes, which are called fraudulent, cast for J. J. Martin. That is the proposition that gentlemen are invited to come up to. It is said that these tickets were fraudulent because they had a "device" on them. Now was there a "device" on these tickets? What was the form of the ticket? It was a very small ticket, having printed at the top of it the words "Republican ticket;" then followed the words "for Congress;" then followed the words "J. J. Martin." The ticket was printed upon white paper, and was in every respect in accordance with the law of the State of North Carolina. There was no "device" on it in the proper meaning of the term. It is claimed that the "device" consisted of the words "Republican ticket" on the face of the ticket and at the head of it. I refer to the law of North Carolina. From section 18, chapter 275, of the laws of North Carolina of 1875, I read all that has any bearing on this question:

The ballots shall be on white paper and may be printed or written or partly printed and partly written, and shall be without device.

The question is whether printing on the face of the ticket at its head in ordinary type the words "Republican ticket" constitutes a device. What is a device? Let us take the definition as given by Webster, and see whether we find anything indicating that the sacred name "Republican," when it precedes the word "ticket," constitutes a "device." A late edition of Webster gives this definition of device:

That which is formed by design or invented; scheme; artifice; artificial contrivance; stratagem; project; generally used in a bad sense.

Worcester gives the same definition. It is a word which had a meaning in heraldry, and it has a well-understood meaning in mechanics. It is a word used sometimes in criminal law. It has no meaning difficult to understand when used in the connection here. It is anything connected with bad. Any scheme, any plan, anything that is intended to operate for evil on the minds of others, might be called a device.

Here is the ordinary ticket such as we find everywhere, and there is nothing in the claim except as it existed in the minds of Martin and his willing tools, the judges down there—J. B. Martin, I mean. There is no decision of any of the courts of North Carolina showing that a heading when printed on the inside of a ticket is a device.

To go into the history of this matter a little, there was a time when they had embellishment, distinguishing marks on the back, especially of tickets in States South, and some of them North, and the legislatures of those States struck at that sort of thing; that is, the use of those emblems, those distinguishing things, and which it was supposed were the means of intimidating voters. It was supposed they worked harm, and I am told some Democrats went so far as to say it was a means by which unlettered whites and blacks were enabled to tell when they were voting the Republican ticket. They used to have large tickets with the face of General Grant in every imaginable shape and form upon the back of them, so that if the voter saw any part of the ticket, if a colored man saw the face of that great war hero and statesman, he knew that he was voting the right ticket; he would know that he was voting the right ticket even if he could not read the face of it. Some of this legislation was on the theory that it was wise to prevent this sort of thing. The law may be all right, Mr. Speaker; I am not here quarrelling with it, but I am only referring to this to show this legislation was not intended or designed to be a blow at the ordinary ticket, such as is voted everywhere all over the country.

I intended, Mr. Speaker, to give the use in which the word device appears in several places in the Holy Bible, and as it lies before me, I believe I will do it now. Job, speaking of the powers of the Almighty, chapter v, verse 12, says: "He disappointeth the devices of the crafty." David, in praising the goodness of God, says, Psalms xxxiii, verse 10: "The Lord bringeth the counsel of the heathen to naught; He maketh the devices of the people of none effect." Paul uses the same word in his second epistle to the Corinthians, chapter ii, verse 11: "Lest Satan should get an advantage of us, for we are not ignorant of his devices." All connect with bad, with evil. Here it is used in the same sense, although used by legislators in the State of North Carolina.

Now to the authorities for one moment. It is claimed on the part of gentlemen who make the majority report in this case that they were unable to find anything that was satisfactory to themselves except where they gleaned it from a private paper of some other gentleman. I have been a little curious to look at some of the authorities which are cited in that printed paper, and I assert—and I wish while gentlemen are correcting me they would go to this and correct it—I assert that every authority cited in that report which the gentleman adopts and takes home to himself—I assert, sir, that every authority cited on the subject of a device is exactly in the face of the conclusion of this report.

I will invite your attention first to the Indiana case, a case in 35 Indiana, 275. Here Mr. Speaker, we get the precise question exactly, where the words "Republican ticket" were printed on the head of the ballot on the same side where the names of the candidates were printed. The statute of the State of Indiana was much more stringent and severe than the state of the State of North Carolina. But I will read an extract from it:

SEC. 23. That all ballots which may be cast at any election hereafter held in this State shall be written or printed on plain white paper, without any distinguishing marks or other embellishment thereon, except the name of the candidates and the office for which they are voted for; and inspectors of election shall refuse all ballots offered of any other description: *Provided*, Nothing herein shall disqualify the voter from writing his own name on the back thereof.

Now, then, the case was exactly like this one. The court said that at the October election in 1870 there were ballots voted for the contestee with the words "Republican ticket" printed at the head and on the same side the names of the candidates were printed. That is exactly our case. Then the court goes on to say that "the only question before us is, Was this such a distinguishing mark or embellishment as to require the inspectors to refuse the ballots when offered? This question was directly before this court in a former case and was answered in the negative." They say in that deci ion they fully indorse the case in 29 Indiana, 308. That decision I have before me; and these two cases, I beg you, Mr. Speaker, and gentlemen of this House to note, are cited in the report of the majority as sustaining their claim that if there be printed on the face of the tickets the words "Republican ticket" it is a device. Neither of them sustain the conclusion of the report of the committee, and it looks to me as if somebody might have been intending to perpetrate a stupendous joke on the majority of the committee.

But there is another authority cited. Section 401, McCrary on the Law of Elections, has been quoted, and we ought to look at that and see how far it supports the claim of gentlemen upon this question. I will read the section referred to:

It has been also held that where the statute provided that all ballots should be written or printed upon white paper without any marks or figures thereon, to distinguish one from another, ballots upon paper tinged with blue, and which had ruled lines, were legal ballots within the meaning of the act.

This case was decided in 15 Illinois, 492:

This ruling, however, went upon the ground that the ruled paper was not used with any intent to violate the statute.

Certainly J J. Martin did not intend to violate the statute of the State of North Carolina, even though J. B. Martin, counsel of Yates in this case, did intend to commit an outrage upon Mr. J. J. Martin by attempting to unseat him; and the voters of that State did not intend to violate the law.

But I continue reading from McCrary:

It is quite clear that when the statute distinctly declares that ballots having distinguishing marks upon them shall not be received, or shall be rejected, it should be construed as mandatory and not simply directory.

And so it was held by the supreme court of Pennsylvania under a statute of this character, that ballots having an eagle printed thereon were in violation of the law and should be rejected.

Now, then, the American eagle was co sidered in the Pennsylvania case in reference to whether it constitutes an embellishment or not. We might draw a fine distinction even about this. We find this cited as authority here, and as conclusive in principle against the voice of the majority, as cited in their report.

Then we are also referred to section 403 of McCrary (and I believe it is the last) which refers to the California cases. This section is as follows:

The supreme court of California has very recently had occasion to consider the force and effect of a statute regulating the size and form of ballot, the kind of paper to be used, the kind of type to be used in printing them, &c. The court held, and we think upon the soundest reason, that as to those things over which the voter has control the law is mandatory, and that as to such things as are not under his control it should be held to be directory only. * * * The conclusion of the court was that the purpose and object of the statute was to secure the freedom and purity of elections and to place the elector above and beyond the reach of improper influences or restraint in casting his ballot, and that it should have such reasonable construction as would tend to secure these important results. And so construing the statute, the court conclude that a ballot cast by an elector in good faith should not be rejected for failure to comply with the law in matters over which the elector has no control, such as the exact size of the ticket, the precise kind of paper, or the particular character of type or binding used, &c.

These references are put into the report and they might mislead; not purposely; but unintentionally put in to make gentlemen believe that there was some authority somewhere that would hold that such a ticket as was rejected in this Merry Hill precinct in Bertie County, North Carolina, was a "device," and that such ticket was cast in violation of the law; whereas every authority upon the subject, including especially those cited by the majority of the committee in their report, supports the contrary doctrine.

I will not pursue this subject further. There is but one other precinct that I need refer to. The contestee claims that there were 139 voters who would have voted for him in Goose Nest precinct of Hamilton County, North Carolina, if they had been permitted to do so in a just and fair election. I believe that the gentleman from Massachusetts [Mr. FIELD] who has given the most attention to the testimony in this case, and given the contestant the advantage of any doubt, cuts this number down to 120.

These 120 persons were refused their ballots in this precinct because they were not registered there. Now, if they were not registered there there was no person registered there, unless perhaps there may have been a few, three or four, or as high as a dozen; but there was no registration of 132 Democrats that voted in that precinct although the majority of the committee do not find any difficulty in counting them, while the votes of these 120 or 132, as the case may be, who were not registered were not received. The statutes of North Carolina, as has been fully and elaborately explained by the gentleman from Massachusetts [Mr. FIELD], that is the statute on the subject of registration of voters in cases where they have removed from the places where they have been properly registered, is clear and plain in the light of that explanation.

But not one of these voters did remove; not a single one of the 120 removed from the place where they had been living and were at the time of the election, and where they lived when they voted or tried to vote. Hamilton precinct was divided and Goose Nest precinct was cut off from it, and these names were transferred to the new precinct rolls. There was no case of removal; they were transferred on the books simply. The judges of election, however, refused to allow the Republicans to vote. A Democrat went the night before the election, and, in violation of the law, as admitted, I believe, by everybody who has examined it, succeeded in getting certificates of transfer for the Democrats from the Democratic registrar of Hamilton precinct on which judges of election in Goose Nest precinct permitted Democrats to vote. But the next day it was "unlawful" for the Republicans to attempt to vote, and certificates were refused to them by the very same persons who gave the certificates to the Democrats. They could not find any authority for giving them to the Republicans.

I put this case on the ground that no action was required on the part of any of these voters; it was not a case of removal; they were simply voting where they were by law placed—in a new precinct—and if we turn to the statute on the subject that will be made quite plain. Section 7 of the law relating to registrars of North Carolina, says:

No elector shall be entitled to register or vote in any other precinct or township than the one in which he is an actual and *bona fide* resident on the day of election, and no certificate of registration shall be given.

Now, section 12 of the same act contains the words which I will ask the clerk to read, down to where provision is made for the form of the oath.

The Clerk read as follows:

And if an elector has previously been admitted to registration in any ward, township, or precinct in the county in which he resides, he shall not be allowed to register again in another ward, precinct or township in the same county, until he produces a certificate of the registrar of the former township, ward, or precinct, that said elector has removed from said township, ward, or precinct, and that his name has been erased from the registration books of the ward, township, or precinct from which he has removed; and the identity of any person claiming the right to be registered in any precinct of the same county, by virtue of such certificate, with the person named therein, shall be proved by the oath of the claimant, and when required by the registrar, by the oath of at least one other elector.

Mr. KEIFER. That is as far as the clerk needs to read. The balance of the section gives the form of the oath.

Now, it will be noted that that section refers to cases of removal. Only when a man removes from one voting precinct to another is it necessary for him to apply in person and have his name erased from the books of the place where he had been registered, and then get a certificate so that he may register in another place. But these voters that tendered their votes in this Goose Nest precinct did not remove. The precinct was established around them.

I come now to the further point that I suggested; the one hundred and thirty-two Democrats who voted in this precinct on certificates that were issued on the application of one person, voted illegally, if it was necessary for this twelfth section of the statutes relating to registers in that State to be complied with. Why? Because each one of them would have had personally to apply and take an oath himself as to his removing, and, if required by the registrar, furnish other evidence of the fact of his removal. So that all the certificates that were used—and this is a fact not disputed in the case—all the certificates that were used by Democrats were certificates that were illegally issued. And although the judges of election were notified of that fact they received the Democratic votes here and refused the Republican voters who offered their votes; and the Hamilton precinct registrar refused to give certificates on the day of election to these Republicans when they applied for them.

In conclusion, I may add that this House is asked and expected to affirm and confirm all these outrages upon the sitting member and vote in the contestant. We are asked now to put our confirmation and our sign of approval upon all these outrages on the people of the first district of North Carolina, on the sitting member, and on the country.

We are asked by our vote here, to-day or to-morrow, whenever we reach it, to say it is all right for contrivances, schemes, acts of omission or acts of commission to be worked out to consummation by officers of election to defeat the voice of the people in that district. We are asked to approve of the premeditated act and conduct of a man who unblushingly appears as an attorney in this case, and comes here swearing that he himself set up a scheme, or device, or plan by which he robbed one hundred and eight men in his own precinct of their elective franchise. And we in the House of Representatives in the Congress of the United States are, by our votes, asked to say that this J. B. Martin did a nice, decent thing, because it only operates to exclude a Republican from his seat. We are asked then to say as to these illegal acts on the part of the judges of election in this precinct, in Hamilton and the Goose Nest precinct, in their refusal to allow these men to vote, they did right in allowing Democrats to vote who were exactly in the same position so far as the law was concerned.

I may have been earnest, and if the gentleman from Mississippi [Mr. MANNING] proposes to say that I have been passionate, I offer this single excuse, that I have been asked as a part of my duty, not alone as a member of a committee, but as a member of this House, by my act and vote to approve of this sort of thing. My voice and vote shall be against such action. I warn gentlemen that whether the day is come now, or whether it is only near at hand, or whether it is still in the remote future—I warn gentlemen that the sooner they put the seal of infamy upon all such proceedings as this and upon all men who countenance them, who aid them, who are auxiliaries to these grave crimes against the elective franchise, the better. I warn them that the day is coming when all such persons will be swept from the Halls of Congress, and forever. The American people South as well as North—I am happy to say I believe that the Southern people are equally ready to do so—will stamp down, in a political point of view, all those persons who are willing to approve of such conduct as we will here approve if we adopt the report of the majority.

My conclusion is that Mr. Martin is entitled to hold his seat, and I find his true majority to be 375.

APPORTIONMENT OF REPRESENTATION.

February 3, 1881.   On the bill for the apportionment of representation in Congress

Mr. KEIFER said:

Mr. SPEAKER. In the midst of this wild confusion I can hardly expect to speak calmly and moderately, as I always try to do, and yet entertain the distinguished gentlemen here.

I shall vote for three hundred and nineteen members in this House for the coming decennial period.   Having announced that, I want to go back and ascertain how far it would be just and equitable for us to accept the original bill introduced into this House by the distinguished chairman of the Census Committee [Mr. Cox], a bill which provides for three hundred and one members of this House.

That gentleman told us yesterday that the number three hundred and one was more convenient and more fair than three hundred and eleven or three hundred and nineteen; that it would produce as little inequality as any other number that could be selected. Now, when we look at this matter on this side of the House in a partisan point of view, we are charged with doing something unfair. Yet examining that bill in that view, it will appear that the number three hundred and one would give to the States which we now commonly denominate the Southern States, to distinguish them from the Northern and free States, an advantage of four members.

Now, the majority of the Committee on the Census concluded that that was not enough advantage; that it would be better to find the only number perhaps that would give to the Southern States the advantage of six members, while the number which I favor, and the number favored by the minority of the committee, three hundred and nineteen, would give to neither section of the country, North or South, any advantage at all. It is the only number, so far as I have seen the figures, that fixes the apportionment exactly on an equality between the two sections so far as gains and losses are concerned. This matter of looking carefully to the interests of the North and South is not an original question with this Congress. It was the first question upon which the first President of the United States took issue with Congress. Out of apportionment legislation grew the first veto message ever signed by a President of the United States, and it was on the theory that the first apportionment bill submitted to him in 1793 was unfair to the South.

If the Clerk will now read the first veto message of April 5, 1792, I will then call attention to the history and the circumstances under which it came to be written and sent to the House.

The Clerk read as follows:

UNITED STATES April 5, 1792.

Gentlemen of the House of Representatives:

I have maturely considered the act passed by the two Houses, entitled "An act for an apportionment of Representatives among the several States, according to the first enumeration;" and I return it to your House, wherein it originated, with the following objections:

First. The Constitution has prescribed that Representatives shall be apportioned among the several States according to their respective numbers; and there is no one proportion or divisor which, applied to the respective numbers of the States, will yield the number and allotment of Representatives proposed by the bill.

Second. The Constitution has also provided that the number of Representatives shall not exceed one for every thirty thousand; which restriction is, by the context, and by fair and obvious construction to be applied to the separate and respective numbers of the States, and the bill has allotted to eight of the States more than one for every thirty thousand.

GEORGE WASHINGTON.

Mr. KEIFER. It will be found that by taking the number three hundred and one as a basis for the future House of Representatives there is "no one proportion or divisor which, applied to the respective numbers of the States, will yield the number and allotment of Representatives proposed by the bill," to use the exact language used by the President of the United States, George Washington.

Before going into a demonstration of that statement, I ask the Clerk to read—and I beg the attention of members to it—what Thomas Jefferson says on the subject of the history of that veto message. He will read an extract from Elliot's Debates on the Federal Constitution, volume 4, page 624.

The Clerk read as follows:

The President called on me before breakfast, and first introduced some other matter, then fell on the representation bill, which he had now in his possession for the tenth day. I had before given him my opinion in writing, that the method of apportionment was contrary to the Constitution. He agreed that it was contrary to the common understanding of that instrument, and to what was under stood at the time by the makers of it; that yet it would bear the construction which the bill put, and he observed that the vote for and against the bill was perfectly geographical—a Northern against a Southern vote—and he feared he should be thought to be taking side with a Southern party. I admitted the motive of delicacy, but that it should not induce him to do wrong; and urged the dangers to which the scramble for the fractionary members would always lead. He here expressed his fear that there would, ere long, be a separation of the Union ; that the public mind seemed dissatisfied, and tending to this. He went home, sent for Randolph, the Attorney-General, desired him to get Mr. Madison immediately and come to me ; and if we three concurred in opinion, that he would negative the bill. He desired to hear nothing more about it, but that we draw up the instrument for him to sign. They came ; our minds had been before made up ; we drew the instrument. Randolph carried it to him, and told him we all concurred in it. He walked with him to the door, and, as if he still wished to get off, he said, "And you say you approve of this yourself?" "Yes, sir," says Randolph. "I do, upon my honor." He sent it to the House of Representatives instantly. A few of the hottest friends of the bill expressed passion, but the majority were satisfied, and both in and out of doors it gave pleasure to have at length an instance of the negative being exercised.

·'Written this the 9th April.

· Mr. KEIFER. My time will not permit me to occupy the attention of the House any further with the history of that matter. It shows that early in the constitutional history of this country this matter of apportionment was regarded as a very grave and important one. It was then believed that it was right and proper to find some common divisor that would be equitable and just to each and all of the States. There was a jealous eye to the interest of Southern States in connection with that matter.

I state this in support of my non-partisan position on the subject of fixing a number for the Representatives of coming Congresses that will give no advantage either to the North or to the South.

If we look over this bill and make calculations upon it we will find some queer figures, some queer results. I refer to the original bill upon the subject before this House. It will strike a man as rather curious, if he were not to go to the very foundation of all these peculiar relations of numbers, how it could happen that Ohio, with an increased population from 1870 to 1880 of 532,979, should under that bill lose one member of Congress, while South Carolina, with an increased population of a little more than one-half of that number, that is, 290,016, should gain one member.

The same thing may be said in reference to Mississippi. With an increased population from 1870 to 1880 of 203,670 that State gains one member under this bill, fixing the number at three hundred and one, while Ohio, with her gain of 533,000, loses one member. But this would lead us into some further explanation about the figures which I do not choose to go into. I simply state these mathematical curiosities in support of my claim that we ought to select a number that will be exactly fair. These singular results are not confined to a comparison of Ohio with other States. New York State, with an increased population from 1870 to 1880 of 701,051, under this bill loses two members, and Pennsylvania, with an increased population from 1870 to 1880, of 760,835, loses one member under the bill, while Mississippi with an increased population in the same time of only 203,670, and South Carolina with an increased population, also for the same time, of 290,016, each gain one member by the provisions of this bill. Other comparisons could be made with like results.

Mr. HAMMOND, of Georgia. Has the gentleman made inquiry whether Ohio has not now more representation relatively to South Carolina than she ought to have ?

Mr. KEIFER. Oh, no ; I have taken the figures of 1870 as a fair apportionment with the ratio then adopted ; then I take the ratio given now ; and taking the difference between the census of 1870 as reported and the census of 1880 as reported, I find these singular results. The matter of fairness or unfairness in the taking of the census for either of the years 1870 or 1880 has nothing to do with the question.

Mr. HAMMOND, of Georgia, rose.

Mr. KEIFER. I cannot yield further ; I have not the time.

Now, I am not quite satisfied with the position of the gentleman from Kentucky [Mr. THOMPSON] when he argues in favor of a large body of men as more likely to be a pure body. While I am not afraid of having the number increased, for other reasons which I will indicate I am not quite satisfied that the reason the gentleman gave—that a large body of men is always the safest—is the right one. I understood him to say that the rule is universal in relation to large bodies of men being safer than small ones. History will prove that to be absolutely untrue, if the gentleman takes into account the fact that in other countries the methods of choosing such bodies and the powers that choose them have not recognized the people as the governing power. I wish to say as I pass along that when we get a perfectly pure body of men in our Republic, large or small, it will be a body representing the people of the several districts of the country who have had a fair opportunity to cast their ballots without fraud or intimidation and to have those ballots honestly counted and fairly returned. When the time shall come that we have that in this country we may expect to have a good and pure House of Representatives. If it has happened in other countries that small bodies of men have been more tyrannical than large, it will be found to be because some concentrated power other than the masses of the people has selected or chosen that small body of men, and therefore directed and controlled them.

I believe, however, in a reasonably large House of Representatives, in view of the great amount of work that we have to perform. The Constitution fixed 30,000 as the ratio of representation for the first apportionment. It was then supposed that one member for 30,000 inhabitants was enough, and only enough.

Now, with all the varied interests of this country, with all the subjects that our constituents are concerned about, with all the multiplication of duties growing out of our business here, it is proposed to adopt the ratio of 164,018 as the basis of representation here. This number is the ratio on which the original bill fixing the number of members at three hundred and one is based. The bill reported by a majority of the Census Committee, fixing the number of members at three hundred and eleven, is based on a ratio of 158,745, and the bill of the minority of that committee, fixing the number at three hundred and nineteen, is based on a ratio of 154,764. The ratio ten years ago was on 135,239, I believe.

We are expected to perform all our many duties promptly and well. There comes requisition after requisition upon members of Congress. It may be that many of these demands upon us are for the performance of duties that do not properly belong to our position here; but custom has made it the duty of every member of Congress to run errands to the Departments—to be a sort of counselor or adviser between the people and the different Departments where the business of the people is pending. If the number of Representatives is to be cut down and our constituencies increased it will be impossible for us to perform the duties that these people expect of us. For that reason I am in favor of an increase on the basis of the figures I have named.

Turning aside for one moment in this discussion, I will say that there are some other remarkable figures and facts worked out under this census. My own State will not suffer on a basis of voting population, if such a basis could be adopted (and I do not say it could) under the Constitution. Ohio, I am happy to say, has a people not only free to vote when election day comes, but a people educated to vote, and who do vote. Let me state a fact that may not have been noted. At the election in November last Ohio cast 103,046 more votes than were cast in the great State of Illinois, with substantially the same population, the population of Illinois being 3,078,769, as against 3,198,239 in Ohio. Now, this larger vote in Ohio comes from the freedom of the people to vote and also (for they are free as in Illinois) from the education of the people in the matter of voting. We have first tried before the people of Ohio the great issue of this country. We have tried the great financial issues there in advance of the nation. First in 1875 we fought the battle, and we won the financial victory as it has been won since by the people of this whole country.

' The election returns coupled with the vote at the late election show some curious results in the North and West in the ability or willingness of the people to vote. Take the table of figures made up in round numbers, as follows:

States.	Vote.	Population.	Per cent.
Illinois	622,000	3,100,000	1 in 5.0
Ohio	725,000	3,200,000	1 in 4.4
Indiana	575,000	2,200,000	1 in 3.4
Iowa	323,000	1,600,000	1 in 5.4
Kansas	201,000	1,000,000	1 in 5.0

It will be seen that Indiana is a good voting State. The now good roads and accessibility of voting places in Ohio and Indiana may have something to do with the voters getting to the polls in a larger per cent. than in some other States.

The gentleman from Michigan [Mr. Horr] has given figures from the Southern States which in comparison to these would astonish the country if it was not already aware that something terrible was the matter with the voting population in those States.

Before taking my seat I wish to say but one other thing in support of my proposition. Taking three hundred and one as the number, Ohio with nineteen members (which would be her apportionment under that number) would have one member for every 168,328; Mississippi one member for every 161,656; South Carolina one member for every 165,937; Louisiana one member for every 156,683. Thus, without taking the time to run through the list, it will be seen that my State is to be put at a disadvantage of several thousand in population (to say nothing of votes) as against these States of the South. Therefore, I protest Mr. Speaker, against a bill such as the one originally offered by the gentleman from New York, and I still more protest against the bill reported by the Committee on the Census, because it is still more unfair. I insist upon a fair number, one that will be just to each section. So far as I am concerned (I do not speak for those around me), I shall oppose, as does the gentleman from Michigan [Mr. Horr], any number that is unfair, and I will do it by every means known to the rules of parliamentary law.

[Here the hammer fell.]

SUPPLEMENTARY FUNDING BILL.

March 1, 1881. Pending consideration of a supplementary funding bill in the House of Representatives, the following colloquy took place :

Mr. KEIFER said :

This Congress first met under most extraordinary circumstances—within less than three weeks of the time it was entitled to meet under any possibility provided by the Constitution—and we then knew that the Democratic party was in power in both branches of Congress, and we knew then as well as at any time since that a funding bill was important and of pressing necessty. The four months of the extra session passed. During that time the Committee on Ways and Means, distinguished because of the great men or the great Democrats upon it, were considering the funding bill.

In the early days, if I recollect aright, of the first regular session of this Congress a bill was introduced providing for the funding of the national debt. Since that bill was printed and laid upon our tables we have had above ten months' continual session of this Congress. And now, within forty-eight hours of the time we are to close this most memorable Congress, a bill of a more than doubtful character has, amid the wreck of hopes and fortunes in some cases, passed, and instantly upon its being passed, before it could be engrossed or enrolled, and before the Speaker could sign his name to it, a distinguished Democratic member of the Committee on Ways and Means [Mr. CARLISLE] arises in his place and introduces a bill which is from the first letter to last a confession that the Democratic party, in above ten months' session and the consideration of a bill, could not pass one that was fit to go to the country. [Applause on the Republican side.] It confesses and admits that it is vile, that it is evil, that it will do wrong and injustice, and that the whole country is to be financially ruined by it.

I do not allow the gentleman from New York [Mr. Cox] to get the gentleman from Kentucky [Mr. CARLISLE] off the track by talking about national banks. I do not believe the national banks in the last week have acted with great prudence or with that courage which should have been displayed by their officers in meeting the great financial problem so unnecessarily forced upon this but recently prosperous country by the Democratic party. I do not believe that at all. But it is not a question of national banks. It is a question of bread; it is a question of labor; it is a question of universal prosperity in this land. That is the question. It is a question of 'cheap money—cheap a few days ago, dear now—because the Democratic party could not pass a law, as it now confesses through one of its distinguished leaders, but what would injure and ruin and unsettle all of the great financial interests of this country. It is a question of value of property; it is a question of labor; it is a question of keeping up and preserving our great and growing manufacturing interests of this country.

We want it understood now that with all the effort and with all the labor of the Democratic majority of this Congress they must go out of it confessing that it is impossible for that party to control and regulate the great affairs of this nation wisely. We have some things to congratulate the country and the Democratic party upon. We have witnessed some things this session which are valuable to be recorded and remembered. We have witnessed with pleasure the Democratic party lay down that spirit that I dare not characterize and bring in here from the Appropriations Committee appropriation bills surrendering the things they said at one time they would have or they would have the nation's life. ["Oh!" "Oh!" from the Democratic side.] They do not even go to that bill to which they clung for so long—the Army appropriation bill; they do not even go to that now. They even come here confessing that they have been wrong on that as well as on all other things which they have been obliged to surrender. They used to put a section into that bill prohibiting the use of the money appropriated for paying, equipping, and transporting troops to be used for keeping peace at the polls on election days; and they have surrendered that and laid it down in the presence of the verdict of the American people. [Derisive cries and laughter from the Democratic side.]

Mr. TALBOTT. And still we had eight thousand majority on the popular vote.

Mr. KEIFER. You are mistaken. Garfield received the popular vote. I expected to hear these groans from the other side. I admit that they surrender and die hard, but the death comes all the same. Now let me, in bidding farewell to this subject, say that the Democratic party, above all other parties that ever existed, is, if possible, to be congratulated more than the country for this verdict of the people.

But I want simply to re-enforce what I said at the beginning of my remarks ; that is, that we have this evening, in the closing hours of this Congress, had a proposition submitted to us boldly and openly confessing that on that subject about which we have been struggling and talking so long the Democratic party has been obliged to offer a new bill, giving construction to the one just passed, which new bill is made up of amendments which were proposed to the original bill by the Republican members of the Committee on Ways and Means. This extraordinary thing is done to perfect, not a law, but to attempt to perfect that which is not, for want of the approval of the President, a law—which may never become a law. [Applause.]

ELECTED SPEAKER.

Monday, December 5, 1881, Mr. Keifer was elected Speaker of the House of Representatives. Mr. Randall and Mr. Hiscock conducted him to the chair, when he addressed the House as follows:

Gentlemen of the House of Representatives:

I thank you with a heart filled with gratitude for the distinguished honor conferred on me by an election as your Speaker. I will assume the powers and duties of this high office with, I trust, a due share of diffidence and distrust of my own ability to meet them acceptably to you and the country. I believe that you, as a body and individually, will give me hearty support in the discharge of all my duties. I promise to devote myself faithfully and assiduously to the work before me. I invoke your and the country's charitable judgment upon all my official acts. I will strive to be just to all, regardless of party or section. Where party principle is involved, I will be found to be a Republican, but in all other respects I hope to be able to act free from party bias.

It is a singular fact that at this most prosperous time in our nation's history no party in either branch of Congress has an absolute majority over all other parties, and it is therefore peculiarly fortunate that at no other time since and for many years prior to the accession of Abraham Lincoln to the executive chair has there been so few unsettled vital questions of a national character in relation to which party lines have been closely drawn.

The material prosperity of the people is in advance of any other period in the history of our Government. The violence of party spirit has materially subsided, and in great measure because many of the reasons for its existence are gone.

While the universal tendency of the people is to sustain and continue to build up an unparalleled prosperity, it should be our highest aim to so legislate as to permanently promote and not cripple it. This Congress should be, and I profoundly hope it will be, marked peculiarly as a business Congress.

It may be true that additional laws are yet necessary to give to every citizen complete protection in the exercise of all political rights. With evenly balanced party power, with few grounds for party strife and bitterness, and with no impending Presidential election to distract us from purely legislative duties, I venture to suggest that the present is an auspicious time to enact laws to guard against the recurrence of dangers to our institutions and to insure tranquility at perilous times in the future.

Again thanking you for the honor conferred, and again invoking your aid and generous judgment, I am ready to take the oath prescribed by law and the Constitution and forthwith proceed, with my best ability, guided by a sincere and honest purpose, to discharge the duties belonging to the office with which you have clothed me.

Mr. KELLEY, having served longest continuously as a member of the House, administered to the Speaker-elect the oath prescribed.

VALEDICTORY.

Sunday. March 4. 1883.

Mr. RANDALL. Mr. Speaker, I submit the following resolution.
The Clerk read as follows: *

Resolved, That the thanks of this House are hereby tendered to the Hon. J. WARREN KEIFER, the Speaker, for the ability and courtesy with which he has presided over the deliberation of the House during the Forty-seventh Congress.

The resolution was agreed to.

Mr. HISCOCK. The committee appointed on the part of the House to wait upon the President of the United States, in conjunction with the committee appointed on behalf of the Senate, have performed that duty, and report that the President has requested them to inform the two Houses of Congress that he has no further communication to make to them.

VALEDICTORY OF THE SPEAKER.

The SPEAKER. Gentlemen, the time has come when our official relations as Representatives in the Forty-seventh Congress are to be dissolved. In a moment more this House of Representatives will be known only in history. Its acts will stand, many of them, it is believed, through the future history of the Republic.

On the opening day of this Congress I ventured the suggestion and the expressions of a hope that it should be marked "as peculiarly a business Congress."

It has successfully grappled with more of the vital, material, and moral questions of the country than its predecessors. Many of these have been settled wisely and well by appropriate legislation. It would be quite impossible at this time to enumerate the many important laws which have been enacted to foster and promote the substantial interests of the whole country.

This Congress enacted into a law the first 3 per cent. funding bill known to this country, and under it a considerable portion of the Government debt has been refunded at lower rates than ever before.

It did not hesitate to take hold of the question of polygamy, and it is believed it has struck the first effective blow in the direction of destroying that greatest remaining public crime of the age.

Laws have been passed to protect the immigrant on his way across the sea and upon his arrival in the ports of this country.

Laws have also been passed to extend the charters of the banking institutions so that financial disorder cannot take place which would otherwise have come at the expiration of old bank charters.

Many public acts will be found relating to the Indian policy and the land policy of this country which will prove to be wise.

The post-office laws have been so changed as to reduce letter postage from 3 to 2 cents, the lowest rate ever known in the United States.

No legislation of this Congress will be found upon the statute-books revolutionary in character or which will oppress any section or individual in the land. All legislation has been in the direction of relief.

Pension laws have been enacted which are deemed wise, and liberal appropriations have been made to pay the deserving and unfortunate pensioner.

Internal-revenue taxes have been taken off and the tariff laws have been revised.

Sectionalism has been unknown in the enactment of laws.

In the main a fraternal spirit has prevailed among the members from all portions of the Union. What has been said in the heat of debate and under excitement and sometimes with provocation is not to be regarded in determining the genuine feeling of concord existing between members. The high office I have filled through the sessions of this Congress has enabled me to judge better of the true spirit of the members that compose it than I could otherwise have done.

It is common to say that the House of Representatives is a very turbulent and disorderly body of men. This is true more in appearance than in reality. Those who look on and do not participate see more apparent confusion than exists in reality. The disorder that often appears upon the floor of the House grows out of an earnest, active spirit possessed by members coming from all sections of the United States, and indicates in a high degree their strong individuality and their great zeal in trying to secure recognition in the prompt discharge of their duty. No more conscientious body of men than compose this House of Representatives, in my opinion, ever met. Partisan zeal has in some instances led to fierce word-contests on the floor, but when the occasion which gave rise to it passed by party spirit went with it.

I am very thankful for the considerate manner in which I have been treated by the House in its collective capacity. I am also very thankful to each individual member of this body for his personal treatment of me. I shall lay down the gavel and the high office you clothed me with filled with good feeling toward each member of this House. I have been at times impatient and sometimes severe with members, but I have never purposely harshly treated any member. I have become warmly attached to and possessed of a high admiration not only for the high character of this House as a parliamentary body, but for all its individual members. I heartily thank the House for its vote of thanks.

The duties of a Speaker are of the most delicate and critical kind. His decisions are in the main made without time for deliberation, and are often very far-reaching and controlling in the legislation of the country on important matters, and they call out the severest criticism.

The rules of this House, which leave to the Speaker the onerous duty and delicate task of recognizing individuals to present their matters for legislation, render the office in that respect an exceedingly unpleasant one. No member should have the legislation he desires depend upon the individual recognition of the Speaker, and no Speaker should be compelled to decide between members having matters of possibly equal importance or of equal right to his recognition.

I suggest here that the time will soon come when another mode will have to be adopted which will relieve both the Speaker and individual members from this exceedingly embarrassing if not dangerous power.

During my administration in the chair very many important questions have been decided by me, and I do not flatter myself that I have in the hurry of these decisions made no mistakes. But I do take great pride in being able to say that no parliamentary decision of mine has been overruled by the judgment of this almost evenly politically balanced house, although many appeals have been taken.

I congratulate each member of this House upon what has been accomplished by him in the discharge of the important duties of a Representative, and with the sincerest hope that all may return safely to their homes, and wishing each a successful and happy future during life, I now exercise my last official duty as presiding officer of this House by declaring the term of this House under the Constitution of the United States at an end, and that it shall stand adjourned *sine die*. [Hearty and continued applause.]

CERTAIN QUESTIONS OF ORDER

DECIDED BY

HON. J. WARREN KEIFER,

SPEAKER OF THE HOUSE OF REPRESENTATIVES, FORTY-SEVENTH CONGRESS.

—

DECEMBER 5, 1881.

Mr. HASKELL submitted the following resolutions, and demanded the previous question thereon, viz:

Resolved, That the rules of the House of Representatives of the Forty-sixth Congress shall be the rules of the present House until otherwise ordered ; and
Resolved further, That the Committee on Rules, when appointed, shall have leave to report at any time all such amendments or revisions of said rules as they may deem proper.

Mr. RANDALL made the point of order that the said resolutions were not now in order for action under clause 1 of Rule XXVIII; when, on motion of Mr. RYAN, at 5 o'clock and 25 minutes p. m., the House adjourned.

DECEMBER 6, 1881.

Mr. HASKELL called up the resolutions submitted by him on yesterday and pending when the House adjourned, on which the demand for the previous question was pending, and renewed said demand.

Mr. RANDALL made the point of order that under the law other business of higher privilege took precedence, viz, the swearing in of the Delegates, as provided by section 30 of the Revised Statutes.

The Speaker sustained the said point of order, and directed the Clerk to call the names of the Delegates from the Territories of Arizona, Dakota, Idaho, Montana, New Mexico, Washington, and Wyoming.

The Clerk thereupon proceeded to call the names of the Delegates from the said Territories in the foregoing order.

. . . .

The House having resumed the consideration of the question as to the Delegate from Utah, Mr. HASKELL submitted the following resolution, viz:

Resolved, That Allen G. Campbell, Delegate-elect from Utah Territory, is entitled to be sworn in as Delegate to this House on his *prima facie* case.

Mr. COX made the point of order that a roll of Members and Delegates elect had been prepared under the law, and that the Members and Delegates thereon were entitled to be sworn in unless objection be made thereto.

After debate, the Speaker overruled the said point of order on the ground that no law known to him required or authorized the Clerk of the outgoing House to make a roll of Delegates-elect of the incoming House, and also upon the further ground that sections 31 and 38 of the Revised Statutes, relied upon to sustain the action of the Clerk of the last House in making a roll of the Delegates-elect, contained nothing in regard to the subject of filing and passing upon the merits of credentials of Delegates-elect ; in which decision of the Chair the House acquiesced.

DECEMBER 16, 1881.

Mr. W. E. ROBINSON proposed, as a question of privilege, to submit a resolution relating to an alleged usurpation of the privileges of the House by an officer of the Government connected with the State Department.

The Speaker held the resolution not to be in order under Rule IX, and also to be in violation of the previous order of the House as to the order of business.

So the said resolution was not received.

JANUARY 10, 1882.

The House then proceeded, as the regular order of business, to the consideration of the following resolution, submitted by Mr. HASKELL on the 6th ultimo, and made the special order for this day, viz:

Resolved, That Allen G. Campbell, Delegate-elect from Utah Territory, is entitled to be sworn in as Delegate to this House on his *prima facie* case.

Pending which Mr. REED submitted the following resolution as a substitute therefor, viz:

Resolved, That the papers in relation to the right to a seat as a Delegate from the Territory of Utah be referred to the Committee on Elections, with instructions to report at as early a day as practicable as to the *prima facie* right, or the final right, of claimants to the seat as the committee shall deem proper.

After debate, Mr. HASKELL demanded the previous question on the resolution and pending amendment.

The previous question was thereupon ordered.

The question being on agreeing to the said substitute; pending which, Mr. HASKELL submitted the following preamble and resolution, in the nature of instructions to the Committee on Elections, viz:

Whereas polygamy has been for many years and is now practiced in some of the Territories o the United States, in contravention of the laws thereof [see section 5352 of the Revised Statutes] ; and

Whereas there has been admitted to former Congresses of the United States a Delegate from the Territory of Utah, who has served in the House of Representatives as such while sustaining polygamous marital relations—

[See the following testimony in the contested election case of Cannon vs. Campbell, now of record in this House :

In the matter of George Q. Cannon. Contest of Allen G. Campbell's right to a seat in the House of Representatives of the Forty-seventh Congress of the United States as Delegate from the Territory of Utah.

I, George Q. Cannon, contestant, protesting that the matter in this paper contained is not relevant to the issue, do admit that I am a member of the Church of Jesus Christ of Latter-day Saints, commonly called Mormons ; that in accordance with the tenets of said church I have taken plural wives, who now live with me, and have so lived with me for a number of years, and borne me children. I also admit that in my public addresses as a teacher of my religion in Utah Territory I have defended said tenet of said church as being, in my belief, a revelation from God.

GEORGE Q. CANNON.]

Now, therefore,

Be it resolved, as the fixed and final determination of this House of Representatives of the Forty-seventh Congress, That no person guilty of living in polygamous marital relations, or guilty of teaching or inciting others so to do, is entitled to be admitted to this House of Representatives as a Delegate from any Territory of the United States.

Mr. RANDALL made the point of order that the said preamble and resolution were not in order, not being germane to the pending proposition.

The Speaker sustained the said point of order, on the ground that said preamble and resolution did not come within the provisions of paragraph 2 of Rule XVII.

Under the operation of the previous question the said substitute was agreed to, and the original resolution as amended was agreed to.

JANUARY 20, 1882.

Mr. CANDLER, from the Committee on Accounts, reported the following resolution :

Resolved, That the committees of this House designated in the foregoing report as entitled to clerks under the legislative, executive, and judicial appropriation bill making appropriations for the year ending June 30, 1882, be, and they are hereby, authorized to employ clerks during the session within the present fiscal year, and any excess of clerks therein authorized over the number provided for by existing law shall, under the direction of the Committee on Accounts, be paid out of the contingent fund of the House.

The House having proceeded to its consideration, Mr. CANDLER demanded the previous question.

Mr. CONVERSE made the point of order that under clause 2 of Rule XVIII the said report, not being printed as therein required, was not in order for present consideration.

The Speaker overruled the point of order, on the ground that the clause of the rule referred to applied only to bills and propositions referred to one of the calendars.

JANUARY 26, 1882.

The House having under consideration the report of the Committee on Accounts authorizing the appointment of committee clerks, and the question being on the substitute submitted by Mr. CAMP, when Mr. CALKINS made the point of order that the motion to strike out that which had just been inserted by the House was not in order. The Speaker sustained the said point of order.

The House then proceeded, as the regular order of business, to the further consideration of the following resolution, reported by Mr. ORTH from the Committee on Foreign Affairs, on the 23d instant, and pending when the House adjourned on that day, viz:

Resolved, That the President be requested to obtain from the British Government a list of all American citizens, naturalized or native-born, under arrest or imprisonment by authority of said Government, with a statement of the cause or causes of such arrest and imprisonment, and especially such of said citizens as may have been thus arrested and imprisoned under the suspension of the *habeas corpus* in Ireland; and if not incompatible with the public interest, that he communicate such information, when received, to this House, together with all correspondence now on file in the Department of State relating to any existing arrest and imprisonment of citizens as aforesaid.

After debate, Mr. ORTH demanded the previous question.

Pending which, Mr. W. E. ROBINSON proposed to submit an amendment to the said resolution.

The Speaker ruled the amendment out of order, on the ground that it could not be offered while the demand for the previous question was pending, under Rule XVII and the practice of the House.

From which decision of the Chair Mr. ROBINSON appealed. And the question being put, viz, Shall the decision of the Chair stand as the judgment of the House? it was decided in the affirmative.

So the ruling of the Chair was sustained.

JANUARY 31, 1882.

The House then proceeded, as the regular order of business, to the further consideration of the joint resolution of the House (H. Res. 91) to declare certain lands heretofore granted to railroad companies forfeited to the United States, and to restore the same to the public domain and to open the same to settlers, introduced by Mr. ROBESON on the 11th instant, the pending question being on the reference of said resolution; when Mr. ROBESON modified the same.

Mr. HUBBELL and Mr. HOOKER made the point of order that the modification proposed was not in order, being in effect a new proposition.

After debate on said point of order the Speaker overruled the same, on the ground that Mr. ROBESON originally obtained leave to introduce a joint resolution for reference to the Committee on the Public Lands, on which question a motion to refer with instructions was not in order, and that before "decision or amendment" was made on the said motion it was in order to modify the said proposition.

FEBRUARY 7, 1882.

Mr. CHALMERS moved that the House proceed to the consideration of business on the Speaker's table; pending which, Mr. PAGE moved that the House proceed to the special order for to-day, viz, the bill of the House (H. R. 3540) to regulate, limit, and suspend the immigration of Chinese laborers to the United States; pending which, Mr. PRESCOTT, as a privileged question, moved that the House proceed to the consideration of the bill of the House (H. R. 3550) making an apportionment of Representatives in Congress among the several States under the Tenth Census.

Mr. ANDERSON made the point of order that the said motion of Mr. PRESCOTT was not a privileged question.

After debate on the point of order, by unanimous consent, the Speaker overruled the said point of order on the ground that clause 1 of section 2, article 14, of the amendments to the Constitution of the United States made it the imperative duty of this Congress to pass an apportionment bill fixing the number of Representatives in the next Congress, and for this reason, and also in view of the fact that under the past practice of the House the question had been treated as one of a highly privileged character, the Chair felt bound to hold that it was a question of high constitutional privilege.

FEBRUARY 13, 1882

The House thereupon proceeded, as the regular order of business, to the consideration of the bill of the House (H. R. 3550) making an apportionment of Representatives in Congress among the several States under the tenth census.

Mr. PAGE moved that all debate on the pending bill terminate at 3 o'clock and 30 minutes p. m. to-morrow; pending which, Mr. KNOTT made the point of order that debate on a proposition could not be limited by a motion, and that under the rules and practice of the House debate could only be closed by the previous question.

The SPEAKER. The gentleman from Kentucky makes the point of order that debate cannot be limited by a motion in the House. The Chair is inclined to think that unless the motion to limit debate be adopted by unanimous consent, the point of order is well taken.

FEBRUARY 14, 1882.

Mr. ORTH also, from the Committee on Foreign Affairs, reported adversely the following resolution, viz:

Resolved, That the President of the United States, if not incompatible with the public service, be requested to communicate to this House all correspondence with the British Government on file in the State Department with reference to the case of D. H. O'Connor, a citizen of the United States, now imprisoned in Ireland.

Mr. ORTH, under instructions from said committee, moved to lay the said resolution on the table; which said motion was disagreed to.

The House thereupon proceeded to the consideration of the said resolution.

Mr. S. S. COX submitted the following amendment, viz:

Strike out all after the word "Resolved," and insert in lieu thereof the following:

That the President be, and be is hereby, requested to obtain for D. H. O'Connor and other American citizens now imprisoned under a suspension of the *habeas corpus* by the British Government in Ireland, without trial, conviction, or sentence, a speedy and fair trial or a prompt release.

Pending which, Mr. POUND made the point of order that said amendment was not in order, not being germane to the subject-matter of said resolution.

The Speaker sustained the said point of order on the ground stated, and also on the further ground that it changed a resolution of inquiry into a resolution directing or instructing the President in a respect which it was not competent for the House to do.

Mr. S. S. COX appealed from the decision of the Chair; when, on motion of Mr. POUND, the said appeal was laid on the table.

FEBRUARY 16, 1882.

Mr. SPRINGER moved to reconsider the vote by which the amendment submitted by Mr. COLERICK was disagreed to; pending which, Mr. BUTTERWORTH moved to lay the said motion on the table.

Mr. SPRINGER demanded the yeas and nays; and, one-fifth of the members present voting in favor thereof, the same were ordered.

The Clerk thereupon proceeded to call the name of Mr. AIKEN.

Mr. SPRINGER asked that the amendment submitted by Mr. COLERICK be read.

The Speaker held that the roll-call having been commenced it was not in order to interrupt it to have said amendment read, except by unanimous consent; and objection being made, the Speaker directed the roll-call to proceed.

FEBRUARY 21, 1882.

The Clerk thereupon proceeded to call the roll of members, and called the first two names thereon; when Mr. ROBESON moved that the House adjourn.

The Speaker held the motion to be not in order, on the ground that it was not in order to interrupt the call.

The Clerk thereupon resumed the call of the roll and completed the same.

FEBRUARY 25, 1882.

Mr. REED, from the Committee on Rules, as a privileged question, reported the following resolution, viz:

Resolved, That a select committee of nine members be appointed to whom shall be referred all petitions, bills, and resolves asking for the extension of suffrage to women or the removal of their legal disabilities.

Mr. McMILLIN made the point of order that under clause 1, Rule XXVIII, the said report must lie over one day.

The Speaker overruled the point of order, on the ground that the pending resolution did not change or rescind any standing rule or order of the House.

Mr. SPRINGER made the point of order that the resolution changed Rule X by increasing the number of committees therein named.

The Speaker overruled the point of order, on the ground that the resolution provided only for the appointment of a select committee and did not increase or decrease the number of standing committees provided for in Rule X.

157

MARCH 8, 1882.

Mr. HASKELL moved that the House proceed to business on the Speaker's table.

And the question being put, it was decided in the affirmative—yeas 111, nays 86, not voting 95.

So the motion to proceed to business on the Speaker's table was agreed to.

The Speaker thereupon laid before the House the bill of the Senate (S. 1692) authorizing and directing the purchase by the Secretary of the Treasury, for the public use, of the property known as the Freedman's Bank, and the real estate and parcels of ground adjacent thereto, belonging to the Freedman's Savings and Trust Company, and located on Pennsylvania avenue, between Fifteenth and Fifteenth-and-a-half streets, Washington, D. C., as the unfinished business on the Speaker's table, and stated the pending question to be on the third reading of the bill.

Mr. SPRINGER made the point of order that the said bill must receive its first consideration in the Committee of the Whole House on the state of the Union.

After debate on the said point of order, the Speaker overruled the same, on the ground that when the pending bill was reached on the Speaker's table, on the 28th ultimo, the bill was taken up, read a first and second time, ordered to be read a third time, and was read the third time. Thereupon Mr. SPRINGER moved to reconsider the vote by which it was ordered to be read a third time. Pending that motion, motions to adjourn and to lay the bill on the table were successively negatived. The vote by which the bill was ordered to its third reading was then reconsidered, when the question recurred on ordering the bill to be read a third time. Pending which, motions to refer the said bill to the Committees on Public Buildings and Grounds and Banking and Currency were successively negatived, when the question again recurred on ordering the bill to its third reading. For these reasons the Chair held that the House had entered upon the consideration of the bill, and the point of order was therefore overruled.

From this decision of the Chair Mr. SPRINGER appealed.

When, on motion of Mr. WASHBURN, the said appeal was laid on the table.

MARCH 13, 1882.

The Speaker thereupon announced as the regular order of business the bill of the Senate (S. 353) to amend section 5352 of the Revised Statutes of the United States, in reference to bigamy, and for other purposes, reached in order when the House was considering business on the Speaker's table on the 8th instant, the pending question being the point of order made by Mr. CONVERSE that the said bill, under clause 3, Rule XXIII, must receive its first consideration in the Committee of the Whole.

After debate on the said point of order. The Speaker said: The Chair has found some difficulty in reaching a satisfactory conclusion upon this question. The discussion upon the point of order has ranged over a very wide field. The point of order made by the gentleman from Ohio [Mr. CONVERSE] is that under paragraph 3 of Rule XXIII this bill must be first considered in Committee of the Whole. The Chair directs the Clerk to read that paragraph.

The Clerk read as follows:

3. All motions or propositions involving a tax or charge upon the people; all proceedings touching appropriations of money, or bills making appropriations of money or property, or requiring such appropriation to be made, or authorizing payments out of appropriations already made, or releasing any liability to the United States for money or property, shall be first considered in a Committee of the Whole; and a point of order under this rule shall be good at any time before the consideration of a bill has commenced.

The SPEAKER. The bill under consideration in section 9 makes provision for a board of five officers to discharge certain election duties, and provides that the members of this board shall be paid a salary of $3,000 a year. The Clerk will read that portion of section 9 which relates to these officers and in part to their duties.

The Clerk read as follows:

SEC. 9. That all the registration and election offices of every description in the Territory of Utah are hereby declared vacant; and each and every duty relating to the registration of voters, the conduct of elections, the receiving or rejection of votes, and the canvassing and returning of the same and the issuing of certificates or other evidence of election, in said Territory, shall until other provision be made by the Legislative Assembly of said Territory as is hereinafter by this section provided be performed, under the existing laws of the United States and of said Territory by proper persons who shall be appointed to execute such offices and perform such duties by a board of five persons to be appointed by the President, by and with the advice and consent of the Senate, not more than three of whom shall be members of one political party, and a majority of whom shall be a quorum. The persons so appointed by the President shall each receive a salary at the rate of $3,000 per annum, and shall continue in office until the Legislative Assembly of said Territory shall make provision for filling said offices as herein authorized.

The SPEAKER. It should be conceded that this proposition does not, within the meaning of the rule, involve "a tax or charge upon the people;" that it is not a "proceeding touching an appropriation of money;" that it does not "make an appropriation of money or property;" that it does not "authorize a payment out of the appropriations already made;" that it does not "release any liability to the United States for money or property."

But it is contended that this bill, if it should become a law, would require an appropriation to be paid out of the Treasury of the United States. The tax or charge referred to in the rule, as the Chair thinks, relates to a direct tax or charge on the people, and has no reference to an appropriation of money from the United States Treasury.

The five members of the board proposed to be created by this bill are to be paid a salary at the rate of $3,000 per annum. The claim is that an appropriation of money would have to be made to pay the members of that board; or, in other words, that the bill, if it should become a law, would require an appropriation of money to be made to execute it.

It is perhaps clear under the rule that if this bill does require an appropriation of money out of the Treasury of the United States to pay the salaries of the officers mentioned, it must be first considered in Committee of the Whole. A very strict construction of this rule would justify the Chair in holding that a bill must by its terms require an appropriation of money to make it liable to a point of order. The Chair, however, is not now disposed to give such a construction to the rule, but is strongly inclined to hold that in case a bill provides for new officers and fixes their salaries, which salaries must of necessity be paid out of the United States Treasury and from money to be appropriated, such bill may be said to require an appropriation of money within the meaning of the rule.

The Chair does not intend to intimate that a bill which if enacted into law would incidentally involve expense to execute it would therefore be subject to the point of order that it should be first considered in Committee of the Whole, unless the bill directly required an appropriation of money to pay such expense. The rule relates to bills "requiring," not "involving," an appropriation of money. Within the construction of the rule indicated, does this bill require an appropriation of money? If the five members of the board provided for in the bill must of necessity be paid their salaries out of money to be appropriated from the United States Treasury then the bill would require an appropriation of money.

To determine the last proposition we must look to the laws in force especially relating to the Territory of Utah, and to the general laws of the United States relating to the organization of all the Territories.

By reference to the charter act of Utah and to the general laws of the United States relating to the organization of Territories it will be found that in the organization of the Territory of Utah Congress provided for a governor, a secretary, a Territorial assembly, justices of courts, an attorney, and a marshal, and their assistants and deputies, and perhaps some other officers for the government of the Territory. The salaries of those officers, including the pay of the members of the Legislative Assembly, are fixed and authorized to be paid out of the Treasury of the United States. A fixed sum is established for the contingent expenses of the governor in each year, and a sufficient sum is authorized to defray the expenses of the Legislative Assembly, including printing and incidental expenses, to be paid out of the Treasury of the United States. All other expenses necessary to carry on the Territorial government not otherwise provided for in the laws of the United States are required to be paid out of a fund to be raised by a tax imposed on property owners in the Territory. By the express terms of the Territorial laws the election officers are required to be so paid.

This bill proposes to depose certain election officers and to provide temporarily a board of officers for the conduct of elections and to execute the election laws of the Territory of Utah. The legislative assembly may again, as provided in the bill, fill the offices declared by this bill to be vacant, and the functions of the board proposed by the bill will then cease.

Such board becomes a part of the election system for the time being of the Territory of Utah; and it may be held that their salaries will be payable out of the treasury of the Territory, either by virtue of existing laws or by laws, either Territorial or Federal, which may hereafter be enacted. If this be true, then it follows that the bill does not require an appropriation of money out of the Treasury of the United States to pay the officers created by it.

The Chair will here observe, with reference to a decision said to have been made by Speaker Blaine, that upon an examination of the then pending bill it seems quite clear that his decision was properly made, and is within the views of the present occupant of the chair. The class of officers that was proposed to be constituted by the bill then under consideration were assistants of the United States attorney and deputy marshals. Those officers by the very terms of the then existing laws would have to be paid out of the Treasury of the United States. They did not belong to any Territorial system, and it could not possibly have been then held that under any state of the law. in the absence of legislation directly upon the subject, any other treasury was to be drawn on for the payment of these assistant attorneys and deputy marshals than the Treasury of the United States.

The Chair cannot agree that any bill which might, if amended, require an appropriation of money from the Treasury of the United States must be first considered in Committee of the Whole. There are a vast number of bills pending that are under our rules and practice not referred to the Committee of the Whole House for consideration which might be amended under the rules so as to finally involve an appropriation of money to execute the laws created should such bills pass.

The Chair is not disposed to hold that if a bill might by possibility require an appropriation of money it must first be considered in Committee of the Whole. The Chair thinks it goes far enough when it holds that a bill must on its face require an appropriation of money to carry it out or to pay the salaries of the officers created by it.

It is not necessary to decide that the officers proposed to be created by this bill are or are not United States officers. They may be both United States and Territorial officers. The Chair has nothing to do with the question of the power or right of Congress to enact such a law as this bill proposes. The Chair is bound to assume that the proposed legislation is within the constitutional power of Congress.

It may be, perhaps, proper to remark that all the laws of the Territory of Utah enacted by its assembly are by the terms of the original act for the organization of that Territory subject to be annulled by the mere disapproval of Congress. Entertaining these views, the Chair overrules the point of order.

Mr. CONVERSE. Inasmuch as the decision of the Chair involves a rule of the House of so much importance to the House itself and the entire country, I desire respectfully to make an appeal.

The SPEAKER. The gentleman from Ohio takes an appeal. The question is, Shall the decision of the Chair stand as the judgment of the House?

Mr. HASKELL. I move that the appeal be laid on the table.

Mr. CONVERSE. In view of the importance of the question to be determined by the House, I demand the yeas and nays on this proposition.

The yeas and nays were ordered.

The question was taken; and there were—yeas 119, nays 80, not voting 93.

So the appeal was laid on the table.

MARCH 20, 1882.

Mr. REED, under instructions from the Committee on the Judiciary, moved that the rules be suspended so as to enable him to report from the committee on the Judiciary and the House to agree to the following resolution, viz:

Resolved, That the House bill 4197, re-establishing the Court of Commissioners of Alabama Claims, for the distribution of the unappropriated moneys of the Geneva award, be taken from the Committee of the Whole and be considered in the House as in committee on the fourth Tuesday of March, and then from day to day until finally disposed of, not to interfere with the revenue and general appropriation bills.

Pending which, Mr. SPRINGER moved that the House adjourn; and the question being put, it was decided in the negative.

. . . .

Mr. BRAGG moved that the House adjourn.

The Speaker held the motion to be not in order, on the ground that under clause 8 of Rule XVI but one motion to adjourn was in order pending a motion to suspend the rules, which motion (to adjourn) had been made and negatived.

From this decision of the Chair Mr. HOUSE appealed; pending which, Mr. CAMP moved to lay the said appeal on the table; and the question being put, there appeared—yeas 79, nays 42, not voting 171.

No quorum voted.

A call of the House was thereupon ordered and had.

The Clerk thereupon proceeded to call the names of absentees for excuses; pending which, Mr. BRAGG moved that the House adjourn, the Speaker having entertained the said motion on the ground that on a call of the House less than a quorum had answered to their names; pending which motion to adjourn, on motion of Mr. REED, by unanimous consent—

Ordered, That the House now adjourn, and that to-morrow, after the reading of the Journal, the motion to suspend the rules and adopt the resolution as modified shall be voted on the same as on a Monday's session.

MARCH 28, 1882.

Mr. CALKINS, as a question of privilege, proposed to call up the report of the Committee on Elections in the case of the claim of M. D. Ball to a seat in this House as Delegate from the Territory of Alaska.

Mr. KNOTT made the point of order that the said report and subject was not a question of privilege, there being no law authorizing Alaska to send a Delegate to Congress, or authorizing an election for that purpose to be held in said Territory.

After debate on said point of order, the Speaker sustained the same, on the ground that said report, with an accompanying resolution providing that M. D. Ball be not admitted to a seat in the Forty-seventh Congress as a Delegate from the Territory of Alaska until the Committee on the Territories shall report thereon, was referred to the Committee on the Territories, which committee had not reported thereon.

APRIL 21, 1882.

Mr. BOWMAN moved that the consideration of private business for to-day be dispensed with, and that the House proceed to the consideration of the special order, the bill of the House (H. R. 684) to afford assistance and relief to Congress and the Executive Departments in the investigation of claims and demands against the Government.

After debate thereon, by unanimous consent, Mr. BOWMAN withdrew the said motion, and made the point of order that the regular order of business was the bill of the House (H. R. 684) to afford assistance and relief to Congress and the Executive Departments in the investigation of claims and demands against the Government, under the order of the House of February 20, ultimo.

After debate on said point of order, by unanimous consent, the Speaker sustained the said point of order, on the ground that the said bill was made a "special order" for the 7th of March, after the morning hour, and from day to day thereafter until disposed of, with certain restrictions, without excepting Friday, and also on the further ground that the said "special order" was made under a suspension of rules, which of necessity suspended all rules in conflict with the terms of said order.

APRIL 25, 1882.

Mr. WILLIAM E. ROBINSON then called up, as a privileged question, the following preamble and resolution, submitted by him on yesterday, viz:

Whereas on the 23d day of January, 1882, a resolution of inquiry was introduced in this House and was on that day referred to the Committee on Foreign Affairs; and

Whereas afterwards, on the 14th day February, 1882, the same resolution having been reported back, was recommitted to the Committee on Foreign Affairs with instructions, all of which will more fully appear by reference to the said resolution and instructions hereto appended and the record of the proceedings of those days; and

Whereas by clause 2 of Rule XXIV every such resolution is required to be reported back to the committee to which it has been referred within one week of such reference; and

Whereas more than one week, to wit, ten weeks, have elapsed since the reference or recommitment of said resolution to said committee, and no report has been made thereon by said committee: Therefore,

Resolved, That the Committee on Foreign Affairs be, and they hereby are, discharged from the further consideration of said resolution, and that the same be now brought before the House for immediate consideration.

Mr. ORTH withdrew the point of order made by him on yesterday, that the said preamble and resolution did not present a question of privilege; when Mr. KASSON renewed the same.

The Speaker overruled the point of order, on the ground that the last paragraph of clause 1 of Rule XXIV required committees to report resolutions of inquiry within one week after their reference, and that as this was a matter affecting the order of business of the House, it had a right to direct and control the action of the committee with respect to the said resolution.

MAY 18, 1882.

The House then proceeded, as the regular order of business, to the further consideration of the bill of the House (H. R. 4167) to enable national banking associations to extend their corporate existence, the pending question being on the amendment submitted by Mr. BUCKNER, to strike out in line 16 of section 1 the word "twenty" and insert in lieu thereof the word "ten," pending when the House adjourned on yesterday, on which amendment the yeas and nays were then ordered.

* * * * * * *

Mr. BLAND moved to amend the said substitute by adding thereto the following words, viz:

Provided further, That said associations are hereby prohibited from issuing circulating notes; and hereafter no national banking association shall increase its circulation or be organized with authority to issue notes to circulate as money.

Mr. DINGLEY made the point of order that the said amendment was not in order at this time.

The Speaker sustained the point of order, on the ground that under the terms of the resolution making the pending bill a special order certain specified amendments were made in order, and the amendment proposed by Mr. BLAND not being so named, it was subject to the provisions of the rule regulating amendments, and not being germane to the pending question was not in order as an amendment thereto or a substitute therefor.

MAY 19, 1882.

The House then proceeded, as the regular order of business, to the further consideration of the bill of the House (H. R. 4167) to enable national banking associations to extend their corporate existence.

*   *   *   *   *   *   *

The question recurring on the amendment submitted by Mr. RANDALL, pending which Mr. CANNON moved to amend said amendment by striking out the following words, viz. "but when bonds are called for redemption, the banks holding such called bonds shall surrender them within thirty days after the maturity of their call;" which said amendment was disagreed to.

The question again recurring on the amendment submitted by Mr. RANDALL, pending which Mr. BAYNE submitted the following amendment thereto, viz:

Provided, however, That said banks may withhold such bonds, in whole or in part, for one year, upon notifying the Secretary of the Treasury of their intention so to do, in which event such bonds shall not be redeemable until the expiration of the year, nor shall they bear interest.

Mr. RANDALL made the point of order that said amendment was not in order, being substantially the proposition just voted on and rejected.

The Speaker overruled the said point of order, on the ground that the vote referred to was to strike out a portion of a proposed section on which an affirmative vote had not yet been taken, and that while it might be inconsistent with the vote last taken, it was for the House to pass upon that question.

And the question being put, it was decided in the negative.

The question again recurring on the amendment submitted by Mr. RANDALL, pending which Mr. SPRINGER moved to amend the same by striking out the words "ninety days" and inserting in lieu thereof the words "six months;" which amendment was disagreed to.

Mr. BLAND moved to amend the pending amendment by adding the following words, viz:

Provided further, That there shall be coined monthly in the mints of the United States standard silver dollars to the maximum amount now authorized to be coined by law, and the same, or certificates therefor, shall be paid out in sufficient quantities to replace the bank notes that may be retired under this act or existing law. And if such quantity is not sufficient for such purpose, then the Secretary is authorized and hereby required to cause to be coined an amount of standard silver dollars sufficient for the purposes aforesaid: *Provided,* That nothing herein shall be construed to limit in any manner the amount of such dollars now authorized and required to be coined.

Mr. DINGLEY made the point of order that the said amendment was not in order, not being germane to the pending amendment.

The Speaker sustained the said point of order, on the ground that the proposed amendment was not only not germane to the pending amendment, but was not germane to the subject-matter of the pending bill, which related to the extension of the corporate existence of national banks.

From this decision of the Chair Mr. BLAND appealed; pending which Mr. BAYNE moved that the said appeal be laid on the table, when Mr. BLAND withdrew the said appeal.

Mr. RANDALL moved to amend by inserting the following words as a new section, viz:

SEC. 11. That from and after the passage of this act the Secretary of the Treasury is hereby authorized and required to receive deposits of gold coin and bullion with the Treasurer or any assistant treasurer of the United States, in sums of not less than $20, and to issue certificates therefor in denominations of not less than $20 each, corresponding with the denominations of the United States notes. The coin and bullion deposited for or representing the certificates of deposit shall be retained in the Treasury for the payment of the same on demand.

Mr. CRAPO made the point of order that said amendment was not in order, not being germane to the pending bill.

The Speaker sustained the said point of order, on the ground that the proposed amendment had no relation to the subject-matter of the pending bill, which related exclusively to the extension of the corporate existence of national banks.

MAY 24, 1882.

Mr. CALKINS, as a question of privilege, sent to the Clerk's desk an extract from a newspaper, relating to the contested-election case of Mackey *vs.* O'Connor.

Mr. RANDALL reserved all points of order as to the said extract.

After debate on the point of order that the said extract did not present a question of privilege, the Speaker overruled the same, on the ground that the extract read alleged fraudulent transactions as to the taking of testimony in said case by the Committee on Elections, and as that charge was made by a member of the House, it presented under Rule IX a question of privilege.

MAY 26, 1882.

Mr. CALKINS, as a privileged question, called up the report of the Committee on Elections in the contested-election case of Mackey *vs.* O'Connor.

*　　　*　　　*　　　*　　　*　　　*　　　*

The question recurring on the motion of Mr. CARLISLE that the House adjourn, on which motion the yeas and nays were ordered, Mr. HATCH asked to be excused from voting on the said question.

Mr. CALKINS made the point of order that the said request was not in order under the rules and practice of the House.

After debate, by unanimous consent, on the said point of order, the Speaker sustained the same, on the ground that previous rulings of Speakers had established the practice as to requests of this character, and that under the terms of clause 1 of Rule VIII, which was identical with Rule XXXI, under which said rulings had been made, it was not in order to entertain and submit the said request.

From this decision of the Chair Mr. BLACKBURN appealed.

Mr. CALKINS moved to lay the said appeal on the table; and the question being put, it was decided in the affirmative—yeas 147, nays 1, not voting 143.

MAY 27, 1882.

Mr. REED, as a privileged question, from the Committee on Rules, submitted the following report, viz:

Amend paragraph 8 of Rule XVI so as to read as follows:

Pending a motion to suspend the rules, or on any question of consideration which may arise on a case involving the constitutional right to a seat, and pending the motion for the previous question, or after it shall have been ordered on any such case, the Speaker may entertain one motion to adjourn; but after the result thereon is announced he shall not entertain any other motion till the vote is taken on the pending question; and pending the consideration of such case a motion to adjourn or to take a recess (but not both in succession) shall be in order, and such motions shall not be repeated without further intervening consideration of the case for at least one hour.

Pending its submission, Mr. KENNA moved that the House take a recess until 8 o'clock p. m.; which motion the Speaker declined to entertain and submit, during the reading of the said report.

From which decision Mr. KENNA appealed; which appeal the Speaker also declined to entertain during the reading of said report.

Ordered, That said report lie over for the present.

MAY 29, 1882.

Mr. REED, as a privileged question, called up the report of the Committee on Rules made on Saturday last; when Mr. RANDALL raised the question of consideration; pending which, Mr. KENNA moved that the House adjourn; pending which, Mr. BLACKBURN moved that when the House adjourn it be to meet on Wednesday next; and the question being put thereon, it was decided in the negative—yeas 2, nays 146, not voting 143.

*　　　*　　　*　　　*　　　*　　　*

So the House refused to adjourn over to Wednesday next.

The question recurring on the motion of Mr. KENNA that the House adjourn; pending which, Mr. RANDALL moved that when the House adjourn it be to meet on Thursday next.

Mr. REED made the point of order that the said motion was not in order at this time, on the ground that pending a proposition to change the rules of the House, dilatory motions cannot be entertained by the Chair.

After debate on the said point of order,

The SPEAKER. The Chair is ready to announce his decision upon this question.

Mr. SPRINGER. Mr. Speaker, will the Chair hear me for a moment?

The SPEAKER. The Chair thinks that sufficient time has been given for this discussion. The Chair has allowed already more than four hours of debate, considerably more than half of which has been given to the gentleman's side.

Mr. SPRINGER. I hope I will not be cut off from the opportunity of being heard. [Cries of "Vote!" "Vote!" and "Question!"]

The SPEAKER. The Chair thinks that sufficient time has been given.

Mr. SPRINGER. I desire to remind the Chair that in the first session of the Forty-sixth Congress a point of order was made in the Committee of the Whole on the Army bill; and that point of order, by the indulgence of the majority, was discussed for one week, and there was no effort to limit debate upon it.

The SPEAKER. The Chair thinks the debate has not been limited; debate has been liberally allowed.

Mr. SPRINGER. I had the honor to occupy the chair at that time, and hope that the same courtesy will be extended to me.

The SPEAKER. The question for the Chair to decide is briefly this: the gentleman from Maine [Mr. REED] has called up for present consideration the report of the Committee on Rules made on the 27th instant, and the gentleman from Pennsylvania [Mr. RANDALL] raised, as he might under the practice and the rules of the House, the question of consideration. The gentleman from West Virginia [Mr. KENNA] then moved that the House adjourn, and the gentleman from Kentucky [Mr. BLACKBURN] moved that when the House adjourn it be to meet on Wednesday next, which last motion was voted down; and thereupon the gentleman from Pennsylvania [Mr. RANDALL] moved that when the House adjourn it be to meet on Thursday next. The gentleman from Maine [Mr. REED] then raised the point of order that such motions are mere dilatory motions, and therefore, as against the right of the House to consider a proposition to amend the rules, not in order.

It cannot be disputed that the Committee on Rules have the right to report at any time such changes in the rules as it may decide to be wise. The right of that committee to report at any time may be, under the practice, a question of privilege; but if it is not, resolutions of this House, adopted December 19, 1881, expressly give that right.

The Clerk will read the resolutions.

The Clerk read as follows:

Resolved, That the rules of the House of Representatives of the Forty-sixth Congress shall be the rules of the present House until otherwise ordered; and

Resolved further, That the Committee on Rules when appointed shall have the right to report at any time all such amendments or revisions of said rules as they may deem proper.

The SPEAKER. It will be seen that these resolutions not only give the right to that committee to report at any time, but the committee is authorized to report any change, &c., in the rules. The right given to report at any time carries with it the right to have the proposition reported considered without laying over. The resolutions are the ones adopting the present standing rules of the House for its government; and it will be observed that they were only conditionally adopted; and the right was expressly reserved to the House to order them to be set aside. Paragraph 1 of Rule XXVIII provides that—

No standing rule of the House shall be rescinded or changed without one day's notice of the motion in writing.

This clause of the rule, if applicable at all, may fairly be construed to make it in order under the standing rules of the House to consider any motion to rescind or change the rules after one day's notice.

But the question for the Chair to decide is this: Are the rules of this House to be so construed as to give to the minority of the House the absolute right to prevent the majority or a quorum of the House from making any new rule for its government; or in the absence of anything in the rules providing for any mode of proceeding in the matter of consideration, when the question of changing the rules is before the House, shall the rules be so construed as to virtually prevent their change should one-fifth of the House oppose it? It may be well to keep in mind that paragraph 2 of section 5 of article 1 of the Constitution says that—

Each House may determine the rules of its proceedings.

The same section of the Constitution provides that—

A majority of each House shall constitute a quorum to do business.

The right given to the House to determine the rules of its proceedings is never exhausted, but is at all times a continuing right, and in the opinion of the Chair gives a right to make or alter rules independent of any rules it may adopt. Dilatory motions to prevent the consideration of business are comparatively recent expedients, and should not be favored in any case save where absolutely required by some clear rule of established practice.

In any case it is a severe strain upon common sense to construe the rules so as to prevent a quorum of the House from taking any proceedings at all required by the Constitution; and it is still more difficult to find any justification for holding that the special resolutions of this House adopted December 19 last, or the standing rules even of the House, were intended to prevent the House, if a majority so desired, from altering or abrogating the present rules of the House.

There seems to be abundant precedent for the view the Chair takes. The Clerk will read from the RECORD of the Forty-third Congress, page —, an opinion expressed by the distinguished Speaker, Mr. Blaine, which has been repeatedly alluded to to-day.

The Clerk read as follows:

The Chair has repeatedly ruled that pending a proposition to change the rules dilatory motions could not be entertained, and for this reason he has several times ruled that the right of each House to determine what shall be its rules is an organic right expressly given by the Constitution of the United States. The rules are the creature of that power and of course they cannot be used to destroy the power. The House is incapable by any form of rules of divesting itself of its inherent constitutional power to exercise its function to determine its own rules. Therefore the Chair has always announced upon a proposition to change the rules of the House he would never entertain a dilatory motion.

The SPEAKER. It will be observed that the then Speaker says he has frequently held that pending a proposition to change the rules dilatory motions could not be entertained. The precedents for ruling out dilatory motions where an amendment of of the rules is under consideration are many.

During the electoral count my immediate predecessor [Mr. RANDALL] decided, in principle, the point involved here. On February 24, 1877, after an obstructive motion had been made, the following language was used, as found in the RECORD of the Forty-fourth Congress, page 1906:

The SPEAKER. The Chair is unable to recognize this in any other light than a dilatory motion.

The mover then denied that he made the motion as such.

The SPEAKER. The Chair is unable to classify it in any other way. Therefore he rules that when the Constitution of the United States directs anything to be done, or when the law under the Constitution of the United States enacted in obedience thereto directs any act of this House, it is not in order to make any motion to obstruct or impede the execution of that injunction of the Constitution and laws.

While this decision is not on the precise point, it clearly covers the principles involved in the case with which we are now dealing.

The Chair thinks the Constitution and the laws are higher than any rules, and when they conflict with the rules the latter must give way. There is not one word in the present rules, however, which prescribes the mode of proceeding in changing the standing rules except as to the reference of propositions to change the rules, with the further exception that—

No standing rule or order of the House shall be rescinded or changed without one day's notice.

But it will be observed that there is an entire absence from all these standing rules of anything that looks to giving directions as to the procedure when the rule is under consideration by the House. This only refers to the time of considering motions to rescind or change a standing rule to the reference of propositions submitted by members, and to the time and manner of bringing them before the House for consideration, and not to the method of considering them when brought before the House.

It seems to purposely avoid saying one word as to the forms of proceeding while considering such motions. This is highly significant.

There is nothing revolutionary in holding that purely dilatory motions cannot be entertained to prevent consideration or action on a proposition to amend the rules of the House, as this right to make or amend the rules is an organic one essential to be exercised preliminary to the orderly transaction of business by the House. It would be more than absurd to hold otherwise.

Rule XL undertakes to fasten our present standing rules on the present and all succeeding Congresses. It reads as follows:

These rules shall be the rules of the House of Representatives of the present and succeeding Congresses, unless otherwise ordered.

If this rule is of binding force on succeeding Congresses, and the rules apply and can be invoked to give power to a minority in the House to prevent their abrogation or alteration, they would be made perpetually if only one-fifth of the members of the House so decreed.

The fallacy of holding that the standing rules can be held to apply in proceedings to amend, &c., the rules will more sharply appear when we look to the case in hand. The proposition is to so amend the rules in contested-election cases as to take away the right to make and repeat dilatory motions, to prevent consideration, &c. And the same obstructive right is appealed to prevent its consideration. To allow this would be to hold the rules superior not only to the House that made them but to the Constitution of the United States.

The wise remarks quoted in debate made long since by the distinguished speaker, Mr. Onslow of the House of Commons about the wisdom of adhering to fixed rules in legislative proceedings were made with no reference to the application of rules which it was claimed were made to prevent any proceedings at all by the body acting under them.

The present occupant of the chair has tried, and will try, to give full effect to all rules whereve applicable, and especially to protect the rights of the minority to the utmost extent the rules will justify.

The Chair is not called upon to hold that any of the standing rules of the House are in conflict with the Constitution, as it is not necessary to do so. It only holds that there is nothing in the rules which gives them application pending proceedings to amend and rescind them. It also holds that under the first of the resolutions adopted by the House on December 19, 1881, the right was reserved to order the standing rules set aside at any time this House so decided, and without regard to dilatory forms of proceedings provided for in them. The Chair does not hold that pending the question of consideration no motion shall be in order. It is disposed to treat one motion to adjourn as proper at this time, as it is a well-known parliamentary motion, and that such motion may be liable at some stage of the proceedings to be repeated if made for a proper and not a dilatory purpose.

The Chair feels better satisfied with its ruling in this case, because the rule proposed to be adopted is one which looks to an orderly proceeding in the matter of taking up and disposing of contested-election cases, a duty cast directly on the House by the Constitution of the United States, and an essential one to be performed before it is completely organized.

The Chair is unable to find in the whole history of the Government that any dilatory motions have ever been made or entertained to prevent the consideration or disposition of a contested-election case until this Congress. The point of order has not yet been made against obstructive motions to prevent the consideration of a contested-election case, and the Chair is not now called on to decide whether such motions are in order or not where they would prevent a complete organization of the House. The principle here involved will suffice to indicate the opinion of the Chair on that question.

The question here decided the Chair understands to be an important one, because it comprehends the complete organization of the House to do business, but it feels that on principle and sound precedents the point of order made by the gentleman from Maine [Mr. REED] must be sustained to the extent of holding that the motion made by the gentleman from Pennsylvania [Mr. RANDALL], which is in effect a dilatory motion, is not at this time in order.

It has been in debate claimed that on January 11, 1882, the present occupant of the chair made a different holding. The question then made and decided arose on a matter of reference of a proposition to amend the rules to an appropriate committee as provided for under the rules, and not on the consideration of a report when properly brought before the House for its action. The two things are so plainly distinguishable as to require nothing further to be said about them.

Mr. RANDALL. From your decision, Mr. Speaker, just announced, I appeal to the House, whose officer you are.

Mr. REED. I move to lay the appeal on the table.

The SPEAKER. The gentleman from Pennsylvania [Mr. RANDALL] appeals from the decision of the Chair, and the gentleman from Maine [Mr. REED] moves that the appeal be laid upon the table.

Mr. SPRINGER. Before that question is taken——

The SPEAKER. The motion is not debatable.

Mr. SPRINGER. I rise to a question of privilege, not to debate anything. The gentleman from Maine [Mr. REED] has moved to lay the appeal on the table, and I ask to be excused from voting on that motion.

Mr. REED. I make the point that that is not in order.

The SPEAKER. That is not in order.

Mr. SPRINGER. I appeal from the decision of the Chair.

The SPEAKER. The Chair will not entertain the appeal. The question is upon laying on the table the appeal of the gentleman from Pennsylvania.

Mr. BLACKBURN and others called for the yeas and nays.

The yeas and nays were ordered.

Mr. SPRINGER. I want a ruling upon the question I have raised.

The SPEAKER. The Chair has ruled upon it.

Mr. SPRINGER. I want to know whether the Chair holds that I have not the right before this question is put to ask to be excused from voting on it?

The SPEAKER. The Chair so holds.

Mr. SPRINGER. I appeal from that decision.

The SPEAKER. The Chair cannot entertain two appeals at the same time. The question is upon the motion of the gentleman from Maine [Mr. REED] to lay upon the table the appeal of the gentleman from Pennsylvania [Mr. RANDALL] from the decision of the Chair. Upon that motion the yeas and nays have been ordered; and the Clerk will call the roll.

The question was taken; and there were—yeas 150, nays 0, not voting 141.

So the appeal was laid on the table.

The names of those voting were read, after which the result was announced as above stated.

The SPEAKER. The question now recurs on the motion——

Mr. Cox, of New York. I rise, with all respect to the Chair, upon a question of privilege on behalf of one hundred members on this side of the House. I desire to make the paper which I hold in my hand a part of my statement of the question of privilege, and wish to have it read from the Clerk's desk.

Mr. REED and others objected.

Mr. KASSON. On this paper, which is understood to be a protest, I make a point of order, saving rights in that respect.

Mr. COX, of New York I make it a part of my remarks.

The SPEAKER. The gentleman from New York states that he rises to a question of privilege. The Chair wishes to say that while he does not know there is anything in the Constitution or the rules providing for making a protest a part of the proceedings, the Chair, so far as he is concerned (and he is assured the protest is in respectful language), is willing that it should be received and go upon the records.

Mr. REED. Let us not waste time by reading it.

Mr. COX, of New York. I have a right to have it read.

The SPEAKER. The Chair does not think the reading is a matter of right, except so far as it may present a question of privilege; and the Chair does not understand that a mere protest is a question of privilege.

Mr. REED. I have no objection to its going into the RECORD.

Mr. COX, of New York. I want it read.

The SPEAKER. It may be read so far as the Chair is concerned. [Cries of "Read!" "Read!"]

Mr. KASSON. I wish to save all rights.

The SPEAKER. Undoubtedly; all rights will be reserved.

Mr. BURROWS, of Michigan. I suppose it is understood that this is to be read not because it is a question of privilege, but by unanimous consent.

Mr. COX, of New York. We l, let it be read.

The SPEAKER. The Chair does not object.

Mr. COX, of New York. I do not wish to take any advantage of gentlemen on the other side. Let the paper be read.

Mr. VAN VORHIS. I object. [Cries of "Don't object!"]

The SPEAKER. The gentleman from New York [Mr. Cox] has informed the Chair that this is a protest. The Chair is quite willing that it should be read and go upon the records. [Cries of "Read!" "Read!"]

Mr. KASSON. Mr. Speaker, I wish to say a word upon the point of order.

Mr. COX, of New York. I distinctly stated that I made this paper a part of my remarks on the question of privilege. Whatever it may turn out to be hereafter, it is a part of my remarks, and I have the right, which the Chair has conceded, to have it read.

Mr. REED. There is no question of privilege that can interrupt the present business of the House.

Mr. KASSON. What I wish to call the attention of the Speaker to is on page 333 of the Manual, where it is stated that it has been ruled——

The SPEAKER. The Chair is quite willing that the body of this paper should be read.

Mr. WILSON and others. Let it be read. [Cries of "Read!" "Read!"]

Mr. COX, of New York. It is a respectful paper, coming from over a hundred members.

The SPEAKER. The House will come to order. The paper will be read, points of order being reserved.

The paper is as follows:

* * * * * *

During the reading, when the Clerk had read the words "because a proper hearing has not been granted to the contestee by the Committee on Elections as to the allegations of forgery and fraud,"

Mr. HAWK said: I "object."

The SPEAKER. The House will be in order. The protest will be read to the end.

The Clerk concluded the reading of the body of the paper, and was proceeding to read the signatures when

The SPEAKER said: The names need not be read.

Mr. KASSON. I insist on my point of order and ask to state the reasons for it.

Mr. COX, of New York. Before that is done I desire to say——

Mr. KASSON. I am on the floor.

The SPEAKER. The gentleman from Iowa [Mr. KASSON] makes a point of order, and is entitled to the floor on that point.

Mr. KASSON. I do not wish to prevent the gentleman from New York from answering my point, but I think I ought first to state it before he replies.

* * * * *

Mr. REED. I now ask the previous question upon the report.

The SPEAKER. The Chair thinks that this is not a question of privilege, but one which should not be ruled out by the Chair. The Chair thinks, although he has no more interest in it than any other member, as so many gentlemen have signed it and desired it go into the record, that it should go.

Mr. REED. Let it go to the record.

The SPEAKER. Names and all.

Mr. COX, of New York. Certainly, names and all.

The SPEAKER. It will then be printed in the RECORD.

Mr. REED. I now call the previous question.

Mr. BLACKBURN. I rise to a parliamentary inquiry.

The SPEAKER. The gentleman will state it.

Mr. BLACKBURN. I wish to know whether under the ruling of the Speaker, which seems to have been supported by the House, without regard to parties——

Mr. REED. Unanimously by the House.

Mr. BLACKBURN. Unanimously; whether any member of the House chooses to sign that protest, whose name is not now on it, shall not have the privilege of doing so at any time hereafter?

The SPEAKER. The Chair thinks that at any time during this afternoon, if any gentleman desires to sign the protest, he should be allowed to do so.

Mr. HAZELTON. Certainly, let it be done.

The SPEAKER. There will be no objection if any gentlemen desire to append their names to it.

The gentleman from Maine now demands the previous question. The Chair will now, however, submit the motion made by the gentleman from West Virginia that the House adjourn, and which motion was pending. That motion was entertained this morning, and was entertained on the ground, as stated by the Chair, that it was an ordinary parliamentary motion, and was not ruled out under the decision of the Chair.

Mr. KENNA. I rise to make a privileged motion. It is now five o'clock. I do not understand——

The SPEAKER. The gentleman can have his motion which was pending under the rule submitted to the House; that is, the motion to adjourn.

Mr. KENNA. Does the Chair hold that the motion that the House shall adjourn over to-morrow cannot be entertained?

The SPEAKER. The motion to adjourn will now be submitted.

Mr. KENNA. I move that when the House adjourn it be to meet on Thursday.

The SPEAKER. The Chair has just ruled, and the House has sustained the ruling of the Chair, that that motion would not now be in order, and therefore cannot be entertained. The motion that the gentleman formerly made, that the House do now adjourn, being in order, will of course be submitted to the House.

Mr. KENNA. On that motion I demand the yeas and nays.

The yeas and nays were ordered.

The question was taken; and there were—yeas 6, nays 152, not voting 133.

So the motion was not agreed to.

Mr. CAMP. I ask unanimous consent that the reading of the names be dispensed with.

Mr. SPRINGER. I object.

The names of members voting were read, and the result of the vote was then announced as above stated.

Mr. REED. I now call the previous question upon the adoption of the report made by the Committee on Rules.

Mr. SPRINGER. I move to lay the report on the table.

The SPEAKER. That motion is not entertained.

Mr. SPRINGER. I move to lay the report of the Committee on Rules on the table.

Mr. CONVERSE. I ask the gentleman from Maine permission to make a motion to amend the report so far as it relates to suspending the rules, so that it shall apply only to cases of election contests.

Mr. ROBESON. That is in the rule now. This incorporates the existing rule, so far as that is concerned.

Mr. SPRINGER. I move to lay the report on the table.

The SPEAKER. The motion is not entertained. The gentleman from Illinois is not recognized to make it.

Mr. SPRINGER. I have a right to make it under the rules. Does the Chair refuse to entertain a motion to lay on the table?

The SPEAKER. The Chair entertains the motion of the gentleman from Maine, which is a demand for the previous question.

Mr. SPRINGER. I rise to a question of order.

The SPEAKER. The gentleman from Maine demands the previous question.

Mr. SPRINGER. I raise the question of order that the motion to lay on the table takes precedence of the motion for the previous question.

Mr. CAMP. There is no such motion before the House.

The SPEAKER. The ruling of the Chair was sufficiently broad to cover all these questions.

Mr. SPRINGER. The Chair has not ruled a motion to lay on the table is out of order.

The SPEAKER. The Chair has ruled that dilatory motions are not in order.

Mr. SPRINGER. I deny that this is a dilatory motion, and the Chair has no right to say I am making a dilatory motion. I am making a motion that is always recognized as in order.

The SPEAKER. The gentleman from Illinois is not in order.

Mr. SPRINGER. I am in order; and I appeal from the decision of the Chair and desire to state the reasons for that appeal.

The SPEAKER. The Chair declines to entertain the appeal.

Mr. SPRINGER. I desire the Chair to hear me.

Mr. TUCKER. Does the Chair hold the motion to lay on the table is out of order?

The SPEAKER. The Chair holds that the motion is not in order on the question of the adoption of this proposed rule.

Mr. TUCKER. And does the Chair refuse to entertain an appeal from its decision?

The SPEAKER. Unquestionably.

Mr. SPRINGER. I call the attention of the Chair——

The Speaker proceeded to put the question on Mr. REED'S motion for the previous question.

Mr. SPRINGER. I call the attention of the Chair——

The SPEAKER. The gentleman from Illinois is not in order.

Mr. SPRINGER. I desire to state the question——

The Speaker rapped to order and said: The Chair has heard the question and overrules it.

Mr. SPRINGER. I rise to a question of privilege.

The SPEAKER. The Chair cannot entertain it now. The Chair is very indulgent to the gentleman from Illinois, and has heard him on his application, but the gentleman must now desist from further insisting on this matter.

Mr. SPRINGER. I have raised a privileged question, and desire the Chair to rule on it.

The SPEAKER. The Chair has ruled on it.

Mr. SPRINGER. I appeal from the decision of the Chair.

The SPEAKER. The Chair declines to entertain that appeal,

Several MEMBERS (to Mr. SPRINGER). Sit down.

Mr. SPRINGER. I will not sit down, but will stand up and will protest against such ruling as long as I am a member.

The SPEAKER. The question is on the motion of the gentleman from Maine [Mr. REED], who demands the previous question on agreeing to the report of the Committee on Rules.

Several members called for the yeas and nays.

The yeas and nays were ordered.

Mr. KENNA. I desire to make a parliamentary inquiry.

The SPEAKER. The gentleman will state it.

Mr. KENNA. I desire to ask whether under the present ruling and conduct of the Chair it is of any use to amend the rules as suggested by the report of the committee; if the Chair is not doing under the present rules what is sought to be accomplished by the amended rule?

The SPEAKER. That is a question to address to the gentleman having the report in charge.

The question was taken; and there were—yeas 151, nays 3, not voting 137.

So the previous question was ordered.

Mr. REED. I ask unanimous consent that the reading of the names be dispensed with.

Mr. RANDALL. I have no objection to that, but we desire the yeas and nays on the adoption of the new rule.

Mr. REED. That is all right.

Mr. SPRINGER. If I may be permitted, I object to dispensing with the reading of the names.

The SPEAKER. Objection is made, and the names will be read.

The names of those voting were read, after which the result was announced as above stated.

Mr. SPRINGER. I now rise to a privileged motion, which is to commit this report with instructions which I send to the Clerk's desk.

The SPEAKER. The Chair holds that the motion is not in order.

Mr. SPRINGER. I call the attention of the Chair to the language of Rule XVII.

The SPEAKER. The Chair remembers the rule very well.

Mr. CAMP. Debate is not in order.

Mr. SPRINGER. I ask that the rule be read. It shows that "it shall be in order, pending the motion for or after the previous question shall have been ordered on its passage"——

The SPEAKER. On the passage of a *bill*.

Mr. SPRINGER. On the passage of any motion—"for the Speaker to entertain one motion to commit, with or without instructions." I submit that motion under the rule and ask that the instructions may be read.

The SPEAKER. The Chair has heard the gentleman's statement, and rules his motion out of order.

Mr. SPRINGER. The Chair cannot rule upon it until it is read.

The SPEAKER. The Chair has heard the gentleman's statement, and it was quite intelligible. [Laughter.]

Mr. SPRINGER. Will the Chair allow the motion to be read?

The SPEAKER. The Chair will not.

Mr. SPRINGER. Then I move that this report be recommitted with instructions to the committee to report the same back with an amendment so that it shall be in order pending a contested-election case to move to amend, to recommit, or to lay the subject on the table.

The SPEAKER. The Chair thinks that the motion to recommit a contested-election case would be in order under the rules.

Mr. SPRINGER. That is what I desire to have incorporated in the new rules.

The SPEAKER. The gentleman's motion is not in order. The question is upon the adoption of the report from the Committee on Rules.

Mr. RANDALL. And on that I call for the yeas and nays.

Mr. SPRINGER. I appeal from the decision of the Chair.

The SPEAKER. The Chair does not entertain the appeal.

Mr. SPRINGER. The Chair does not?

The SPEAKER. The Chair does not.

Mr. SPRINGER. Then the Chair [cries of "Order!"] is violating the plainest rules of the House, and ought to be deposed.

The SPEAKER. The Chair can only say to the gentleman that his motions have been clearly out of order, even under the rules, if they were applicable at all. But the Chair has made a ruling which has been affirmed in the most extraordinary manner by the House, and the Chair will certainly be bound to stand by that affirmation of its own ruling.

Mr. SPRINGER. If we have no rules the Speaker is right.

The SPEAKER. The question is upon ordering the yeas and nays upon agreeing to the report of the Committee on Rules.

The yeas and nays were ordered.

The Clerk began the calling of the roll, when

Mr. HOOKER said: I rise to a point of order.

The SPEAKER. The gentleman will state it.

Mr. HOOKER. I understand that the gentleman from Illinois [Mr. SPRINGER] has submitted a proposition to the House. Now, I demand under the rules that that proposition be reduced to writing.

The SPEAKER. The Chair has ruled on that point. The Clerk will proceed with the roll-call.

Mr. HOOKER. Wait a moment. I want to understand, and I will understand, whether the Speaker means to rule that the proposition of the gentleman from Illinois shall not be reduced to writing.

The SPEAKER. The Chair has ruled upon all those questions.

Mr. HOOKER. And the Chair will not allow——

The SPEAKER. The gentleman from Illinois was not recognized to make any such proposition. The Clerk will proceed with the call of the roll.

The question was taken; and there were—yeas 150, nays 2, not voting 139.

So the report of the Committee on Rules was adopted.

Mr. CALKINS. I now desire to call up the contested-election case of Mackey *vs.* Dibble.

Mr. RANDALL. If I correctly understood the Chair a moment ago, he stated he had not yet decided that a motion to recommit this case with instructions would be out of order under the rule just adopted.

The SPEAKER. The Chair incidentally stated it had not held that the rule proposed to be adopted would exclude at the proper time a motion to recommit an election case.

Mr. RANDALL. I desire at the proper time to submit the following resolution

Mr. CALKINS. Until the question of consideration is determined by the House I object to that proposition being considered. Whenever the House has agreed to consider the case, of course I have no objection to having the motion voted upon.

The SPEAKER. Is the question of consideration raised?

Mr. BLACKBURN. I raise the question of consideration.

The SPEAKER. The gentleman from Kentucky raises the question of consideration as against the contested-election case.

Mr. SPRINGER. I move that the House now adjourn.

Mr. CALKINS. Before any action is taken it is desirable that the gentleman from Ohio [Mr. ATHERTON] and myself should reach some agreement about this matter, which I trust will be satisfactory on both sides.

Mr. HOOKER. I call for the regular order.

The SPEAKER. The gentleman from Illinois [Mr. SPRINGER] moves that the House adjourn.

Mr. BLACKBURN. On that motion I call for the yeas and nays.

The yeas and nays were ordered.

The question was taken; and there were—yeas 2, nays 149, not voting 140.

So the motion to adjourn was not agreed to.

Mr. CALKINS. I now call up the contested-election case of Mackey vs. Dibble; and I desire to say——

The SPEAKER. On this case the gentleman from Kentucky [Mr. BLACKBURN] has raised the question of consideration. The question recurs, Will the House proceed to consider the contested-election case named by the gentleman from Indiana?

Mr. BLACKBURN. On that I call for the yeas and nays.

The yeas and nays were ordered.

The question was taken; and there were—yeas 150, nay 1, not voting 140.

So the House determined to consider the contested-election case.

Mr. RANDALL. I would like now to have read for information the resolution which I send to the desk, which I propose to offer at the proper time.

The SPEAKER. The Chair will cause it to be read for information.

The Clerk read as follows:

Resolved, That the report in the case pending be recommitted to the Committee on Elections, with instructions to inquire into the authenticity and integrity of all depositions, returns, and evidence of whatever character produced in the case of Mackey vs. O'Connor, and inquire into all alterations, destruction, loss, or mutilations of the original notes of the same, or of any transcript of such notes; and when, where, or by whom such alterations, destructions, loss, or mutilations were made or caused to be made.

Resolved, That said committee shall have authority to visit such places and compel the production of such persons and papers as may be necessary to carry out the purpose of their appointment, and may sit during the sessions of the House.

Mr. CALKINS. I yield of course, Mr. Speaker, to have this read for information. I now desire that the House give unanimous consent to adjourn over until the day after to-morrow.

Mr. BLACKBURN. That is right.

Mr. CALKINS. I ask this for the reason that is known to every gentleman here; and I desire further to supplement the proposition with the request that the previous question in this case may be called on Thursday afternoon, without fixing the hour.

Mr. KENNA. We would rather that the gentleman would not designate now the time when he will call the previous question.

Mr. REED. If an arrangement can be made by which the previous question can be ordered or considered as ordered at a specified time, I hope the House will adjourn over to-morrow.

Mr. RANDALL. We had better consider that hereafter.

Mr. REED. I want to be very frank with gentlemen on the other side of the House, and I want them to understand what difficulties there are upon our side, and the imposition which we are necessarily forced to make upon some of our members by requiring a quorum to be present here during the whole time, if this debate shall be prolonged.

Mr. TOWNSHEND, of Illinois. You can agree to adjourn over.

Mr. REED. That is not the difficulty. We have not many more than a quorum, and if we are compelled to keep that quorum present all the time during the consideration of this case until the previous question is ordered, of course it operates as an undue hardship upon some of our people. It is not fair to our sick members to allow a great length of time for discussion upon this subject if you force us to keep a quorum. I am talking now as a reasonable man.

Mr. RANDALL. You had better keep your quorum.

Mr. REED. Very well; we will have, then, to pursue our own course in this matter.

Mr. CALKINS. Then I desire, Mr. Speaker, to yield the floor now to the gentleman from Pennsylvania [Mr. MILLER] to enter upon the debate on this election case, after which the gentleman will yield to me for a motion to adjourn.

Mr. MILLER took the floor.

Mr. CALKINS. If the gentleman will yield now I will make a motion that the House do now adjourn.

Mr. MILLER. I yield for that purpose.

The SPEAKER. The Chair will entertain the motion to adjourn.

JUNE 3, 1882.

The House proceeded, as the regular order of business, to the further consideration of the report of the Committee on Elections in the contested-election case of Lowe es. Wheeler, from the eighth Congressional district of the State of Alabama, the pending question being on the following resolutions, reported by said committee, viz:

Resolved, That Joseph Wheeler is not entitled to a seat in this House as a Representative in the Forty-seventh Congress from the eighth Congressional district of Alabama.

Resolved, That William M. Lowe is entitled to a seat in this House as a Representative in the Forty-seventh Congress from the eighth Congressional district of Alabama.

After debate, * * * Mr. HAZELTON demanded the previous question; pending which, Mr. SPRINGER moved to recommit the pending report to the Committee on Elections, with instructions contained in a preamble and resolutions.

Mr. KASSON made the point of order that the said preamble was not in order, being in the nature of argument or debate, which was not in order pending the motion for the previous question, and asked for an inspection of the paper by the Chair before being read to the House upon that point.

After debate on the said point of order, the Speaker sustained the same, on the ground that the motion to commit with instructions could not, either by the terms of the rule or by the practice of the House thereunder, be permitted to include either an arraignment of the committee or an argument as to the merit of the instructions proposed. For this reason the Chair held that the proposition as submitted by Mr. SPRINGER was not in order under clause 1 of Rule XVII.

Objection having been made to the reading of the proposition submitted by Mr. SPRINGER, the same was suspended when partially read; when Mr. KENNA appealed from the foregoing decision of the Chair and demanded the reading of the paper in full. Whereupon the Clerk, under the direction of the Speaker, resumed and concluded the reading of said paper.

Mr. REED moved to lay the said appeal on the table; which said motion was agreed to.

So the decision of the Chair was sustained.

JUNE 6, 1882.

Mr. WHITE, as a question of privilege, called the attention of the Speaker to the fact that a resolution of inquiry submitted by him on the 11th day of April last, and referred to the Committee of Ways and Means, had not been reported to the House until this morning, though clause 1 of Rule XXIV required a report to be made thereon within one week, and that, having been made, it was entitled to immediate consideration.

Mr. HISCOCK made the point of order that no question of privilege had been presented.

The Speaker sustained the said point of order on the ground that the said resolution had been reported to the House, ordered printed, and laid over for the present, and was not now before the House.

JUNE 13, 1882.

Mr. BREWER called up the report of the Select Committee on Ventilation and Acoustics submitted on yesterday and laid over for the present.

Mr. CANNON having objected to its consideration, the Speaker held the said report to be of a privileged character, on the ground that the committee had been specially directed to consider the subject-matter of the resolution submitted, and report their conclusions thereon to the House, and although authority had not been specifically given that committee to report at any time, it was still the duty of the committee to report at as early a day as practicable, and having so reported, the said report was properly before the House; and also on the further ground that the pending resolution related to the convenience of members and comfort of the employés of the House.

JUNE 26, 1882.

The Speaker having announced as the special order of business such business as may be presented by the Committee on the District of Columbia, under the resolution of the 5th instant, Mr. KELLEY having proposed to raise the question of consideration as against the consideration of business under the foregoing order, the Speaker held that this day being set apart for the consideration of such business as might be presented by the Committee on the District of Columbia, the question of consideration could not be raised against such special order, but could only be raised as against a particular bill or measure. The Speaker further held that a motion to postpone the said special order was not in order, and that the Committee on the District of Columbia could not be dispossessed of their rights under the terms of said special order so long as the committee had any business to present, and claimed their rights under said order.

In which decision of the Chair the House acquiesced.

On motion of Mr. HOGE, the bill of the Senate (S. 1158) to authorize the supreme court of the District of Columbia to appoint two additional criers was taken from the Speaker's table and read twice.

Mr. CANNON made the point of order that under the terms of the special order it was not in order for the Committee on the District of Columbia to take business from the Speaker's table for present consideration.

The Speaker overruled the said point of order, on the ground that the said special order in terms set aside this day " for the consideration of such business as may be presented by the Committee on the District of Columbia," and that committee having asked the consideration of the said bill, it was in order to proceed thereto.

<h3 style="text-align:center">JULY 8, 1882.</h3>

Mr. CRAPO, as a privileged question, from the committee of conference on the disagreeing votes of the two Houses on the amendments of the Senate to the bill of the House (H. R. 4167) to enable national banking associations to extend their corporate existence, submitted a report.

Mr. RANDALL made the point of order that the said report was not in order for present consideration, on the ground that no "detailed statement" accompanied said report, as required by Rule XXIX.

The Speaker sustained the said point of order.

The SPEAKER. The rule requires such a statement to be submitted with the report; and if objection is made the report cannot be received at this time.

<h3 style="text-align:center">JULY 15, 1882.</h3>

Mr. CANNON, from the committee of conference on the disagreeing votes of the two Houses on the amendments of the Senate to the bill of the House (H. R. 6244) making appropriations for the legislative, executive, and judicial expenses of the Government for the fiscal year ending June 30, 1883, and for other purposes, reported that the committee were unable to agree.

After debate, by unanimous consent, Mr. CANNON moved that the House further insist on its disagreement to the said amendments of the Senate to the said bill, and ask a further conference with the Senate on the disagreeing votes of the two Houses thereon.

After debate thereon, Mr. CANNON moved the previous question; which was ordered, and under the operation thereof the said motion of Mr. CANNON was agreed to.

Ordered, That Mr. CANNON, Mr. HISCOCK, and Mr. ATKINS be the managers at the said conference on the part of the House of Representatives.

Ordered, That the Clerk acquaint the Senate therewith.

Mr. McCOID submitted the following resolution, viz:

Resolved, That the committee on the part of the House is instructed to agree to such modification of the bill as will equalize the salaries of the Senate and House by an increase of the pay of House employés if necessary.

Mr. GEORGE D. ROBINSON made the point of order that the said resolution was not in order, for the reason that it proposed to instruct the conferees on the part of the House on a subject not submitted to them or in disagreement between the two Houses.

The SPEAKER. The Chair is not at present prepared to hold that the House might not instruct the committee to recede or to insist upon some matter which was particularly before it. But this resolution the Chair thinks goes further and proposes to instruct the conference committee to take up a new matter not referred to it; and therefore it is not in order.

<h3 style="text-align:center">JULY 19, 1882.</h3>

Mr. CALKINS, as a privileged question, called up the report of the Committee on Elections in the contested-election case of Smalls *vs.* Tillman, from the fifth Congressional district of the State of South Carolina.

The House having proceeded to its consideration, after debate, Mr. CALKINS moved the previous question; which was ordered.

＊　　　　＊　　　　＊　　　　＊　　　　＊　　　　＊

The question recurring on the resolutions reported by the Committee on Elections; when Mr. ATHERTON demanded a division of the question.

And the question being first on the following resolution, viz:

Resolved, That George D. Tillman was not elected as a Representative to the Forty-seventh Congress from the fifth Congressional district of South Carolina, and is not entitled to retain the seat which he now occupies in this House—

And being put, viz, Will the House agree thereto? it was decided in the affirmative—yeas 141, nays 1, not voting 146.

So the said resolution was agreed to.

The question recurring on the following resolution, viz:

Resolved, That Robert Smalls was duly elected as a Representative from the fifth Congressional district of South Carolina in the Forty-seventh Congress, and is entitled to his seat as such—

And being put, viz, Will the House agree thereto? it was decided in the affirmative—yeas 141, nays 5, not voting 145.

So the said resolution was agreed to.

Mr. WAIT moved to reconsider the vote just taken, and also moved that the motion to reconsider be laid on the table; which latter motion was agreed to.

The Speaker stated that an error had been discovered in the vote taken to-day on the first branch of the resolutions reported by the Committee on Elections, and that instead of being yeas 145 and nay 1, as announced, the correct vote was yeas 144, nay 1. The Speaker thereupon claimed and exercised his constitutional right to vote on any question before the House, and directed his vote to be recorded in the affirmative on said resolution.

Mr. BLACKBURN, having called for the reading of clause 1 of Rule XV, made the point of order that under said rule it was not in order for the Speaker to have his vote recorded after the completion of the roll-call and the announcement of the result to the House.

The SPEAKER. The House will be in order. There is no complication about this proposition. The Chair understands that it has the right and is required under the rules to vote in order to make a quorum or to give a result when there is a tie vote.

Mr. RANDALL. Does the Chair state that after the result has been announced and accepted by the House as the result of a yea-and-nay vote by the House the Chair can come in and change the result, as in this case presented?

The SPEAKER. The vote of the Chair did not change the result. It simply makes a quorum; and the gentleman from Pennsylvania, when Speaker, as the Chair is informed, exercised this right one day after the vote had been taken.

Mr. RANDALL (amid great confusion.) I never did, under such circumstances as here presented.

The SPEAKER. It is stated here, and the record will show it.

Mr. RANDALL. I ask the Chair to produce the full record. The Chair nowhere can find any such decision. There is no warrant for such construction or decision referred to, as I believe.

Mr. CASWELL rose.

The SPEAKER. Gentlemen will come to order.

Mr. ATHERTON. I rise to a question of order.

The SPEAKER. The gentleman will be heard later. The Chair now recognizes the gentleman from Wisconsin.

Mr. CASWELL. The gentleman from Pennsylvania cannot have forgotten the fact that in the Forty-fourth Congress he voted the next day to carry a measure.

Mr. RANDALL. I never voted when there was objection, as there is here. The gentleman will produce the record.

Mr. BLACKBURN. I rise to a parliamentary inquiry.

The SPEAKER. One at a time. Gentlemen will be heard patiently, but the House must come to order.

Mr. BLACKBURN. I will abide the Chair's pleasure.

Mr. TOWNSHEND, of Illinois. I desire to read Rule XV, which absolutely prohibits it.

Mr. BLACKBURN. Just wait a minute.

Mr. TOWNSHEND, of Illinois. It requires that every member shall answer to his name at the roll-call.

The SPEAKER. The Chair will direct the Clerk to read certain paragraphs from the Digest.

Mr. KASSON. I ask that gentlemen shall be seated, so members may hear what is going on.

The SPEAKER. Members will resume their places. The Clerk will read from the Digest, page 354.

The Clerk read as follows:

On a very important question, taken December 9, 1803, on an amendment to the Constitution, so as to change the form of voting for President and Vice-President which required a vote of two-thirds there appeared 83 in the affirmative and 42 in the negative; it wanted one vote in the affirmative to make the constitutional majority. The Speaker (Macon) notwithstanding a prohibition in the rule as it then existed, claimed and obtained his right to vote, and voted in the affirmative; and it was by that vote that the amendment to the Constitution was carried. The right of the Speaker as a member of the House, to vote on all questions is secured by the Constitution. No act of the House can take it from him when he chooses to exercise it.

(See latest instance by Mr. Speaker RANDALL—Journal, 2, 44, pages 23, 24.)

The SPEAKER. The Clerk will now read from the Journal the case cited under Mr. Speaker Randall.

The Clerk read as follows:

Pending which, Mr. Banks moved that the Journal and RECORD be corrected so as to include the name of Mr. Plaisted in the negative on the vote on the adoption of the resolution submitted on yesterday by Mr. ABRAM S. HEWITT.

After debate the Speaker decided that it was the right of the gentleman from Maine to have his vote recorded upon the said resolution upon the statement made by Mr. Plaisted that he did vote in the negative when his name was called.

Mr. Fuller asked that the Journal and RECORD might be further corrected so as to show that he voted in the affirmative upon the aforesaid resolution, stating that he was present and so voted when his name was called.

The Speaker decided, as in the case of Mr. Plaisted, that the gentleman from Indiana was entitled to have his name recorded.

And therefore the names of Mr. Plaisted and Mr. Fuller were recorded, the first in the negative and the last-named member in the affirmative, upon the adoption of the aforesaid resolution.

The Speaker thereupon claimed and exercised his constitutional right to vote upon any question before the House, and voted in the affirmative upon the said resolution.

[Applause and laughter.]

The SPEAKER. This right of the Speaker to vote was exercised the next day after a result had been announced.

Mr. RANDALL. That was not a question of a quorum nor a majority. I believe it was done by consent of the House, while in this instance there is objection.

Mr. HAZELTON. The question is of the right of the Speaker to vote.

Mr. RANDALL. I had a right to vote as Speaker. Gentlemen's votes were added which changed the result, and the case is entirely dissimilar.

The SPEAKER. The gentleman then Speaker claimed the right to vote and exercised it. It was not done by unanimous consent, or the Journal does not show it.

Mr. RANDALL. Gentlemen's votes were added which changed the result, and there was no objection.

Mr. REED. Regular order!

Mr. RANDALL. The changes made in fact produced an even tally, and the Speaker had a right to and did vote.

The SPEAKER. The principle is exactly the same in the present case.

The Clerk will now read from what occurred Monday, January 8, 1849 (Mr. Winthrop, Speaker).

The Clerk read as follows:

MONDAY, *January 8*, 1849.

As soon as the Journal of Saturday had been read,

The SPEAKER said: The House will remember that the vote on the passage of the bill for the relief of the representatives of Antonio Pacheco was originally made up by the Clerk—ayes 90, noes 89; and this record having been handed to the Speaker and by him announced to the House, the Speaker proceeded to make some remarks upon the bill preparatory to giving the vote contemplated in such cases by the rules of the House. While in the act of explanation, the Speaker was interrupted by the Clerk, who stated that on a more careful count the vote was found to be—ayes 91, noes 89. The intervention of the Speaker was therefore no longer allowable; and the bill was declared to have passed the House.

The Chair takes the earliest opportunity to state to the House this morning that upon a re-examination of the yeas and nays the Clerk has ascertained that an error existed in the announcement of the vote on Saturday. The vote actually stood—ayes 89, noes 89. The correction will now accordingly be made on the Journal: and a case is immediately presented, agreeably to the twelfth rule of the House, for the interposition of the Speaker's vote.

The SPEAKER. At this stage of the proceedings the Speaker was interrupted by Mr. Farrelly, who rose and called for a further correction of the Journal, stating that he voted in the negative on Saturday last, and his vote appeared not to have been recorded.

The Speaker decided that it was the right of the gentleman from Pennsylvania to have his vote recorded if he voted on Saturday last; and the correction was accordingly made.

The vote was then finally announced—yeas 89, nays 90.

Mr. TOWNSHEND, of Illinois. Rule XV determines that matter.

Mr. BLACKBURN. I ask the Speaker to have the rule indicated by the gentleman from Illinois read; and I ask further that the Speaker will remember that notwithstanding he has been made Speaker and the presiding officer of this House by its votes, that still, even as presiding officer, under the law he is but a member of this House.

The SPEAKER. The gentleman will allow the Chair to state that it has never been the rule or practice for the Speaker's name to be called in the regular roll-call; and therefore the Speaker does not respond to the roll-call as other members do, nor does he come within the provision of the rule which is applicable to other members whose names are upon the roll. The rule, paragraph 6, Rule I, provides when the Speaker shall vote. It is as follows:

He shall not be required to vote in ordinary legislative proceedings, except where his vote would be decisive or when the House is engaged in voting by ballot; and in all cases of a tie vote the question shall be lost.

Rule XV may be read, but it has no possible application.

Mr. BLACKBURN. May I ask then, Mr. Speaker, another question as to the construction given to this rule by the Chair on the subject of voting, or on the right to vote?

Does that position elevate the Speaker of the House one inch above the plane occupied by other members of the House.

The SPEAKER. The Chair does not disagree with the gentleman in that respect. The Chair claims no higher right or privilege than is accorded to other members, except in cases when by the rules, law, or Constitution other or higher rights are given it.

Mr. BLACKBURN. Then would any other member of the House, after the ruling and the construction applied to this rule frequently by the present occupant of the Chair, have the right to rise in his place and ask even unanimous consent to have his name recorded after the second call of the roll has been completed?

The SPEAKER. Certainly not; the rule is very clear and prohibits that.

Mr. BLACKBURN. Then by what authority does the Chair claim the right to vote?

The SPEAKER. Under the rule applicable to the Chair. The rule which the gentleman invokes has no sort of application to the Chair, but to the members whose names are called.

Mr. BLACKBURN. Then may I ask this further question: Is the Chair, the Speaker of this House, by his election to that position elevated above all rules, and does he know no rule?

The SPEAKER. The rules do not require the Speaker's name to be called, nor does his name appear upon the roll. That is the practice of the House, and has been, as far as the present occupant of the chair knows, for all time.

Mr. BLACKBURN. What rule does that?

The SPEAKER. The rule to which the gentleman refers.

Mr. BLACKBURN. I ask to have that rule read.

The SPEAKER. The rule is very clear.

Mr. BLACKBURN. But after the Chair has announced the result of a vote, I ask if, under that rule, he has the right to vote; and I ask to have the rule read.

The SPEAKER. The rule is familiar to everybody; but the Chair will of course have the rule the gentleman refers to read if he so desires. It has no application to the Speaker.

Mr. ROBESON. I rise to a parliamentary inquiry.

The SPEAKER. The Chair can recognize but one.

Mr. HAZELTON. No Speaker's name has ever been called upon the roll.

Mr. BLACKBURN. My friend will allow the rule to be read?

Mr. ROBESON. I want to know whether the vote on the passage of the resolution to which reference is made was not 144 to 1; and whether that was not a majority?

Mr. BLACKBURN. It was not a quorum.

Mr. ROBESON. And whether the point of no quorum was made? Further, I wish to ask whether, that point not having been then made, it can be made now; and if the gentleman claims the right to make the point of no quorum now, because of the fact that the House was misinformed as to the vote, has not the Speaker the right to vote now to make a quorum?

The SPEAKER. It is not only his right, but he must exercise it under the rule.

Mr. TOWNSHEND, of Illinois. The rule is explicit that no member shall even be permitted to ask unanimous consent to record his vote after the announcement of the vote has been made.

Mr. ATHERTON. The question is whether when a wrong has been done there is any way of righting it. [Cries of "Regular order!"]

The SPEAKER. The Chair thinks that there is no question before the House. No wrong was done to any one, but the vote was corrected at the earliest possible time.

Mr. REED. I demand the regular order.

Mr. HAZELTON. The only question before the House is the regular order.

The SPEAKER. The regular order is the call of committees for reports.

Mr. BLACKBURN. Does the Chair decline my request to have Rule XV read?

The SPEAKER. The Chair has no objection to having the rule read.

Mr. BLACKBURN. I ask to have it read.

The SPEAKER. The Clerk will read Rule XV.

The Clerk read as follows:

Upon every roll-call the names of the members shall be called alphabetically by surname except where two or more have the same surname, then the whole name shall be called; and after the roll has been once called, the Clerk shall call in their alphabetical order the names of those not voting; and thereafter the Speaker shall not entertain a request to record a vote or announce a pair

Mr. BLACKBURN. I thank the Chair for having the rule read. I only desire further to ask a question as to fact in the shape of a parliamentary inquiry.

The SPEAKER. The gentleman will state it.

Mr. HISCOCK. I demand the regular order.

The SPEAKER. The gentleman from Kentucky rises to make a parliamentary inquiry, which the Chair will hear.

Mr. BLACKBURN. The gentleman from New Jersey [Mr. ROBESON] has said that upon the report of the voting it stood 144 yeas and 1 nay. I now desire to know whether the clerks of this House did not report 145 yeas instead of 144?

The SPEAKER. Undoubtedly, and solely through a mistake.

Mr. WAIT. As a question of privilege I ask that Mr. Smalls be sworn in.

Mr. TOWNSHEND, of Illinois. I rise to a question of order.

[Cries of "Regular order!"]

The SPEAKER. The gentleman from Illinois will state his question of order.

Mr. TOWNSHEND, of Illinois. I raise the point of order that a quorum not having voted on the resolution unseating Mr. Tillman as a Representative from South Carolina the present applicant to be sworn in has not been lawfully declared elected a member of this House.

The SPEAKER. That vote has no reference to the one declaring Mr. Smalls elected. The point is overruled.

Mr. TOWNSHEND, of Illinois. I have not finished stating my point of order. My point of order is that through the error of the Clerk in reporting that a quorum had voted when a quorum had not done so, the House was deceived into proceeding to the consideration of the second resolution, and that now, it having appeared that a quorum did not vote on the resolution unseating Mr. Tillman, the gentleman from South Carolina, Mr. Tillman, is still entitled to retain his seat.

The SPEAKER. But the result of the vote had been announced, and there was no question about it.

Mr. TOWNSHEND, of Illinois. It was because the House was misled by the report made by the Clerk.

The SPEAKER. That does not apply to the resolution declaring Mr. Smalls entitled to a seat. The Chair wishes to state again that it simply exercised, at the earliest time the case arose, what it believes to be a constitutional right, and it acted in accordance with the rule in the light of various precedents, some only of which have been cited.

Mr. RANDALL. I find the precedent, as far as I am concerned, is not at all like the present case. In the instance which was cited, other gentlemen (Messrs. Plaisted, of Maine, and Fuller, of Indiana) whose votes had not been recorded presented themselves on the following day and said they had voted. Their votes were received, changing the result, and the Speaker under these circumstances had, as he had a right to do, then voted, making a two-third vote, and it was done without objection; in fact this controversy is quite different as I consider it.

The SPEAKER. The principle is precisely the same, and both arose in consequence of unintentional mistakes or omissions of the Clerk.

Mr. SMALLS appeared, and qualified by taking the oath prescribed in section 1756 of the Revised Statutes.

JULY 22, 1882.

On motion of Mr. BINGHAM, the House proceeded to the consideration of the bill of the House (H. R. 859) regulating rates of postage on second-class mail matter at letter-carrier offices.

Mr. TOWNSHEND moved to amend by adding thereto the following as additional sections, viz:

SEC. 6. Strike out the word "three" and insert "two" on the eighth line of section 3903 of the Revised Statutes.

SEC. 7. Strike out sections 3905 and 3906 and insert "that the postage on second-class mailable matter be, and the same is hereby, abolished, and that such mail matter shall be conveyed in the mails of the United States free from postal charges."

Mr. PEELLE made the point of order that the said amendment was not in order, not being germane to the subject-matter of the bill.

Mr. MONEY made the further point of order that the said amendment, being the substance of a bill referred to the Committee on the Post-Office and Post-Roads, was not in order under clause 4 of Rule XXI.

After debate on said points of order,

The SPEAKER. The Chair does not think it matters whether the proposition is one that is to be found in several bills pending before the House or in only a single bill. But let us look at the question a little closer. The bill before the House is a bill to regulate the rates of postage on second-class mail matter at letter-carrier offices. The amendment proposed by the gentleman from Illinois is to reduce the rate of postage upon ordinary letters and newspapers. It undertakes to amend the statutes in another respect and entirely different from that proposed by the pending bill. The Chair is by no means satisfied that the amendment would be germane to this bill. This is not a general proposition to revise the postal laws of the United States; but if it be a fact that any portion of this amendment is, in substance, included in a pending bill or bills, then that portion would clearly not be in order. But there being a portion of the amendment not in order, as must be conceded, it is perfectly clear that the whole amendment must go out. If a portion of a proposition submitted is clearly not in order, the whole must be rejected, for under no cover of including that which is not in order with that which is, could such an amendment be admitted.

The Chair holds, therefore, the amendment is not in order under the point of order made against it.

JULY 21, 1882.

Mr. PAYSON, under authority granted on the 6th ultimo, submitted the views of the minority of the Committee on the Judiciary, to accompany the report (No. 1253) of said committee submitted on said date, in relation to land grants to the Northern Pacific Railroad.

Ordered, That said views of said minority be printed as part 2 of said report.

Mr. KNOTT, under the same authority, submitted the views of a further minority of said committee on the same subject, accompanied by a proposed joint resolution attached to said views.

Mr. KNOTT moved that the said views of the said minority be referred to the House Calendar and printed.

Mr. CASWELL made the point of order that the said motion was not in order, for the reason that the views of a minority of a committee could only be submitted by unanimous consent, which was all that was granted the minority of the Committee on the Judiciary.

After debate on the said point of order,

The SPEAKER. The Chair is ready to rule upon the point of order.

With the importance of this question the Chair has nothing whatever to do. The gentleman from Kentucky [Mr. KNOTT] presented the views of certain members of the Committee on the Judiciary, not a majority of the committee, under permission granted when the report of the committee on this subject was presented, and moves to have a resolution accompanying the views placed upon the Calendar. Now, there is no doubt but this belongs to the minority of the committee as a matter of right if it is to be regarded as a report at all. This question has frequently been raised, where a minority of a committee proposed to make a report and claimed the right to bring a subject before the House; but it has been always rejected and treated as though no such right existed, the majority of the committee alone being competent to bring in a report and submit it to the House for its consideration.

There is no case known to the Chair, and certainly none has been cited in the discussion of this point of order, to indicate that under any circumstances these views of the minority are to be regarded as a report.

As Cushing says in his admirable work on parliamentary law, "these views are sometimes submitted under the somewhat incongruous name of minority reports, when they are in no sense reports.

Now, to go back, at the time the report was made upon this subject the gentleman from Massachusetts [Mr. ROBINSON] stated to the House that there were certain views of the minority which they might desire to present to the House, and asked on behalf of the minority that these should be printed, which request was granted. And it was then ordered, not that they should come in as a report, but that their views, dissenting from the report of the committee, should be received and printed, and, to use the exact language of the record, "the views will be received and be printed with the report of the majority." Consent was given for this and nothing more.

Now, the gentleman from Illinois [Mr. TOWNSHEND] has cited Cushing's Manual of Parliamentary Law, and the Chair thinks it would be well enough to examine it further and have read a little more from the same paragraph and sentence from which the gentleman has already quoted. The Clerk will read.

The Clerk read as follows:

* * They [minority views] are received by the courtesy of the House, expressed by the ordinary vote of a majority and usually receive the same destination with the report, that is, they are printed, postponed, and considered in the same manner. But they are not in any parliamentary sense reports, nor entitled to any privilege as such; and their only effect is, in the first place, to operate upon the minds of members as arguments, and, secondly, to serve as the basis for amendments to be offered on the resolution or other conclusion of the report. If they contain a recommendation of a resolution as a bill, but as part of the report and for the information of the House

Mr. TOWNSHEND, of Illinois. Let the whole paragraph be read.

The SPEAKER. That is the whole of this chapter.

Mr. TOWNSHEND, of Illinois. I desire to have read the first portion of the paragraph.

The SPEAKER. The Chair will state that the portion of the paragraph just read which used the word "majority" has distinct reference to a majority of the House as a matter of courtesy having the right and power to allow the views of the minority to be presented, and had no reference to the disposition of them on the House Calendars.

The Chair will cause the Clerk to read now from the House Journal proceedings in

1836, where the question was made whether or not the minority of a committee could make a report.

The Clerk read as follows:

Mr. HALL, of Vermont, a member of the Committee on the Post-Office and Post-Roads, to which was referred so much of the message of the President of the United States, at the commencement of the session, as relates " to the report of the Postmaster-General, the condition and operations of the Post-Office Department, and everything connected therewith," offered to submit to the House a paper, in the form of a report, which he stated contained the views of the minority of the committee on that part of the said message which suggests " the propriety of passing such a law as will prohibit, under severe penalties, the circulation in the Southern States, through the mail, of incendiary publications, intended to instigate the slaves to insurrection."

The Speaker decided that, when reports from committees are called for, a report cannot be made from a minority of a committee, as a minority is not a committee; that the paper offered was not a report authorized to be made to the House by authority of the committee, and could not be received as a report from the minority, and that consequently it was not in order to offer the same.

The SPEAKER. The Chair thinks that under what seems to be the uniform practice all the Chair can do is to indicate that the action shall be taken which was directed to be taken on the 6th of June last when the majority report was introduced; and that is that the views of the minority shall be printed with the majority report.

Mr. KNOTT. I desire to ask what is now the parliamentary status of the joint resolution presented by the minority?

The SPEAKER. It has no possible parliamentary status except that when the majority report shall come up for consideration it might be referred to only as a matter of information to the House; and it might furnish a basis upon which amendments might be offered to the action of the majority, if action can ever be taken on that. It is now on the table and it seems to call for no action on the part of Congress.

That report concludes as follows:

We can conceive of no legislation which would hasten the completion of the road, and therefore recommend none.

Mr. KNOTT. It is then in no sense a pending proposition before the House?

The SPEAKER Independently of the majority report, it is not, as the Chair apprehends.

Mr. HOLMAN. I rise to make a parliamentary inquiry.

Mr. COX, of New York. I desire to take an appeal from the decision of the Chair.

Mr. REED. I move to lay that appeal on the table.

Mr. HOLMAN. My parliamentary inquiry is this: it is shown from the record that the gentleman from Kentucky [Mr. KNOTT] had the floor properly by consent of the House to submit this report.

The SPEAKER. It is not a report.

Mr. HOLMAN. To submit whatever he has submitted. And having the floor, I claim he had a right to make, under that consent, the statement or report or whatever else it may be called—that having the floor rightfully he had the right to make whatever was the proper motion touching the subject-matter. Therefore he had a right, having the floor by consent, to move to refer that joint resolution to the Calendar.

Mr. POUND. But the subject-matter is not before the House.

The SPEAKER. The gentleman had only the right, except by unanimous consent, to have the resolution offered and printed. The gentleman from New York [Mr. COX] states that he appeals from the decision of the Chair, and the gentleman from Maine moves to lay that appeal on the table.

Mr CASWELL. I do not understand there is anything to appeal from.

The SPEAKER. The Chair understands the gentleman from New York to appeal from the ruling of the Chair, in which the Chair holds a minority of the committee cannot make a report and have it referred to the Calendar.

Mr. TOWNSHEND, of Illinois. But the Chair goes further than that——

Mr. ROBESON. Did not the Chair also decide that at this time, this not being a privileged motion, and no unanimous consent having been given for that motion, it is not in order if an objection be made?

The SPEAKER. The Chair does not hold the gentleman is out of order in presenting the views of the minority; but the Chair holds the gentleman from Kentucky did not present any report in the proper sense of the word.

Mr. COX, of New York. I make my appeal from the ruling of the Chair, which I understand to be this: that the Chair rules out of order the motion made by the gentleman from Kentucky to refer this joint resolution to the Calendar. From that decision of the Chair I respectfully appeal.

The SPEAKER. And the gentleman from Maine moves that the appeal be laid upon the table.

Mr. HOLMAN. I call for the yeas and nays.

Mr. CANNON. I wish to know whether the majority resolution accompanying the report of the majority of the committee is now on the Calendar.

The SPEAKER. It is not.

Mr. HAMMOND, of Georgia. That is the trouble. We want to get something on the Calendar.

Mr. COX, of New York. And that is what they are dodging.

The SPEAKER. The Chair understands if the report of the committee had been accompanied by a bill or joint resolution, and had gone to the Calendar, then this matter would have taken the same course. It would have been printed and would have accompanied the majority report. Wherever the majority report went, under the uniform practice the minority views must go also. The gentleman from Maine [Mr. REED] moves to lay upon the table the appeal taken by the gentleman from New York from the decision of the Chair.

Mr. HOLMAN. And upon that I call for the yeas and nays.

The yeas and nays were ordered.

Mr. KASSON. Is it in order now for me to ask to have a statement read from the Digest?

The SPEAKER. The Chair thinks the question is not debatable now.

The question being taken, there were—yeas 97, nays 70, not voting 123.

So the said appeal was laid on the table.

SAME DAY.

The House then proceeded, as the regular order of business under the resolution of the 21st instant, to the further consideration of the bill of the House (H. R. 3902) permitting the use of domestic materials in the construction of steam and sail vessels for foreign account, the pending question being on the amendment submitted by Mr. TUCKER to said bill, on which question the yeas and nays were ordered on yesterday.

After debate, by unanimous consent, Mr. KASSON moved to reconsider the vote by which the yeas and nays were ordered.

Mr. TUCKER. I ask the Speaker this question: If the Speaker is right, as I think he is, that it is out of order for the gentleman from Pennsylvania [Mr. KELLEY] to make the motion to recommit to the Committee on Ways and Means, is it not equally out of order for the gentleman from Iowa [Mr. KASSON] to move to reconsider the vote of the yeas and nays when we are acting under that order, and taking the yeas and nays on the amendment which I have moved? Will not the Speaker see that if his present decision is right that the motion to reconsider is out of order and cannot be entertained.

The SPEAKER. The Chair thinks that is not so. It gives the House a right to reconsider its action.

Mr. KNOTT. The Speaker holds it is in order to entertain the motion to reconsider the call for the yeas and nays. Suppose that motion prevails, does not the question immediately recur on ordering the yeas and nays?

The SPEAKER. Yes, when the question comes up on the amendment. Then any member can demand the yeas and nays, and on the order of one-fifth of those present, the yeas and nays can be ordered. But if the gentleman has the right, as the Chair has indicated, to make the motion to refer, that would take precedence of the motion to amend, because paragraph 4 of Rule XVI provides expressly for it.

Mr. KNOTT. With the permission of the Chair I wish to submit this point of order.

Mr. TUCKER. I raise the question of order on my friend from Iowa [Mr. KASSON].

The SPEAKER. The gentleman from Kentucky has the floor.

Mr. TUCKER. I raise the question of order on the gentleman from Iowa, and that is whether he can move to reconsider the ordering of the yeas and nays when he did not vote on that question.

Mr. KASSON. There was no record of the vote on that question, and it does not matter how I voted.

The SPEAKER. There has been no record on ordering the yeas and nays, and therefore the point does not lie. But only one point of order can be pending at the same time.

Mr. HAMMOND, of Georgia. There was a call of the yeas and nays, and on that call of the yeas and nays the gentleman from Iowa declined to vote.

Mr. ALDRICH. I move to reconsider the vote ordering the yeas and nays.

Mr. KNOTT. I believe, Mr. Speaker, I have the floor.

The SPEAKER. The Chair has recognized the gentleman from Kentucky on the point of order.

Mr. ALDRICH. The yeas and nays were ordered and the yeas and nays were called, but there was no quorum.

Mr. KNOTT. Mr. Speaker, the Constitution of the United States guarantees to one-fifth of the members of the House the right to demand and have put on record the yeas and nays on any proposition. That being so, no majority of this House, however large, unless by unanimous consent, can deprive that one-fifth of that constitutional right. That being so, a motion to deprive them of that right is in derogation of the Constitution, and is manifestly out of order.

Now, let us look at this proposition *ab inconvenienti*. I make a motion, for instance, for the yeas and nays, one-fifth of the members present second it, and the demand is sustained. A gentleman moves to reconsider the vote by which the yeas and nays were ordered, and a majority vote to sustain the demand for reconsideration. I call for the yeas and nays on that demand, and one-fifth of the members present order them. Another gentleman rises and moves to reconsider the vote by which that demand was sustained and it is carried, and one-fifth of those present again demand the yeas and nays upon that.

Is it not evident that you can go on, sir, without limit, until the crack of doom, working in a complete circle, in a vain attempt to get a vote upon any question at all as long as one-fifth of the members present see proper to insist upon their constitutional right which neither you nor any majority of the House can deprive them of. I maintain that the very absurdity of the proposition is so patent that I cannot see how it can possibly be entertained at all. By what authority can a majority of the House say to one-fifth of those present, "You shall not exercise your constitutional right?" If they have no authority to do that, what authority have they or has the Speaker to submit a question to the House which contemplates depriving them of that right?

Mr. BURROWS, of Michigan. Will the gentleman from Kentucky allow me to send to the desk and have read a ruling bearing upon this point?

Mr. KNOTT. I have no objection.

Mr. ATKINS. I rise to a parliamentary inquiry.

The SPEAKER. The gentleman will state it.

Mr. ATKINS. What is the question before the House, and how did that question get before the House? Is not the *status quo* of Saturday, when we adjourned on this question, the *status quo* of this moment, the unfinished business coming over and occupying the present consideration of the House? If that be so we were dividing at that time, and a motion was made to reconsider another motion while we were dividing.

The SPEAKER. The Chair will state in answer to the gentleman from Tennessee that the yeas and nays were ordered. The roll-call is not going on, and if it is in order to move to reconsider at any time it is in order now.

Mr. ATKINS. It is going on, I beg pardon of the Speaker; we are dividing.

The SPEAKER. Does the gentleman hold that the roll-call is going on?

Mr. ATKINS. Yes, sir.

The SPEAKER. The Chair thinks not.

Mr. ATKINS. It ought to be going on at this moment.

The SPEAKER. As a matter of fact it is not going on, however.

Mr. TOWNSHEND, of Illinois. I rise to a parliamentary inquiry.

The SPEAKER. The gentleman will state it.

Mr. TOWNSHEND, of Illinois. There was no vote ordering the yeas and nays on Saturday. There were some thirty-odd members of the House who constituted one-fifth of the members of the House and who demand their constitutional right to have the yeas and nays entered upon the Journal. There was no vote, however, upon it. Therefore my colleague who makes a motion now to reconsider that vote by which the yeas and nays were ordered has no right to make it.

The SPEAKER. There is no question about the fact that the yeas and nays were ordered.

Mr. TOWNSHEND, of Illinois. But not by a vote of the House.

Mr. BURROWS, of Michigan. I ask now to have read, as bearing upon the point of order, what I send to the desk.

The SPEAKER. The Clerk will read.

The Clerk read as follows:

Mr. Kellogg moved that the order by the House of the yeas and nays be reconsidered.
Mr. Pollock raised the question of order that it required four-fifths to reconsider an order for the yeas and nays.
The Speaker decided that according to the precedents a majority might reconsider the order, but that the question would immediately recur on ordering the yeas and nays, when one-fifth would be sufficient for that purpose. (February 14, 1848.)

The SPEAKER. The Chair thinks that, following the precedents, it must entertain the motion. There seem to have been precedents during the entire history of the Congress of the United States in favor of entertaining the motion to reconsider a vote ordering the yeas and nays. The Chair might agree with the gentleman from Kentucky if this was an original question; but the decisions are all one way. It is very true, as has been stated, that after such a vote is reconsidered one-fifth of those present would still have the constitutional right to again order the yeas and nays on the same question.

Mr. KNOTT. I call for the yeas and nays on that motion.

The SPEAKER. The gentleman from Iowa [Mr. KASSON] moves to reconsider the vote by which the yeas and nays were ordered, and the gentleman from Kentucky [Mr. KNOTT] calls for the yeas and nays on the motion to reconsider.

The yeas and nays on the motion to reconsider were ordered—42 members voting therefor.

Mr. DUNN. I move now to reconsider that vote by which the yeas and nays have been ordered on the motion to reconsider.

The SPEAKER. The Chair thinks the gentleman from Arkansas can hardly be in earnest about that.

Mr. DUNN. I want to run the rule to a ridiculous result.

The SPEAKER. All parliamentary rules that are followed out improperly may run into absurdities.

Mr. DUNN. The position I take is that this runs into an absurdity.

Mr. ROBESON. It cannot be in order to reconsider a vote to reconsider.

Mr. DUNN. If any one makes the point of order on my motion let the Chair rule upon it.

The SPEAKER. The Chair has simply ruled, following a line of precedents through the entire history of the House, that a motion to reconsider the vote by which the yeas and nays were ordered was in order. The Chair cannot entertain two motions of that kind at the same time.

Mr. DUNN. But this was a vote ordering the yeas and nays. Now, I move to reconsider that vote; and if a point of order is made on my motion I ask the Chair to rule upon it.

The SPEAKER. It is like making several appeals at the same time. The Chair cannot present any such absurdity under the rule. The Clerk will call the roll.

Mr. KENNA rose.

The Clerk proceeded to call the roll, and called the first two names.

Mr. KENNA. I rose to a point of order before the call of the roll began. I ask the Chair to rule upon the motion of the gentleman from Arkansas.

The SPEAKER. That motion would undoubtedly be in order, but the Chair cannot entertain two motions of the same kind at the same time.

Mr. KENNA. This motion does not apply to the same vote as the other. The one is to reconsider the vote ordering the yeas and nays on the amendment of the gentleman from Virginia [Mr. TUCKER]. This does not apply to the same vote at all. The motion of the gentleman from Arkansas applies to the vote last taken.

The SPEAKER. The Chair understands that perfectly well. But it is the same character of motion.

Mr. KENNA. Does the Chair hold it out of order?

The SPEAKER. The Chair does not hold it out of order. But the Chair holds it cannot entertain two motions of the same kind at the same time.

Mr. KENNA. Does the Chair hold it to be in order?

The SPEAKER. The Clerk will call the roll.

Mr. KENNA. I ask the Chair to decide whether the motion of the gentleman from Arkansas is in order or is not in order.

The SPEAKER. The Chair would hold it would be in order if the House was not proceeding to vote on a similar motion.

Mr. KENNA. If the Chair holds the motion is out of order I desire to appeal from the decision of the Chair.

Mr. HISCOCK. I made the point of order that the Clerk had commenced the roll-call and that two names had been called.

Mr. KENNA. I rose before the Clerk began, and was recognized.

Several members called for the regular order.

The SPEAKER. The regular order is the call of the roll.

Mr. KENNA. Does the Chair entertain my appeal?

The SPEAKER. The Chair can submit no appeal pending the roll-call.

Mr. KENNA. I rose in my place and was recognized by the Chair.

The SPEAKER. There need be no difficulty about this. The Chair followed the precedents in entertaining the motion of the gentleman from Iowa. In every session of Congress, so far as the Chair is able to learn, certainly in all the Chair is familiar with, the practice has been to allow a motion to reconsider a vote by which the yeas and nays have been ordered. If presented as an original question the Chair might hold otherwise. But when the yeas and nays have been ordered on a motion of that kind the Chair does not think it can entertain a similar motion and so put the question on that, going on indefinitely. In this the Chair follows exactly the precedent that two appeals cannot be submitted at the same time.

Mr. KENNA. I only desired the Chair to pass on that because it is a new proposition.

The SPEAKER. The Chair would hold the proposition of the gentleman from Arkansas in order for the same reason that it has entertained the other motion; but it cannot entertain the two at the same time.

Mr. KENNA. And from the ruling of the Chair that the motion of the gentleman from Arkansas is out of order I desire to appeal, in order that there may be a decision of the House on this novel proposition.

The SPEAKER. The Chair did not so rule. The Clerk will proceed with the call of the roll.

The Clerk resumed and concluded the call of the roll.

The question was taken; and there were—yeas 94, nays 78, not voting 117.

So the order for the yeas and nays was reconsidered.

JULY 25, 1882.

Mr. MILLER, as a question of personal privilege, sent to the Clerk's desk and had read the remarks made in the Senate on the 21st instant by Mr. BUTLER, a Senator from the State of South Carolina.

Mr. BUCKNER and Mr. CARLISLE made points of order that no question of personal privilege was involved in the publication read, and that controversies between Senators and Representatives, of this character, were in gross violation of parliamentary law and propriety.

The Speaker overruled the same, on the ground that the attack was made upon Mr. MILLER in both his individual and representative capacity, and that he was entitled to make an explanation of the speech for which he had been criticised by Senator BUTLER.

SAME DAY.

The Speaker, at 11 o'clock and 58 minutes a. m., announced the regular order of business to be, under the special order of the House adopted on the 21st instant, the further consideration of the bill of the House (H. R. 3902) permitting the use of domestic materials in the construction of steam and sail vessels for foreign account. the pending question being the motion of Mr. KELLEY to refer the bill and pending amendment to the Committee on Ways and Means; pending which, Mr. TUCKER moved to amend the said motion by adding thereto the following instructions, viz:

With instructions to report a bill which shall allow, under proper regulations, a drawback or rebat equal to the whole amount of duties paid or chargeable thereon on any and all imported materials which shall be used in the construction and equipment of any steam or sail vessel constructed and equipped within the United States for any citizen of the United States or for any foreign citizen or subject: *Provided*, That the same shall not apply to any such vessel to be engaged in the coastwise commerce of the United States

Mr. HASKELL made the point of order that the said amendment submitted by Mr. TUCKER was not in order.

After debate on the said point of order, the Speaker overruled the same, on the ground that the said motion was in order as an amendment of the motion to refer, under clause 4 of Rule XVI, the previous question not having been ordered or moved.

In which decision the House acquiesced.

SAME DAY.

Mr. SPRINGER, from the same committee, reported without amendment the bill of the Senate (S. 329) to authorize the preparation and publication of a classified, analytical, and descriptive catalogue of all Government publications from July 4, 1776, to March 4, 1881.

Mr. HOLMAN made the point of order that the said bill must receive its first consideration in the Committee of the Whole House.

After debate on the point of order, the Speaker overruled the same, on the ground that as the Committee on Printing had the right to report at any time, it carried with it the right of present consideration in the House; which was in harmony with the past practice of the House, and with this view the Chair was inclined to adhere to that practice, and consequently overruled the said point of order.

From this decision of the Chair Mr. HOLMAN appealed; pending which, on motion of Mr. VAN VOORHIS, the said appeal was laid on the table.

SAME DAY.

Mr. PAGE, as a question of privilege, from the committee of conference on certain amendments of the Senate to the bill of the House (H. R. 6242) making appropriations for the construction, repair, and preservation of certain works on rivers and harbors, and for other purposes, submitted a report.

Mr. KASSON moved to recommit the said bill to the committee of conference, with instructions to report the same with the following proviso at the end of the bill, viz:

Provided, That the Secretary of War, with the approval of the President, may limit any expenditure provided by this act to any less sum than that authorized therefor during the current fiscal year in any case where in their opinion the public interest does not require the entire expenditure.

* * * * * * * *

The SPEAKER. The Chair thinks it would not be in order to so recommit the report to the conference committee. It is never in order to instruct the conference committee to do that which it could not do under the reference made of the matter to the committee in the first instance.

AUGUST 2, 1882.

Mr. PAGE, as a privileged question, called up the message of the President returning the bill of the House (H. R. 6242) making appropriations for the construction, repair, and preservation of certain works on rivers and harbors, and for other purposes, without his signature and with his objections to its passage, and moved that the House proceed to reconsider the said bill, on which motion Mr. PAGE moved the previous question.

Mr. KASSON moved to refer the said message and bill to the Committee on Commerce, with instructions; which motion he subsequently modified by withdrawing said instructions.

Mr. PAGE made the point of order that the said motion was not now in order.

The Speaker held that the motion to refer would be in order but for the pendency of the motion for the previous question on the first motion submitted by Mr. PAGE.

Mr. KASSON made the point of order that the motion to refer was in order, under the practice of the House, and particularly under clause 1 of Rule XVII, which permitted a motion to refer with or without instructions pending the demand for or after the previous question shall have been ordered.

After debate on said point of order,

The SPEAKER. The Chair is ready to dispose of this question. Since the inquiry was first made whether it would be in order to move to refer, and since the motion which the gentleman from Iowa [Mr. KASSON] proposed to make was sent to the Clerk, the Chair understands the gentleman from Iowa to have withdrawn that part of his motion which included instructions to the committee. Clearly that would be out of order. The House could not instruct the committee to report the bill back with amendments, as it is a bill which the House itself could not amend when it was being considered. What the House cannot do itself it cannot instruct a committee to do.

This bill comes back to the House by reason of the veto message of the President of the United States, and under the Constitution, paragraph 2, section 7, article 2, the House must proceed to reconsider it. That does not necessarily mean that the House may debate it. Reconsidering may be voting on it; and perhaps that was all that was intended by the language of the Constitution. The Chair would not intimate that if the House desires it may not debate; but reconsideration might be had by simply voting on the bill.

It is settled, the Chair thinks, by the practice, that a motion to refer—a simple motion to refer—to a committee may be entertained. But the Chair thinks that that motion to refer must come in at the proper time. It is the first duty of the House, under the Constitution, as the Chair interprets its language, to reconsider and proceed to vote upon the vetoed bill. If the House chooses, by ordering the previous question, to cut off debate upon this matter of reconsideration, that is within the power of the House. If the House does not order the previous question, the Chair would hold that a motion to refer would be in order. It is claimed that under Rule XVII of the House the motion to refer, being, as the Chair holds, equivalent to a motion to commit, is in order. The Chair does not think so. Rule XVII speaks entirely of the proceedings governing the ordinary passage of the bill. If the whole rule is read it will appear that a motion for the previous question is made, first, upon the engrossment and third reading of the bill. Then, that having exhausted itself upon the third reading of the bill, the second step is a motion for the previous question upon the passage of the same bill, such a bill as the House has ordered to be engrossed and read a third time. This rule refers to the passage of a bill in the ordinary sense. The bill before us is at a different stage. It is in consideration of a bill which the House and Senate have already passed, and for the purpose of determining whether the House will by a two-thirds vote pass the bill, notwithstanding the President's veto as provided by the Constitution.

The Chair feels bound to hold that the demand for the previous question having been made first, must be first submitted to the House. If that be voted down, the Chair will entertain a motion to refer the bill.

JANUARY 4, 1883.

Mr. KASSON, as a privileged question, under the order of the House of the 2nd of December last, from the Committee on Reform in the Civil Service, to which was referred the bill of the Senate (S. 133) to regulate and improve the civil service of the United States, reported the same without amendment, for previous consideration.

Mr. CULBERSON made the point of order that under the special order heretofore made, the bill of the House (H. R. 3123) to amend sections 1, 2, 3, and 10 of an act to determine the jurisdiction of the circuit courts of the United States and to regulate the removal of causes from State courts, and for other purposes, approved March 3, 1875 was the regular order of business and entitled to precedence.

After debate on said point of order, the Speaker overruled the same, on the ground that the said Senate bill was referred to the Committee on Reform in the Civil Service with leave to report thereon at any time, and that under the uniform practice of the House the right of consideration followed when reported.

*   *   *   *   *   *   *

Mr. BLAND made the point of order that under clause 3 of Rule XXIII the said bill, must receive its first consideration in a Committee of the Whole House.

The Speaker overruled the said point of order on the ground heretofore held, and, on appeal, sustained by the House, that where a bill has been made a special order the rule above cited was thereby waived.

JANUARY 11, 1883.

The House then proceeded, as the regular order of business, to the further consideration of the bill of the House (H. R. 7061) to remove certain burdens on the American merchant marine, to encourage the American foreign carrying trade, and to amend the laws relating to the shipment and discharge of seamen, pending when the House adjourned on yesterday, the pending question being on the amendment submitted by Mr. CANDLER to the substitute submitted by Mr. PAGE for section 18 of the bill.

*   *   *   *   *   *   *

The question recurring on the amendment submitted by Mr. CANDLER to the substitute submitted by Mr. PAGE, and being put, viz, Will the House agree thereto? it was decided in the affirmative.

*   *   *   *   *   *   *

The question recurring on the substitute submitted by Mr. PAGE, as amended; pending which, Mr. ROBESON moved to amend the same by striking out the words "free of duty as to," and inserting in lieu thereof the words "upon payment of an import duty of 20 per cent. upon the value of."

Mr. SPRINGER made the point of order that the said amendment was not in order, for the reason that it struck out a proposition words to which the House has just agreed.

After debate on said point of order, the Speaker overruled the same, on the ground that the amendment submitted by Mr. CANDLER had not been finally adopted by the House but only as an amendment to a proposed substitute for a section of the pending bill.

JANUARY 12, 1883.

Mr. S. S. COX moved to recommit the said bill with instructions to report back to the House without delay a bill providing for the purchase, free admission, and registry of foreign-built vessels, and for the free admission of the material used in the construction and repair of vessels in American yards, to be used in the foreign and not in the coastwise trade of the United States.

Mr. COX having proposed to modify the said motion by adding the words "with leave to report at any time." Mr. REED made the point of order that the said modification was not in order, for the reason that the House was dividing when the said modification was proposed, and also on the further ground that leave to report at any time was a change of the rules.

The Speaker overruled the first point of order and sustained the second, and held the said modification to be out of order.

JANUARY 13, 1883.

Mr. FORNEY moved that the House resolve itself into the Committee of the Whole House on the state of the Union for the purpose of considering the bill of the House No. 7191 (fortification appropriation bill); when Mr. WHITE made the point of order that the regular order of business was the consideration of unfinished business.

The Speaker held the motion of Mr. FORNEY to be of higher privilege, under clause 9 of Rule XVI.

Mr. R. W. TOWNSHEND, as a privileged question, submitted the following resolution, to amend the rules.

*　　　　　*　　　　　*　　　　　*　　　　　*

Mr. MILLS made the point of order that the resolution was not in order except by unanimous consent.

The Speaker overruled the point of order, on the ground that a motion to amend the rules could be made on one day's notice, as provided by clause 1 of Rule XVIII, but also held that it was in order to move to refer the resolution to the Committee on Rules.

FEBRUARY 26, 1883.

Mr REED, as a privileged question, called up the following resolution reported by him on Saturday last from the Committee on Rules, viz:

During the remainder of this session it shall be in order at any time to move to suspend the rules, which motion shall be decided by a majority vote, to take from the Speaker's table House bill No. 5538, with the Senate amendment thereto, entitled "A bill to reduce internal-revenue taxation" and to declare a disagreement with the Senate amendment to the same, and to ask for a committee of conference thereon, to be composed of five members on the part of the House. If such motion shall fail the bill shall remain upon the Speaker's table unaffected by the decision of the House upon said motion.

Mr. BLACKBURN made the point of order that the said resolution was not a rule or an amendment to the rules of the House.

After debate on said point of order,

The SPEAKER. The point of order made by the gentleman from Kentucky the Chair would hold was made too late if it were not for the fact that the gentleman would have the right to claim that he reserved the right to make it before the question of the consideration of that rule was submitted to the House. The Chair was not advised of the nature of the point of order reserved by the gentleman; and the Chair is clearly of the opinion that it ought to have been stated before the House decided to go forward with the consideration of the resolution; for that is now the action of the House, and the Chair does not very well see how his decision now would affect that order or override the action of the House, even if it should be held that the point of order was good. The Chair, however, will take no advantage——

Mr. BRAGG. Let me inquire, Mr. Speaker, if the Chair did not state to the gentleman from Kentucky that the point of order could be reserved?

The SPEAKER. The Chair does not intend or propose to take any advantage of the condition in which this resolution has been placed by the action of the House. But at the time that this reservation of the point of order was made of course it could not be foreseen what action the House would take on the question of consideration.

Mr. BRAGG. But the Chair expressly stated that the reservation of the point of order would be observed.

The SPEAKER. The Chair repeats that it has no intention of taking advantage of the situation, and remembers very well all that took place.

It is proper for the Chair to say that with the question of the constitutional prerogatives of the House, in the matter of originating revenue bills, the Chair now at least has nothing to do. That question does not enter into the decision of the point of order made by the gentleman from Kentucky. The gentleman from Kentucky makes the point of order and rests his point solely upon the claim that this resolution, if adopted, would not be a rule of the House. It would be rather early for the Chair to undertake to decide on that which is not before the House. It is reported as a rule from the Committee on Rules.

But passing that, it is perfectly competent, as the Chair thinks, for this House, when the subject is properly brought before it, to change every rule of the House and all of the rules that have been adopted by the House. And early in this session a resolution of the House was adopted authorizing the Committee on Rules to report at any time any change or modification of the rules or any new rules. That right of the committee has been exercised perhaps in this case. But in this case the Committee on Rules has reported this rule as a substitute for various propositions of a similar character that have been introduced in the House and referred to the committee. This comes from the committee as a substitute for them all.

Its effect, if the Chair is to look to that, may be, in this exceptional case, indeed, to put aside other rules which would prevent the motion that the rule proposes to allow. But the greater certainly includes the lesser. It was in the power of the committee to report a rule to suspend the whole of Rule XX, which would require an amendment of the Senate, on the point of order being made, to go to the Committee of the Whole House on the state of the Union. It is in the power of the committee to report to the House a proposition to suspend the rule or rather to allow a suspension of the rules by a two-thirds vote. In other words, it might have been —

ported from the committee, and properly, which would suspend or repeal or annul or set aside every rule of this House, standing or special; and if the House so decided to affirm that report by a majority vote it could do so. In this case, though it may apply to a single great and important measure now pending before Congress, it seems perfectly clear to the Chair that it would be a rule to the extent that it goes; and perhaps gentlemen, on consideration, may see that in this particular case it goes far enough.

The Chair overrules the point of order.

From this decision of the Chair Mr. BLACKBURN appealed, pending which Mr. REED moved that the said appeal be laid on the table; when, the hour of 5 o'clock and 30 minutes p. m. having arrived, the Speaker, in accordance with the order of the House of February 7, instant, declared the House to be in recess until 7 o'clock and 30 minutes p. m.

AFTER THE RECESS.

(7 o'clock and 30 minutes p. m.)

   *   *   *   *   *   *

The regular order being insisted on, the Speaker stated the same to be the motion to adjourn, on which tellers had been demanded, pending when the House took a recess.

By unanimous consent the said motion was considered as withdrawn.

The question recurring on the motion of Mr. REED to lay on the table the appeal taken by Mr. BLACKBURN from the decision of the Chair, and being put, it was decided in the affirmative.

   *   *   *   *   *

So the said appeal was laid on the table.

The question recurring on the said resolution, when Mr. REED moved the previous question; and the question being put, viz, Will the House order the previous question? it was decided in the affirmative.

Mr. CARLISLE submitted the following resolution, viz:

Resolved, That the proposition now under consideration be recommitted to the Committee on Rules, with instructions that if the same shall be again reported it shall be so amended as to permit the House to vote upon a motion either to concur or to non-concur in the amendment of the Senate to the bill of the House No. 5538, entitled "An act to reduce internal-revenue taxation."

Mr. REED made the point of order that the said resolution was not in order under Rule XVII, for the reason that the motion to recommit therein authorized, with or without instructions, did not cover or include the pending proposition.

After debate on said point of order,

The SPEAKER. The Chair will state that thus far no precedent has been cited that sustains the right to recommit in the present instance. The Chair will state further, with reference to the case cited by the gentleman from Kentucky [Mr. CARLISLE], that it turns out, on examination of that precedent, that it is not a precedent in support of the right to recommit, as cited here, for two reasons: First, that when that motion was made to recommit the previous question had not first been ordered.

Mr. CARLISLE. But, Mr. Speaker——

The SPEAKER. One moment, if the gentleman please. The motion to recommit was made on the 18th day of January, 1882, and, according to the RECORD, it appears that it was arranged between the gentleman from New Jersey on the one part and the gentleman from Vermont [Mr. JOYCE] that he should have that right after the time had arrived (January 19, 1882,) when the previous question was ordered, as stated by the Chair at the time the motion was made. The Chair will quote the exact language used:

The SPEAKER. Under the arrangement made between the gentleman from Vermont and the gentleman from New Jersey there has been a motion made to recommit.

That was made upon the previous day. So that for that reason it is not a precedent. And for the further reason that the Chair would have entertained the motion to recommit now as it did then if no member had made the point of order. The language of Rule XVII was not called to the attention of the Chair, and no member made a point of order. For that reason the case cited is not a precedent.

Now, the difficulty seems to be in there not being time to look up the precedents. The Chair feels quite certain that the motion was made by the gentleman from Indiana [Mr. HOLMAN] to recommit a proposition that was presented here. The point was made and decided in this session or in this Congress—the Chair thinks in this session, but it may have been in the last. And there the Chair decided according to its then opinion of the fair reading of this rule.

Mr. HAMMOND, of Georgia. Will the Chair permit me to suggest, as it is late, that he yield to a motion to adjourn and have the precedents to-morrow. It is now after 9, and this is a very important matter.

The SPEAKER. The Chair understands its importance and does not desire to be hasty about it. If there be any general disposition on the part of the House to adjourn the Chair will not proceed. [Cries of "No!" "No!"]

Mr. HAMMOND, of Georgia. To test the sense of the House on that point I make the motion that the House do now adjourn.

Mr. KASSON. I make the point of order that while the Chair is addressing the House a motion to adjourn is not in order.

The SPEAKER. The gentleman from Georgia asked permission of the Chair to make the suggestion. But the Chair does not feel inclined to yield unless such is the general desire of the House.

Mr. HAMMOND, of Georgia. I am sorry the Chair retracts its admission. How can we ascertain whether the sentiment be general or not unless by a vote?

The SPEAKER. Gentlemen indicated what was the sense of the House by cries of "No," &c. The Chair does not say the gentleman from Georgia interrupted the Chair improperly.

The effect of the motion for the previous question is very clearly stated in the first paragraph of Rule XVII:

There shall be a motion for the previous question, which, being ordered by a majority of members present, if a quorum, shall have the effect to cut off all debate and bring the House to a direct vote upon the immediate question or questions on which it has been asked and ordered.

There can be no doubt but what the previous question can be asked and ordered upon a single motion, whether in writing or orally, or upon a series of motions, or upon an amendment or amendments; and it may be made to embrace all authorized motions or amendments and include the bill to its engrossment and third reading.

The principal purpose of the previous question is to bring the House to a direct vote upon the pending question, and if other things intervene to delay such vote it must be by virtue of a plain provision of the rule.

And then—

The rule goes on to say—

on renewal and second of said motion—

After the previous question has been ordered on a bill, before engrossment and after it has been engrossed and read a third time, which is only usual with bills or joint resolutions, which under the Constitution of the United States have the effect of bills and are treated as bills for all purposes of legislation—the rule then provides that—

on renewal and second of said motion—

The previous question on the passage or rejection may be ordered. Now, the plain reading of this part of the rule is that it is dealing with the passage of a bill. Then the rule further provides:

It shall be in order, pending the motion for or after the previous question shall have been ordered on its passage, for the Speaker to entertain and submit a motion to commit, with or without instructions to a standing or select committee.

It would be wholly unnecessary to use any such language in a rule if it were not for the fact that a bill has several stages through which it must pass before it can be brought to its passage. This refers, in the opinion of the Chair, to the passage of a bill, and only a bill.

Then the motion to commit with or without instructions, in the opinion of the Chair, can only be made pending or after the previous question has been ordered on the passage of the bill, and it is only by virtue of the rule that that motion can be entertained.

The latter clause of this same paragraph seems to make this perfectly clear. It states that—

A motion to lay upon the table shall be in order on the second and third readings of a bill.

The Chair is of the opinion that but for that clause, after the previous question is ordered a motion to lay upon the table would not be in order. It is only such motions as are expressly authorized to be made by this rule after the previous question is ordered that can be made at all, and a motion to recommit a single proposition, a single verbal motion, or a written motion cannot be made, because it is obvious that it can it be said, within the contemplation of the rule, to be on its passage. But on a bill which goes through its various stages to its final passage, the rule provides for a motion after the previous question has been ordered on its passage to recommit with or without instructions.

In the opinion of the Chair the point of order made by the gentleman from Maine [Mr. REED] is well taken, and it is therefore sustained.

Mr. CARLISLE. I take an appeal from the decision of the Chair.

Mr. REED. I move to lay that appeal on the table.

The question was taken; and there were—yeas 125, nays 102, not voting 41.

So the appeal was laid on the table.

FEBRUARY 27, 1882.

Mr. N. J. HAMMOND, as a question of privilege, submitted the following resolution, viz:

Resolved, That the substitute of the Senate bill (H. R. 5538) entitled "An act to reduce internal-revenue taxation, and for other purposes," under the form of an amendment to the bill of the House (H. R. 5538) entitled "An act to reduce internal-revenue taxation," containing a general revision and repeal of laws imposing both import duties and internal taxes, is in conflict with the true intent and purposes of that clause of the Constitution which requires "all bills for raising revenue shall originate in the House of Representatives;" and that therefore said bill so amended do lie upon the table.

And be it further resolved, That the Clerk of the House be, and is hereby, directed to notify the Senate of the passage of the foregoing resolution.

Mr. CALKINS made the point of order that the said resolution was not in order either to be offered or considered until the bill to which it refers was brought before the House for consideration.

After debate on said point of order, the Speaker overruled the same, on the ground that the resolution submitted was one relating to the constitutional privilege of the House as to its sole right to originate revenue bills. The House had taken notice of the amendment of the Senate to said bill, and if the House were to proceed to its consideration it would then be too late to raise such question against the Senate amendment.

The House having proceeded to its consideration, after debate, Mr. KASSON submitted the following substitute for the said resolution, viz:

Resolved, That this House, insisting always upon its privilege under the Constitution to originate all bills for raising revenue, and waiving its right thereunder in respect to House bill 5538 with Senate amendments thereto, hereby declares a disagreement with the Senate amendments to the same, and asks for a committee of conference thereon, to be composed of five members on the part of the House.

Mr. CARLISLE made the point of order that the said resolution was not in order, for the reason that the said bill was not before the House for present consideration.

The Speaker sustained the same, on the ground that the proposition submitted by Mr. HAMMOND presented solely the question of the right of the House exclusively, under the Constitution, to originate revenue bills. The substitute offered by Mr. KASSON is a proposition to waive whatever rights the House possesses under the Constitution in reference to this particular bill, and embodies a proposition to declare at once a disagreement with the Senate amendments with a view of immediately putting the bill and amendments in conference. On the ground, therefore, that the question of constitutional privilege must be disposed of independently of any collateral or subsidiary questions, the Chair held the proposed substitute not in order.

Mr. HASKELL submitted the following preamble and resolution as a substitute for the said resolution, viz:

Whereas House bill 5538, entitled "An act to reduce internal-revenue taxation, and for other purposes," under the form of an amendment in the Senate to title 33 of the Revised Statutes, which provides for duties on imports, has been so modified and changed by the introduction of new provisions, containing, among other things, a general revision of the statutes referred to, so as both to increase and reduce duties on imports, and in many instances to repeal and in others to amend the laws imposing import duties; and

Whereas in the opinion of this House it is believed that such changes and alterations are in conflict with the true intent and purpose of the Constitution, which requires that all bills for raising revenue shall originate in the House of Representatives: Therefore,

Resolved, That if this bill shall be referred to a committee of conference it shall be the duty of the conferees on the part of the House on said committee to consider fully the constitutional objections to said bill as amended by the Senate and herein referred to, and to bring the same, together with the opinion of the House in regard thereto, before said committee of conference, and if necessary, in their opinion, after having conferred with the Senate conferees, said conferees on said committee may make report to the House in regard to the objections to the said bill herein referred to.

Mr. CARLISLE made the point of order that the said proposed substitute was not in order, for the reason that it not only proposed to submit the question of constitutional privilege of the House to such conference, but also to consider the subject-matter of such Senate amendment.

After debate on said point of order, the Speaker overruled the same, on the ground that a fair reading and construction of the proposed substitute would show that it provided only for referring to a conference committee the constitutional objections to the bill such as grow out of the alleged violation of the Constitution by the Senate in passing an impost bill as a portion of an amendment to an internal-revenue bill proposed by the House.

From this decision of the Chair Mr. N. J. HAMMOND appealed; pending which, on motion of Mr. REED, the said appeal was laid on the table.

MARCH 2, 1883.

Mr. BUTTERWORTH, from the committee of conference on the disagreeing votes of the two Houses on the amendments of the Senate to the bill of the House (H. R.

7077) making appropriations for the support of the Army for the fiscal year ending June 30, 1884, and for other purposes, submitted the following report, viz:

*   *   *   *   *   *   *

The accompanying statement having been read, Mr. BRAGG made the point of order that the statement accompanying the said report was not in order, for the reason that it was not in compliance or conformity with Rule XXIX, and also the further point of order that the report itself was not in compliance with the said rule.

The Speaker overruled the point of order, on the ground that it was not for the Chair to decide whether a conference report and accompanying statement was or was not in strict conformity with said rule, that being a question of fact.

MARCH 3, 1883.

Mr. KELLEY, as a privileged question, from the committee of conference on the disagreeing votes of the two Houses on the amendment of the Senate to the bill of the House (H. R. 5538) to reduce internal-revenue taxation, submitted the following report, viz:

*   *   *   *   *   *   *

Mr. BAYNE made the point of order that the said report was not in order for present consideration, on the ground that the detailed statement required by Rule XXIX did not accompany said report.

After debate on the said point of order, the Speaker sustained the same, on the ground that the paper submitted by Mr. KELLEY, entitled "Index to changes proposed by the committee of conference," though signed by the majority of the conferres on the part of the House, was not in compliance with the last clause of Rule XXIX.

Mr. KELLEY thereupon submitted a detailed statement accompanying said conference report, as required by said rule.

Mr. CARLISLE made the point of order that the said statement was not such a statement as is required by the rule, for the reason that it only states the effect of the amendment proposed by the Senate, whereas the rule requires a statement sufficiently explanatory to show the effect of the propositions reported by the committee.

The Speaker overruled the point of order.

INDEX TO SUBJECTS.

INDEX TO PARLIAMENTARY DECISIONS.

ADDENDA.

195

○

www.ingramcontent.com/pod-product-compliance
Lightning Source LLC
Chambersburg PA
CBHW030542040726
47497CB00008B/2557